JOURNEY OF THE SHADOW

JOURNEY OF THE SHADOW

Volume One

Warith Stone Abdullah

ISBN: 1548745944
ISBN-13: 9781548745943
Library of Congress Control Number: 2017912808
CreateSpace Independent Publishing Platform
North Charleston, South Carolina

I dedicate this book to the youngest of my six older sisters,
Sakeena Abdullah.
Thanks for convincing me to pursue this work.
Sorry it took fourteen years, sis.

CHAPTER ONE

There was *something* about late-autumn nights that made Tsumisu, the nineteen-year-old commander of the Sonzai clan, appreciate them more than any other time of the year. Nature bustled with activity, aware that winter would approach soon; wasps suddenly turned unbelievably hostile toward you. And every now and then, particularly with the advent of a changing global climate, those *warm* nights, which capped humidity inland from the Sea of Japan, gave the grandest symphony of confused insects anyone could witness. Fortunately, on such a night of spiritual observation of the southern region of Okayama, Japan, Tsumisu found a tree branch strong enough to support his 1.92-meter, one-hundred-kilo body...and share with a curiously peering barely quarter-kilo squirrel.

"This will sound unusual, but hear me out for a second," Tsumisu muttered in a joking manner.

His voice was a deep tenor, clear-cut and refined, albeit with a hint of swagger.

The fuzzy creature, carrying nuts within its cheek, standing up on its hind legs, intently listened to him.

"We're alike, you and I," he continued. "Just trying to get *something* accomplished before the night is over, right?"

It chattered, somewhat nervously, and scurried away and above him to its home. Strange, it seemed relaxed before. What changed its disposition so quickly? Another earthquake tremor? Not likely. Otherwise, the deer nearby would have made haste elsewhere—well, there they went. Tsumisu sighed, having gotten comfortable on this newfound favorite branch that haphazardly matched his brown-skinned complexion.

"Hundreds of recorded quakes per year, they said..."

The expression covering Tsumisu's softened yet prominent-cheekboned face was one of subtle annoyance as he performed a front flip and landed crouched on the partially leaf-covered ground. At this moment, the Sonzai commander postulated that if a dust mite lived on his stomach, would it get equally annoyed each time he ate the wrong food? Wow, talk about thought digression...this sucked.

"Say, uh, Commander, you there?" a man asked over Tsumisu's embedded earpiece. "Heh, are you bored yet?" he asked, bearing a young midalto, albeit strong, voice.

"*Yes,* Lieutenant," he responded quickly. "I just get this awful feeling like I'm about to take out some misdirected hostility on the ground...Anyway, what've you got, Wanako?"

Twenty-three-year-old First Lieutenant Wanako Satsuno, a fellow Sonzai clansman, chuckled. "Dude, I *told* you to get a smartphone. But nooooo—"

"And I asked *you* to find us a bass player *weeks* ago!" Tsumisu proclaimed in defense. He exhaled afterward while running his hand through his shoulder-length black hair. "Besides, I tried playing that candy game the other day? And *now* I owe Shujin a new phone! Soooo, I'm done with frustrating, tedious-ass 'apps' or whatever."

"You got issues, man. Well, you know what they say, right?"

"No, I don't, sir."

"It's better to have smashed a phone than to have smashed a portion of the planet…or *something* like that—"

Suddenly, a calm though slightly amused sigh came over the channel.

"Lieutenant? Up for your nightly antagonizing, again?" said a more mature male voice, though not necessarily in a worn tone.

"Pfft, *no* idea what you're talkin' about, Captain," Wanako replied with clear and heavy denial. "See, I'm *assisting* the commander. Don't get jelly on me, sir!"

"It's good to hear you, Goshinfuda," Tsumisu responded with a stifled laugh. "Seriously, I'm crying out here!"

"Hmm, late-season allergies maybe?" Goshinfuda Hanai, who was thirty-six years old and captain of the Sonzai clan, asked in serious inquiry. "Because I couldn't imagine you implying *appreciation* of Wanako's services right now."

Tsumisu was pacing around, his black boots crunching the newly decaying leaves, as he observed the continuous disappearances and reclusive behavior of nearby wildlife. "That's *exactly* what I'm saying!" he replied with honest enthusiasm. "Yet I have one observation that I trust you gentlemen will find thought-provoking at this late hour."

"Great!" Wanako remarked ecstatically. "'Cause I'm not gettin' *any* action on my end tonight. Ha ha! Did you guys hear that?"

The three Sonzai warriors were indeed on observation duty, continuing their investigation of humans at risk for abduction or possession. Typical profiles included but were not limited to the spiritually misguided, those tormented by some perturbation or another, and those inclining toward serious, perpetual abuse of the evil within their own souls. This was a global effort, stretching their three-hundred-plus group of talented spiritual warriors, all infiltrating various nations in areas for which their combined intelligence guided them—of course, with absolute direction from the clan leader, Grandmaster Sonzai himself. As such, First Lieutenant Wanako was positioned near a military outpost in Northern Russia, and Captain Goshinfuda was stationed in the Midwest of the interior United States.

Their actions were incontrovertibly necessary, as the last few months had stirred inconsistencies within the spiritual energy complex encompassing the planet. Phenomena of this nature could only stem from the clan's avowed enemy: Nyugo. Though subtle, the interruptions in ethereal string frequencies were enough to grasp the grandmaster's attention; after all, Nyugo was a foe not seen in existence for the last three thousand years. If the Sonzai clan was to be tasked with protecting mankind and all life on the planet, every potential red flag should be investigated to ensure this vicious entity would *not* be resurrected.

Despite their expansive efforts, the secretive organization of spiritual warriors had few strong leads, for each locale assigned to each warrior was based on the most stringent theories of greatest likelihood a possession on behalf of Nyugo could arise. The grandmaster detested stretching his clan out so far on glorified assumptions. Yet the proverbial red flags were *so* subtle they were forced to act in spite of the magnitude of difficulty they encountered in acquiring solid evidence. Nevertheless, there was an unusual lead—a "Shujin Iwato" individual, who Tsumisu convinced the grandmaster would be of importance.

Shujin, an eighteen-year-old man of incredible docility and a kindred spirit, defeated their profile for observation. However, Commander Tsumisu *swore* that Shujin bore repressed spiritual talents—such that he had willingly registered for the high school Shujin attended, Okayama High, and monitored him for the last three years. As of yet, the Sonzai clan had not detected any suspicious activity—good *or* bad—from Shujin, though Tsumisu had continued to cling to his instinct, even befriending him.

"Wow," the captain lamented Wanako's crude humor, drawing a hand over his face. "I really didn't need to hear that. Please, Commander, what has captured your attention? Say it quickly!"

Tsumisu, laughing aloud, shook his head in disbelief. "Cheer up, Cap'n! He's just sore after his last date...I think."

"*No*!" Wanako forcefully replied. "Just an error in judgment on my part for movie choice—"

"Riiiight. So, anybody notice the animals taking shelter all of a sudden?" Tsumisu began. "Sure, you guys aren't in my location, but it's worth asking...global-phenomena potentiality and whatnot."

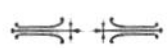

Goshinfuda looked around his environment; he saw closed shops in need of an aesthetic fixing up and heard loud mufflers on pick-up trucks blaring *early* in the morning down a two-way street and suspicious, yet well-meaning individuals who walked by every once in a while.

"Not much wildlife near me," he said. "Sorry, can't confirm. What about you, Lieutenant?"

"Well, if you consider military personnel barbaric animals, then *yes*! Lots of activity. If not, then the answer is no," Wanako frankly explained. "Besides, it's relatively cold where I am. Most nocturnal hunting critters are farther away from my position. Earthquake coming maybe?"

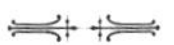

The Sonzai commander's spiritual senses suddenly got a ping, like an unexpected muscle spasm, yet the sensation registered within his soul. "*Negative*, Lieutenant," he responded sternly, hazel eyes looking in the direction he detected a rather significant power arise. "I think I've just found the cause."

"Hey, return your copy, Commander," Goshinfuda responded in concern. "There's definitely something on the planet generating a worthy source of energy. Is that what you're detecting?"

"Copy, Captain."

Tsumisu strode over to the tree he had previously sat on and retrieved his weapon, Akari—a straight-edge katana—as it leaned against the trunk. The scabbard was colored silver, and so was its hilt. Grooves existed for finger placement.

"Hey…that feels awfully unusual yet *awfully* familiar. What the hell *is* that?" Wanako asked with confusion. "What's your assessment, Commander?"

"Your guess is as good as mine, brother," Tsumisu replied, attaching the custom-made harness of his weapon to his back, the hilt protruding above his right shoulder. "Assessment is that the power is a threat if left uncontained. So! I'm not bored now…and… *no way*!" A grin arose as he stared into the distance. "Gentlemen? Keep this channel open; this will be *interesting*."

"You got it, Commander," Goshinfuda responded, his voice indicating he was smiling as well at his comrade's genuine amusement. He too could detect the spiritual signal in Japan, even from his position in the United States. "Is backup necessary? I'm sure you can scramble a team to your position."

"Naaahh!" Tsumisu chuckled with a bright tone. "I think backup is already *there*. Over and out."

The Sonzai commander leaned forward and dashed off into the forest; his footsteps were feather light, yet he accelerated with tremendous speed as his body shone with a soft white aura—a product of spiritual energy emanating into the physical realm. He *knew* he detected Shujin, located at or near their high school's location some ten kilometers away. At his rate of speed, he'd be there in approximately two minutes.

As the world passed him by in a blur, Tsumisu had to consider the lieutenant's question: Just *who* would attract this power to the earth? Chances were it took either a mastermind of spiritual ferocity *or* an idiot to cause such an event. Well, the good news was (given the commander's insight) he knew *just* the friendliest idiot this side of the mountains who would do such a thing.

Finally arriving at his location, Tsumisu scaled another tree and stood on a branch. As he observed the scene, there appeared to be *fire* billowing out of the chemistry lab. Yikes. Good thing he had turned *his* Bunsen burner off earlier—no culpable negligence here. Oh great, there appeared to be a large, aggressive-looking aircraft vessel of some kind parked on the school roof. Geez, how many man-hours did it take to put the black-metallic shine on *that* hull? Additionally, the roof was collapsing from the vessel's weight.

Oh well, no sense panicking yet over catastrophic structural failure. Coming to a crouched position, Tsumisu scanned the area for his buddy…

"Waah! Get away from me!" Shujin screamed as he suddenly bolted outside, stumbling over himself. "Noooo!"

Well, that didn't take long. Tsumisu surmised he was one hundred meters from and twenty meters above Shujin's position and *also* detected a fierce presence bearing down on his friend quickly, but! Curiosity begged him *not* to intervene just yet.

"Dude!" Tsumisu shouted, cupping both hands over his mouth.

Shujin stopped in his tracks, swearing he heard a familiar voice. "Tsumisu? Hey! Where are ya, man?"

"Up here, sir!" Tsumisu bore a wide grin. "See why you need a curfew? Now you're gonna face criminal charges!"

Diligently holding on to his book bag, Shujin was jogging in place—as if he really needed to pee and the world just had to wait. "*Help* me!" he cried. "Get down here! She's chasing me! I dunno why!"

Suddenly, the double doors to the rear of the school blew open with a ball of flames to follow, and out of the plume emerged a female figure. This blue-skinned female levitated in the air quite forebodingly, wearing a glistening black-and-gold-lined full-body latex outfit that sported a rather generous V-cut for her rather *generously sized* breasts. And from what Tsumisu could tell, she was about 1.8 meters tall, possessed two tanto short swords holstered at her waist, packed a revolver holstered on her right thigh, and had voluminous blue hair.

On a lesser note, she *was* smoking hot, though.

"What is indigo again? Ugh, I *hated* art class," he muttered, recalling his inability to remember fancy color names as the image of an artist's paint palette blossomed. "Bro! Run to the gym! I'll be right behind you!"

"Waaahhh! There she is! Oh my God!" Shujin kept hollering in dire panic, jogging faster. "What the hell are you doin'? Get down here!"

"*Shujiiinn...*" seethed the female attacker, unsheathing her tanto swords, which shone with an energized hue. "You cannot escape from me, Shujin! Ha ha ha ha!" she continued, staring him down while bearing her fangs. "Face your fate!"

Tsumisu looked on in amazement. What *was* this entity? She was *powerful* indeed, and as stated previously, something like her could cause much destruction if left unchecked. *But!* Tsumisu just *didn't* have the heart at this moment to accompany his buddy, so he gestured in rejection.

"No, no! It looks like you got it covered, dude!" he called. "I'm just gonna go back home!"

"*What*? Tsumisu, that's not funny!" Shujin was struck with disbelief that he would encounter *jokes* at a time like this. "Ahhh! I'm outta here! Noooo!"

Tsumisu ran a hand over his face and shook his head, equally amazed at Shujin's running speed. "Poor guy." He sighed, watching the unknown assailant twirl her weapons and fly after. "I suppose my boredom is seriously affecting my judgment tonight."

Shujin, meanwhile, figured running to the gym wasn't such a bad idea, as it required him to reenter the school and make his way there with plenty of corners and doors to impede the progress of his attacker. *Why* wouldn't Tsumisu help him out, though? After all, he had all the muscles and whatever! Shujin's rather thin 1.77-meter frame wasn't built for this. Ah well, guess heading to the gym was an ugly reminder of succumbing to protein shakes and extra push-ups.

Turning a corner and narrowly missing a large, collapsing piece of roofing, Shujin threw his back against a wall and caught his breath. No *way* could this be happening to him right now. And all he wanted to do was take a nap earlier. Maybe Tsumisu was right: Shujin needed some self-restraint, and if he had enforced a personal curfew days ago, this probably would never have happened. Maybe.

"I can *smell* you, Shujin!" the sinister voice of the female attacker cried from afar. She discharged her revolver to send an energy blast into a hallway behind him. "Show yourself *now*!"

Crap. As sweat bullets rolled from his brow, Shujin *knew* his ninja-mode technique for sneaking away would be invaluable, but with all this broken glass around, was it better for him to stay still? Could she *really* smell him?

"Dude!" Tsumisu whispered suddenly, poking his head around a corner. "*This* way!"

Shujin feverishly shook his head, making him aware of the broken glass.

Undeterred, Tsumisu widened his eyes in arm-twisting encouragement. "Get over here *now*, dude!" He signaled to move his way. "She's like *right* there!"

Sure enough, Shujin was against the wall that the fierce woman was passing from behind; a convenient hole granted up-close viewing access to the entity who had been chasing him this entire bizarre occasion. Shujin's rounded blue eyes inspected his hunter. Damn, would you look at the *hips* on her? *OK*. Not the right time.

Drumming his fingers on his forehead now in impatience, Tsumisu picked up a rock and tossed it away from the hiding duo—instantly catching her attention. In short celebration, the Sonzai commander once again signaled his friend to come toward him.

Cautious yet hopeful now, as he saw the woman fly away, Shujin slid against the wall until he finally grasped a helping hand, instantly seeking reprieve within a semidemolished janitor's closet.

"Finally!" Shujin exclaimed under whisper. "What do we do? How'd you get here?"

Tsumisu placed a finger over his mouth to signal his buddy to be silent; then he directed Shujin's attention to the creepy ability of the woman to *completely* cloak—as if she were a ghost. She did so, they assumed, as she approached the region of their distraction.

With book bag clenched awkwardly between his legs, fear gripping his boyish face, Shujin tightly covered his mouth with both hands to work on some breathing techniques—Tsumisu assisted with his pacing. But upon looking back at the woman's last-known location, Shujin realized she was *gone*!

"She's close," Tsumisu whispered, checking the surroundings now.

Several dozen slashing sounds could be heard, and perfect cutouts of Tsumisu and Shujin fell from behind them, revealing a smirking assailant.

"I'm right *behind* you," she remarked, twirling her weapons. "Now, where were we?"

"Waah!" Shujin bolted away, dropping his bag, but responsibly ran back to pick it up as the hell-bent-on-destruction entity gave chase once more. "Tsumisu! We gotta get outta here, dude!"

"Hey!" Tsumisu asked casually, running beside him. "Do you, uh, know that *thing* back there?"

"Do I what? Uh…I-I dunno!" Shujin desperately responded as the two rounded a corner, evading an energy blast that tore open another gaping hole in the building. "How am I supposed to know her?"

"You *do*, don't you?" Tsumisu laughed humorously, once again scanning his surroundings. "Look! We *literally* don't have anywhere to run! This would've been a great time to have that smartphone, huh?"

"Oh har-har, thanks! W-what about *your sword*?" he cried, stumbling over some debris. Tsumisu immediately assisted him. "Why don't you use it?"

"It's not necessary!" Tsumisu assured him with a thumbs-up.

"What?"

"Let's try negotiating first!"

Shujin dropped his arms to his sides in utter disbelief. "*Negotiating*?" he cried. "She's trying to *kill* us!"

Sure enough, the crazed woman darted around the corner, wearing a wide and sinister grin. "I've found you, Shujin! Surrender now!" She single-handedly aimed her revolver at him. "And *you*," she seethed at Tsumisu, "stay out of my way if you know what's good for you!"

"Pardon me, ma'am." Tsumisu had both hands clasped behind his back, his tone sounding official. "But could you kindly *stop* destroying our facility of institutionalized learning? For you see, we cherish it dearly—"

She shot another explosive round at Tsumisu, barely missing his head as he dodged it just in time.

"*And* we intend to graduate on time," he finished.

"Silence, you! I said stay outta my way or else!" she roared, charging him with dust blown from behind. "Raaaggh!"

"Ah, nnoooo!" Shujin yelled, shielding himself.

Tsumisu exhaled and stepped to his side at the last second, allowing the woman to pass him, but in doing so, something activated in Shujin's bag.

"Dude, check it out!" he exclaimed.

"Am I dead?" Shujin cautiously asked.

Tsumisu snatched his arms away from his face. "*No*, genius, look between your legs."

Shujin looked down and witnessed a glowing object of energy pulsating from inside the bag. Rummaging through it, he retrieved a crystal orb and held it before him. "Wow," he said, eyes illuminated, "I never thought it could do *this*."

"Huh, that thing could light up a city." Tsumisu stood with a slightly twisted mouth, thinking. "Isn't that your grandma's?"

"I-I mean…yeah!" The object began to levitate. "OK, uhhhh, you think she makes these things like bars of soap?"

"You *might* wanna stand back a sec," commented the woman instructively.

"Oh really? Why—whaaa!"

Sure enough, the orb transformed into a single-edge, two-handed sword, having a blue shine to its brilliant blade. For Tsumisu, his suspicions were more than correct, and this mysterious latex-clad lady did just the trick…somehow.

"Woohoo!" he cheered, slapping his shoulder. "You look all Jedi knight now!"

Shujin took hold of the weapon and blinked a few times, inspecting it closely. "Whoa…I *am* all Jedi knight…Think I can face her?" he asked, turning to him. "And I-I know this is wishful thinking, considering…"

Tsumisu nodded in extreme confidence. "Hey, this night *couldn't* get any weirder," he replied. "Besides! We won't have education for a *long time* now, might as well, sir."

Shujin exhaled, and for the first time, he felt like he didn't need to run. "OK!" he said, clenching the weapon with both hands, awkwardly positioning it before him. "Let's do this!"

"Aww, *no*!" Tsumisu shook his head as the powerful woman began boiling over with anger a few meters from them. "Sir, we *really* have to work on your aggressive stance."

Shujin shrugged it off, unoffended. "What?" His voice broke. "This is my *Jedi* stance, dude. Where's yours?"

Tsumisu scoffed with a grin. "Don't need one! I'm gonna try the Obi-Wan mind trick technique; see if she'll complete my homework assignment."

The female entity clenched her fists, her yellow eyes burning with rage. "You're *welcooome*!" she cried.

"Oh! Thank you for your warning earlier!" they said in unison, bowing.

"Dude, how do you think she knew about the sword?" Shujin frantically asked in a whisper.

"Well, have you seen those hips?" Tsumisu nonchalantly muttered back.

He was silent.

"C'mon, man…"

"*Yes*, I've noticed them. How is that relevant?"

"Pfft, with 'dat ass'?" Tsumisu chuckled. "Anybody could've predicted your reaction."

Shujin rolled his eyes. "Out of context—oh God, you're saying because the sword *extended*…" He groaned.

"Heh-heh, ask her to drop her gun—"

"Well, *well*!" she began. "Let's see how experienced you are with that thing, Shujin." She lowered her body into an aggressive stance. "After all, why tease a lady if you ain't gonna use it?"

"Aww, c'mon! Don't encourage him!" Shujin pleaded.

She blew after Shujin first, using her short swords to unleash a ferocious barrage of strikes at him, creating a blinding display of sparks. However, Shujin's newly formed weapon dutifully deflected each attack she initiated. His fourth dan kendo training kicking in, Shujin managed to perform a counterattack, forcing her to retreat. Surprised, she drew her revolver and proceeded to lay out a series of energy blasts; however, Tsumisu, previously dancing around the two in an effort to engage the "mind trick," parried her hand as she fired off each shot.

"You're starting to feel very *sleepy*," he chanted, the gun discharging over his shoulder to obliterate an outer wall. "There is no resistance to the force—"

"Graah! Stop interfering!" she growled, landing a solid and energy-packed punch on Tsumisu's abdomen, only to look up in utter astonishment. "What the *hell*?" she exclaimed, looking at his slightly wincing face.

Having both index fingers placed on his temples, Tsumisu persisted in pseudo-Jedi mind summoning—unaffected by her attack. "Um, you are going to dooo my homewooorrk..." he continued with a haunting chant but slowly opened his eyes. "Yeah, this isn't working, is it honey?"

Having her arm outstretched while levitating midair, the woman retracted her fist. "Who *are* you?" she asked through gritted teeth.

"A responsible student of Okayama High School!" He saluted, looking to Shujin now to repeat the gesture.

"Oh!" Shujin too was quite impressed by the feat of strength he had just witnessed. Was it due to the push-ups? "Um, yes! I'm not sure...h-how you knew my name, ma'am, b-but we are students of knowledge!"

"Indeed we are!" Tsumisu comically crept toward his buddy to stand beside him, maintaining the odd salute. "And our favorite subject is uh...underwater basket weaving!"

Shujin had enough comfort to laugh aloud. "It is a graduation requirement! Yet you have callously destroyed our materials facility—dude, I can't keep this up!"

Tsumisu slapped his back. "Ha! You did good, dude! OK, listen." The Sonzai commander turned to the slowly not-seething and increasingly confused woman. "I'm Tsumisu! This here is... Shujin, of course. And, uh, who are *you*, by the way?"

The woman made a fist multiple times, evidently checking herself to ensure she hadn't made a mistake in her last attack. "That's none of your business! Raggh!" she yelled, charging Tsumisu this time.

"Agh, crap!" Shujin yelled as well, noticing Tsumisu drew her ire away. "Er, you got it?" he called out.

"Uh!" He engaged in martial-arts combat, noticing she was excellent in her technique. "Y-yeah! Hey! Her power is in this—*whoa*!" Tsumisu exclaimed, dodging a beautiful roundhouse kick that leveled a nearby wall. "Wow, you're *good*, lady! You know that?"

"Shut up!" she roared, bearing a fierce scowl. "Why won't you go down? Graah!"

"Power in the what? The *what*?" Shujin called, involuntarily slicing a falling piece of ceiling in half. He stared at it. "Whooaa…did I do that?"

Grinning the whole time, Tsumisu was striding backward as she furiously continued her attacks. "This, uh, jewel thing in her chest!" he answered.

"Oohhh! That glowing thing is a jewel?" Shujin chased after them—feeling sorry he had overstarched his pants that morning. "Hey! We gotta get rid of it then!"

Tsumisu ducked one of her straight-left fists and quickly went to stand beside Shujin once more. "That's the idea! However, her level of strength is *fantastic*…You know that whole spay-neuter campaign for household pets?"

Shujin looked at him with a most peculiar expression. "I-I mean, *yeah* but…?"

"I don't think it'd be ethically right to get rid of it, you know what I mean? Kinda like a male dog missing his balls? Look, just *be* the dog for a second—"

"She'll get *our* balls if we don't do something soon, dude!" Shujin desperately screamed, trying to reach his friend's practical thinking.

Meanwhile, the indigo-haired entity only stood fuming as she overheard Shujin and Tsumisu's unusual conversation; steam poured from her ears as her body shook in fury.

"Aggh! What the hell is *wrong* with you two?" she said. "Shujin! I'm coming for *your* balls! Raaarrggh!" she declared and vanished into thin air.

"Oh no!" Shujin hollered in fright. "I can't see her!"

"Can you feel her?" Tsumisu strafed around, keeping track of her movements. "Hey! I can see you, magic lady! Aaand Shujin? You should look out..."

"What?"

At that moment, she reappeared before Shujin, bearing down on him with a spinning attack. With quick reflexes, Shujin performed a sidestep maneuver and evaded the attack, following up with an energy-laden palm strike to her chest, sending her flying back and onto the ground—the diamond-shaped item fell, bounced a few times, and rolled across the ground, bumping against Tsumisu's foot.

"Aggh!" she cried, immediately withdrawing while inspecting her damage. "Wow! That really smarts, Shujin!" she exclaimed, having a hole where the jewel once sat.

"Wuuahh!" he cried as well, not expecting to do such a thing. "I'm sorry! *Tsumisu*!" he said as he bowed.

"Right!" the Sonzai commander exclaimed, stuffing the gem into his pocket and then bowing alongside Shujin. "Please accept our apologies for desecrating your body, ma'am! As honorable students of knowledge, we, uh...c'mon, dude, a little help?"

"Uh-whuh, we will make it up to you somehow!" Shujin concluded. "That sounds awfully weak, doesn't it?"

Tsumisu gave him a quick glance, nodding. "Well, there go your balls, sir. Eye for an eye, you know..."

"Shh! Stop—are you insane?"

The woman laughed aloud now—in a bright and cheerful manner. "Hey! Take a look, boys!"

As Shujin and Tsumisu cautiously looked up, they witnessed the strange and powerful woman simply materialize the wound away! Needless to say, they were both speechless as they exchanged curious expressions.

"See?" She smiled warmly, dusting off her chest. "All better now!"

Tsumisu calmly turned to Shujin as they stood upright. "That look odd to you?"

"Well, *you* said it couldn't get any weirder tonight, remember? So no, no, it does not." Shujin shook his head, waving with a wince-grin. "Nothing's weird anymore."

"Dude, put your hand down," Tsumisu said with annoyance. "Where's your integrity?"

Shujin scoffed. "*She's* waving too! What? You want her to start attacking again?" he intensely whispered. His nerves were clearly shot for the night—or month.

Soon, the wailing sound of multiple emergency response vehicles could be heard in the distance. The mysterious, body-part materializing, revolver-wielding, powerful flying woman cupped a hand over her twitching ear as she listened curiously—having an innocent expression.

"Oops! Guess that's my cue to get outta here!" she said. "Bye, Tsumisu! Bye, Shujiiin! I'll see ya later, OK?"

She vanished into thin air once again. Mashing his lips together with a frown, Tsumisu stuffed a hand into his pocket and reached for the two-centimeter-in-diameter gem.

"You know something, dude?" he began casually, a gas line exploding in the background as he inspected the object.

Shujin was startled beyond reason, expecting her to show up again. "God…" He sighed, a hand over his heart. "*What,* Tsumisu? That we should get outta here too? I don't wanna go to jail for somethin' *she* did!"

"Ah *besides* that, I think she likes you." He grinned, slapping his back unnecessarily hard. "Now, I'm not a *connoisseur* of the female species—"

"H-how can you—know what? I'm not asking," Shujin remarked with conviction, only to notice he somehow deactivated his weapon into the crystal sphere.

"Shiny thing this is," Tsumisu further muttered, rubbing his chin. "OK, let's say we go grab some nachos."

"Finally! Let's get outta here, dude!"

Fleeing their burning institution of higher learning, Tsumisu comforted his buddy later on by actually stopping by a fast-food chain for fish nachos. After ordering to go, Shujin asked if Tsumisu would accompany him on the way home—fearing Tsumisu's assessment about that crazed killing-machine woman liking him. The Sonzai commander complied, and the two tried their best to inconspicuously walk the streets as if nothing had happened a few blocks away. Who would suspect them? It wasn't as if Tsumisu was carrying around a reflective silver weapon on his back while five-alarm flames sent black plumes of soot and ash into the sky.

Nevertheless, the heavens evidently smiled on Shujin, in particular, for half an hour later, they returned to his domicile on the outskirts of town.

"Dude…" Shujin muttered, hands smashed against his face and leaning wearily on the couch. "What…the hell…happened?"

After taking in a deep breath and exhaling, Tsumisu laid his weapon on a special sword rack Shujin's grandmother provided for his visits.

"Ha, you're gonna make me lie to you, bro." He smirked, rubbing his forehead. "I swear there's so much *plaster* in my teeth. Can you see it?"

"Uggh, I'm not looking in your mouth, sir." Shujin waved his hand in dismissal. However, he did notice a suspicious *crunch* on clenching his own jaw. "Yeah, I'm gonna go change. Help yourself to some drinks in the fridge, man. I'll be back."

"Thanks, sir," Tsumisu acknowledged, grabbing the remote to a flat-screen television. "Guess I'll put it on the ever-so-special-news program that is *no doubt* on."

Shujin scoffed in humor. "I mean, sure, but do we really need an update? It's not like we should anticipate school tomorrow."

Tsumisu nodded. "Yeaaah, I'll just find a nature program about…whale mating calls or something."

Shujin brushed lingering dust from his brown hair. "Pfft," he rhetorically replied, walking upstairs. "Mating calls…"

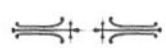

Inside his bedroom, Shujin exhaled deeply, slightly shaking his head in reflection of the night's events. Man, if there was ever a time he needed a reality check, this was *definitely* it. After setting his book bag aside and placing the crystal orb on a nightstand, Shujin stood at the foot of his bed…and fell down face first. Ah, such a warm feeling—nurturing, welcoming. But seriously, who *was* that woman? At times, Shujin swore she really had no intention of hurting him—in fact, it felt like she was…testing him for some reason. Mysteries continued to pile up for the young man.

Hmm, that's funny—he felt cushioned, *especially* his face. But why wasn't he making contact with the sheets? Uh-oh…

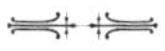

Meanwhile, Tsumisu pressed the device in his right ear. "Captain? Lieutenant? Did you gentlemen catch *all* of that excitement?" he asked.

Snickering childishly once more, Wanako clapped politely. "Commander, that's a big fat copy. What the *hell* was that woman again? And that was a woman?" he asked, raising his pitch unnecessarily.

"Copy here, Commander," Goshinfuda responded. "Apparently removing that jewel of hers reduced her power by an order of magnitude or more…at least that's what I detect. Such a *curious* spiritual signal as well."

"Not sure *what* she was, Wanako, but she was certainly curious," Tsumisu agreed. "I've obtained a gem—"

"Waaahh!" A cry from Shujin suddenly interrupted. "Aaghh! Lemme go!"

Overhearing Shujin's voice, Wanako exhaled in realization. "She *is* a lady of her word, apparently," he remarked. "Good call, Commander. Not sure what to make of it! But good call."

Tsumisu chuckled as he looked upstairs. "Thanks, sir. Please hold for the next customer service representative."

"Pssh, I'm hanging up. I ain't got time—"

"You've got *no* patience, sir."

Tsumisu quickly leaped from the first floor and up to a walkway, expecting the worst. He rushed to Shujin's bedroom, where he found him struggling in bed...or at least his face struggling between the mysterious woman's breasts.

"Not a chance, Shujin!" she said playfully. "You know how long it took me to find ya, babe? I'm not lettin' go! Ha-haa!"

"C'mon now; this can't be legal!" Shujin pleaded. "I'm gonna go blind or something!"

"Hmm..." Tsumisu mashed his lips together and nodded in understanding. "I *don't* know whether I should call for help or giggle aloud."

Shujin found the willpower to break her grasp. He fell on the floor in a seated position, catching his breath. "Tsumisu," he wearily responded, eyes closed as he placed his hands together. "She... can cloak."

The once seemingly bloodthirsty woman sat up and crossed her legs, casually moving her extended bangs.

"Sooo..." she began, her eyes—prominently yellow—capturing the sight of the taller warrior.

Tsumisu clapped twice before placing his hands together. "And here we sacrifice what *would've* been a normal night of fish nachos, for the company of..." He paused. "I'm sorry, what's your name again?"

She raised a thinly shaped eyebrow. "Tetyanaaaa…" she responded.

"Tetyana! Fantastic. So in exchange for fish *nachos,* we have Tetyana…Say, that almost has a nice ring to it, dude."

"She's *living* here, dude," Shujin quickly muttered.

Tsumisu gasped slightly. "Oohhh, I thought this was just temporary lodging—"

Shujin shook his head.

"Hmph, OK. I'm gonna go back and search for that program now…"

"Nope!" Tetyana leaped from the bed and took hold of Shujin and Tsumisu, laying her arms around their necks. "Saaay, you guys brought food? Hell yeah! I'm hungry!"

"I mean, it was literally enough for two people. You know that, right?" Shujin tiredly lamented. "Like, we didn't expect any company?"

Tetyana's expression lit up in surprise. "You didn't? But I thought I told ya I was gonna see you in a minute, Shujin?"

Tsumisu cleared his throat, catching an enormous whiff of her underarm. "Umm, let's see…I dunno how to *say* this, Tetyana—"

"Don't *tell* me you would let me starve!" she exclaimed, eyes sorrowful. "Shujin! I'm huuungryyy!"

"*All right* already! Fine, you can have mine…and Tsumisu's," Shujin muttered quickly with conniving eyes.

"Yay! Ha ha! You're the *best*!" she instantly pulled Shujin toward her, rubbing the top of his head aggressively. "Shujin loves me! Shujin loves me!" she chanted.

"Ow! Cut it out, Tetyana!" he exclaimed with arms flailing about. "Aahhh! Lemme go!"

Tsumisu exhaled in a deep sigh of relief. "Woo! That is a *whole* lot of female musk—how long were you looking for him again, Tetyana?"

Tetyana kept holding Shujin in a submissive position as she looked up. "Me? Hmm, about eight hundred years, give or take a couple," she said. "Why do ya ask, big guy?"

"Oh, n-nothing! Dude, I'm going downstairs to covet my nachos," Tsumisu remarked calmly. "Um, I *told* you so. Good luck taking a shower *alone*. Thanks for your time." He patted his head and politely left the room, slowly closing the door behind him. "*Wow*, Febreze is strangely calling."

⟿ ⟾

Shujin reached out. "Uh, hey! Come back, man! Arrgh! Tetyana?"

He found it immensely difficult to escape her grasp; she seemed genuinely *strong*. Despite his eagerness, Shujin decided patience might work this time around—although he noticed her left breast becoming exposed, so it wasn't exactly the most prudent option.

"Uh-uh, what say we call it a night, huh?" Shujin inquired, sweat beading on his forehead.

"He's gonna do *what* to the nachos?" Tetyana pulled him up with a curious expression. "Stay here, babe! Don't move!" she exclaimed and chased after Tsumisu.

Immediately slumping on his bed, which now smelled like her, Shujin fell backward in a heap, arms outstretched. "Aww man, I *do* have to shower..."

⟿ ⟾

Meanwhile, Tsumisu was only seconds away from radioing his clansmen in, but a quickly charging Tetyana came out of nowhere and ran straight into him.

"Gotchaaa!" she sang, knocking them both off the second floor. "Prepare yourself!"

"Oh nooo!" Tsumisu hollered, landing on his back. "Agh! Dang, Tetyana! What the hell was that for?"

She sat cross-legged on his chest. "Mwahaha! Gimme those nachos, ya greedy bastard!" she pointed to him valiantly with a big grin.

Rolling his eyes, Tsumisu reached into his pocket and pulled out the gem. "I'll trade you this *shiny* diamond for my nachos? See how pretty it is? Ooooo…"

Her eyes became wide with anticipation. "That's *mine* too!" She tried snatching it from him but noticed his speed outmatched hers. "Cut it out!" She attempted again but to no avail. "Grrr, why are you so darn mean? Shujin is nice to me!"

"Yeah, nice enough to offer my nachos for ransom? Agh, who am I kidding? Here, Tetyana." He laid the gem in her hand. "I don't want you feeling like a ball-less dog."

"Gee, thanks! That was easy," she remarked sort of taken aback, implanting the diamond in her chest once more. "Yeah! There we go! Now, gimme those *nachos,* ya greedy bastard!"

Tsumisu repeatedly banged the back of his head against the floor. "Shujin! Would you come and get your violent girlfriend, please?" he called, but there was no response. He turned his sight back to Tetyana. "You knocked him unconscious, didn't you?"

Tetyana blinked twice. "Never! Hey! How come you could withstand my attacks? I oughta beat you up right now." She leaned forward with an aggressive grin, cocking a fist back. "C'mon, you!"

"*No*!" Tsumisu declared. "You can't make me, and I-I'm not gonna fight a girl again! That's unethical!"

"Ethical, shmethical!" she proclaimed, charging her fist now. "You owe me an explanation!"

Tsumisu banged his head several more times in frustration. "Sh-Shujin! *Damn it,* get down here, sir!"

Suddenly, there came a stumbling sound, accompanied by a roughly opened door, and Shujin leaned against the railing—worn, mangled, and out of sorts.

"What did you say…dude?" he wheezed.

Tsumisu's eyes widened, but his expression remained blank. "Hmm, *nope.* Just don't worry about it." He turned to Tetyana. "W-why are you still on top of me again? Oh…nachos. They're in the kitchen—"

"Woohoo!" She celebrated and vanished. She grabbed Shujin and then reappeared with him over her shoulder. "What? You're not coming with?" She sassily laid a hand on her hip and smirked.

Tsumisu rose to his feet, only to realize there was even *more* eight-hundred-year-old-lady musk on him now. Fantastic. "If not just to watch you eat, I wouldn't miss this entertainment." He grinned humorously, noticing the gurgling sounds from his buddy. "Er…you sure that's *safe* for him now?"

Tetyana's expression lit up in surprise again. She had not particularly been paying attention to the cues of Shujin's enervated disposition. "Oh! Hey, Shujin? Shujin, honey bunny?" She started patting his face repeatedly. "Hmm, that's strange. Wonder what's wrong with 'em?"

"Say, *that's* what the ruckus is all about!" said a jolly voice from upstairs.

It was a slightly overweight Japanese man in his early forties—Mr. Komaru Iwato, Shujin's father. He strolled out of his room in red-and-white-striped pajamas, sporting the cheesy striped cap with fuzzy ball at the end too.

"Hiya, Tsumisu!" He waved.

Tsumisu meekly saluted him. "Evening, Mr. Iwato! Sorry to disturb you at this late hour."

"Agh, it's not a problem." He waved his hand in pleasant dismissal. "I see you brought a *lady* friend over, huh? Ha ha! *And* I see Shujin is gettin' to know her the old-fashioned way!" His laugh was loud and infectious.

Tetyana smiled with confidence. "Yup! Sure are gettin' to know each other *real* well!" she agreed, suggestion behind her voice.

"Saaay! This is a nice place ya got here! Hope ya don't mind me stayin' awhile?"

"Nope! Don't mind at all! You're just what the doctor ordered for Shujin, so make yourself at home, uh..."

"Tetyana!"

Mr. Iwato gave an enthusiastically appreciative thumbs-up. "Tetyana! Well, it's nice to meet ya, and the guest room is open... unless you plan on spendin' the night with Shujin there? Ha ha ha!"

"If I may offer a *better* suggestion, could you convince her *not* to steal my nachos?" Tsumisu threw it out there just to see if support would come his way. "Right..."

"Don't mind if I do, Mr. Iwato!" Tetyana returned the greeting with a thumbs-up of her own.

"Okeydoke, good night now!" He gave a friendly wave good night. "Er, Tsumisu, you *don't* have a lady friend with you?"

He forced a smile. "Not tonight, I fear."

"Hey, don't sweat it! I couldn't score on my first try either! Ha ha! All right, good night, guys!"

Tsumisu exhaled in disbelief, watching the jolly man return to his room as the new and *apparently* amorous woman stood before him. It was astounding how far Mr. Iwato was willing to go in order to ensure his son...became a man. Evidently, such a measure was the acquisition of a "lady friend." Sure, it wasn't a mystery that Shujin and Tsumisu were the *worst* virgins ever, though neither man was inclined to end such a position anytime soon.

After all, the whole high school...or what was left of it, knew Shujin was especially notorious for being an awkward gentleman—he had lots of nice speech but always failed to put the moves on the ladies. Tsumisu, in contrast, was literally *never around* long enough to engage in such activity. Top-secret global missions and the like made him such a *mystery* among the ladies. Well, they weren't alone in that regard. Either way, it was clear that relationship building had its hang-ups, but Tsumisu knew he was absorbing more of the *social* attributes surrounding it than his fellow man.

And just look at him now, drooling all *over* that poor woman's outfit…and not awake to enjoy the fruits of his labor. Stop staring, Tsumisu; it's weird.

CHAPTER TWO

The high school building was still undergoing repairs, and this left time for the Sonzai commander to review some spiritual information he had acquired from being in contact with Shujin and the—according to the parked ship he had observed—*visiting* warrior woman named Tetyana. Unfortunately, Tsumisu's opportunity to gain *further* information about the origin and spiritual structure of her power was squandered by his chivalry, which prompted him to return the gem to Tetyana—a futile exchange for fish nachos. All was not lost, however, for a key moment arose during their battle: the repressed talent he had detected within Shujin became active on her proximity.

Truth be told, this sounded *really* sordid.

Nevertheless, such a phenomenon provided some registry of information with respect to the *only* strong lead the Sonzai clan possessed to the interruption of ethereal string frequencies within the earth's spiritual energy complex.

The three-hundred-strong clansmen returned from their global assignments, pooling information on what they could find, but again, everything was speculation in the end. Damn it all, they needed *direction.* Seemingly in perpetual thought, Tsumisu walked along the modestly busy streets of Okayama during rush hour, hands stuffed into black-jean pockets. At this point, he couldn't be bogged down in what he couldn't control, not while he had something to work with.

For example, *eight hundred years* was a long time, especially for someone outside of their knowledge of energy acquisition, to be in pursuit. Preliminary conclusion? This must mean Tetyana was from *outside* their domain of observation. Hell, all the senior clansmen *and* the grandmaster unilaterally agreed on the "curious" nature of such power—it was complex, like there was a *design* behind it, like the Egyptians' construction of the pyramid of Giza. You understood it served a particular *function,* just not what that function *was.*

On another lesser note, folks, Tsumisu's first deep inclination about a lady was considering her as a damn *machine.* Wow. Maybe he shouldn't have burned those magazines from his perverted school associate, Asaka.

Leaning against a crosswalk sign, he scoped his surroundings, as he always did, making his way to his apartment—Akari on his back, but no one gave him a second look. Speaking of a second look, what was that fiery streak across the sky? Tsumisu peered at it for a few more seconds, adjusting his position to blot out the bending rays of the setting sun.

Was that a *plane* of some sort? No, it looked to be military in nature...but definitely not *people-grade* military. *Crap. It's going to crash land, isn't it?* And here he was, standing on the stairs leading to his apartment door, just three *measly* meters away. Well, at least he didn't have to get dressed again.

Another advantage? The density of people and their natural propensity to be distracted by such an event provided the right amount of cover the Sonzai commander needed to turn his boosters on. Leaping into the air, he took off at a speed of three hundred kilometers per hour, heading toward the landing point he roughly calculated from the flaming craft's speed and trajectory, hoping to intercept it in time.

He detected *one* soul on board. *That's it?* By observational estimates alone, this thing was large enough to accommodate a whole flight crew to swap the International Space Station team… and *then* some. No matter, Tsumisu bolted into the woods once more, his right hand steadily hovering above the hilt of Akari—who knew? He might have to improvise to alleviate some damage or in case the Japanese military decided to scramble jets and intercept this foreign vehicle. Speaking of which, how many people would be filming this on their smartphones and posting videos to social media in the next six minutes? Ugh, he could just envision the slew of alien-conspiracy-nut shows exploding on Netflix now…

"Commander Tsumisu? This is the captain. Do you read me, sir?" Goshinfuda suddenly radioed in.

"Loud and clear, Cap'n!" Tsumisu was barreling along, pacing his breathing. "Kinda occupied, my brother! What've you got?"

"*Aha*! So it *is* the ship you're going after?" he replied with insight.

"Sure is! I, uh, I'm not trying to play Superman here, Captain, but it'd be nice if we could assemble a *medical* team at the coordinates you will see me stationary at in the next…two minutes. Persons on board I detect are *not* human and…scared as hell!" Tsumisu tried to stifle his laughter. "Gracious! That is some *serious* spiritual outlet. Do you copy, Captain?"

Goshinfuda motioned to his preassembled medical team nearby, signaling them to hold on. "Copy! I'm ahead of you, Commander! I've got a team on standby, waiting for your order to move in. Lieutenant Kadochi *is* reporting military action thirty kilometers to our south and east on the array. I suggest you intercept the nonhuman subject and *disappear*. Copy?"

Tsumisu grinned with confidence, knowing the Sonzai had outsmarted every government piece of equipment for decades. "Copied..."

Breaking through a clearing within the forest, the Sonzai commander placed himself at about his best estimate of the vessel's impact point. It had lost all control moments past, and now the gravity of earth was doing its work, pulling the object in with tremendous velocity. Slowly, Tsumisu unsheathed Akari and let the blade ring as he placed it before him in perfect vertical positioning. Glimmering in a brilliant silver finish, the blade was engraved with a forked lightning bolt from the hilt to its tip. And in the next moment, Tsumisu placed his left hand at the blade's middle, bracing himself with a planted foot. The vessel was *fast* approaching.

"T minus five, four...three...two..."

With a mighty crash and compression wave, Tsumisu ensnared the object within the field of energy he amassed between himself and the weapon, suspending the vessel at a forty-five-degree angle from the surface. Indeed, he was pushed several meters backward; however, the energy field was more than sufficient to withstand the titanic kinetic energy behind the imperiled 130-meter-long vehicle.

Using the field once more, he traced its physical energy to shut off the burners and set it down gently—the residual heat more than seared the ground, charring the grass and evaporating whatever water remained.

"Captain?" Tsumisu radioed, sheathing his weapon without looking. "Cancel that medical team. How long before the jets get here?"

"You've got...six minutes and counting, Commander," Goshinfuda promptly responded. "Good to hear on the negative medical team, but whatever you have to do, *do it.* Copy?"

"Loud and clear as always." Tsumisu nodded and approached the vehicle. "Woo! That's some *stupid* heat. O-K, let's see...red paint stripped here...that's a funny insignia," he muttered, noticing the partially smudged acronym "DMP."

His expression lifted in piqued interest. He was trying to avoid the military only to save a *foreign* military space vessel? No way.

"Well, I hope the passenger is friendly," Tsumisu muttered as he cautiously hopped up on the nose. "Hello in there!" he yelled in a welcoming tone. "I won't hurt you! As a matter of fact, we're going to have some unwelcome company in a few—"

At that moment, the front hatch began to open with a mechanical whirring, lifting from right underneath him. Tsumisu immediately leaped off and ran to the front, noticing there was a frantically shouting, high-pitched female voice emanating from within—this was coupled with a frantically *repeating* autonomous voice, apparently giving instructions.

"Um." Tsumisu hopped up once more, figuring the ship was in such disrepair the magically extending ET stairs wouldn't work anyway. "Excuse me? Ma'am? Are you OK in there? We've gotta get *moving* like...really, really soon."

Within the technologically advanced cockpit was a chocolate-skinned woman with long, partially curly yellow hair and elfin ears, awkwardly plopped on the floor. Her arms drooped at her sides, and tears flew out like steam from Old Faithful. Her red-and-black uniform was in pretty good condition—despite some stocking splits.

"Oohhhh, I knew I shouldn't have gotten up todaahaaay!" she wailed. "Now I'm gonna dieee-hieee-hieee!"

The tinny nature of her voice really made the scene that much more dramatic.

"*Whoa.*" Tsumisu was trying to shroud his fear on entering the cockpit, enjoying the flowery smell. "Ma'am! Excuse—damn it."

Finally kneeling in front of her, Tsumisu noticed she looked far more human than his imagination had earlier surmised. He caught sight of a name tag on the left side of her chest: "Arlette Sauveterre, First Lieutenant."

"Arlette, is it?" he began kindly.

"Huh?" She instantly ceased her intense crying, though a stray tear here and there strolled down her puffed cheeks. "Yes? That's me!"

Wow. Oh sweet mercy, wow. Blushing, he noticed her unusually big eyes were the deepest blue he had *ever* seen. OK, Tsumisu, she's *definitely* extraterrestrial.

"We have to get you out of here, Arlette. My name is Tsumisu. It's great to meet you!" He offered an assisting hand.

Arlette sniffled once and then twice…"Oh, *thank you*! Oh my God, you saved my life! Ah ha ha haaaa!" she celebrated, bringing with it a mighty hug that well-oiled vise-grips would be proud of. "Yaaaay! You're my herooo!" She stopped *very* suddenly. "Uummmmm, *what* did you say your name was? And where am I?"

Tsumisu tried to readjust himself in the wake of her impressively devastating hugging technique; given her legs and arms were clasped around him, it made things a *tad* awkward to move about.

"Ha! Who needs compression clothing?" he muttered, wresting his arms free. "I'll explain in a second. Captain? Time!"

"Time is *up*, Commander! *Move*!" Goshinfuda instructed with great haste.

"Copy! Hang on, sweetheart! I have to make this quick!" He smiled, grasping on to her.

Arlette blinked curiously, twitching her nose a few times. "Make it quick? *Hey*! How dare you! We're not even dating!" she fussed in her high-pitched tone. "How can you make it quick?"

Wow again. Tsumisu's expression said the same. Leaping from the cockpit, they landed beside the vessel; there, the Sonzai commander initiated an energetic cloak for the both of them and

Arlette's ship. The very moment he did so, three fighter jets flew overhead at low altitude, clearly on a search-and-intercept mission. Their movements indicated a second pass, so Tsumisu remained still with an incredibly interested lieutenant continuing to display her talent of strength sans fatigue.

"Oh my!" Arlette exclaimed, watching the jets make their coordinated turns, maintaining the roar of their fierce engines in the air. "Is that for us?"

"Sure is!" Tsumisu happily responded, realizing she was easily excited. "Sooo…we're staying *here* until they're finished! Think of it like a…uh…"

"Ooo! I know!" she peeped brightly—you could've mistaken it for a baby chicken. "Hide-and-seek game! Yay!"

Tsumisu laughed aloud, failing to stifle it in fear she might be sensitive to laughter. "OK, I'm sorry, but it is *exactly* like hide-and-seek, Lieutenant." He managed to compose himself. "That's a cute description too. You often do that?"

"Yeah!" She made herself comfortable, taking hold of his broad shoulders just as the jets made a second flyby. "You like it?" she shouted.

"*What*?" he replied in humor. "I-I can't hear your face!"

"My what?" Arlette grabbed her red uniform cap sitting on her professionally pinned-up hair. "What?"

"Ha ha, you can stop shouting now." Tsumisu grinned, having too much fun. "Our, uh…unwanted neighbors have given up hope it seems. We win!"

Arlette gasped enough to nullify the oxygen concentration within a square kilometer. "Yaaaaaaayy! We win! That's so *awesome*! Umm…" Her propensity for immediately halting thoughts was apparent as a finger lay on her bottom lip. "What did we win? Oh my *goodness*! We've won together, and I don't even know your name!"

"I think that's a Goo-Goo Dolls tune…Oh, it's Tsumisu."

Arlette blushed with a smile, shapely eyebrows accentuating her eyes as she gave him an infatuated gaze.

"Really? Tsumisu? That's a *cute* name..."

The wind blew in a moment of awkward silence.

"Yeeaaaahh, say, we've gotta get *you* somewhere less conspicuous," he replied, dodging her sudden, if he was correct, come-on by observing the area around them. "And I think I know just the place too."

"B-b-but what about my ship?" Arlette was reaching for it. "We can't just leave it!"

"Nah, it'll be fine." Tsumisu pulled her waving arm back gently. "Now, I hope you don't get motion sickness, my dear..." He sighed, leaning forward.

"What do you mean? Waaahhh! Tsumisu! Slow down!" she hollered as he took off.

Indeed, he was headed toward one of the only places where he deduced the hospitality was uncannily benevolent...and he was a bit nervous.

"Really, dude?" Shujin threw up his arms as he stood at the front door in a T-shirt and pajama pants. "*All* the way out here? You carried her all the way here? Why not a local hospital or somethin'?"

"Eww *no*, not a hospital, but certainly, sir!" Tsumisu brightly exclaimed, trying to instill reassurance in his panic-stricken friend. "And this lady is a little shaken up, as you can tell from the *swirliness* of the subject." He nodded to the lieutenant's face. "So! Here you go. Now be careful. She's taller than you, so watch that center-of-gravity...thing."

Shujin shook his head. "I-I feel like this will be a refugee camp in a second," he muttered, helping him take the dizzied Arlette to the couch. "Could you at *least* tell me how you got here like this?"

"Ah ha ha! *That's* not the point!" Tsumisu proclaimed like an overexcited game-show host. "Besides, I just bumped into her on my way to get nachos, as usual, and boom! I said to myself, 'My place has one bedroom…Shujin's place has a *thousand*,' and *that* idea alone brought me here."

Shujin kept a straight face, not blinking.

"And the rest, as they say…" Tsumisu laid a hand on his shoulder, speaking solemnly. "…is *history*!"

"Did, uh…anyone ever tell you how horrible a liar you are?" Shujin folded his arms and twisted his mouth. "Seriously."

"In all honesty? I *did* technically bump into her…It was one hell of a bump!" He rubbed the back of his neck, pondering the magnitude of energetic release on said collision. "Oh well, I suppose I should get the poor woman some water. Oh, her name is Arlette, by the way, and she's a *lieutenant*. How freakin' *cool* is that?"

He swiped Tsumisu's *consoling* hand away. "Great, now I can finally update the sign-in sheet with an 'occupation' section."

"Shujin? What's all this about?" asked an investigating Tetyana, flying into the living room, wearing his pajamas. "Honey? What's that strange lady doing here?" She danced around him midair, hands on her hips with a grin.

Exhaling, arms at his sides, Shujin closed his eyes. Evidently, the previous week had been an enormous trial. "Tetyana? I-I dunno what to tell you, OK?" he said. "Tsumisu just *shows* up, and now she's there, but in the meantime, we gotta look after her until—"

"It snows," Tsumisu finished quickly. "Which may be quite soon. Or was that for Europe? Yikes, getting my geography mixed up."

Taking advantage of the altogether disadvantaged Shujin, Tetyana clamped on to him suddenly, nearly pulling him to the floor. "Shujiiin! She's one of those mean ol' *military* officers! She can't be around here, Shujin!"

"Waah! Cut it out!" He wore an exasperated, irritated expression while attempting to break her grasp. "And what do you mean she can't?"

"But she'll try to *detain me*, Shujin!" Using her well-developed strength, she finally pulled him to the floor and began rolling *everywhere*. "And you don't want me to go to some stinky, run-down prison, right, Shujin?"

"Nooo! Agghh! Stop, Tetyana!" he cried, arms and legs helplessly sprawled out.

Subtly rubbing his chin with a frown, Tsumisu verified some additional energetic reactivity between the persons of interest; close proximity *did* initiate a particular sequence of events. And why was she wearing his clothes again? Geez, this was a lot worse than Tsumisu had previously estimated. But…

"Dude!" Tsumisu approached them, not bothering to help. "Dude! Think of it like that Twister game."

"*Help* me!" Shujin pleaded.

"In a few, I'm just gonna walk to the kitchen and fetch a glass of water. *Meanwhile*, why don't you ask ol' Tetyana there about that jail talk! Pardon me," he muttered, stepping over both of them carefully. "Just gotta get something…"

"Tsumisu!" Shujin reached out desperately as if he were being pulled underwater. "Come back, man!"

"Ha ha! Ya can't get away, Shujin!" Tetyana remarked brightly, throwing her chest on his face now. "Isn't this *nice*? See how we get to play around and not go to jail?" she remarked, pushing up and down against him. "*Agh!* Oh you like that, huh? Horny devil—"

"N-no! You've got it all wrong!" he cried.

"Don't be shy." She grinned slyly, lowering her hips. "I won't say no to you, Shujin…"

"Hiya, son, I'm back! Sorry for being late—hey-hey! Nice *job*, son!" Mr. Iwato proudly exclaimed, walking through the front door with briefcase in hand. "Now *this* I gotta keep for my records." He quickly reached into his jacket pocket to whip out a smartphone.

"Dad! Glad to see you!" Shujin was trying to return his father's greeting, but his voice was obviously muffled. "Uh, hey! What're you doing?"

"Say cheese!" he directed.

Tetyana paused for a really wide grin, throwing a peace sign. "Ha ha! Aww, it's our first picture together, Shujin! See that?"

Mustering the strength to escape her deadly-ish grasp, Shujin slid away to catch his breath and propped himself against a wall. "Whuh! Hey, Dad! I ordered…a pizza…for us…" His head drooped in his weary state.

"Say, that's fine, son!" Mr. Iwato continued to speak proudly while approaching but not before noticing the curious new individual drooling badly on the couch. "I'm willing to bet that's *Tsumisu's* lady friend huh? Ah ha ha! He can't stand to be one-upped by ya, eh, son?"

"No, Dad. That's a…semiabandoned military lady or something, according to Tetyana there—nooo! I'm just making a statement, Tetyanaaaa!" Shujin rolled out of the way as she began attacking once more.

Returning to the chaotic living room with dissolvable nausea medicine in one hand and a glass of water in the other, Tsumisu blew some hair out of his face and shook his head.

"Evening there, Mr. Iwato," he said courteously. "Yeah, that's *not* my 'lady friend'…"

"Are ya *sure* there, Tsumisu?" Mr. Iwato asked suggestively. "She's a damn good looker if ya ask me!"

"*Yes,* she certainly is a gorgeous woman." He nodded. "At the moment, she needs some medical attention—as will Shujin in a minute! Ha ha!"

"Ha ha!" Mr. Iwato laughed in response, catching on to the joke. "Haaa, that's why I like you guys! Well, I'll be back in a few. Gotta get changed!"

"Uggh, Tsumisu, you're not *helping*, dude!" Shujin lamented. Tetyana was sitting in his lap and mussing his hair nonstop. "S-stop it, Tetyana! What's gotten into you?"

She stared at him with a super innocent expression. "Oohh, Shujin, I'm just afraid you're gonna let that mean ol' *military* woman wake up and find out I'm *here*." She nodded to him to follow along. "See what I'm saying?"

Adhering to her words finally, he raised an eyebrow. "What kinda trouble are you in, Tetyana?"

"Bingo!" She pointed enthusiastically. "That's why *she* shouldn't be here, baby! Ugh! Tsumisu! D-don't give her that!"

"Uuuhhh." Tsumisu's eyes widened, looking quickly between her and Arlette. "It's too late?" He winced. "Besides, you need to fess up anyway, lady-who-likes- destroying-school-buildings."

"Nooo! You don't understand!" She flew up to the Sonzai commander and grasped his shirt. "She'll take me back to that awful planet, and they'll want to do all kinds of crazy stuff to me!"

"Experimental or otherwise? 'Cause prison is no fun either way," Tsumisu nonchalantly responded.

"I mean…" Her ears twitched at the sound of Arlette moaning to consciousness. "All I did was help my little empire attack *another* little empire! That's all!"

"Aha!" Tsumisu's expression grew insightful. "I *knew* you weren't from around here, Tetyana. That being said, how long ago was this 'horrible act of aggression' on your part, my dear?"

Arlette was rubbing her face, trying to get her bearings together now.

"Uh, um! About eight hundred years ago now?" Tetyana's voice became desperate. "She's waking up, guys! C'mon! Do me a favor, pleeease?"

Rising to his feet and dusting his pants, Shujin approached the couch. "Now look, I'm sure we can work this out some way, Tetyana." He gestured with a negotiating hand. "All we gotta do is talk this over, right? I'm sure—"

Tetyana flew toward her apparent love interest and hid behind him, grasping onto his shoulders. "You have to protect me, Shujin! You don't know these people!"

Shujin rolled his eyes but then greeted the alert lieutenant. "Hey there!" he began. "Sorry for the rude awakening, but I hear from my friend that you've had quite the time getting here!"

Her eyes wide and curious now, Arlette looked at the shorter man before her—noticing incongruously blue hair poking out from behind.

"Yeah! It was really traumatic! Thanks for helping me ummm…"

"Shujin!"

"Yay! Hi, Shujin!" She beamed brightly, hands clasped together and laid on her lap. "I'm First Lieutenant Arlette Sauveterre of the Devonian Military Police! Hee-hee! Sooo…what's that fuzzy stuff behind you?"

"Uhm, this is Tet—agh, c'mon now," Shujin groaned as she prevented him from turning around. "Cut it out!"

Tsumisu grinned, being humored. "I got it, dude." He rose to his feet and plucked her up. "Ta-da!"

"Hey! What did ya go and do that for, Tsumisu? Oooo, I *knew* you were a mean one!" She scowled, kicking her legs furiously. "Put me down!"

Tsumisu comically dodged as he continued displaying her. "OK! Yikes…but see? Where's the fire now?"

Arlette's eyes grew wide as her jaw dropped. "Oh my gosh! That's *Mercenary Tetyana*!" She pointed in exclamation. "Wow! I was *looking* for you!"

"See?" Tetyana flew up to Tsumisu's face with a clenched fist. "What did I say, ya moron?"

He fearfully held his hands before him, looking for support. "Uhh, there *still* isn't a fire?"

"I'm on it, dude." Shujin sat down beside the suddenly shocked lieutenant. "Sooo, what were you doing looking for Tetyana, Arlette?"

"Ummmm..." She looked to the ceiling, a finger on her bottom lip. "Oh yeah! She's a most-wanted criminal for...let's see...violent war crimes against the Devonian Empire." She was counting on her white-gloved hands. "Reckless endangerment, destruction of imperial property, attempted theft of imperial property, traversing the sixth sector without proper identification! That's a *bad* one," she whispered to Shujin with all seriousness.

"Er...and the *first* one wasn't?" He grew a sweat drop, smiling nervously.

Tetyana was pacing around, pulling on her hair. "OK, look! Let's just say that *none* of this happened, yeah? Aaannd then we'll all go to bed tonight and wake up the next morning with a brand-new day! What do ya say?" she stated in a bright and cheerful manner.

Tsumisu pumped his fist in wholehearted agreement. "I think that's a *swell* idea, Tetyana!" he declared.

"Really?" She grew glittery eyes. "You mean there's hope?"

"Um, you *might* have to pay for that traveling violation." He winced and grinned.

"I didn't come here to arrest you anyway, Tetyana!" Arlette assertively stated. "I came here because I needed to warn you that um...ummm..."

"Gee, did you have a rough landing, Lieutenant Arlette?" Shujin asked courteously, noticing she had trouble remembering things. "Dude? I told you she needed a hospital!"

Tsumisu fervently shook his head. "Dude…that's just how she *is*…" he whispered intensely.

With mouth slightly open, Shujin nodded in understanding. "Oohh…"

"I got it!" she exclaimed suddenly, startling everyone. "Tetyana! I have to put you under protective custody!"

Tetyana laid both hands on her hips, twisting her mouth with a reproachful frown, apparently she was trying to shake the fact swirling in her mind about being arrested…and *replace* it with protection.

"Are ya *sure* you didn't have a rough landing?" She peered at Arlette in doubt.

"Yep! See, *Tsumisu* stopped my ship from crashing!" Arlette enthusiastically began to explain, looking to everyone intently as she acted out the event. "I was all, 'Ahh! Oh my gosh!' and on my monitor, I saw this man on the ground, holding a sword! And then before I knew it, *smack*!" She slapped her hands together, once again startling everyone. "And here I am! Soooo…I think my ship is not doing so well, but I'm just fine! Hooray!" She genuinely beamed. "Isn't that great? Oooh, Shujin didn't you say you ordered pizza? I swear I heard pizza being mentioned somewhere," she stated eagerly, licking her lips.

Shujin looked at Tsumisu, giving him a most peculiar expression. "Wait! Stopped your ship from crashing? Rewind that again? Tsumisu! What aren't you tellin' me, dude?"

"Ah ha ha ha ha ha ha!" he exclaimed in an annoying, cheesy tone. "Got stuff to hide? Me? Naahh!" He waved his hand in dismissal. "Look, the point is Tetyana is *not* going to jail, and Arlette is not gonna vomit all over the place! And…and I say *that*, my friends, is a victory."

Tetyana turned to Tsumisu with the consistent, doubtful eyeballing. “Yeaaah, you’re hidin’ stuff all right, big guy.” She cocked her fist back and psyche-out threatened him suddenly.

Tsumisu stumbled backward, shielding himself. “Don’t even joke about that, Tetyana! What the hell, girl?”

“C’mere you!” She began to give chase. “Fight me right now!”

“No! I’m not fightin’ a girl again!” he exclaimed, childishly running around the couch now. “Especially not *you*!”

“So you’re yellow-bellied *and* a liar!” Tetyana cried, cutting off his path to confront him.

“And you’re a *name*-caller!” Tsumisu pointed out in retaliation.

Meanwhile, Shujin laid a hand on his forehead, trying to absorb all the out-of-place information he had encountered just now.

“OK, why does Tetyana need protective custody?” he asked. “I mean, she just about leveled me and Tsumisu’s school! Is somebody after her?”

“Ummm…” Arlette searched her mental registry once again. “Yep! It’s a wicked individual named Taras Ganymede! He’s a *real* nasty one.” She leaned toward Shujin as if she were recalling looking at the reports. “Some say he’s turned himself into a super cyborg—”

“S-super cyborg?” Shujin’s voice broke, and he cleared it, not realizing what physiological stage of development he was in. “Coming *here*?”

Tsumisu was being put into a standing choke hold now. “What’s this about Taras again? Tet-Tetyana! My gosh! You’re a *violent* lady!”

“Explain yourself! Who the heck are ya?” she demanded, legs clasped around him as she tried a submission move from behind. “Grrr, start talkin’ or face the…consequences!”

Tsumisu sniffed the air—finally, a fresh floral scent encompassed her presence. “Hey! You took a bath? I’m proud of you!”

"What?" Tetyana's expression was awkwardly surprised. "Of *course* I did! What're ya doin' sniffing on me anyway? Take this!" She began crawling over him to get a better grip. "Damn it!"

Arlette looked on, impressed. "Wow," she remarked. "Say, can you do that too?"

"Uh-uh, you mean the wrestling part or the *non*wrestling part?" Shujin answered with a nervous question, rubbing the back of his head.

"Here, lemme show you!" Arlette offered, suddenly bringing the poor man, who was a half-meter *shorter* than she, into a C-clamp-style submission. "Like this! I'm first place in all the DMP wrestling competitions, professional circuit—oh! Across all seven sectors..."

Shujin's face was turning red, then blue, and then polka-dotted. "Y-yeah! I can tell! Um, thanks for the demonstration, Arlette!" he wheezed out. "C-can you let me go p-please?"

"Yep!" she happily complied, returning to her seat as if nothing had happened. "I can teach you if you'd like!"

"Wuuhhh, yeah...much later." He tried to get his senses and blood circulation back to normal operating condition. "Tsumisu? Stop playing around with Tetyana and help me figure this out, please?"

Tsumisu exhaled, slightly disappointed. "Fine, man. I was *trying to* earlier until your misplaced-hostility girlfriend started challenging me...again," he explained as he approached, Tetyana, who was still at it.

"Sh-she's *not* my girlfriend, dude! You need some nausea medicine too?"

"Ha! I bet your *face* needs medicine." The Sonzai commander pointed, sitting to Arlette's right as he plucked Tetyana off with a "pop." "Playful critter..."

Tetyana punched his chest. "I don't wanna hear it!" She stuck her tongue out and flew away to land on top of Shujin.

"Ow! Tetyanaaa," he lamented once again. "I can't catch a break, I swear!"

She had both hands in his hair, twirling strands around her fingers. "I'm *giving* you a break, Shujin, sweetie pie! Aww, you don't like it?"

"*Not* your girlfriend, right?" Tsumisu gave his buddy a straight face and adjusted his seat on the couch, legs crossed, gentleman-like. "Now um, Lieutenant Arlette, you mentioned a name earlier...Taras? Who is he, and why does he want to come *here* again?"

She happily turned to him. "What's this now? You wanted a demonstration too, cutie?" She beamed, cracking her knuckles.

"Nooooo," Tsumisu replied in a monotone, backing himself further into the couch just as she readied herself. "I-I'm asking about the really evil guy you mentioned before—"

"Oooh, *him*!" Her expression turned serious, though her face was too adorable for the point to be driven home. "Taras is the *worst* of criminals—he's been terrorizing multiple regions of the galaxy for hundreds of years, all to fulfil his *dastardly* quest to gain as much power as possible!"

Tetyana, for the first time, grew a stern disposition. "*Taras*," she growled, a clenched fist following her remark. "*Now* it makes sense why you're here..."

"You two have a history, I assume?" Tsumisu inquired, trying to cover his Sonzai-conditioned interrogative tone.

"Yeah, if that's what you wanna call it," Tetyana affirmed. "Damn it, you know you can't do much to offer 'protective custody,' right?" she looked at Arlette, speaking with certainty.

"Weelll, the idea was to bring you back to headquarters! But... I'm *not* sure how we're gonna do that now," Arlette said regretfully, looking at the clearly troubled Tetyana. "Sorry."

Regaining the force the of Jedi-Knight syndrome he and Tsumisu had experienced recently, Shujin gave the two women a confident expression.

"Hey, super cyborg or not, I'm sure we can take this guy should he wanna show his ugly face around here." He smirked.

Tsumisu returned the sentiment, nodding with conviction. "Shujin has a point—nothing will escape our terrible wrath!"

"Nothing shall!" He quickly followed with a voice of justice. "But, uh…can you give me an indication of just *how* strong this guy is?" he asked Tetyana, knowing she'd be the best gauge.

"Are you kidding? This bastard is a *powerhouse* if I've ever seen one." Tetyana clung onto Shujin dramatically. "I've fought against him before and only escaped with my wits at times…"

"What?" Shujin's tone was concerned, catching her gaze. "You actually fought with him?"

She nodded. "He's a *traitor*, baby. Yes, it's true that I'm on the run, but only because I'm a mercenary for the long-conquered empire of Ordovicia." Tetyana frowned. "Taras…he sold us out to the Devonians."

"Eight hundred years ago," said Tsumisu.

"Yeah…now he's got this horrible ship, the *Leviathan*. Rumor has it he constructed it after stealing technology from the very civilizations he wiped out." Tetyana shook her head, regretful. "Who knows how many millions died 'cause of him. Here's what I don't get, though: I thought Taras was on *your* side," she said to Arlette.

The lieutenant confidently shook her head. "Not anymore. I'm not sure of all the details behind his motives, but apparently, the empire knows Taras is working to eradicate the Devonians, the Ordovicians…*everybody*!" she exclaimed. "He's just a raving…madman now. And to be honest, nobody knows how to stop him."

Tsumisu had gained an understanding. "Now it makes even *more* sense why you're here, Arlette," he said. "Whatever Tetyana's made of, and looks like Shujin too, the Devonians don't want Taras's hands on it. Am I right?"

She nodded. "That's right, Tsumisu."

Tetyana place a gentle hand on Shujin's cheek. "Listen, honey, I-I spent my whole *life* searching for you. I don't want you to face him!" Her eyes grew compassionate. "I still have my ship, so we could find a way to get outta here, no problem, yeah?"

"Pfft, are you kidding? We *live* here!" he replied brightly, wanting to lighten her mood. "We're not about to allow some creep in the galaxy push us around, Tetyana!"

"Gotta love that swagger, sir!" Tsumisu snapped his fingers and pointed with gusto. "As far as I'm concerned, the guy sounds like an intergalactic robo-*chump* with a peashooter! And so he shall *fall* like a chump. We'll avenge *every* last person he's ever terrorized!"

"Oh my gosh, you boys are so brave!" Arlette clasped both hands before her, dreamily staring at Tsumisu, stars and twinkles littering her expression. "*Wooow...*"

"Er..." He waved a hand in front of her face, getting no response. "Shujin and I don't...take kindly to chumps, is all."

"Hey..." Shujin suddenly remembered something at that moment. "Like...a chump?" He grinned in amusement, a beat coming to him.

"Like a chump, hey!" Tsumisu returned the acquainted lyrical phrase. "Perchance we do it all for the—"

"*Not,* a heh, in front of *her,* please?" Shujin exhaled in well-founded relief.

"All for the what?" Tetyana asked, pinching Shujin's cheek. "All for *what*? C'mon! Tell me! You're hiding somethin', Shujin!"

"Ow! Stop it, Tetyana!" He swiped her hand away but in vain.

Arlette blinked a few times, biting her bottom lip as her glance shifted between the two young men. "Did I miss something?" She tilted her head.

"Nope! Not a thing, my dear. Just make yourself at home...*here,*" Tsumisu responded frankly, rising to his feet to stretch. "Agghhh, OK. Sir? I'll see you tomorrow or something. When are you getting another phone?"

Shujin scoffed at the fact his friend would just *leave* him and also that he'd bring up a problem that wasn't his fault.

"Really?"

"Yes. Really."

"Man! Just…make sure you stop by tomorrow, 'cause I'm gonna need some help!" Shujin's tone held annoyance within it. "Obviously?"

Tsumisu pushed out his bottom lip as he shook his head. "Nah, I disagree. Now, for *chumps*? Sure. Ladies? Noooo." He walked over to the sword rack and retrieved Akari. "See ya, dude! Bye, girls!"

And with that, Tsumisu darted quickly out the front door.

"Tsumisu! Unbelievable," he muttered, looking at an enamored Tetyana. "I'm *locking* the door tonight, just so you know."

"That can't stop *me*, Shujiiin!" she responded brightly, tapping his nose with a finger. "I'm comin' to get'cha! Ha ha!" Tetyana gave him another breast-defying hug. "C'mere, baby!"

"Aggh, noo!" Shujin hollered desperately as she overpowered him. "Tetyana, I can't breathe!"

"Oh my," Arlette gasped in sudden insight, being shaken up by the ferocious tussling right beside her. "Wah! Does Tsumisu have a *last* name?"

CHAPTER THREE

During midmorning of a new day, the Sonzai commander sat cross-legged at a table in his humble apartment, meticulously analyzing the data his clan collected during Tetyana's rampage. Spiritual frequency estimates and comparisons with respect to their previous global reports were printed on several dozen sheets, and Tsumisu, pen in hand, frowned in deep thought. There *had* to be something he was missing—at least that was what he surmised.

Dwelling on what he *didn't* have wasn't doing him much good, so Tsumisu pieced together what information he had managed to collect. No more theories regarding Tetyana's origins—her verbal revelations told she was from an Ordovician civilization, obviously outside of earth and the solar system, and the Ordovician civilization was evidently attacking *another* civilization, the Devonians. Not only that, Tetyana's energy had to have been of significant importance if some intergalactic asshole was spending hundreds of light-years in search of her. Yeah, Tsumisu sensed an interrelationship somewhere, a connection…

Tsumisu's hunch that Shujin was a lead for his clan's investigation was heating up; however, it remained unclear as to *why* he was a lead or what both Tetyana and this Taras Ganymede knew about him. Tetyana had spent her entire eight-hundred-year existence in search of Shujin. Why? Did *she* even truly know? Hell, for all intents and purposes, what she did possess in terms of information was enough to make Tetyana devoted to finding him. Additionally, since she had started searching so long ago, that inherently meant Shujin was *not* who he appeared to be. And that being said, where the hell did *he* come from? Ha, Tsumisu chuckled at the thought of asking Shujin what antiaging face cream he applied each morning.

All right, Taras had a ship that could wipe out a civilization. Boring. Asteroids could do that. Nevertheless, such energetic capabilities on a technological level were certainly worthy of applause. Further, Tetyana was all too aware and afraid of the *Leviathan*—not that she'd be a victim but…something worse. So the question arose: With all the power Taras had amassed, there had to be an even *greater* power he sought, right?

Tsumisu chuckled again, bringing the video-game character Kirby to mind. Maybe Taras figured sucking everything up would make him stronger? Ha, if he absorbed Tetyana, he'd transform into a *girl*. Giggling childishly and then sighing in elongated humor, the Sonzai commander realized his train of thought was signaling him to take a break.

Aahh, television. What better way to destroy brain cells? Not moving from his seat, Tsumisu turned his flat-screen on. Wouldn't you know it? The news…

"…where Japanese military spokesman Ichiro Nanaki said yesterday's events were, quote, 'A secret training exercise gone wrong,' and offered an apology to the public for the scare."

"Incredible," he muttered in disbelief. "Well, at least they apologized about it."

Not bothering to flip through channels, he immediately turned it back off and figured throwing some tunes on would suffice—besides, getting up to stretch both his legs and his mind would do some serious justice...*unlike* the truth behind Lieutenant Arlette's sudden appearance on earth. Approaching a cherrywood-substitute bookshelf, Tsumisu programmed a small MP3 player-speaker combo to the music genre metal and pressed play. The first song in the playlist? "Make Me Bad" by the band Korn.

A smirk came to him as he head-banged to the rhythm, briefly playing air guitar. "Much better," he said, having to adjust the volume before he disturbed the downstairs residents again.

Tsumisu thought while strolling to the kitchen that perhaps he should check on his buddy. Would it, perchance, "make him bad" if he didn't? Laughing aloud in utter self-amusement, Tsumisu figured it best to abstain from further personal jokes, lest it inhibited his judgment more among his fellow clansmen on their next meeting.

After all, he never *really* apologized for sitting pretty in that tree during Shujin's time of need; he never really apologized for deserting the poor man while Tetyana investigated Shujin's hair follicles one by one. A *galactic* wrestling champion lieutenant had sat idly beside him. But setting personal accountability aside, Shujin *did* have more rooms than he; Tsumisu's six-hundred-square-meter domicile could only accommodate one person half-comfortably, such was the purpose of leasing it during his three-year investigation within Okayama High. And upon looking himself over, Tsumisu knew he was *a lot* of person. So, twisted logic dictated that he didn't *really* need to call Shujin...

He placed a pan atop his flattop electric range, and his fish filets began to grill nicely. At least he wasn't contemplating his existence this time. However, such a willingness to discard responsibility over the newly acquainted alien ladies prompted Tsumisu to wonder where he may have inherited such behavioral characteristics. Brushing off a clear and present threat from said alien ladies *didn't* seem natural; was it arrogance? Or simply knowing something they didn't…and it came off as arrogant? Maybe it was the product of training he received from Grandmaster Sonzai and Captain Goshinfuda over the years; yet any prudent warrior knows gracefully wielding a sword doesn't necessarily explain *why* you're wielding it.

Great. He was contemplating his existence. The next song on the playlist was Metallica's "Sad but True." Oh the irony.

As his meal simmered, Tsumisu forced himself to walk to the digital phone. Pressing redial, he waited…and waited. Strange, no answer? Hmm, maybe Tetyana was chasing him around *again*. Even so, the man should seriously set up his voice mail for once. Just when he was setting the receiver down, it rang. The caller ID displayed "Iwato, Komaru."

"Is that you, sir?" he answered.

"Shh! You gotta keep your voice down!" Shujin responded in a whisper. "I'm hiding from Tetyana, but it's not easy!"

Tsumisu snickered. "Dude…where are you?"

"In the hall closet! Listen, I knew you'd call eventually 'cause you've got a loud moral conscience!"

"I *would* publicly admit to that," Tsumisu firmly replied. "However, I'm not the one seeking shelter in a closet."

"What's that got to do with anything?" Shujin sighed in exasperation. "So you're not gonna apologize?"

Silence.

"Shujin! Ooooh, Shujin! Where are youuu, honey bunny?" called a nearby Tetyana in a playful tone, though it harbored some mischievously ill intent. "Don't be scared. I won't hurt ya, baby! Well, not *much*! Ha ha ha!"

Exhaling through his nose, Tsumisu clenched his jaw once or twice in contemplation. "All right, dude. I'm sorry."

"*Thank you.*" Shujin's breathing slightly shuddered.

Tsumisu could hear footsteps, no doubt Tetyana's, in the background. Tsumisu found himself captivated by the moment, wondering if she'd pull that cloak-and-capture trick. Now, just how *big* of a jerk would he be if he...yelled out loud? Don't do it, Tsumisu, tempting as it may appear. Just spare the man some angst.

"Whew." Shujin exhaled cautiously. "OK, she's gone."

"Has this been going on all morning?" Tsumisu had to ask.

"*Yes.* To be honest, I was gonna call earlier for assistance... which I can't count on nowadays," he grumbled. "W-wait..."

"What? Look, don't move!"

"I'm *not*!"

"Tetyana, dear, was that you calling earlier?" asked Mrs. Himaki, about to head out.

"Yeah that was me; I'm trying to find Shujin!" she explained, sensationalizing her demeanor. "I haven't been able to find him, Grandma. Did you see him leave?"

"Aww, he's a *shy* creature," the amiable woman reassured her. "And to answer your question, I'm very certain Shujin remains here. But perhaps you can draw him out by utilizing the stereo?"

Tetyana was silent for a moment, probably thinking and subtly twisting her mouth. "Stereo...*oh*! The karaoke machine is hooked up to it, right?"

"Oh God," Shujin muttered in steep concern. "My grandma is helping her. This can't be happening."

Tsumisu winced heavily. "Is she on your side?"

"Explain 'side,' because I don't see you holding up your end of the bargain."

"OK...why are you bringing up old issues?"

"That's right!" Mrs. Himaki brightly affirmed. "There's nothing a little serenade can't fix. Good luck now, Tetyana. And if that doesn't work, my hot springs are always open!"

The lovestruck mercenary waved. "Appreciate it! Ha ha, this oughta coax my little sugar-snap out of hiding..."

Tsumisu was struck with realization. "It's just you and her?"

"*Yes.*" Shujin used a coattail to wipe his brow. "Geez, I-I can't stay in here forever."

"Well, since clothes are made of fiber and since fiber is a good source of nutrients—"

Suddenly, microphone feedback reverberated through the house. "Hey! *Woohoo!*" Tetyana cheerily did her sound check. "Shujin, baby! I know you can hear me! And sooo I made a little song like forty seconds ago in my head? But I think you'll like it!"

"I didn't know she was talented," Tsumisu remarked, anticipating the tune. "Did you know? Ooorrr…"

"Are you making light of my situation?" Shujin wearily whispered. "Damn it! Just be honest!"

"I am sincerely trying to help here!" Tsumisu chuckled. "You gotta believe me. Now just enjoy the song and make peace with yourself!"

"I swear, why do I even bother—"

Tetyana blew into a harmonica, matching her tone. "Ah OK. Ooohhh, where is my baby, Shujin? He's really sweet to mee," she sang, twirling around as a ballad ensued.

Tsumisu bobbed his head to the beat, catching a groove, though his expression was *dead* serious. Shujin, in contrast, sweat even harder and was helplessly embarrassed.

"And when I find my baby Shujiinn," Tetyana continued, "well, he'll just wait and *seeeeeeee!* Yeah!"

"You're gonna die," Tsumisu remarked flatly. "It was nice knowing you—"

"Arlette is headed your way for your information, sir," Shujin quickly retorted. "To *your* apartment! You're welcome."

Tsumisu was just about floored. "Y-you told her where I lived? How *could* you, dude?"

Shujin's eyes widened in shock. "You *brought* her to where I live! I'd consider that a fair trade! You see what I'm dealing with—oop…"

"Shujin?" Tetyana called out again, taking in a *long* sniff of air. "Hmmm…"

Suddenly, there came a knock at Tsumisu's door; rather, it was an interesting series of rhythmical knocks.

"Well, I hear music playing," said a soft female voice from outside. "Maybe I'll try picking the lock! Hee-hee!"

"Fu—OK, so," Tsumisu began in whisper, starting to sweat under his arms. "I understand your vengeance reaction, and I've also apologized…which you've accepted."

Shoved in the far corner of the closet behind cases of luggage, Shujin carefully pulled his legs up to reduce his size—watching that door as if his life depended on it.

"And um…" Tsumisu's thoughts raced with visions of bizarre extraterrestrial technology capable of evaporating simple metal compounds in seconds…just to pick a lock. But didn't abductions happen by beams of light levitating the victims into a ship? *Stop.* "Sir, I pray for the both of us—"

"Got'chaaaa!" Tetyana declared in a singsong voice, snatching the door open. "You're gettin' better at this sneakin' around, Shujin!"

"Waahh! Oh nooo!" he cried, dragging and tumbling noises sounding throughout his ordeal. "Tetyana, I'm on the phone!"

Dial tone. Wow! Was Tsumisu's hand shaking as he stared at the receiver? No time! Carefully setting the phone down, he rushed to the door, quickly opened it wide, and put on a nervous smile—fearing the worst.

Sure enough, there stood Lieutenant Arlette, holding an advanced, personal-data-assistant-style device, entering a flurry of instructions.

"Now, let's see here," she muttered. "I thought I had—yep! Here it *is*!" she exclaimed happily, bringing forth a materialized key for the door. "He won't know what—"

"Uhm, A-Arlette!" Tsumisu greeted her, locking eyes with her, pretending to be surprised to hide his trepidation. "What are you doing here? I mean, it's nice to see you again!"

"Yay! Hiya, Tsumisu! How are ya?" she quickly hid the key behind her back.

Without a second thought, Tsumisu attempted to get a closer look at the results of her magic trick from an array of angles, some awkward, yet she perfectly obstructed his vision by keeping them face-to-face.

"You're lucky I'm a lieutenant, Tsumisu!" she responded with a giggle. "Can you guess why?"

All right, first inquiry from an alien girl whereby there is no immediate support. Answer it with caution or—Wait! Is that your fish burning? Girl does *not* equal burning fish! Get it together, dude!

"Uhhh, w-why don't you come in?" Tsumisu answered with a question and bolted toward the kitchen. "Ha! Just super-extra crispy on one side, it'll be fine!" he cried in relief, an overhead stove fan coming to life as he fanned smoke away. "Woo! Uh, just make yourself at home!"

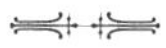

Arlette, helplessly curious, stepped inside, closed the door, and immediately began *touching* random things. Since the area was illuminated by incoming sunlight, she had zero issues investigating and shifting the few available pieces of furniture around.

"Don't touch the sword, please?" Tsumisu kindly yet cautiously requested, still salvaging his fish. "Thanks!"

Darn, it was the *very next* thing she wanted to investigate. But it was sooo *shiny*! Oh well. Reluctantly drawing her hands away from the sword rack, Arlette then noticed inscriptions, numbering about twelve or so, in black ink beautifully written on white parchment paper hung on each wall. Even more intriguing was the fact they were all in *perfect* alignment in spacing and height, regardless of their location with respect to one another. What could they all mean? she wondered. A belief system maybe?

While poking each and every last inscription, Arlette observed the accompanying items on the walls. They were positioned *far* less meticulously. There hung posters of various musicians (Van Halen's *Women and Children First* stood out the most), framed high-definition satellite photos of weather phenomena, and a printed slogan in red text stating, "No Matter, No Fear," above his sword. Wow, there *had* to be more to him than possessing the ability to stop crashing space vessels.

"Ooo, what's *this*?" her eyes were drawn to the data printouts on the table. She crouched down to shuffle through them. "Hmm, looks serious…Hey, is that my name?"

Moving sans friction, Tsumisu sloppily scooped up his clans' top-secret documents, wearing an innocent grin. "Y-your name? That's just plain crazy talk, Arlette. I-I mean, if it *were,* it's probably because I was just…uh…copying it *down* so that I could *remember* what your name was!" He shrugged.

The lieutenant smiled, staring at him with great interest. "You're not a good liar, cutie! Hee-hee!"

⁂

Dang, was he *that* obvious?

"Ha-ha! Whatever do you mean?" he cheerily responded in denial, scurrying away to temporarily dispose of the documents in his bedroom before scurrying back. "Listen, uh," he began, nervously rubbing his hands. "Why don't you just…have a seat? Are you hungry?"

Arlette simply giggled in amusement, not saying anything as she continued to stare.

"Um…is that a yes or a no?" Tsumisu gave her a grin-wince, still not accustomed to her unusually large, ocean-blue eyes. Why was she *staring* like that? Would she stop? "Right. So! How was your trip here? I mean, did you walk or…fly?"

"I walked the *whole* way!" she happily replied, rising to her feet to stand in front of him.

Tsumisu's eyes fell to her *impressively* fit legs, and he mildly scoffed in realization. "*Indeed*—no wait, what am I saying?"

Arlette noticed his line of sight drift down and immediately recaptured his gaze with her own. "Soooo…do ya know why you're lucky I'm a lieutenant now?" she sweetly inquired.

Tsumisu slapped his forehead in recollection-slash-thought-redirection, only to *additionally* realize he had forgotten to wash his hands after handling the fish filets earlier. What was more, his sweaty hands weren't improving the situation. Well, on the bright side, this was the *best* liquid solution project he had developed outside of chemistry class.

"*That* was the question, wasn't it?"

"Suuurre was!" Arlette affirmed.

In a cruel twist of environmental conditions deteriorating (at least in Tsumisu's mind), the next song on the playlist? Korn's "A.D.I.D.A.S." Life often proved to supersede coincidence at the most inopportune moments—particularly *now.*

"Well?" Arlette continued to smile, but finding her attention drawn to the background music, her elfin ears twitching. "Oh *wow,* all day?" she gasped. "My gosh, is that *true,* Tsumisu?"

He took one giant step to the side and shut off the MP3 player, standing in front of it nervously. "Why, yes, I *am*…I-I mean, I'm *not*!" He clenched his eyes in regret. Always think before you speak, dude. "That is to say I *have* infrequently dreamed about it sometimes…"

Hands innocently clasped before her, Arlette intently listened but with confusion written on her face.

"But not *all day*! Ha! Especially not *to*-day! Ah ha ha!" Tsumisu subtly shook his head, still regretful. "Eeehhhhh...God, I'm such an *idiot*."

"Uuummm," she responded, clearly sifting through information in her mind. "Is *that* your answer to my last question?"

"No! I mean, *no*. Listen, to walk this entire way proves your devoted nature to get things done as a...uh...lieutenant of the Devonian Military Police?"

"Yay!" she cheered with applause. "That's right! So, if you were wondering why I'm still wearing my uniform, it's because *somebody* hid my ship from me. And guess what my ship has?"

Tsumisu rubbed his fish-juice-and sweat-ridden hand on his chin, thinking. "Er...all your stuff?"

"Yep! Like a change of clothes for a few weeks, shampoo, conditioner, body lotion—ooo! My shaver, that one's *important*." Arlette counted on her fingers as she spoke. "Nail polish, lipstick, rollers, hairdryer...uuumm, was I finished?"

Tsumisu exhaled, piecing together what she was saying. "Shujin didn't *really* tell you how to get here, did he?"

Arlette approached him, beaming. "Nope! Well, I think he was trying to tell me. But I knew I could track ya down, for a true first lieutenant *never* loses her suspect!" She stood to attention in serious declaration and salute, giggling afterward. "Aawww, you're so *cute* when you're nervous!"

Indeed, Tsumisu cowered back into a strange position, caught off guard by her sudden change of attitude. "Cute? Uh, wait..." He stood upright now. "Are you s-saying that because of your nature to be a 'lady on a mission,' you utilized that device to find me...and *would* have found your ship earlier, spare finding me, if not for the energetic barrier...hiding your ship?"

"Uuumm..." Arlette pressed a finger on her bottom lip, staring at him blankly as she tilted her head. "I think so? But that sounds way too complicated, Tsumisu. I just wanted to see you again!

Why'd you leave so soon yesterday? I wanted to talk to you some more!"

Gosh, why'd she have to push her arms together and squeeze her *anatomy* like that? Stop staring, Tsumisu. Oh no, did she catch you staring? Whew. Fate, it seemed, was leaving him well-written postcards without the cheesy palm trees.

In an effort to dismiss self-accountability and dump it on Shujin, he inadvertently set *himself* up to have Arlette at his apartment anyway—regardless of whether she understood the circumstances surrounding *why* she was standing before him. There...she...was.

Horrible thoughts began to swell within his virgin mind. Did she intend to sleep here? Where? Oh gosh, she had to shower too, right? She'd have to be *naked* in order to get *clean* in his *shower.* What if her towel fell in some incongruous scenario? OK, defuse those consternations and redirect. Prove that fate is freakin' *wrong* and steer this situation back on course, Commander! Gosh, that *fish juice* though...

"Well, um, it was just some *ninja* business I had to attend to; that's all!" he innocently replied.

Tsumisu noticed she *closely* followed him down the short hallway to the bathroom as he strolled backward. Seriously, he just needed to wash his hands. A simple task, right? So why increase the difficulty by reversing natural humanoid movement? *Fear.*

"I-I mean, it had nothing to do with writing your name down... which I-I've never done on ninja business."

"So you *do* have something to hide, don't you, cutie?" she stepped even closer to him, hands behind her back. "Can't tell me, huh? Hee-hee! I bet it's a big *secret*!" Arlette gasped in realization. "Wow! Like your *sword*, right?"

The diminutive size of his apartment granted quick access to the bathroom, and he stumbled through, reaching for the light switch and successfully turning it on.

"A-Arlette, look..."

Tsumisu gained the will to turn his back to her, reaching the lavatory sink, not *quite* understanding what he was afraid of in the first place; but he couldn't shake the feeling of foreboding. Was it because of the Tetyana-stalking-Shujin incident? Was Arlette stalking *him*? Stop. Control your damn thoughts already.

"I'm more than happy to take you to your ship, OK?" he said.

"OK!" she responded brightly, walking inside the bathroom. She stood beside him, her white knee-high boots audible against the hard floor. Arlette stared at Tsumisu with a smile. "You're *really* nice, Tsumisu."

What was *that* supposed to mean? It's a general statement, dude. Calm down. Or is it?

"Oh! Uh, am I now?" he asked in an effort to maintain subject defusion, gaining a good lather now. "Thank you, Arlette. Er, you are too! I suppose this mutuality of niceness is representative of uh…a committee of 'nice people' in this country somewhere?" Tsumisu hated his convoluted explanations sometimes. "And would you believe it?"

She was essentially shoulder to shoulder with him. "What?" she enthusiastically inquired.

"They are even *nicer* than me!"

Arlette gasped. "No way!"

"I'm dead serious!" he exclaimed.

Tsumisu finally felt "right" in his head now that his hands were clean. He could only hope they wouldn't get dirty by some other unethical means that exceeded both his control and judgment—*stop.* Redirect.

"Now since you're interested, I can tell you where these *other* nice folks are located."

"Wow." The lieutenant stared dreamily, yellow stars encircling her head. "I'll bet they learned it from *you* first, huh?"

Good *heavens* this girl had a one-track mind…and he could *really* see those stars. OK, just dry your hands and pretend as if all is as it should be. Why is she standing so close? Not saying Arlette's scent—*leagues* better than Tetyana's lady musk, he might add—wasn't enjoyable, but *why* was his back against the wall? *Why* wasn't he handling this better internally?

"Whuuhh, I might've sent a strong letter of benevolent expressionism once or twice…in the past." Tsumisu grinned, clearing his throat politely. "Do…you realize how close you are? I feel troubled with peculiar tingles—I said that *aloud*."

Arlette sighed audibly, starting to blush. "*Yeeaah*…we're pretty close, huh Tsumisu?" she said, pressing herself against him.

Alien boobs! *Alien boobs*! His eyes widened, sweat droplets glistening on his brow like fresh morning dew.

"Weeeeell, I'm ready to go if you are!" he remarked quickly. "No wait! Not ready to 'go' but t-to physically *exit*! Fu—"

"Hmm?" She snapped out of her daydreaming. "Aren't ya gonna eat first?"

"*Eat*? Pfft, I've got a whole 'nother stomach of material to metabolize!" he proclaimed, patting his lower abdomen. "Trust me; it's only a *mild* condition."

Arlette covered her mouth, laughing in hilarity. "Aww, you're really funny too! I think I'll come back here and stay with *you* from now on!" she stated concretely, locking eyes with him. "Yep! Suuuure am! Guess you'd better make some room, cutie!"

Dude, you're making things worse. Either shut up or use some of that Sonzai methodology to figure this out. All right, try diplomacy but *don't* stutter.

"W-well, fu—" he began, stuttering. "Listen, Arlette, since you've got 'lady operations' to attend to…" Tsumisu gestured with his hands. "You'll need sufficiently *better* accommodations to… uh…to do that. Besides, just look around!"

Arlette blinked once and then twice and smiled pleasantly. "I don't mind that your place is small, cutie!" she said. "Besides, it's kinda *intimate*, don't ya think?"

"And our current situation isn't?" Wrong answer, Tsumisu. You've scored a negative F on your test today. "Intimately *humble* that a lady—"

"I can still do all of my 'lady business' *here*, silly! See? You've got a shower..."

Fate is farting twenty-four-hour-old nacho binge in your face right about now, Tsumisu. Diplomacy isn't working.

"But it's *bro*ken." Tsumisu nodded steadily, noticing her eyes following his movements. "So I've recently resorted to using either Shujin's shower or...theeee *sprinkler system* outside! Er, whichever is most convenient for the occasion, of course...?"

Needless to say, the lieutenant was struck with astonishment. "Wow, so the entire neighborhood watches you take a shower sometimes?"

"Y-*yes*." He winced badly, praying this story would succeed. "Just don't tell anyone."

"OK!" She happily saluted. "Your secret is safe with me! But oh my *goodness*! With so many people watching, how is it a secret, Tsumisu?" Her expression was adorably inquisitive and filled with genuine concern.

He sighed, relaxing his shoulders in a slump. "W-we just won't say this to anybody *else* then?"

"Yay!" Arlette grasped onto his hand, leading him out of the bathroom. "Well, c'mon, Tsumisu! Don't just stand there! Let's get to my ship already!"

"Whoa! Wait a second! I gotta get my keys!"

"You won't need 'em if I come back with you!" She giggled.

Wow. That was awfully clever. Tsumisu found it mentally strenuous to formulate a rebuttal.

"I-I mean the keys for my motorcycle," he responded, in truth. "The only reason why I had to 'improvise' last time was because I didn't...uh...have an opportunity to *use* it. But now..." He paused patiently, watching her eyes study him with love. "Since we're here, we can use…the motorcycle."

"Uummmm, nope! I like it when you carry me, Tsumisu!" She whipped out dissolvable nausea medicine from out of nowhere. "See? A first lieutenant is *always* prepared! Yay!" Arlette happily proceeded to leap into his arms. "Wow, you're really *strong* too…"

Upon one final gargantuan fart from fate, the stench of reality, as it were, explained that Arlette *did* have a rebuttal for just about everything. Was this epiphany something she too encountered? Hmm, why is she handing you nausea medicine? Whatever, somebody open a window…please.

CHAPTER FOUR

"Huh," muttered a thoughtful Goshinfuda, setting his shovel aside. "Would you take a gander at that?"

"Gandering mode activated," replied Wanako, doing the same. "This ain't made by human hands, I'll tell you that much right now."

"And that only means *this* is our source." Tsumisu wiped his brow, propping his shovel in the ground. "Transmission frequency matches our previous reports, Lieutenant Kadochi?"

Kadochi Owaru held a laptop in his hands, checking readings. "Affirmative," the seventeen-year-old technical officer said, crouched above the pit they had dug out. "That capsule has been broadcasting an indiscriminate high-intensity radio signal into space for about three months now. Anyone wanna guess how Tetyana knew where Shujin was located?"

"Or why Taras is headed this way," said Wanako. "That explains the elevated extraterrestrial activity earth's been encountering—it's a damn buffet invitation."

No more than eighteen hours of investigative work on behalf of the Sonzai clan turned up a strange and clearly foreign module buried underground in the forests of Okayama; it looked aged, yet that was likely due to natural weathering and erosion processes. Nonetheless, the module was fitted with a host of technologies; the most interesting of these were life support and cryogenic suspension. At this point, it didn't take a genius to put two and two together...

"This is too small for a young adult to fit in," began Goshinfuda, crouching to investigate it. "The obvious guess is that whoever sent this capsule intended for something like a *child* as a passenger."

"That's ya boy," Wanako commented, looking at Tsumisu.

"Yep." He nodded with a sigh. "Something tells me we've stumbled on an ongoing interstellar conflict between the Devonians and Ordovicians..."

"In other words, what kind of shit did we step into *this* time?"

Tsumisu chuckled. "Precisely, Lieutenant. I've got a supposition: if Tetyana is Ordovician, and the Devonians conquered *them*, and she's been charged with *attempted theft* of imperial property..." He looked at his fellow warriors. "Shujin is Devonian, gentlemen."

"Damn. The Devonians have no doubt sent someone to retrieve him for their empire," concluded Goshinfuda.

"Exactly. We'll get another guest soon."

"Hmph. Let's assemble a team to contain this area; we must meet with the grandmaster with our findings."

"Agreed, Captain." Tsumisu's eyes rose to the heavens. "It may only be a matter of time before things start getting *real* ugly. I hope Shujin's prepared..."

A warm breeze overtook the night air as a young woman with fierce blue eyes, 1.81 meters tall, wielding a dual-edge katana, stood valiantly before a battle-ready Tetyana...behind Shujin's house. She wore purple fitted Devonian armor, elegant in design with imprinted symbols. It attached to her shoulders, chest, and forearms as well as from her waist to her feet, leaving her midriff exposed.

Tetyana summoned her own armor. It was similar in style, though gold in color. Shujin, who was conveniently confined to an energetic sphere (courtesy of Tetyana), could've sworn there existed deep similarities between the Devonians and Ordovicians... but at this point? He *reaaaallly* thought they were taking this too seriously.

"Um," he began, voice slightly muffled. "I'm sure we could just talk this over! Like I can call my grandma to make tea and—"

"It's nice to see you again, Princess *Suzuka*." Tetyana smirked, unsheathing her tantos and materializing a single-edge katana with a dark blade. "I beat ya to the punch, so he's *mine*. Got it?"

Suzuka also gave a smirk, twirling her weapon once as the wind blew her *long* arcing pigtails behind her. "You may have won the battle, Mercenary Tetyana, but you shall certainly lose the war," she declared. "Shujin belongs to *me*. It is naught but fate!"

"Really? So fate told you to throw him away and leave him to the wolves?"

"How dare you!" Suzuka raised a clenched fist. "It was *your* actions that spurred his discharge from the Devonian Empire! It is *you* who are responsible for imperiling his life!"

Suzuka rested her weapon on her right shoulder, her jet-black hair glistening against the moonlight. "Now, hand over what is rightfully mine...and I *might* spare you harm."

"Ooohh-hooo, you must have me mistaken." Tetyana brought her weapon into a samurai-style position. "Because you're gonna have to *take* my sugar from me..."

"Actually, too much sugar can cause type-two diabetes!" Shujin comically interjected. "C'mon! Everybody is gonna see these *huge* ships just hovering around! That'll draw the police and news crews, and I-I don't have the nerves for that today, girls!"

"You're really funny, Shujin!" said a little girl, poking his transparent prison. "Say something else!"

"I'm glad you appreciate my efforts, Dahlia, but I just wish they'd work on your sister and Tetyana for *once*!"

"M-maybe you should keep trying?" suggested an equally concerned Arlette. "Why don't *you* give it a shot, Dahlia?"

Dahlia's green eyes looked at the lieutenant. "I don't think it'll make a difference," she said, her tone bearing confidence. "When Sister Suzuka has her mind made up, it's pretty tough to change it!"

"My man ain't gon' make it," muttered a nervous Wanako, hidden and watching from a distance. "*Not* trying to sound pessimistic..."

"Copied, sir," replied Tsumisu. "You're doing *great* out there, by the way—"

"Can't I just *save* the dude?" he asked. "I mean, being trapped in a bubble can't *possibly* feel honorable in a situation like this."

He chuckled. "Negative, Lieutenant! Remember, our job is infiltration, information acquisition, and oversight...OK?"

"Well, call the grandmaster and ask if he can bend the rules a bit." Wanako shook his head, doubtful. "Shit, we might need to call his grandma for that tea."

The inevitable came to pass; twenty-four hours after the Sonzai clan excavated Shujin's suspected transport capsule, they were indeed met by more outside visitors—Suzuka and Dahlia Devonia, princesses of the very empire responsible for sending Shujin to earth. Needless to say, their presence brought even *stranger* occurrences into the Sonzai commander and his clansmen's ethereal energy array.

With Wanako deployed in the field, Tsumisu, Goshinfuda, and Kadochi remained at the encampment, monitoring the incoming readings. The frequencies of the energy complex they utilized were converted into data, thus translated into coherent information. And the results? The spiritual power output of Tetyana and Suzuka with their respective ships. It was obvious they were engaged in a (so far) intense standoff.

Strangely enough, *no* indications of Japanese military intervention were detected by the Sonzai—a stark contrast to Arlette's entry, given her ship was significantly smaller. Nevertheless, they were finally retrieving much, much-needed information.

"See that peak here?" Kadochi pointed out on a computer monitor as he sat between Tsumisu and Goshinfuda. "That's the precise signature of Tetyana—enhanced by two orders of magnitude. If I weren't having astigmatism issues, I'd swear there were *two* signals integrated into a single propagation."

The captain rubbed his short black goatee in thought as he stood to Kadochi's left, watching the analysis as it came in. "No, you're right, Lieutenant; it *is* a merging of the two sources of energy. Symbiotic, Commander?"

"Or pseudosymbiotic," Tsumisu replied at Kadochi's right, leaning against the table by which their equipment was placed. "Almost like the energetic interaction is preengineered. Either way, Tetyana and her ship, the *Diablo,* share the same origins. Now, we could say the same for Suzuka there…" He pointed to her energy signal. "Baseline spiritual integration in my observation."

"Extremely harmonious," agreed Goshinfuda. "In fact, that's *so* harmonious I'm willing to bet the Devonians are well-versed in spiritual energy manipulation."

"The surprises just keep on coming." Tsumisu grinned. "Case in point, Kadochi, overlap that small signal with our warrior ladies. Anything look familiar about that?"

Kadochi, adjusting his glasses, pressed a few keystrokes and hit the enter key. "Say, that's *Shujin,*" he remarked in a calculated yet soft-spoken tone. "But…his signal looks like Suzuka's *and* Tetyana's."

Tsumisu nodded with internal resolution. "We need more data, of course, but gentlemen, I think we've found ourselves a relationship here with respect to my blabbering on of repressed talents."

"Impressive," Goshinfuda acknowledged as he tossed his ponytail behind him with a grin. "I'll inform the grandmaster of our preliminary results."

"Understood." Tsumisu patted his slightly shorter comrade's back once and turned toward the monitor again. "Lieutenant Wanako, you still there, brother?" he radioed in, amused.

Diligently on the ground and observing the scene, Wanako provided visual confirmation to the clan's proxy data retrievals. "Wish I had some popcorn!" he replied, shouting over the noise. "These ladies would make *scintillating* Sonzai warriors! Hot *damn*!"

Indeed, Princess Suzuka and Mercenary Tetyana commenced their fierce sword battle, committing strikes multiple times a second as energy flares were sent in all directions. Each time their weapons met, a sonic wave like that of a thunderclap was released, shaking the ground in its wake. At once, they drew into a stalemate test of strength, grinding blade against blade. Their history of battle became very apparent as Suzuka's intense gaze met Tetyana's; it seemed to all observers that neither woman could cripple the other's poise.

Unfortunately for one observer, Shujin, he feared going bald because of the conflict. "Hey! You girls know *I'm* gonna be responsible for filling those holes you're leaving!" he called.

"F-fear *not,* my prince!" Suzuka gritted out, eyes steady on her foe. "I shall deal with this nuisance accordingly...and we'll fill them together if that be your wish!"

"In your dreams, Suzuka!" Tetyana retorted. "The only one allowed to make plans with Shujin is *me*!"

In that moment, Tetyana cloaked and reappeared behind Suzuka to initiate an overhead strike; Suzuka, without turning around, held her weapon above her to block the attack, subsequently sending a back kick to Tetyana's abdomen. The counter was in vain for Tetyana evaded the move, spinning away to return with a powerful sword strike to stagger Suzuka. Though the mighty princess blocked the attack, she had to kneel down momentarily; Tetyana was hurling forward once again, and on a missed horizontal strike, Suzuka launched into the air, Tetyana giving chase.

The two barreled into the sky briefly as Suzuka flipped twice and propelled herself from her ship, *Ivan.* She charged toward her opponent. Tetyana was prepared for the onslaught, and the two took to airborne combat; their sword strikes were *much* heavier than before, creating shock waves that bent and snapped the treetops below.

"Wow, look at 'em go," Arlette whispered, though having to cover her head. "It's *always* been like this, Dahlia?"

The little princess was also shielding herself, her black and typically straight-pressed hair getting tossed around by the vicious wind. "Yeah, I'd hate to say it, Ms. Arlette!" she replied. "Nobody's ever won though!"

"What?" cried Shujin. "Like *never*?"

Another heavy exchange brought the warring women to part a distance from each other, levitating midair. Frustrated, Suzuka snapped her fingers to open the hatch to *Ivan*'s bridge and quickly flew inside. Tetyana's eyes narrowed, realizing what the battle had escalated to and waved her hand to teleport herself inside the *Diablo.*

"We settle this once and for *all,* Mercenary Tetyana!" Suzuka declared over her ship's loudspeaker. "Now I'll show you *why* Shujin is mine and mine alone!"

"Bring it on, Princess!" Tetyana retorted, arming her dozens of proton-laser turrets. "I've been waiting *too damn long* for this day! I want my baby to see how miserably you're gonna lose!"

"Oh, sweet merciful..." Shujin muttered, hands pressed against his bubble prison. "*Please* don't tell me they're about to have a dogfight! My house will get destroyed! *Hey*!" he cried as loud as he could. "Girls, you gotta stop it alreadyyy!"

⥈ ⥈

"What my man don't realize is that at *least* he's in the countryside!" Wanako radioed in with enthusiasm, his oval-shaped, light-blue eyes illuminated by their ship's thrusters. "And, uh, I think the earth is in more danger from Princess Suzuka than the Taras guy! Er…over?"

Tsumisu laughed aloud. "Copy that, Wanako! Still no word on military intervention, by the way," he replied. "You're officially on your own out there!"

"*What*?" his voice broke as explosions erupted overhead. "This is not madness; this is *Sparta* out here! Throw me a guess, somebody! Over!"

Kadochi looked to Tsumisu, shrugging. "Fear? Perhaps the Japanese government knows that such activity is a representation of possible premenstrual syndrome for both female entities concerned?"

He firmly shook the hand of his comrade. "Wise! Very, *very* wise hypothesis," he proudly stated. "You hear that, dude? New orders: stay the *hell* out of their way! Copy?"

"Shit, you ain't gotta tell me that twice!" Wanako sarcastically remarked. "Hey! Think your boy will be all right?"

Tsumisu and Kadochi snickered.

"Nope!" the Sonzai commander responded, amused. "This is out of our hands, technically, so he should know as well as *we* do: When that time comes, you just gotta let nature take controoool."

"Ha! Ha ha ha! Damn, he's gonna die!" Wanako sighed pleasantly, until he witnessed the vessels charging toward each other. "Waaaaiiit a minute!" he radioed, his 1.75-meter-tall body rising from a crouched position. "Make sure you got our stellar medical team on standby *again*!"

"Why? What's the situation?"

"Uh, the situation is that these are some *seriously crazy* women—oh, I'm sorry!" Wanako muttered. "Correction, prepare for contact!"

"Contact?" Tsumisu looked at the chief technical officer in shock. "Boost the array by sixteen petaHertz, now! Focus it on their coordinates!"

Kadochi quickly turned to his keyboard. "The targeted energy should dispel some of the physical ramifications! You got it, Commander!"

"Captain! You copy on the medical team? Sorry for the short notice!" Tsumisu immediately radioed.

"Done! Lieutenant Takashi is leading them en route now!" Goshinfuda promptly responded. "ETA fifteen minutes, Wanako!"

In the next moment, Princess Suzuka was steering her extraterrestrial, technologically advanced, sleekly designed, white-and-purple-hulled vessel *straight* into Tetyana's similarly advanced, shimmering black-metallic-hulled and aggressively designed vessel...directly over Lieutenant Wanako's head. Seconds later, they collided with tremendous force, sending debris from Suzuka's vessel raining down on earth as the energy that sustained each ship seemed to interfere with the other's as well; large, electromagnetic discharges of gold and purple twisted round in a vicious nature as the two hulls ground together in violent collision. Fortunately, the energetic damper initiated from the Sonzai clan provided enough of a reversal of potential energy, allowing the now-crippled warring women to fall square into a natural lake, not far from Shujin's house, subsequently displacing enough water to douse Lieutenant Wanako.

Then, as quickly as the action began, it ceased altogether. The gurgle of air pockets escaping from the vehicles, accelerating their descent, filled the night air and was almost in synchronicity with the crickets! As far as the Sonzai lieutenant could spiritually detect, everyone involved was alive and well…and like a thunderstorm rolling in from afar, the inexplicably *livid* voices of Suzuka and Tetyana could be heard for *kilometers* if one paid close enough attention.

Wringing out his shirt and shaking the water from his hair, Wanako knelt to the ground and radioed in.

"Gentlemen?" he began, spitting out a tadpole and brushing his tongue off. "I uh…think my work here is done."

"Copied, my brother!" Tsumisu responded with a chuckle. "Nice job. Come on back!"

Wanako noticed an equally flustered Arlette run to the lakeside, apparently trying to negotiate with the other two; meanwhile, Shujin was desperately trying to get away, yet Dahlia was playfully keeping him around—or rather, rolling him around.

"*Damn*," he muttered in concern, a frown coming to him as he recalled what Kadochi hypothesized earlier. Shouldn't each component of alien-PMS be multiplied by *three* now? "Commander?" he began with a painful realization swelling in his conscience. "Are you, uh…gonna *help* your boy anytime soon?"

"Naahh." Tsumisu was arranging some papers of their analysis now, stapling a certain stack. "Know something? Shujin asked me the *exact* same thing a couple of days ago…You think I should, sir? Copy."

"*Yes*, copy! What the fu—well, forgive me." Wanako calmed himself at Tsumisu's comfortable denial of Shujin's clear and present danger. "Commander? I'm gonna say it like *this*: if a battle doesn't kill him, these *women* will." He was sure to keep his voice low as he sneaked away. "Headed back now, over and out."

Kadochi looked at the commander with humor. "I suppose Wanako's previous relationship attempt is still biting hard. Poor guy…" He sighed, wincing a bit.

"Yeaaah, he should speak to someone about that." Tsumisu nodded to the insightful, fair-skinned lieutenant. "Don't get me wrong;

I've attempted to assist his plight! Yet, I've realized my advice is far too…convoluted. I dunno if that's the proper terminology."

"You could always consult Captain Goshinfuda?" Kadochi used his hands to make a circling motion.

"Pssh, he *wishes* I would talk to him about women." Tsumisu widened his eyes, shaking his head at the embarrassing conversation that would transpire. "OK, guess that's a wrap for yours truly. We're leaving the array's data collector ensemble on tonight, right?"

"That's affirmative, Commander. I still don't like that the skies remain absent of *any* military investigation after that display. Aren't you bothered?"

He sighed, a solemn expression coming to him. "Indeed, Lieutenant. I've no idea what to make of it…Humans are intrinsically curious beings, regardless of what the underlying context may be. It would take some *direct* stimuli to avert such action." He ran a hand through his hair. "Anyway, we've at least got this data to work on; in the morning, I'll speak with the grandmaster and see if we can get some clarification. Cool?"

"Sounds like a plan." Kadochi shook his friend and comrade's hand. "Always a pleasure working with you, Commander."

"Feeling is altogether mutual, sir." He grinned. "Get some sleep—ha, I'm gonna tell Shujin I was asleep this *whole* time when he asks. That's gonna be epic on so many levels."

"You're a real heartless bastard!" Kadochi laughed aloud in disbelief. "One of these days, that'll be *you* getting dragged or chased around. Karma, right?"

So, did Karma equal fate? Because the last thing Tsumisu needed was to be farted on again. Not wishing to divulge his recently nerve-racking encounter with Lieutenant Sauveterre he decided to play it cool. Besides, it wasn't like she *purposely* flew her space vessel into him…

"You worry too much, dude!" He patted his shoulder and left their technology command center. "But I'll keep a look out for that karma!" he called before closing the door.

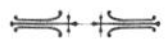

There was *something* about leaving the curtains almost closed when your window was facing due east; mysteriously, from one-hundred and fifty million kilometers away, the sun finds a means to encroach on your face and *in your eyes* just to let you know it's time to get up. Who wanted to on the first coldish day of November? And in the twenty-first century, human beings *just* hadn't adapted eyelids to block out such light.

Was that Tsumisu's VoIP phone ringing in the living room? Was *that* why he kept having these *weird* dreams about bells and screaming battle cries? Wow. Somebody needed a vacation. At any rate, the Sonzai commander rubbed his face, threw on a worn-out Van Halen shirt and black jeans to stumble into the living room. Plopping on an at *least* comfy half couch, Tsumisu pressed a button on the receiver to check his digital messages: twenty-six. Yikes. Were they *all* from Shujin? What *time* was it? Eight forty-five.

Rather than have the patience to sit and listen to every last one of them in chronological order, Tsumisu, like a good friend, picked up the phone and called the man.

"H-hello?" a weary, worn, tired voice answered. "Dude, is that you?"

Tsumisu cleared his throat. "N-no it's *me*! The magic tooth fairy!" he replied in a raspy, squeaky voice. "I'm calling to remind you of your next dental appointment!"

"Damn it, Tsumisu! This is *not* a laughing matter today. Where the hell were you man? Have you *any*...*any* idea what I've been through in the last several hours?" Shujin's tone was frantic, and Tsumisu could hear glass being broken and an argument of some sort taking place in the background. "Oh God, wait let me go into another room—Wahh! Tetyana, no! I'm on the phone!"

"Shujin! Tell this *demon* of a woman to stay the hell out of our lives!" she growled.

"I shall not allow you to corrupt Shujin!" said the dignified, articulate, yet spastically upset Suzuka. "You release him this instant, or you shall pay dearly, Tetyana!"

"M-Ms. Suzuka! Look I'm not gonna get corrupted! I'm just tryin' to use the phone!" Shujin pleaded desperately. "Besides, you girls are tearing up the house!"

Yawning yet continuing to hold the phone to his ear, Tsumisu was impressed by the nature of ongoing conflict between Suzuka and Tetyana. Evidently, Suzuka hadn't given up on calling dibs on Shujin, but Tetyana wasn't backing down because she *did* get her mittens on him first, by Tsumisu's surmising—thus, the battle continued. *Meanwhile…*

"Corrupt? You're the one bargin' in here like nobody's business!" Tetyana retaliated, pointing vindictively at Suzuka with Shujin in her grasp. "Ya home wrecker!"

Suzuka's eyes, accented by thick eyebrows, flared with rage. She clenched her fists and pressed them to her sides. "Ooohh, how *dare* you accuse me of such a vile disposition!" she retaliated, one meter from her opponent. "*You* are the one who has defiled Shujin's mind by your incessant, discourteous behavior! Take your *filthy* hands off him!"

"Waaah!" Shujin cried, helplessly being pulled around by the powerful females.

Tetyana gasped in utter disbelief, meeting eye to eye with Suzuka. "I'll have you know I washed my hands this mornin', Princess!" She quickly snatched him away. "Give 'em back!"

"Waaahh! Noo!" Shujin cried yet again.

"You've *no right* to Shujin in the least! Fate has already decided our union, Tetyana!" Suzuka continued. "Now, I command you in the name of the Devonian Empire to unhand *my* beloved!"

"I think I'm gonna be sick!" Shujin further exclaimed, his body limp.

"Like I give a damn about fate *or* the empire, Princess!" screamed Tetyana with an aggressively raised fist. "Now, *you* keep *your* stinkin' paws offa *my Shujin*!"

Shujin began gurgling aloud, his face changing colors. "Uuurrgghhh! C'mon! I'm serious!"

"Guys, you have to be careful with him!" cried a worried Arlette from a safe distance. "Can't we just have breakfast and be nice for once?"

"*No*!" Suzuka and Tetyana proclaimed in angry unison.

Wow, this was *really bad.* Tsumisu exhaled, shaking his head, and looked at the time again. Eight fifty. Damn, has it really been five minutes of this?

"Uh, excuse me, ladies and gentlemen..." He finally spoke normally into the receiver. "Is this on speakerphone?"

Suddenly, it became eerily silent.

"Who is this?" asked Suzuka inquisitively, an authoritarian royal inflection wrapped her words. "Speak *now*!"

Yikes.

"Uhhh...my name is Tsumisu, Ms. Princess Suzuka, ma'am. I'm, um...a friend of...of Shujin's," he cautiously replied, hoping she didn't possess technology to snatch people through phones. "He *will* vomit, by the way—"

"That's you, big guy?" Tetyana interrupted. "Why don't ya bring your *shady ass* over here and help me kick this lady outta the house, huh?"

"What? You shall do *no* such thing, Mr. Tsumisu!" Suzuka *seriously* declared. "Mark my words, if you are an accomplice of Tetyana's, I will most certainly have you reprimanded!"

"Aaaghhh!" Shujin hollered as Suzuka sought her opportunity to snatch him back. "Ms. Suzuka! He's not an accomplice I swear! We're best friends!"

"Do not feel as if you should cover for those who commit ill against you, Shujin!" she graciously explained, keeping him back in an extremely covetous nature. "Such that you should not defend this…this heinous *succubus*!"

"Heinous *what*?" Tetyana's voice reached a new limit as she threw her fists out angrily. "Come over here and say that to my face!"

Suzuka dragged Shujin along, stomping a short distance toward her. "*Heinous*! *Succubuuuus*!" she hollered in Tetyana's face, reaching a new level of hormonal power.

"Tsumisu, just get over here, man!" Shujin asked wearily. "*Please*?"

On the other side of the phone, Tsumisu gulped once, not necessarily sure what to say. "Uhh…ummm…" he muttered.

Miraculously finding a means to drag himself away from the scene as thuds, shrieks, and random material breakage ensued in the background, Shujin spoke with a clearly shaken tone.

"C'mon, dude!" he continued to plead. "I-I can't hold on any longer!"

In disquieting indecision, Tsumisu, commander of the Sonzai clan, capable of stopping *flaming* ships from outer space and running at speeds of three-hundred kilometers per hour…gently *hung up*.

Sure, it wasn't the *best* course of action. His eyes were as wide as saucers, his hands were pressed together and against his lips, and a frown overwhelmed him. All the while, Tsumisu felt afraid as he reclined in his at *least* comfortable half couch. Yes, the sun arose to a brand-new day, granting him exclusive access to one gentleman's *uncomfortable* situation. Was it worth going over there? Should he heed the call of his endangered fellow man? *Should* he pick up the phone that seemed to ring with increasing desperation on each subsequent call? Well, that was what the digital answering service was for! So that was twenty-six messages, twenty-seven messages… wow, twenty-*eight* messages…

CHAPTER FIVE

The days grew shorter, and the climate turned cold—winter was on the denizens of the Northern Hemisphere. It was a snowy day in Okayama, Japan, and for several hours, Tsumisu had been sitting on the roof of his apartment, legs crossed, shirtless, with arms placed in his lap, spiritually training both mind and body while withstanding the below-freezing temperatures. Eyes closed and wearing an expression of deep concentration, Tsumisu could mentally visualize the surroundings—sensing energies near and far of varying degrees, humans to animals, vegetation, and even the snowflakes themselves. However, it wasn't long until Tsumisu felt an unusual and foreign energy source somewhere on the planet. What it lacked in strength, it made up for with its ominous nature. And, given his business was dealing with these types of presences, his concern was easily captured.

Ending his meditative posture, the Sonzai commander stood up and looked at the sky. "It's a lifeless form," he said aloud but in a whisper. "Strange, this thing is headed in Shujin's direction? I'd best get to him quickly...Hope the neighbors won't mind a little noise today."

Removing the tied Slipknot "Iowa" T-shirt from around his brow, Tsumisu put it on and retrieved the sword of light, Akari, lying on the roof narrows. Flipping into the air, he traveled with great speed to his friend's location. Darting among the trees along the way, Tsumisu detected this presence was *indeed* the "super cyborg" Lieutenant Arlette mentioned before: Taras Ganymede.

Fantastic.

Although Taras's strength increased as he approached the planet, it wasn't enough to make Tsumisu nervous. Seriously, this guy was a robo*chump*.

Upon arrival at the Iwato residence, he stopped for a moment and searched the area for Shujin's location. "Tending to the garden in a snowstorm?" he said aloud, clearly confused. He ran in Shujin's direction.

Passing behind the house, he caught sight of a happily waving Dahlia; Tsumisu waved in return but continued running, as Taras was only three miles from their location by this time.

Meanwhile, Shujin was planting sweet potatoes for his grandmother's garden when he heard Dahlia call out. But by the time he turned around, Tsumisu stood at his side.

"Oh! H-hey, man! What're you doing here?" he greeted with a smile, shoving his aerator into the snow-laden ground.

Tsumisu was searching the skies now. "Dude," he began, "I have strong reasons to believe that Taras has finally made his unwelcome visit to earth...That's the good news. How are *you*?" he brightly finished.

"Er, wait…Could you back up just a second?" Shujin's face nearly turned white. "Taras has made it to earth? *Already*?"

"Oh of this, I'm certain." He nodded confidently. "*Bad* news is he's headed this way soo…"

"W-*what*? *Now*? But—"

"I haven't the slightest. Apparently, Taras dropped his wallet during his last visit and *really* wants it back now. Point is, go inside and inform the others; I'll stay out here and keep watch, all right?"

"Damn it." Shujin frowned as he clenched a fist. "This isn't good at all…"

Tsumisu placed a reassuring hand on his shoulder. "Don't worry; we've *got* this, man! And hey, I'll deal with him first, test his power a bit. That way, we can strategize the world's most generous ass-kicking!"

"OK…" He exhaled, trying to steel his nerves. "But you sure you can take him alone? Remember what Tetyana said? Taras sounds pretty suited to fending for himself. Not to knock the Jedi—"

"That's a relative assessment, yeah? Depends on who he is 'fending' against." Tsumisu threw up air quotes. "At your stage of development, combat engagement warrants much caution on your part. *Don't* let your guard down when you fight, OK?"

"I got it, bro." Shujin nodded, building confidence. "Hey, you watch your back too."

Tsumisu shook his friend's hand, following with a hug that broke into them snapping their fingers in unison. "Will do. Now get inside already, dude!"

"All right, I'm going!"

Once Shujin departed, Tsumisu also bolted away to continue tracking Taras's ominous spirit. In a moment's time, the trail led him into densely populated forestry. As his footfalls barely touched the deep, powdery snow, Tsumisu began assessing the situation. Could Taras be one of Nyugo's minions? Well, the correlation between somebody like Taras, who was just bent on becoming a ruthless killer or what have you, and somebody like Nyugo, who wished to dominate every soul in the universe, was off by a factor of *eight* or more.

Still, the Sonzai commander could not rule out any possibility; if Taras proved to be a soldier of Nyugo, and perhaps his best one, why the *hell* would he be coming there? Hoping for answers soon, Tsumisu finally came to a clearing and saw the form of Taras descending from the sky. Standing motionless, he awaited Taras's landing, and the moment he did, Tsumisu took a seat on a nearby fallen log.

Taras was an individual standing over *two meters tall*, pale with obviously artificial skin and wild bleached hair—perhaps a byproduct of chemical degradation over time. Sensing something was amiss, he turned to catch sight of a casually seated visitor.

"Great. I'm already joined by the damn locals," Taras said in a guttural, tenor voice. "All right then, who might *you* be?"

"Who I am is not important," Tsumisu replied calmly, a hand propping his chin. "Now, let-me-see-passporrrt! Otherwise, I throw you in *gulag*!" he said, faking a horrible Russian accent. "Ahrm, I'm sorry. Why are you here again?"

"Here's a comedian!" Taras proclaimed in amusement. "My arrival here is none of your damn business, boy. Now you'd better get the hell out of here before I kill you and everything else on this miserable planet."

He smiled humbly. "Man, that's too bad actually," he said, leaving his seat. "I was looking forward to meeting *the* Taras Ganymede! I might not even get this chance again, and here you are chasing me away. I can't get an autograph? Sell it on Amazon?"

Taras laughed, cracking his knuckles. "Talk about interesting! Who told you about me, boy? I know damn well you ain't psychic."

"That's none of your business…*boy*," Tsumisu remarked sarcastically. "I'd like to carry on with this conversation, but we're running a little short on time. I'll ask you again: What are you doing here?"

Taras noticed Tsumisu was carrying a weapon. "You intend to use that thing?" He pointed.

"What, this?" He casually looked over his right shoulder. "Well, Mom says I shouldn't use weapons on total strangers," he continued, quickly unsheathing Akari, twirling it around, and placing it at his side. "And heaven *knows* you're a stranger. So, if we get to know each other, I can use this 'thing.' Sound fair?"

"You don't bear the weapon of a *Devonian* warrior—you ain't that legend from earth I keep hearing about?"

Tsumisu eyed Taras with a frown. "Legend? I haven't heard of any legends. Those belong on maps." He scoffed. "Evidently you need one to find out how to answer a question—"

"Long ago, there was a great power detected on this planet, and reports suggest its origins didn't come from the empire." Taras wore another evil grin. "But I highly doubt you'd be that source. Hell!" He chuckled. "You ain't even registering enough energy to make a mouse piss himself, boy. Perhaps I'm mistaking you for someone who arrived at the wrong time." His tone grew cold as he materialized a long energy blade. "Goodbye, boy, it was a good conversation after all."

"I see all of those shiny circuits failed to make you smarter." Tsumisu sighed as he *sheathed* Akari. "But you're right, Taras. I'm just a poor guy who got lost in the woods, in the middle of a pleasant snowy day...*and* happened to be carrying an ancient sword. Alien algorithms sure give the most plausible results..."

Taras was preparing his attack, yet when Tsumisu mentioned "ancient" he changed his mind.

"What'd you say?"

"Oh nothing!" Tsumisu replied dismissively. "Go ahead and do your thing, man."

"You'll regret that smart mouth of yours. Die!"

Taras laid a hand in front of him to send forth a transparent wave of energy, yet Tsumisu only placed a hand forth to cancel out the attack, slowly drawing his hand away afterward. An awkward moment ensued on Taras's part, while Tsumisu took a seat on the log again and propped his chin.

"Oh no, have mercy…" he mumbled. "Hey! That spot in the gulag is still up for grabs…if-if you're interested."

Seething underneath, Taras glared at him with clenched fists. "Who *are* you? How the *hell* did you nullify my energy?" he growled. "You couldn't have parameterized a reversal so quickly! And *what* is this *gulag*?"

"Oh right, you're from space! So naturally, you *suck* at world history." Tsumisu shook his head. "If only you were familiar with Metallica, this would've been easy to deduce—"

Tsumisu was cut short by the arrival of Shujin, Suzuka, Tetyana, and Arlette; Tetyana and Suzuka summoned their armor, Arlette was in uniform dress, and Shujin donned a traditional Devonian battle garb gifted to him courtesy of Suzuka.

"Taras Ganymede!" cried Tetyana, her expression filled with anger. "Your time has come, you son of a bitch!"

Arlette firmly placed her footing and drew out her standard-issue pistol. "Taras! I am First Lieutenant Arlette Sauveterre of the Devonian Military Police!" she declared. "You are under arrest!"

"Sorry, I ain't interested! Damn, more of the locals?" Taras growled with annoyance, yet his solid-red eyes fell on someone familiar. "But I can't say I'm *totally* disappointed. Never in a million years would I think *you'd* team up with that crazy princess, Tetyana!" he addressed her, an eager fist clenched. "What? Couldn't find more of your Ordovician sympathizers to help?"

A gold aura began to emanate from Tetyana. "Bastard," she seethed, knowing the atrocities he had committed. "You *disgust* me!"

"Charmed! And, uh, I guess you're on another 'high-priority mission,' Princess?" Taras continued. "Mommy and Daddy send their little girl out to do their dirty work like *always*."

"Silence, pig!" Suzuka drew her weapon. "You can *never* lecture me on matters of honor!"

"Oh, y-you wanna talk about honor? How's about when your daddy spit in my face when I served *your* pathetic empire!"

"I've heard enough from you, Taras!" said Shujin, materializing his weapon to stand ready. "I wonder if you can fight as much as you talk!"

Taras flashed a glare at him. "Whenever you're ready to die, cockroach, I'll be happy to oblige," he said. Stopping short, he observed Shujin's weapon. "You bear the Mark of Evelyn, boy; you're that 'Chosen One' the Devonians kept rambling on about, ain't you?"

Shujin steeled his resolve, recalling all the information Princess Suzuka had given him previously. He was the product of Evelyn, Mother of Souls and Overseer of the Devonians, sent to bring about solidification of the generations-long warring civilizations. Perhaps Tetyana and Suzuka at his sides was a direct product of his purpose, and though Shujin hadn't fully ascertained the depth of his powers, it didn't serve as a motivational deterrent to face the clearly merciless adversary before them.

"I'm glad you recognize me," Shujin replied. "And I won't accept repayment for your crimes unless it's in your blood!"

"Ha! You *dare* threaten me, boy?" Taras challenged, hearing the mention of his demise. "I shall absorb the very essence of your energy—daaghh!"

In that moment, Tsumisu landed a powerful blow against Taras's chin, standing before him as the cyborg reeled backward.

"That was for not answering my questions, *boy*," Tsumisu said in a stern tone, performing a backflip to return as his fist discharged sparks. "Sorry, had to get it out of me."

Everyone simply looked at Tsumisu, staring in awe.

"Wow..." Arlette whispered, mouth open. "How did you *do* that?"

Tsumisu looked at the lieutenant with widened eyes and a comically blank expression. "Oh you should see me at *Call of Duty*!"

"Really? I've heard of that!" she brightly replied. "We should play once Taras is arrested!"

"Or dead." Tetyana shook her head, trying to recount Tsumisu's movements.

"Whichever comes first will be fine with me," Suzuka said with confidence. "Our alliance is certain to prevail against him!"

Taras wiped his lip to check for bleeding. "Ha, not *bad*. Yeah, I'll admit you've got some skill," he complimented, noticing green stains against his brilliant-white glove. "Guess you've got *something* to hide after all."

"Yep! Glad you noticed. Don't wear it out." Tsumisu patted Arlette's shoulder and turned to her. "Let's *try* to arrest him first, OK?"

Her eyes lit up in admiration, glittering with those twinkles again. "Wow...OK, Tsumisu. I'll do it!" Arlette built up her confidence again and aimed her weapon. "Taras! You have the right to remain silent! Anything you say can and will be used against—"

Taras simply laughed at her.

"...you? Hey! Do you hear me?"

"So I'm just gonna hand myself over to the 'authorities'?" he proclaimed. "Forces better than *you* have tried, and lemme tell you—the results weren't pretty."

Tetyana smirked deviously. "Thanks for the heads-up," she remarked. "Now splitting you open will be even *more* enjoyable."

"Damn, you remind me of this *one* Van Halen song," Tsumisu commented in gratification. "But you're right! Just wanted to avoid any legal trouble from the Devonians..."

"Oh! Well, that was really thoughtful," Arlette expressed. "Court isn't fun for anybody, I hear...especially all that nasty paperwork, right?"

Taras glared at them all, displaying poises of victory. "Well then, I guess it's time to put your money where your mouth is." He grinned, grasping his weapon from the middle to form blades at opposite ends. "It won't be a minute until all of your powers are mine!"

"All right guys, Taras has 'magic tricks,' like controlling energy," Tsumisu instructed the others in a calculated tone. "Assume he can absorb too, so don't let him land whatever that technique is on you, got it?"

"Loud and clear, bro." Shujin nodded in conviction. "You're OK, Ms. Suzuka, Tetyana?"

"As long as you're here, Shujin," the princess responded kindly. "Let us begin…"

"Ha! A strategy! Ain't that cute?" Taras applauded generously. "Well, less work for me to slaughter you, I guess…"

"Shujin! Suzuka! Tetyana! Flank him while I provide support! Go!" Tsumisu grasped the hilt of Akari and flipped into the air, suddenly disappearing.

"Shujin! On my mark!" Tetyana said and charged toward Taras, flying to his right as Suzuka darted to his left. "Let's see what you've got!"

Taras prepared for the onslaught; though backpedaling, he did well to defend himself from both Tetyana and Suzuka's simultaneous attacks, and the three immediately engaged in airborne combat. By no means were they being soft on Taras; the scene was littered with flares emitted from weapon contact, each blow a potential life-threatening injury or instant death.

"Hmm, now *what* intensity setting should I use?" the yellow-haired lieutenant scratched her head, inspecting her proton pistol. "Hey! Where *are* the settings anyway?"

Instantly, Tsumisu appeared beside the slightly befuddled woman. "Arlette, sweetie, slide your finger across the left color bar, where it says 'intensity,'" he patiently explained, Akari's brilliant steel blade propped on his shoulder while he kept up with Taras's movement. "Ha, does it say 'kill' anywhere on there?"

Arlette's big blue eyes peered at the weapon. "Oh *yeah*! Hey, thanks, Tsumisu! How'd you know that?"

"No worries. Just keep shooting at this bastard." He nudged her shoulder with a grin and leaped into the air, disappearing once more.

Her cheeks grew flush as she smiled. "Wow…dreamy," she whispered, snapping out of it to aim her weapon. "Right! Here goes!"

The cover fire served as a split-second distraction, allowing Tetyana and Suzuka to weaken Taras's poise; a heavy blow from Suzuka allowed Tetyana to disassemble her katana into short swords and charge Taras, unleashing a flurry of attacks.

Shujin stood at ground level and studied the fight; weapon clutched in hand, he eagerly wished to join them. The moment he intended to launch himself up, he was stopped by Tsumisu.

"Tetyana said wait for her mark," he reminded him.

"Yeah." He sighed, regaining focus. "They're setting him up."

"Exactly, man. Let's expedite the process."

In that instant, Tsumisu vanished. Meanwhile, Taras found it troublesome detecting his mysteriously powerful opponent and paid for it; all it took was one lapse in concentration, and during Tetyana's relentless barrage, Tsumisu perfectly timed a quick slash to his shoulder, throwing the cyborg off balance.

"Damn it!" he growled. "I can't read his movements. *Why*?"

Princess Suzuka charged her weapon, bringing it over her head. "Read *this*!" she yelled.

With a mighty swing, Suzuka struck the cyborg midair, splitting his skull, and sent him spiraling down; this granted Tetyana an opening to draw her revolver. She discharged it six times to empty the weapon. The projectiles screamed toward their target; drawing out his hand, Taras held back the contact explosions yet was being dramatically accelerated toward the ground.

"*Now,* Shujin!" Tetyana cried. "Finish him off!"

"You've got it!" Shujin was positioned right underneath Taras and leaped into the air, intending a vertical strike; after all, the momentum from Tetyana's shot would all but solidify a clean attack. "This is your end, Taras!"

But when all seemed of a surety, Taras drew in the energy from Tetyana's shot, abruptly halted himself from falling, and twisted his head around 180 degrees, facing Shujin. The wound inflicted by Suzuka began to stich itself back together, strung by neural wires.

"*Surprise...*"

Shujin's eyes flew wide as Taras quickly grasped his neck, choking him as the cyborg drained his energy.

"Shujin!" yelled Tsumisu, heading full speed toward him. "I'm coming, brother!"

"Ah no you don't!" Taras countered.

With the snap of his fingers, Taras set off a series of immense explosions that obliterated the surrounding forestry. Where snow once existed, flames now roasted foliage and embers danced among the air currents. All were forced to retreat and shield themselves, while Tsumisu barely retrieved Lieutenant Arlette from the blasts, taking her to safety. All the while, Shujin remained in danger as a smirking Taras stood with the young warrior suspended by his throat.

"Shit, boy," he began, disappointed by the degree of energy absorbed. "When you see Evelyn, tell her I said, 'Better luck next time.'"

For the unfortunate and horrified observers, Taras released an energy blast into Shujin, killing him instantly. A loud clank of metal rang through the air as Shujin's weapon fell to the seared bare ground, retracting into a crystal orb. Taras casually strolled up to the item and retrieved it.

"That's too bad!" He chuckled, smashing the object. "I guess he wasn't cut out for the job."

"No..." Tetyana muttered, tears welling while she looked on. "*No...Nooooo*!"

CHAPTER SIX

A shaken Suzuka fell to her hands and knees, punching the ground once with clenched eyes. "Shujin," she whimpered, a tear falling. "You *monster...*"

Tsumisu held a sorrowful Arlette in his arms, her face pressed against him as his gaze was cold on Taras...and he stared back.

"Bastard, I'll have your head!" screamed a furious Tetyana, charging straight for him. "I'll cut your heart out!"

"I shall see you *die*!" yelled Suzuka, picking up her weapon to join the assault.

Taras didn't bother to summon his weapon. "Now all that sounds lovely," he remarked.

Tetyana cloaked to leave a ghostly afterimage and reappeared behind Taras to initiate an attack; however, Taras sidestepped into thin air and reemerged some distance away from her.

"Graah! Come back and fight, you coward!" she said, fluidly reloading her weapon and pulling the trigger.

Taras took one step backward and disappeared, cackling with amusement; seconds later, an explosion was making its way just centimeters from Tetyana's right.

"Get down!" said Tsumisu, reacting quickly to shield her from the blast overhead. "Suzuka, you must *not* pursue him!"

"What madness is this?" Suzuka asked aloud, frantically searching for her opponent and finding nothing.

Suddenly, a straight right from Taras flew literally out of nowhere, catching Suzuka off guard and knocking her down. Before she could recover, Taras reemerged again with weapon drawn, attempting to impale her. At that instant, Tsumisu parried the attack away—having removed his opponent's blade in the process. Even so, the Sonzai commander did not follow Taras; rather, he kept his menacing glare imposed on the cyborg, Akari placed before him as he stood guard over a temporarily defenseless Suzuka.

"Ha, you seem to have a lick of common sense on you, boy." The super cyborg smirked. "It'd be a shame just to kill you outright like I did yer friend."

Tsumisu narrowed his eyes, not responding. But inside of him, he could feel his anger broiling—no, this was *hatred*. This surpassed the pain of loss or even the desire for vengeance. It was pure, *uninhibited* hatred of such a nature that called for more than death for Taras. No. Such dishonor in his horrific treatment of women, such disregard for life itself, such arrogance of Taras to *think* he had a right to continue perpetrating such tumult and violence.

And he slaughtered his *friend*...No.

This wicked being must *suffer* in the most heinous, incontrovertibly excruciating and humiliating manner imaginable—such that the universe would remember the name of Tsumisu. And so, he began plotting *not* Taras's death, but the very cradle of his utter ruin.

"Tell you what I'm gonna do!" Taras continued. "You like bad-guy clichés? Well, here's one for you..." He slipped into thin air again, yet his wicked laugh echoed across the burned area. "I invite you to my humble abode, the *Leviathan*, and let's see if you and yer vengeful posse can tickle my fancy! Ah ha ha haaa!"

As his voice faded, Tsumisu sensed Taras's energy descending from within earth's energy complex. Sheathing his weapon, he assisted Suzuka to her feet while Arlette and Tetyana approached—their expressions sorrowful.

"Tetyana," Suzuka finally said, fighting emotions, "I..."

"I know...it's hard," she replied, tears welling. "It's *so* hard."

"I-I just wish there was something we could've done," said a somber Arlette. "I'm sorry."

"None of this is anyone's fault. *Taras*." Tetyana looked at her clenched fist, tears falling. "I swear I'll bury my hand in his chest and rip out his heart for what he's done...He stole what meant everything to me! *Everything*!"

"This is simply not fair!" Suzuka exclaimed with a shaky voice, unable to restrain herself as the horrible moment replayed in her mind. "Prince Shujin...I loved him! I *loved* him!"

Arlette was equally distraught, unable to open her eyes. "He... he didn't deserve this! Why, Tsumisu, *why*?" She gasped and shuddered, tightly holding onto him for reprieve.

Tsumisu took them into a collective embrace, placing a kiss on the tops of their heads, wishing he could remove their pain from them. A bitter wind did not aid their souls, nor did the fire that surrounded them grant warmth of comfort.

Perhaps reality manifested in such a manner—sometimes alleviating burden and otherwise enhancing it with stinging cruelty. Solace was hard to find, and Tsumisu knew it—his heightened senses absorbed the damage of Suzuka, Arlette, and Tetyana, as well as his own seething fury. So, for a time, no one spoke. And what could they say? Yet the silence had to be broken. Taras was still an ongoing threat, and Tsumisu needed answers.

"Yes, we will grieve for Shujin now," he began, "but I assure you, punishment is near for what has been done to him. Indeed, *punishment* is near..."

"Punishment..." Tetyana reiterated, struggling to settle down. "That's all I can think about, Tsumisu."

"Don't feel blameworthy, as dark thoughts consume me too—but I wish not to share them with any of you."

"It is too late to rescind your influence," Suzuka replied, turning to him with determination. "We shall demonstrate to Taras the meaning of vengeance. He shall *pay* for his deeds."

Wiping each of their tears away, the Sonzai commander bore a little grin. "That's all I needed to hear from you." He proudly looked on the three women standing before him. "I have *never* seen such resilience in the face of overwhelming difficulty, and though in my heart, I ache to envision any of you facing Taras, knowing his penchant for suffering, I know your combined strength is far greater than any threat he could throw at us."

Eyes blurry, Arlette looked at him in admiration. "You mean it?" she asked.

"Every word. In fact, take a look at yourselves, Arlette."

Suzuka, Tetyana, and Arlette did as suggested, realizing their unspoken bond was definitely a manifest reality. And despite the atrocity before them, they continued to stand united and ready to face the next adversity—Taras had *not* taken their spirit away.

"Thank you for your kind words, Tsumisu," Suzuka said softly. "Indeed, Prince Shujin chose you as a friend for a reason."

"And he's *still* with us." He nodded in affirmation. "Taras can take away only so much in this life, but our hearts will retain Shujin forever." He laid a hand out before them. "We go in for Shujin's honor together, and we *leave* together. Understood?"

Tetyana smiled, feeling a sense of relief for the first time. "Yeah, I think we can handle that, right?" she said, placing her hand atop Tsumisu's. "Let's get this killing party moving!"

Suzuka placed her hand atop Tetyana's. "Absolutely, we shall not fail!"

"Let's do it, guys!" Arlette proudly cheered, doing the same.

Tsumisu smiled, looking each of them in the eye. "That's what I'm talking about. On three, we break and give Taras hell, all right? One, two, three..."

"Break!" they yelled in unison. Their lifted morale brought welcome positive emotion to the air.

Suzuka knelt down to retrieve her katana. "I'll admit," she said, blowing dirt from the blade, "he's *far* stronger than he was the previous time I encountered him. You detected the same, Tetyana?"

She nodded. "I don't get it, though," she said, spinning the barrel of her revolver and holstering it. "Sure, he was tough, but I can't figure how he gained so much power in such a short amount of time."

"Let alone his magic tricks," Tsumisu added. "I could tell that was something neither of you were familiar with."

"Such is the reason why you suggested we desist attacking him?" asked Suzuka.

"Exactly. I read his movements too." Tsumisu frowned in recollection. "Taras's powers are bizarre, like trying to drink water with chopsticks. Just…out of place." He folded his arms. "And that disappearing trick was dimension-based, so unless machines figured out a way to manipulate spiritual-physical energy somehow, they *shouldn't* be able to pull that off."

"Maybe he had help, somehow?" inquired Arlette. "I mean, we saw him absorb one of Tetyana's attacks; do you think that's a clue?"

"The ability to borrow or even mimic is what you're saying." Tsumisu followed her deduction. "Look, it's obvious we need a plan. Arlette, try to pull up some of your military records, please. Perhaps the intelligence on this guy can steer us in the right direction…"

"OK, I'm on it, Tsumisu!" Arlette saluted, granting him a sweet smile. "Thanks for your help, by the way."

"Hmm? Help? Oh yeah." Tsumisu grinned, dismissing his serious thoughts. "Anytime, my dear. Uh, you OK? The cold getting to you?"

"What? Oh! No, it's nothing like that." Arlette was obviously masking her thoughts.

She drew out her military-issued equipment—an advanced personal data assistant device—and pressed two sides of it to bring up an eight-screen holographic display of Taras's file.

"Here ya go," she said, adjusting their alignment. "You could imagine how hard it is to scrape info about him, so I hope this is enough to help us out."

"Impressive," commented Suzuka, analyzing the records. "I've no doubt it shall, Lieutenant."

"You're a *boss* with this police stuff," Tsumisu complimented her, nudging her shoulder.

She sighed, blushing. "Aww, Tsumisu…"

"Check out the behavior profile," said Tetyana. "Seems Taras loves attacking imperial military installations and torturing his imprisoned victims. Can't say I'm surprised about that. Hm?" She pressed the bottom left screen, sliding it to the right. "Suspected kidnapper regarding 'high-value target'? What the hell does that mean?"

"Let me see," said Arlette, using her credentials to investigate the file. "Huh? I can't access that information!"

Suzuka gave it a closer inspection. "Your authorization has been revoked, it appears," she said. "I'm not aware of this decision, by the way," she further elaborated.

Arlette smiled. "You're commander of the Imperial Army, Your Highness—not a policy pusher."

"That leaves *you* for that job, your Mercenary-ness," Tsumisu joked.

Tetyana shook her head. "Don't start with me," she said, grinning. "And ya *still* owe me an explanation for those moves you pulled off."

"Hey, all in due time!" Tsumisu played innocent. "But on the matter of this 'classified target,' I'm sure once we're up there, we'll release every prisoner and build our own files of them."

The lieutenant couldn't help it if her heart skipped a beat, making her breaths a bit shuddered, if only momentarily. "Yeeaahhh… our own file," she whispered.

"It has *got* to be this cold weather," Tsumisu muttered, self-affirming his diagnosis. "Now, Princess Suzuka?"

"Yes, Tsumisu? Are you prepared now?" Suzuka wore a dignified air about her.

"Not quite. Could you salvage anything from *Ivan*?" he asked. "It's possible we'll need extra firepower in case Taras decides to attack during our approach."

"I salvaged some components, but perhaps we needn't be concerned," she replied. "To this day, neither Devonians nor Ordovicians could reverse engineer the technology of Tetyana's ship. In short, we've more than enough to test Taras's mettle."

"Say, how come you've never told *me* that?" Tetyana inquired, hands on her hips. "And all this time, I figured you were too dang sore to admit it!"

"Though I know when I've been bested, I remain a woman of great pride, Tetyana." Suzuka smirked, raising an armor-clad hand. "Yet this means I'm placing all trust in *you* to escort us to Taras's demise. Understood?"

Tetyana nodded in solemn acknowledgment, taking her similarly armored hand to grasp Suzuka's. "Crystal clear," she said.

"Commander! Commander, come in!" radioed a frantic Goshinfuda. "Do you read me?"

Tsumisu quickly snapped around and paced away, pressing the device in his ear. "I'm here, Captain!" he whispered, keeping his head low.

"Status report, man, we lost contact with you for several minutes!"

"Our bad guy, Taras, made his way to earth, set off some fireworks—Shujin is a casualty," Tsumisu explained. "There was nothing we could do."

Meanwhile, Arlette, Suzuka, and Tetyana were curious as to why Tsumisu had walked away so suddenly—let alone muttering to himself. So, they cautiously stood by to eavesdrop.

"Good news, I can't confirm on that casualty, Commander," the captain replied. "We've still got residual readings of Shujin on earth—even the grandmaster can't explain it."

Tsumisu's eyes flashed with renewed hope, though he refrained from jumping to conclusions. "Listen, I'm currently..." He briefly looked over his shoulder, noticing the audience. "I'm 'occupied' at the moment, OK, er...Mom?"

Tsumisu could envision Goshinfuda's wince of confusion.

"What? Ooohhh...OK, son," he joked, having gotten the message. "You'll pay Taras a visit, I suppose?"

"He must be destroyed at all costs," Tsumisu affirmed. "I-I mean, we'll smoke them online, Mom. I'll be back by sundown?"

"That was weak."

"Ugh, I'll contact you when I get to my friend's place, OK? Geez..." Tsumisu cleared his throat and turned around, wearing an innocent expression. "My mom," he said nonchalantly. "She's just checking up on her favorite child, ya know?"

"You're not a good liar," the group of women said in unison.

"*I know that*!" he cried and then recomposed himself. "Tetyana, be a dear and summon the *Diablo*?"

"Who was that?" she asked, smirking, arms folded.

"My mom—I already said that. Hellllooo?"

"Oh my God." She rolled her eyes. "You're such a dork..."

"And you're a *name-caller*. So there."

As she stretched out her right hand, the diamond-shaped gem embedded in her chest began to glow; as she lifted her arm, a geometric mesh-grid outlining a ship took shape overhead, and in a bright flash, the *Diablo* hovered in all its menacing glory.

"Wow, that's amazing, Tetyana!" began Arlette. "Buuuuuut *why* won't you tell us anything again?" she asked Tsumisu, stepping before him. "C'mon, cutie!"

"No! Y-you can't make me!" he said, shielding himself. "That is to say, I've got nothing *hide*..."

Suzuka was far from convinced. "Your mysteries shall soon come to light, Mr. Tsumisu. Mark my words!" She shook a clenched fist.

"Whuh, duly noted!"

The Sonzai commander was grateful to have their spirits elevated; it made no sense heading straight into battle with heavy hearts, lest they risked a lapse in concentration or judgment under such dispositions. Maybe they mutually appreciated his efforts too.

"And you're gonna keep fightin' in your house clothes, I guess?" Tetyana remarked, observing Tsumisu's attire. "Or is that T-shirt impenetrable?"

He winced. "I *didn't* want to add to the mystery," he began, assuming an aggressive, wide-foot stance with fists at his hips, "but since you're concerned..."

At that moment, Tsumisu's body began to glow with a white ethereal energy, initiating prominent black, highly reflective exoskeleton armor to materialize over him, starting from his feet and continuing to his chest, dancing down his arms and hands. Finally, the armor covered up to the lower half of his face.

Tsumisu exhaled, standing upright. "My mom got it for my birthday—"

"Shut up!" Tetyana threatened, grinning.

"Oh my, that's not too heavy, is it, Tsumisu?" asked Arlette.

"Naaah." His voice was reassuring. "My mom got it on sale—*ow*! OK, Tetyana!"

Suzuka rubbed her chin, inspecting him closely. "This exceeds even Devonian armor," she muttered. Then they locked eyes. "And because no known civilization has surpassed us, you are clearly *not* who you appear to be, Mr. Tsumisu."

"Sooo, I've definitely added too much mystery is what you're saying?" Tsumisu replied, chuckling. "Don't stare, Princess—uh, let's get outta here, yeah, Tetyana?"

The Ordovician mercenary snapped her fingers, bringing a light over the group to transport them into the *Diablo.* Once they arrived, Suzuka, Arlette, and Tsumisu felt strangely comfortable—there was a functional living room inside the vessel, outfitted with furniture (bolted down for obvious reasons) and a room-length viewing window on the port and starboard sides.

"Huh, nice place," Tsumisu complimented her, taking a stroll. "But I gotta say it smells awfully feminine in here—I'm gonna stop messing with you. I swear it's only temporary!" he jested, defensive hands before him.

"You're lucky I'm nice to you, big guy," she replied and then released a deep sigh. "I unwind in this space, in case you guys are wondering—*yes,* those are scented candles, Tsumisu."

"I didn't say anything!"

Arlette had a seat and rested her head back. "No, this is really welcoming, Tetyana," she said, observing the river-tributary-like designs on the ceiling. "Chances are we're gonna run into trouble the minute we leave earth."

"Precisely, so it helps to take a breather," said Suzuka, leaning against a wall, noticing Tsumisu tinkering with the waxless candles. "I couldn't keep up with your movements, Mr. Tsumisu, and your blade cut through Taras's weapon like butter. Tell me, where did you learn to do that?"

"Same here!" Tetyana followed in remark. "You gotta be a pretty cold-blooded warrior to anticipate attacks on that level."

He dematerialized his facial armor. "I'd be lying to you if I said I knew," he replied with sincerity. "Quite simply, I only use what I've been given."

"And what've you been given?" asked Arlette, recalling the pictures on his apartment walls.

Tsumisu smiled softly. "Perhaps a gift, perhaps a curse. I'm not sure which is truer."

"But you've been living with this for a good minute, yeah?" said Tetyana. "Nobody's filled you in up until now?"

His sight drifted out the window. "Ha, that'd be great. I sometimes wonder if there's anybody...or any*thing* in existence that can." Tsumisu subtly shook his head. "Nevertheless, 'no matter, no fear'; I won't let that stop me, especially not now."

"Whatever the case, we're definitely gonna need you against that asshole." Closing her eyes and taking one final deep breath, Tetyana nodded to herself in confidence. "OK. Everybody ready?"

"And willing, Tetyana," said Suzuka.

"Just give the word!" replied Arlette.

"All right." Tetyana gave a smirk. "Follow me!"

Tetyana led the group to the bridge of the *Diablo*, where four seats were present—one at the front with the main controls, two at the sides, and one at the back. A 180-degree heads-up display faced forward, granting the pilots and operators a generous field of view.

"Typically, I let the *Diablo*'s AI handle the turrets," Tetyana began, "but on this occasion, it'll be best for some instinct to man the guns. Any questions?"

Tsumisu raised his hand.

With a smile, she feared the worst. "*Yes*, big guy?"

"Um, h-how can I call shotgun given this seating arrangement?" he winced. "*Can* I call shotgun? No?"

"Okaaaay," she said, holding a hand up to block his face from sight. "Anybody with a *real* question?"

"Actually, I was wondering the same!" chirped Arlette. "Oooohh, maybe if I sit across from you, Tsumisu, that'd be shotgun. Right?"

He gave the lieutenant a high five. "Sweet biscuits, that's correct! I was totally thinking one-dimensional with the front-seat thing...Right." He cleared his throat. "I'll sit portside—*What*, Princess? It's important."

Suzuka chuckled. "I shall take care of the stern then," she said. "I assume you've fought Taras previously with your vessel, Tetyana?"

She nodded. "Precisely why I need you guys as gunners. He might be a cyborg, but I doubt his ability to anticipate four different offensive styles at the same time."

Tsumisu took his seat, familiarizing himself with the controls. "Excellent point. And if our approach is swift, we diminish his chances of adapting." He gasped comically. "I get to fire *six* cannons? Whaaaaat?"

"Oh my gosh!" She laughed. "I can't take you seriously sometimes, big guy!"

"I know! Isn't it great? And *that's* the punch line: We confuse and obscure our opponent, ladies! We bank like hell and alternate suppressive fire. Might feel some serious G-force." He smirked. "But that's nothing we can't handle."

"Though your methods are unorthodox, I could not agree more, Mr. Tsumisu," Princess Suzuka said with clenched fists. "Let us proceed!"

Soon they all took their seats and strapped in, and Tetyana brought up a holographic control panel beneath each hand; her eyes glistened as she established synaptic connectivity. Depressing a sequence of instructions, Tetyana shot the *Diablo* out of earth's atmosphere in a matter of seconds. It didn't take long for the group to see a truly massive object sitting ominously in the black of space. It was the *Leviathan*, a weapon feared across the galaxy.

"Can't say I'm happy to see that damn thing again," Tetyana muttered, a frown across her brow. "Distance one hundred and fifty kilometers and closing, ETA ten minutes."

"His arsenal can hit us from this range," remarked Suzuka. "Don't let your guard down, all right?"

"You got it!" Arlette replied, taking in a deep breath.

"We'll be fine, ladies," said Tsumisu, sensing their tension building. "Chances are we should do enough damage if we find the right weaknesses in that ungodly behemoth." His eyes fell to the *Leviathan.* "We'll try to punch one hell of a hole in it, and it'll serve as our docking port."

"Hey…" Tetyana turned to him. "Thanks."

Tsumisu gave a thumbs-up. "Don't get mushy on me." He grinned.

"I will, and you'll take it, dude. You stacked the odds we have?"

"Not just that." Tsumisu shrugged, watching the *Leviathan* become larger as they approached. "Something on a philosophical level, I guess. Taras amasses such an impure soul, though his strength is great. Given his kind of disposition, it will afford you few friends, and I *doubt* he's smart enough to pull off an engineering feat like the *Leviathan* single-handedly. It forces me to wonder how he came into possession of such a powerful ship."

Suzuka's expression rose in piqued intuition. "Point taken," she said. "Whoever built this ship hadn't intended for it to be in the hands of somebody like him. Of that, we can be certain."

"Maybe he forced many of his victims to build it," Arlette remarked. "Even though it's really big and powerful, it looks like a lot of people influenced the design."

"Yeah, slave labor wouldn't shock me in the least, Arlette," Tsumisu concurred. "Let's mark that as yet another reason to kill Taras."

At that moment, warning alarms sounded within the cockpit.

"Looks like we'll get that chance soon!" announced Tetyana. "Incoming fire! Taking evasive maneuvers!"

Indeed, the *Leviathan* discharged several dozen proton-based turrets at the *Diablo,* forcing Tetyana to bank *hard* and away. Even so, they took a hit.

"Aaghh! Impact, starboard!" reported Arlette. "Shields are holding!"

"Send that bastard a thank-you note!" Tetyana yelled.

"Repositioning weapon systems to bow face!" said Suzuka.

"Fire!"

As the *Diablo* continued to bank, a spiraling stream of turret fire came from its stern and starboard side, canceling out incoming beams to leave explosions in their wake as well as burdening the *Leviathan*'s shield.

"One hundred kilometers and closing!" said Tsumisu. "We gotta reverse direction, Tetyana!"

"And risk degradation to the shield?" she cried. "I can't do that now!"

"Yes, you *can*! You've got a rail-gun on this thing, right? Get it charged, and I'll concentrate fire on his shield! Suzuka, I'll need your help!"

"Roger!" she confirmed.

"Hey, I'm trusting you, big guy!" Tetyana gritted her teeth, initiating her cannons charging parameters. "Let's go!"

Tetyana stomped her foot on the accelerator and plowed forward with full thrusters, narrowly escaping the *Leviathan*'s arcing fire; in the next moment, she pulled the *Diablo* portside, drawing significant gravitational forces on the ship and causing shield failure. At the same time, Tsumisu laid down suppressive fire on a particular section of the *Leviathan* while Suzuka provided cover fire.

"Shields down to sixty percent!" cried Arlette, bracing herself for an impact. "Fifty percent!"

"Tetyana, lock the rail gun onto my area of fire!" Tsumisu instructed, launching a payload of missiles twenty kilometers ahead of the *Diablo*. "What's the time on that charge?"

"T-minus fifteen seconds!" she replied, struggling to maintain the ship's heading. "Whatever you're planning to do, it's gotta happen *now*!"

Another impact to the hull damaged the stern weapons system.

"Damn it!" exclaimed Suzuka. "We lost four turrets!"

"Shields at thirty percent and dropping fast!" cried Arlette, beginning to panic. "Oh my God, Tsumisu?"

A devious smirk crept across his lips. "Fear not, Arlette! Detonating missiles!" he said.

In that moment, ten warheads exploded before the *Diablo*, creating a particle screen between them and the *Leviathan*; for a moment, incoming fire ceased. Tetyana saw her chance.

"Take this, Taras!" she declared.

A mighty blast of highly charged electromagnetic energy tore through space and impaled the *Leviathan*'s shield; the sustained beam finally struck the ship's hull, creating a gaping hole.

"*Now,* Tetyana!" yelled Tsumisu.

"All right you son of a bitch, here I come!" she declared, putting the *Diablo* at full capacity. "*Raaaghh*!"

Everyone braced for impact as they were fast approaching, and in the next few seconds, the *Diablo* barreled through the *Leviathan*'s hull, digging several hundred meters into it before finally coming to a stop. The cockpit was silent; circuits popped, lights flickered, and the group looked around them.

"Heh…heh…heh." Tetyana was in disbelief. "Ah ha ha haaa!"

Tsumisu quickly undid his restraints. "C'mon!" he cheered, freeing Arlette and Suzuka. "We did it! Whoaaa!"

"Yaaaay-haaay!" said Arlette, pummeling him over…with Tetyana and Suzuka piling in afterward. "You're the *best,* Tsumisu!"

"That was simply brilliant, Mr. Tsumisu!" Suzuka exclaimed, planting a kiss on his forehead. She was wearing the biggest smile. "Absolutely brilliant!"

"I knew you were crazy, but that was crazy, dude!" said an equally elated Tetyana. She kissed his cheek.

In that moment, Tsumisu had to remind himself that these highly talented extraterrestrial beings *were* girls at the end of the day. And though his heart raced with the excitement of accomplishment, Tsumisu was similarly warmed (in more ways than one) by their happiness—especially after facing such pain earlier.

"Hey! I couldn't have done it without you lovely ladies!" he replied, still pinned down. "Being honored to fight alongside all of you is an understatement; I couldn't ask to be with a more stellar team—Arlette, Suzuka, Tetyana."

The three of them awed in adoration, sending another group hug his way before finally helping Tsumisu to his feet.

"You're *just* as mushy," said Tetyana.

"Correction, I'm *puréed*," he joked, nudging her shoulder. "OK, ladies, when we get out there, keep your head on a swivel and stab *or* shoot anything that moves."

"Sounds like a plan to me!" said Arlette, arming her pistol. "Ready when you are."

Suzuka checked her katana's scabbard, ensuring it was secured. "If we encounter resistance, I'll leave *nothing* left," she said with a nod.

"Great." Tsumisu returned the gesture, materializing his facial armor. "Let's move out."

Tetyana transported them out of the *Diablo*, and the group secured their location, finding that the *Leviathan* was indeed a conglomerate of varying technologies. Unfortunately, it made landmarks indistinguishable.

"Now, where could Taras be located?" Suzuka asked, observing the immense structure. "Have we any idea where to start?"

"Not me," Tsumisu responded, clearly bothered. "This will be a challenge all right."

"Why, Tsumisu?" Arlette curiously asked, standing beside him.

"Well, my dear, I can detect specific energy from matter *and* beings; yet there's something about this ship that's screwing with my abilities..."

She gasped. "You can tell where somebody is just by thinking?"

"Yeah." He nodded, inspecting their surroundings. "It feels like a symmetric energy pattern is distorting the spiritual plane...as if it has been disrupted by another *physical dimension*. But how could that be? Gosh."

"I'm surprised you can *see* all that crap," Tetyana muttered, taking a look around but only seeing the depressingly repetitive decor of the ship. "Anyway, is that good or bad news? 'Cause if *we* can't tell where the bastard is, we're sitting ducks."

Tsumisu scoffed with humor. "With mango salsa at that, but you're right. We'd better come up with something soon."

"Why don't we divide into groups?" suggested Suzuka. "I'm sure Arlette has communicators on hand, so when one group is about to approach Taras's position, we can inform the others of our location and meet up to face him together!"

"Good idea." Tetyana snapped her fingers, pointing. "OK, Lieutenant, you heard the lady. Hand 'em over."

"Um, now *where* did I put those communicators?" Arlette started rifling through her stash of equipment. "Nope not here…not here either!"

Suzuka had a worried expression. "At least I *thought* she had communicators—"

"Hey! Here they are!" she exclaimed brightly, startling everyone. "Now who's gonna be in which group?"

"I'll go with you, Arlette," Tsumisu directed, his Sonzai conditioning on full alert. "Tetyana? You go with Suzuka."

Tetyana nodded in affirmation. "Yeah, I get ya. That way, if we find Taras first, it won't be as if we can't hold our own. And if you two find him first, Tsumisu can handle him like he did—which I'll ask you about later." She eyed him suspiciously once again. "See, I *know* you're hiding a lot of stuff from me, big guy…"

"And yet I'm hiding right in *front* of you, Tetyana." He nudged her shoulder with a smirk. "I love fighting with you…just saying."

"Hey! The feeling is mutual." She punched his chest again. "But ya *still* owe me an explanation…"

The embattled group made its way in a direction Tsumisu suggested, and it wasn't long before they encountered a two-way tunnel, like a fork in the road.

"Guess this is where we split up," Tetyana remarked, exhaling thereafter. "Remember, if any of us see 'the bastard,' we won't engage. Get coordinates and regroup. Got it?"

"Copy that," Tsumisu replied, hoping his clansmen could still pick up his transmission from their location.

"Understood," Suzuka acknowledged firmly. "We shall take the right hall. Arlette, Tsumisu? Take the left."

"Got it." Arlette nodded. "See you guys soon, hopefully, OK?"

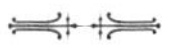

Traversing their designated tunnels and proceeding forth, Suzuka and Tetyana immediately ran into an area completely overrun with a barrage of the ship's defenses—bipedal machines armed with antipersonnel armaments, laser mounts on the ceiling, and levitating bombs that would detonate at a certain proximity. Tetyana softened countless targets with her revolver, while Suzuka brought up the rear by cutting down any reinforcements or stragglers. The powerful warriors had *much* work ahead of them; the tunnel extended as far as the eye could see.

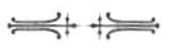

Meanwhile, Tsumisu and Arlette navigated one-fourth of the way into their tunnel, yet did not journey further as the Sonzai commander instantly sensed impending danger and ordered Arlette to stand behind him.

"What danger are you talking about, Tsumisu?" she asked, closely following. However, she was trying to avoid staring at his exoskeleton-molded butt, blushing at the sight. "Oh my..."

"Probably Taras's home-made version of a security system," he replied, right hand resting on Akari. "Speak of the devil. Here they come…"

"Wha-*what*? Oh no! Do something!"

Tsumisu turned around. "Could you stand back a little bit, sweetie? This won't take long."

"Ummm, OK," she said, instantly calming down with hands behind her back, blushing again. "Wow…*dreamy*."

Tsumisu drew his weapon and placed it to his side, twirling it as he waited for the right moment. "C'mon…C'mon…" he mumbled as machines drew ever closer. "*There*."

At that moment, Tsumisu made a slash in the air from the bottom right to the upper left, sending a tremendous wave of energy throughout the *entire* hallway. The white, arc-shaped pulse narrowed inside the tunnel and wrought absolute destruction to it and everything inside, leaving a V-shaped gouge to serve as their new pathway through.

"Pathetic," Tsumisu muttered, twirling Akari back into its sheath. "C'mon; it's safe to go now."

Arlette stood with starry eyes and dropped jaw.

Not hearing her response, Tsumisu quickly turned around to see what the matter was. "Hey, uh…you OK, Arlette?" he asked, waving a hand in front of her. "The ship's air getting to you now?"

"Tsumisu-do-you-have-a-girlfriend-and-if-so-would-you-dump-her-for-me? *Please*?" Arlette spat off her words like an auctioneer, eyes shivering with anticipation. "Pleeease?"

He took a few steps backward, eyes wide. "*Whoa*! Wait a minute, what? Uh, what's happening again?" he cried.

She gasped in desperation. "Oh! Oh my gosh, I just ruined it, didn't I? Oh noo!"

"*Wait* a minute!" Tsumisu grabbed her shoulders, trying to diffuse her before it was over-the-edge time. "You didn't do anything wrong, OK? I was uh…just…caught off guard, all right?"

She sniffled. "So...you don't hate me for asking?"

"Heavens no! That'd be horrible of me."

All right, Tsumisu, diplomacy doesn't work here. Lying is just plain awful. Omission is *probably* worse. There she is, waiting for an honest-to-goodness answer, and you can *clearly* ascertain the level of anxiety she's undergoing. You've *no* reference to work from... just try your best.

"Whuuhh no, I currently *don't* have a girlfriend." He was cautiously pacing his words. "But could you give me some time to *think* about your request?"

Arlette, whimpering a little, stared in stark anticipation. "Y-you mean it?"

"Yes." Tsumisu patiently nodded, granting a reassuring smile. "*Yes*, I mean it."

"Yaaaaay!" Arlette leaped to give him a huge, blood-circulation-endangering embrace...even through his exoskeleton armor. "Yaay! Thank you, Tsumisu! OK, I feel better now," she cheerily responded. "Let's go?"

"Er..." he muttered, watching the lieutenant walk past. "S-sure, after you."

CHAPTER SEVEN

Taras was located within a huge room resembling a well-kept graveyard on a sunny day. Standing among the marked headstones, he noticed a violent tremble coming from the midchambers of his ship.

"I'll be damned," he said with a chortle. "They actually made it this far. I might get my money's worth after all." A monitor hovering above showed an approaching Suzuka and Tetyana, and a sinister grin surfaced. "*Just* who I needed to see. Guess I'll show 'em the front door..."

At the same time, Tetyana and Suzuka made it to the end of the tunnel and came across a hallway. At its end was a large wall, covered in bloodstained engravings depicting Taras—however the trill of birdsong emanated from behind.

⸻

"He's in there all right," said Tetyana as she clenched her fists. "I'm not sure where the entrance is, and that wall looks sealed up tight...See if you can reach Tsumisu and Arlette."

"I'm already trying, but it seems something is interfering with the communicators," Suzuka replied. "Perhaps this is the distortion Tsumisu was mentioning earlier."

"Damn it! The hell is with this ship? I swear, every step forward is a step back..."

"I'm not sure..." Suzuka looked at the wall again, and it slowly began to open. "Should we proceed? It isn't as if we have another choice."

"You're right. As much as I wanna stick to the agreement, we can't afford to go back now..." Tetyana gave her comrade a glance of confidence. "To hell with it, Princess, we can do it."

Suzuka nodded in return. "For the honor of Prince Shujin."

"For Shujin's honor," she agreed, shaking her hand.

Risky as it seemed, they went through the wall, watching it mysteriously close behind them as if the passage never existed. On the other side, Tetyana and Suzuka found themselves stunned by the sight of a massive graveyard that spanned as far as they could see. In the middle of the area lay a brick path leading to a patiently waiting Taras—his back turned to them, Tetyana and Suzuka approached. Cracking his knuckles, he turned around with a sinister smirk.

"Well now, if it ain't my favorite company in the whole galaxy: Suzuka and Tetyana!" he began. "How'd you two figure out where I was so damn fast?"

"Silence, you misogynistic, murdering asshole!" shouted Tetyana, furiously pointing. "We're here to avenge the death of Shujin!"

"Murdering? Shit, I'm glad you noticed!" Taras replied in jest. "You like the scenery then, huh?"

"What?" she gasped, observing the headstones. "You...sick monster!"

"All of those victims," Suzuka said, clenching her fists in rage. "Must you torture them in life and death? Haven't you done enough?"

"Call it a hobby." He casually shrugged. "See, I like to keep my trophies around; it helps to remind folks like you where *you're* gonna be when all is said and done."

"Our fates have been decided," Suzuka valiantly disagreed, "and this day, you shall die as restitution for the suffering you've committed!"

"Now let's be reasonable here! Doesn't it seem pointless to waste your life over a bunch of cockroaches?" Taras chuckled. "*Especially* that joke of a 'Shujin' fellow?"

"Prince Shujin was not weak!" she protested, drawing her weapon. "He devoted his life to us!"

Taras laughed at her remarks. "Ain't that cute? Well, once I've reduced you both to a pulp, I'll consume your powers and *finally* be rid of the Devonians and Ordovicians and claim this galaxy for myself." He materialized his dual-bladed weapon. "See, now *that's* devotion to be proud of."

"Are you ready?" asked Suzuka, preparing herself in a fighting stance.

Tetyana nodded, weapon drawn. "Let's finish him! Rraagh!"

They charged their enemy once again, engaging in two-on-one sword combat with the merciless cyborg.

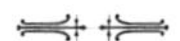

Meanwhile, Tsumisu and Arlette made it to the end of their new canyon-carved tunnel and waded through the debris. However, they appeared to arrive at the same place they started from.

Tsumisu shook his head. "I could've sworn this was the right direction, yet Taras's signal wasn't getting any stronger."

"Maybe it was just the wrong tunnel?" asked Arlette, directing her device around but in futile effort. "Darn it! Is it broken or something?"

"Perhaps—ah shit," he lamented, looking in another direction. "I just felt Tetyana's energy flare up…and…Suzuka's there too! They *can't* be fighting Taras now!"

She gasped. "Fighting Taras? B-but why didn't they contact us?"

"Maybe they tried, and we didn't know? Check the communicators."

"OK!" she replied and dug into her stash of equipment again. Bringing out the communicator, she tried to reach them but ended up getting nothing but static. "I think we're out of the service area," she said regretfully.

"No, there's no service area, my dear." Tsumisu shook his head, the truth hitting him. "It's this God-forsaken *ship*. The energy construct is like walking through a hall of magic mirrors of the *worst* kind!" he grunted in frustration. "All right, Arlette, if Tetyana and Suzuka took that other tunnel, then that must be the right way…"

"Hmm, maybe not, Tsumisu," she replied, standing several meters from him. "Check it out! My scanner is picking up something strange behind this wall."

"What *isn't* strange about this ship that qualifies as strange now?" he muttered, defeating his internal irritability. Standing by Arlette's side, Tsumisu observed nothing strikingly extraordinary about the structure. "Are you sure?"

Arlette nodded. "See?" She showed him her readings. "Crazy, huh?"

"Yeah, now I understand what you're saying. A secret room maybe?"

"That's the thing! It doesn't register anything except empty space back there." Arlette placed a finger against her bottom lip and messed with her device once again. "Maybe there's an activation protocol needed…"

"Hey, don't try it if you're not sure—Arlette!" he called, failing to reach her. "What's happening?"

"Waaah!" she cried, being drawn through the wall. "Tsumisu!"

Tsumisu leaned forward and rushed the wall, intending to break through with his shoulder, to no avail. "Damn it!" he grunted, even *more* frustrated. "This makes absolutely no sense! I seriously don't need any *Chronicles of Narnia* bullshit today! But…I must assist Tetyana and Suzuka." Tsumisu sighed, shaking his head. "But I can't just lose Arlette in this nightmarish vessel. I've *got* to save her. Where could she have gone?" he muttered, leaning against the wall for a few minutes.

"Perhaps there really is more to this ship than I imagined; the inability of my direct senses to determine the exact locations of spirits must be due to a sudden shift of energy patterns within this dimension—like an autocorrection mechanism that can't quite get it right in spiritual parameters." Tsumisu snapped his fingers. "There *must* be another dimension on this damn thing! I gotta find it!"

The Sonzai commander placed a hand against the wall to perhaps locate Arlette energetically. "Right here. Wow, I can barely feel her…"

He paused, sensing a *very* distinguishable spirit alongside Arlette's.

"That does it. I'm breaking in." Taking time to work out the mental details, he cracked his neck. "Here goes nothing. Grandmaster Sonzai? I know what you said…but I'm trying this technique if you're watching me."

Tsumisu slowed his breathing and began amassing energy; recognition, communication, and exchange parameters were taking place. The physical realm had its set of boundaries, so the Sonzai commander could siphon necessary energy sources to *find* the elusive and theoretical alternate physical dimension. The issue was breaking through it without damaging his body—and other matter within the physical dimension—at the same time.

He groaned as the collection of energy became greater and the entire wall began to flicker, briefly displaying another side.

"It's *there*!"

But he couldn't reach it at the moment; he needed more energy still.

Placing both hands against the wall, Tsumisu concentrated more intensely, and the wall flickered dramatically, a product of abnormal energy deconstruction. At this point, Tsumisu could visualize the other dimension for longer lengths of time. Soon, he saw his opportunity—focusing the previously amassed energy into one key frequency, he ripped open a hole into the other side. In a dizzying light display, all the stored energy was released and catapulted him into the next dimension, violently tossing him on the floor.

After tumbling over several times before coming to a stop, Tsumisu landed on his back and stared at the gigantic new area. At least it had a pretty ceiling.

"*Ow...*" he muttered feebly.

Arising, the Sonzai commander gazed on a massive room with erected pillars composed of varying circuitry and cables; the area was dark at the far ends yet illuminated by diffuse light coming from a series of rectangular panels extending the middle of the hall.

"I need a vacation after this place—makes you want to shoot yourself," he scoffed in humor, but his expression suddenly turned to anger. "That's one score for *me*, you piece of shit machination! Did you see that?" He immediately raised a vertically aligned right hand to his face, praying. "It *can't* hear you, dude."

"Well, *he* didn't sound too happy!" said a mature but strong and unfamiliar female voice. "Seems you and I have something in common with the *Leviathan*, handsome!"

"Over here! Hey!" Arlette was jumping up and down, standing beside another person. "Look! I found somebody!"

Tsumisu exhaled, settling his nerves. "All right just stay there, and don't move!" he called, dashing over on his approach to meet them.

On his way, Tsumisu noticed an elegantly elevated glass spherical chamber surrounded by massive cables that extended into the ceiling; screens and monitors coupled with the technological array to display various attributes, which, at that moment, were flatlined. And beneath it all was a wide, multicolored control panel which, in Tsumisu's deduction, served an obvious purpose: to *control.*

Nevertheless, there stood before him a woman about a meter-eighty, with fair skin and deep orange hair; she had an *impressively* long braid behind her, two unabashedly curly locks reached past her shoulders, draping over her bosom, and piercing pink eyes. She wore a solid and flowing black dress of pleasing design, complete with padded shoulders and a V-cut for her *generous* cleavage.

Yet, what Tsumisu found most interesting about this individual was her *perpetual stare.* Why was she staring at him like that? And so…

"Umm, what're you doing?" asked Arlette, watching curiously.

"Gimme a second, dear," he replied, taking small steps in all directions to test the woman's eyesight. "C-could you stop?"

"Why?" she asked, smirking. "What's more uncomfortable for you? Crashing through alternate dimensions or my gaze?"

"*Both.*" He winced, finally standing still. "*Anyway*! Arlette, wow, I'm glad to see you're OK!" Tsumisu officially greeted her, albeit with caution. "You totally freaked me out up there, and I had to break into this dimension—which I had to *verify* was another dimension to find you!" He caught his frustration release and forced a smile. "Gosh, I hate earlier assumptions being correct sometimes."

"I'm impressed you could *do* such a thing," commented the woman. "Sure would take a whooooolle *lotta* energy to make it happen! As a matter of fact, it should be *improbable* to do by *hand* given the right equipment isn't on your person, I see." She continued looking him over, a finger on her bottom lip in meticulous observation. "Have I heard of you before, handsome?"

"Er…there are few who have, I'm afraid," Tsumisu replied, taking a few steps back. "Just how'd you get stuck down here, Little Lady?"

"Please, call me Nataliya! I'm *the* femme fatale of science and *your* worst nightmare." A bolt of lightning struck from out of nowhere and added to the dramatics. "If you get in trouble with me, that is…"

"Uhhh—"

She gasped. "And wouldn't you know it?"

"I'm afraid to guess?"

Nataliya narrowed her eyes. "You're in *deep* trouble."

Arlette smiled as she stood beside her, applauding. "Yep! I'm glad you noticed! He's *super* sneaky!" she said.

"Oh yeah? Think you can provide a full report about that?" she brightly asked. "I've got an inkling I'll need it!"

"Ummm…sure! I can do that!"

Nataliya instantly glanced back at the towering, exoskeleton-outfitted, weapon-carrying warrior, trying to piece things together.

"She's with you?" She pointed behind her.

"Couldn't hurt a fly, but she's a damn good shot." Tsumisu grinned with folded arms. "You know, aside from the *sudden* underhandedness taking place, Taras should *really* put that shit to rest—pardon my language, but I'm assuming you are yet another victim of his, yes?"

"Well, if you wanna put it like *that*, then absolutely." Nataliya raised an instructive finger to him. "Seems like you got a big problem with him on an existential level by my observation, yeah?"

He chuckled in amusement. "I like how you speak, Little Lady. Well, my tremendous romp through this place has benefitted me greatly. Question: is this *your* ship?"

"Oooo, you're a clever one. I *like* it!" Nataliya began rubbing her hands, apparently plotting something. "Well, technically, it isn't; despite my knowledge of the *Leviathan*'s functionalities in all parametric, dimensional, transdimensional yada yada…" She noticed his disposition not changing much. "Long story short, this glorified prison behind me is the product of information sequestration over time."

"On behalf of Taras? So, he literally kept you around to use you for his purposes…but his technical knitting practices pale in comparison to someone of your caliber?" The Sonzai commander brought an aligned right hand to his face once again, praying. "The ancients may fail to forestall my anger this day…"

"Oh my gosh, that's terrible, Nataliya," sympathized Arlette. "Are you OK?"

She looked herself over, subtly bobbing her head. "For the most part, thank goodness," she muttered, placing a hand on her brow. "But I am feeling…*faint*…"

"Hey!" Tsumisu exclaimed, moving quickly to catch her. "Maybe you should take it easy—wait, *really*?"

She was comfortably in his grasp but wore a mischievous grin. "Mm-hmm, strong with *sharp* reflexes," she analyzed. "I sense a soft spot too."

"The underhandedness continues it seems." He sighed.

"Oh, you have *yet* to see me underhanded…"

Tsumisu cleared his throat and helped Nataliya to her feet. "Do you mind enlightening me about this Taras guy?" he inquired. "Trust me; the more I know, the easier his ruin will be exacted."

"Well, Taras was…I *thought* I knew him, a long time ago," Nataliya explained, her tone shifting to a somber one. "Trust me; he wasn't the animal you see today. Actually…" She paused, turning to him. "He's *always* been an animal."

Tsumisu placed a hand on her shoulder. "You were betrayed?"

"Who told you that?" Her eyes widened. "Have you encountered Tetyana?"

"Yeah, we have and Princess Suzuka. They're fighting Taras right now, as a matter of fact."

"Wow…" Her gaze drifted in thought. "It's been so long…"

"You two are familiar?"

"I'm Ordovician, and so is she…as you're probably aware by now." Nataliya gave a little smile. "Tetyana is my creation."

Tsumisu looked at Arlette, stunned. "Y-you…*created* her?" he asked. She *had* to be the classified target!

"Oh yes," Nataliya confirmed. "Before the Age of Conflict, I was chief researcher for the Ordovician government, tasked to develop a weapon capable of defending against the Devonian imperial threat. And so…" She sighed. "That's what I did…Taras worked under me. We spent six hundred years testing prototype after prototype, and we finally got it right with Tetyana."

"What happened?" asked Arlette, hands clasped together.

"Taras was actually a spy for Devonia, and, well…the rest is history."

The time reference took Tsumisu off guard momentarily. "So…you were Taras's lab boss, and an apparently innate psychopathic characteristic of his went unnoticed by everyone else for six hundred years, leading to an interstellar conflict?"

Nataliya nodded in the affirmative. "That about sums it up! Don't get me wrong; I tried to stop him—"

"Blame is not on you, Little Lady, or any of us," he interrupted, a polite hand raised. "Despite Taras's 'knowledge,' his despicable nature makes him nothing more than an ordinary jewel thief wielding a big gun."

"Oh, he's more than just your 'ordinary villain,'" Nataliya cautioned, her expression turning to concern. "And by the looks of it, you're a man on a mission, am I right? Don't get *too* cocky, Mister…?"

"Wow, after all this time, I didn't tell you my name? Sorry, it's Tsumisu." He finally allowed his demeanor to lighten up, dismissing dark thoughts. "It's a pleasure to meet you, Little Lady."

"So 'Tsumisu,' eh? Hmm…" The scientist was in thought. "Nope, your name doesn't come to mind. No last name?"

"None. Sorry to deepen the mystery for you…as I've done for *many* today." Tsumisu shrugged as he exhaled, taking another look around. "So how long have you been down here, Little Lady?"

"Ha, just *can't* say my name, can ya?" She laid both hands on her hips. "C'mon now; give it a shot."

"Naaa…Naaaa…" Tsumisu practiced.

"Yeah, yeah, you're almost there…"

"Natal—*Little Lady*." He winced, sounding defeated. "I *did* try."

She laughed aloud. "Is it because I'm so pretty? So pretty you could just pinch my cheeks and allow me to conduct multiple life-changing experiments on you?"

"Brutally honest! I appreciate it." Tsumisu took another step back in subtle fear. "So, yeah, how long again?"

"About eight hundred years now!" she exclaimed, taking a step toward him. "Taras nabbed me while the proverbial 'shit' was hitting the fan. Things starting to add up for you, handsome?"

Tsumisu snapped his fingers—Taras really *was* a misogynistic asshole. "Wow, that's a long time. Aren't you hungry or something?"

"Maybe." Nataliya bit her bottom lip, mentally turning those potential experiments over. "After all, there's *so much* of the main course to explore, it'd be rude if I didn't eat…don't ya think?"

"Oh my—hold that thought." He dematerialized his exoskeleton armor, revealing normal clothes. "All this new and intricate information makes me *frisky* for action, so in times like these…" He paused, reaching into a pocket to whip out chewing gum. "This stuff really comes in handy. Take one."

Nataliya removed a piece from the package, her eyes noticing something completely different about him than before.

"You're human?"

"As far as I can tell," he said with humor, rubbing the back of his head. "It's spearmint, by the way. Hope you like it. Arlette, take one or two if you need it, dear."

"Yay!" she happily exclaimed, grabbing a piece. "Thank you, Tsumisu!"

"Aww, you're welcome."

Nataliya inspected the food nonsubstitute, sniffing it with a curious expression. "Spearmint?"

"Yeah, you don't like it?" Tsumisu reached for the gum. "You can just hand it—"

"No! It's *mine*! You gave it to me!" She took a few steps back defensively.

He raised his hands in defense. "Whoa! Hey, it's cool, Little Lady! Gosh, you're feisty too."

Nataliya eyed him in severe reproach, shoving the gum into her mouth. "Yeah, and *you* haven't told me how ya pulled off that trick earlier. Trying to hide something from me, Mr. Tsumisu?"

The Sonzai commander noticed that *four* people had asked the same question that day.

"Given your obvious ability to construct something like Tetyana, I'd be an idiot to do such a thing!" Tsumisu replied, chewing some gum as well. "That being said—and I'm not trying to get in deeper trouble with you—"

"Mm-hmm..."

"How good are you with respect to dimension manipulation?"

"Oh? Where's this area of doubt coming from?" she approached him with authority. "Care to explain yourself?"

"Errr, *not* doubt. Just trying to get an understanding?" Tsumisu backed away, noticing his next words could result in a fate worse than...something. "Um, obviously you're familiar with designing symmetrical physical dimensions, yes?"

"That's correct," she succinctly replied. "As well as their components of physical, astral and biastral energy products to correlate the parameters each symmetric dimensional field contains. And?" Fists clenched, Nataliya wasn't letting up. "You're implying what

Taras sucked outta me was insufficient to build this alternate dimension we're in, is that it?"

"Wait a second! I'm not trying to make you upset—"

"Spit it *out* already!"

"Whaa!" he cried. "Uuhhh, four times four is sixteen!"

"Oh my!" Arlette gasped. "Tsumisu! Maybe you should just leave it alone?"

"I can't now, Arlette; it's too late for me," he replied, eyes wide. "OK, that's what I was saying: each dimension parallels the other on the order of subatomic accuracy—this is indeed a tremendous physical matter and energy accomplishment. However..." Tsumisu paused, looking toward the ceiling. "The *spiritual* energetic parameters have not been synchronized as meticulously; therefore, it's thrown out of whack, so to speak. Sort of like...retaining the top and bottom cookies of an ice cream sandwich, but the filling is scattered all over the room."

Nataliya was rubbing her chin and tapping her foot. "And you say you're human? What's this spiritual parameter you mentioned? Are you pulling my leg here?"

Tsumisu laughed in relief. "At least you're not mad at me anymore. Look, all I'm saying is that I see this stuff flowing around us."

"That's it?"

"Um, no, I don't know what the naming conventions are, but I understand behavior. Like water. It flows in many, many ways, and some streams are clear while others are murky." He smiled with insight. "Guess my goal is wading through the murky water."

"Mr. Tsumisu..." Nataliya closed her eyes, trying to retain her inner need for reason. "I didn't ask for a sermon; I asked for an *explanation*. You can't just 'see' these dimensions!"

"Sorry, that's about all I can say given the time we don't have. And," he continued, unsheathing Akari and laying the blade on his shoulder, making Nataliya a little nervous, "I've got a lot of work ahead of me to get all that 'ice cream filling' together. Excuse me, Little Lady, Arlette…" He nodded to them courteously.

"Gonna try and *break* us out, I assume?" she called as he walked away.

"Yup! That's the idea," he casually responded, shoving Akari within the floor. "Nope, not there…" he muttered. "Yeah, just leave the same way I got in basically!"

"Who said there *was* a way, hmm?" Nataliya's strong and medium-pitched voice echoed.

"I think it was, uh…Ronald Reagan that did." Tsumisu briefly turned to her in humor. "Oh wait, you probably didn't hear about him…"

Nataliya bore a confident grin. "Well, it's the truth! Or perhaps you'd rather me give you a song of inspiration for your understanding?"

"Yay! A song!" Arlette cheered. "Which song?"

"Think you can handle the tambourine?" she asked worriedly.

Tsumisu held one finger up as he quickly approached. "No, no, no, I have to get back up there. Do you understand?"

"Of course I do," Nataliya responded, her arms folded. "Taras designed this place as a *prison*, handsome. It's a one-way access; once you go in, nothing comes out."

"But we've gotta help out Tetyana and Suzuka!" cried Arlette. "Isn't there anything you can do, Nataliya?"

"Not sure if it'll add or reduce the stress concentration, however…" She snapped her fingers, and out from the ceiling hung several large, rectangular monitors, displaying the situation in the other dimension. "I'd hate to be reduced to an audience; trust me," she continued, "but that's all I can do, I fear."

"Oh wow! Look at that! It's them!" Arlette remarked, excited to see her friends again. "Look at 'em go!"

Tsumisu observed the fierce battle between Suzuka, Tetyana, and Taras. "Those poor girls are just fighting their hearts out!" He shook his head and turned to Nataliya. "You're positive there's no way to escape this dimension?"

"Absolutely none…and I'm *really* sorry about that," she replied. "It would've been better for you to stay up there. Once you're in this dimension, and I'm sure you 'saw' this by now, the parameters are not only reversed, but access to the primary dimension is…cut off." Nataliya noticed his expression deepening. "Hey…talk to me. What are you gonna do?"

Tsumisu was indeed contemplating, sighing momentarily. "Then I guess I don't have any other choice," he said, weapon drawn once more.

"Talk to me already!" she ran before him, arms outstretched to halt his path. "Don't go poking around things that you don't really understand, Tsumisu! Listen to me!"

"Little Lady, you *know* I must annihilate this dimension as fast as I can," he replied with all conviction. "Please, stand aside."

"Yeah, I know what you're gonna do, and it's absolutely nuts!" she cried, her voice filled with desperation. "Such a feat is impossible! The velocity of astroenergy multiplied by quantum-cluster force would send the next dimension haywire, disrupting all of space-time. Not to mention *kill* you in the process. I *can't* let you do that. *If* you can pull it off anyway!"

Shoving his weapon within the floor, Tsumisu knelt before it. "So that's what all that stuff means?"

"Tsumisu, please listen to me! Don't *do* this!"

"I *am* listening! But I also know Taras killed a good man today, a *damn* good man." Tsumisu's gaze into her eyes was intense. "Quantum forces or not, the keepers of *hell* couldn't stop me right now. For this, I owe no apology…Our fates are not left to chance, and I came here for a reason: to see through that murky water."

"Well…" Nataliya dropped her arms and exhaled. "Obviously, *I* can't stop you. But if it means anything, thanks for trying anyway, OK?"

"We cannot fail except to try, Little Lady." Tsumisu nodded and focused his attention on Akari.

Dispelling thoughts of worst-case scenarios, Nataliya patted the warrior's shoulder and approached Arlette. "I hope you know what you're doin'," she whispered, taking one last look at the embattled man.

CHAPTER EIGHT

Nataliya observed the array of monitors. "OK, what've we got?"

"They're still fighting!" Arlette responded, intently watching with hands clasped before her chest. "But I-I think they're in trouble!"

As the battle raged, Tetyana and Suzuka were holding their own against Taras, but many of their tactics were failing against him. Needless to say, they were running out of options. The two warriors stood beside each other among the ravaged graveyard, trying to take a moment's breath.

"OK," began Tetyana, her demeanor undaunted, though fatigue was setting in. "What the hell…is with this bastard?"

"Each wound we inflict heals without delay," Suzuka replied, weapon still readied. "And I've no idea how to cease this ability."

"Here's the good news, though: when's the last time you saw him pull out that magic trick?"

Suzuka glanced quickly from the corner of her eye. "I assumed Taras was merely toying with us," she replied.

Tetyana shook her head. "Trust me, Princess; he would've pulled that move for intimidation. He ain't the type to say it, but somehow or another, Taras's lost that ability."

"It's like I've got a deck *full* of aces!" Taras proclaimed, cracking his neck with a grin. "Now, I don't know how you ladies feel about your chances, but I'm willing to bet you're gonna die in...say, thirty seconds?"

"Energy discharges alone are folly," said Suzuka, ignoring his banter, "yet if we can strike him simultaneously at full charge—"

"Who knows? We might hit 'em where it counts," Tetyana finished, controlling her breaths as her weapon began to charge. "You ready?"

Suzuka gathered her poise once more, drawing energy into her katana. "May Evelyn bring him to his knees," she said through gritted teeth.

An overlap of gold and purple auras commenced from the Ordovician and Devonian women and grew in size.

"Ha!" Taras scoffed in amusement. "One last hurrah, right? Well, let's see it!" he yelled, arms outstretched. "Do the unthinkable! Ah ha ha haaa!"

"*Raaaaggh*!" was their battle cry.

At once, they bolted toward the evil cyborg with blinding speed and sliced through him; a mighty explosion accompanied their onslaught, forcing them to land unbalanced and collapse. In the wake of their violence, Taras was certainly reduced to hundreds of pieces of both metal and man, scattered about in no discernible order; in the silence, shorted wires popped to overlay the labored breaths of Tetyana and Suzuka.

"Did...did we get him?" asked Tetyana, eyes clenched.

Suzuka struggled to turn over and observe the scene. "I think... we've secured victory," she replied, falling down again. "Victory... for Prince Shujin."

Tetyana nodded. "For Shujin..." she whispered. "OK, let's get the hell outta here—"

The sound of slithering wires and tissue cut the mercenary's words short. To their utter horror, Taras Ganymede was *rebuilding* himself.

"Impossible," muttered a watching Nataliya. "What have you become? C'mon, girls. Get up! You must escape!"

"*C'mon*!" cried Arlette, wishing her voice could reach them. "You don't have much time!"

But it was too late. Taras fully regenerated his body, laughing wickedly all the while, and steadily approached the downed warriors.

"Now *that* definitely tickled my fancy!" he said, opening his right hand to materialize his weapon. "But I guess you're gonna have to call that victory back, 'cause your powers are *mine*."

Tsumisu's eyes flashed white as a sensational power suddenly struck him...

"I'm sorry, Shujin," whispered Tetyana, tears welling. "See you soon, sugar!"

"Forgive me," said Suzuka, closing her eyes in preparation. "I've failed you, my love..."

Taras raised his weapon above them. "Time to say goodbye! Graaahh!" he hollered, flying backward.

"Ugly freak...um, *yes*, you're gonna see me soon, Tetyana, like right now, *and* I can't see where you failed, Ms. Suzuka," remarked Shujin, wearing a beaming smile as he stood before the two. "I honestly can't!"

The princess and mercenary could hardly believe their eyes. There stood a young man dressed in full-bodied, majestic blue- and silver-lined armor with a blue scarf tied around his neck.

"Shu...Shujin?" said Tetyana. "Is that you, babe?"

"My prince..." Sighed Suzuka. "Please, let this be true."

"You bet!" he confirmed, helping them to their feet. "Ha ha, I got my Jedi Knight back!"

Jubilant cheers erupted from Arlette and Nataliya and they granted each other hugs.

"That's Shujin! He's alive!" cried Arlette. "I can't believe it!"

"You must!" Nataliya broke their embrace, quickly turning to the many monitors displaying the reemerged warrior. "It's the power of Devonian legend, Arlette," she continued. "Bearing the Mark of Evelyn, Shujin is the Chosen One…"

"That's incredible," Arlette whispered, yet her eyes couldn't help but notice a glowing light nearby. "Hey, wha-what's happening to Tsumisu?"

Nataliya looked on as well, finding herself again stunned. "This can't *be…*" she said. "Somehow, he's drawing energy into *this* dimension. But that's impossible! *Everything* is cut off!"

With hands firmly clutched around a floor-impaled Akari, Tsumisu was subdued by an uncontrollable power; the ghostly embodiment of a young woman with long silver hair and a majestic white dress floated before him. With her hands on his cheeks, her violet eyes gave a piercing stare.

"If you are who I assume you to be," she began, smiling, "take from me this assistance."

"*Evelyn?*" Tsumisu replied, his energy becoming amplified. "I thank you. Perhaps I'd been searching for you this whole time unknowingly."

"Indeed, I am never far from you," Evelyn replied with assurance, fading away. "Remember that…my *keeper.*"

At the moment of Evelyn's release, a powerful shock wave rolled throughout the dimension, illuminating the floor beneath them. Now, Tsumisu's body shone with a soft white aura that pulsated rapidly in sequence with the energy accumulation interacting with the dimension. He clutched his sword tighter with renewed vigor.

"Grandmaster Sonzai!" Tsumisu declared proudly, his voice having a growl behind it. "Keep *this* one for the record books…ah ha ha!"

Staring at the man she had clear affinity for, Arlette felt simultaneously fearful and hopeful, stemming from what she didn't understand of him. Nevertheless, the lieutenant wore a comforting smile.

"He's listening to his *heart*," Arlette began, turning to Nataliya, "and telling us exactly what he's promised to do…"

The scientist's eyes were illuminated as she observed, "Perhaps you're right." The both of them shielded against a growing wind. "Sometimes, the least likely of phenomena holds all the answers…"

Meanwhile, Shujin noticed the environment around them beginning to shift, though it was subtle at the moment. He managed to find a fallen yet sizable pillar suitable enough to prop both Suzuka and Tetyana against.

Tetyana smiled. "Shujin…I don't understand. How did you get here, baby?" she asked.

"Well Tetyana, I guess you could say I had a little help," Shujin replied, sheathing both her and Suzuka's weapons. "And uh, it seems all that stuff about the 'Chosen One' wasn't just a fairy tale, Ms. Suzuka."

"Indeed, you are the Mark of Evelyn," Suzuka began, holding back tears. "Oh, my Prince, I could not be more joyful at this moment to know you're alive."

Shujin knelt down and took her right hand to kiss it and then did the same for Tetyana. "You two have done so much today, but you don't have to worry anymore," he reassured them. "*I'll* deal with Taras."

Tetyana breathed a sigh of relief and gave him a warm smile. "Then you kick his smug ass for both of us, baby."

"And don't hold back," followed Suzuka. "I…can feel that you've everything necessary to defeat him, my prince."

Shujin rose to his feet and gave them a salute. "I won't let you ladies down. I promise."

"Now just because I can reshape my body doesn't mean you can go around *fucking* with it!" yelled a furious Taras, standing upright to regenerate his partially caved-in face. "I ain't having this 'save the damsels in distress' shit today, boy!"

Shujin quickly faced him, his expression stern. "Your time has *come*, Taras!" he proclaimed, extending his right hand to generate a sword of elegant design. "Prepare to face the consequences of your actions!"

"I killed you before, and I'll do it again, boy!"

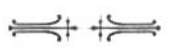

In the middle of the ensuing combat came a faraway cry—the volume of which increased with time, though it held a constant tone and intensity. The mysterious warrior of the Sonzai was summoning a massive surge of energy, which enveloped the dimensional prison. With both hands clutching the hilt of Akari, he knelt before it in prayer...

"Spirits of the Ancients, guide my hand." Tsumisu's words echoed across the parallel dimensions. "Let not my soul fall into transgression, and may no soul perish in the plane that is deemed to extinction..."

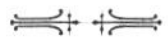

Despite the enigmatically developing events around them, Taras and Shujin stood at a face-off. Taras raised a hand into the air.

"I will not be havin' *any* of this today, boy!" he declared.

Snapping his fingers once, Taras released a powerful explosion on Shujin—and then another. Shock waves rippled through the *Leviathan* as Taras's merciless barrage continued. To all observers, the violent detonations were inescapable, and it was difficult to surmise how any living being could survive. Underneath the malevolent wind, a nearby Tetyana and Suzuka shielded themselves from the debris.

"Shujin!" cried Tetyana. "Please, not again!"

"My prince, no!" Suzuka yelled, her vision obscured.

The environment became increasingly contorted now, the sky beginning to tear in no particular order; the graveyard began disintegrating, as if one were watching sand pour from an hourglass. Yet amid the rising chaos emerged the Mark of Evelyn, bearing a mystic shield—he was simply *unscathed.*

"Incredible!" remarked Nataliya, eyes widening. "That concentrated energy was enough to wipe out planets, And he's not breaking a sweat!"

"Damn you, boy!" Taras roared, eyes flaring. "Damn you to *hell*!"

Shujin dematerialized his shield with a smirk. "Come at me, bro," he muttered, arming his weapon now. "I've got your death wish right *here*."

Enraged, Taras flew toward Shujin with great speed, and their blades collided with vehemence. They faced each other, Taras wearing a scowl and Shujin a focused expression. Taras could not push him away, so he parted swords and changed his strategy. Taras yelled as he made every attempt to strike him, yet Shujin blocked *every* last one. Each time Taras tried to attack, Shujin would devise an excellent counter to drive him back, destabilizing Taras's poise.

Shujin went on the offense with a flying thrust-stab, yet Taras saw the attack and prepared to block it, to perhaps attempt a counter with an energy blast directed at Shujin's face. Reading the maneuver, Shujin leaped away to evade the counter, but Taras transformed into pseudo-shape to reappear behind the Mark of Evelyn—attempting to split him in half. However, Shujin was far too quick, sensing his movements, and made a successful parry, pushing Taras away effortlessly.

Taras clenched his fists and growled in rage, "Why won't you *die*, boy?"

"What's wrong? Are you no match for me?" He smirked. "Not fun anymore now that you can't beat on innocent women, is it?"

"Innocent? I'll show you *yet*!"

Taras tried a speed-cloaking technique, yet Shujin was more than able to keep track of his movements and simply blocked the barrage of blindside attacks when Taras reappeared again, but in return for Taras's flawed tactics, Shujin made several dozen gashes into his body. Taras backed away for a moment to inspect the damage and realized he could not heal a wound made from Shujin's blade, and the bleeding was profuse.

Undeterred, Taras once again challenged him to another round of sword combat; with all of his might did Taras try to break through Shujin's defenses. The clashing swords put great cracks in the floor as energy waves were emitted. Suddenly, Shujin brought his weapon against Taras's, submitting it toward the floor. Then, as Shujin placed a foot atop the subdued weapons to hold them in place, he sent Taras stumbling backward as he charged with an elbow to his chest, knocking him down.

Shujin flipped some yards away where Taras fell. "I told you before: I will *not* leave here until I see that your crimes are punished!" he said.

Without warning, the entire area began to flicker and blur simultaneously; images of celestial bodies were displayed across the floor and stretched in contortion as energy flowed from the mirror dimension.

"What is this?" Taras was stunned. "You! What the hell are you doing?"

"No, Taras, it's *worse...*" Shujin remarked confidently, taking a few steps back. "*Much* worse, I'm afraid."

Seconds later, a pulse of energy dramatically pushed outward and onto the floor of the great hall; it was like the obliteration of a massive dam, releasing great torrents of floodwater therefrom. A distinct, agonized scream became audible among the energetic chaos. As the voice appeared to reach its peak, it suddenly slowed to an indistinguishable low frequency as time stood still. At once, time released with a violent vengeance, sending an astronomical surge of energy throughout the entire ship as the prison dimension shattered like glass, creating a cascade failure around them and obliterating the morose graveyard—leaving behind a barren hall littered with conglomerate circuit-paneled walls and pillars.

Finally, the waves of energy faded away, revealing Tsumisu, Arlette, and Nataliya.

Taras looked on in utter incredulity, his face taken over by fear. "*I-impossible...*he..."

Shujin dematerialized his weapon. "Yeah, *he* is my friend," he said proudly. "My brother."

"Everybody, *shut up*!" Tsumisu yelled as he arose quickly, arms outstretched while frantically looking around, electricity discharging from his body. "I love you, but seriously shut up! J-just pretend like it's a small golf tournament!"

The Sonzai commander made calculated paces, pointing in what appeared to be arbitrary directions.

"*Yes...*" He nodded, a grin coming to him. "Yes! Ha ha haaa! Shujin! Brother!"

"Tsumisu!" he called back. "Arlette! Uh, er...*new* person! You guys are OK!"

They met and shook hands, embraced one another, and snapped fingers in unison.

"Dude! We did it!" Tsumisu shouted happily. "And *then* you lost your damn mind Jedi Knight style! For example…"

Shujin stood back and intently listened, bowing. "Drop the album, my good sir."

"Look at all this *power*!" he exclaimed, slapping his shoulder. "What is that velvet? Versace?"

"What *is* this? Gucci? Is it Prada?" Shujin punched his shoulder in return. "Wait…It looks waaay too good!"

"You look waaay *too* good, man!" Tsumisu laughed, giving him another hug. "God *damn* am I glad to see you, sir!"

"Hey, the feeling is mutual, bro!" Shujin turned to the women. "I was almost lost for a moment there. Sorry for the scare, everybody!"

"Don't ever do that again, Shujin!" cried Arlette. "I'm so glad you're OK!"

"Trust me, Arlette. I'm not planning on it soon. Oh, let's join up with Suzuka and Tetyana?"

Tsumisu pointed to his head in recollection. "Right you are! Uh…" He paused, knowing Nataliya was right behind him. "*Wasn't* trying to leave you, ladies—"

"Nope! I'd count that as abandonment," she replied. "Just gotta stay in trouble today, huh?"

Completely ignoring a seething Taras nearby, the group rejoined Suzuka and Tetyana, who had gained the energy to stand without assistance, especially after witnessing the incredible feats displayed by Shujin and Tsumisu. Immediately, Nataliya and Tetyana gave each other a warm embrace, and the scientist looked over her creation.

"You haven't lost one iota of fight in you," she said proudly. "How've you been?"

Tetyana exhaled. "All those years might've held some relief in there somewhere," she began, "but none of them compares to this. After that day, I didn't know what happened to you."

"Sorry to keep you worried, dear." Nataliya smiled. "Thanks to your friends here, I reckon I made it out OK despite the previously *one-star* accommodations." She turned to Suzuka. "Many thanks to you as well, Your Highness."

Suzuka courteously nodded. "I consider it an honor, Ms. Nataliya," she replied.

"Wait...You guys know each other already?" asked Shujin, mouth slightly twisted. "Like *know* each other?"

"Absolutely, my prince," Suzuka kindly replied. "Sure, we've had our differences in the past, yet destiny ceaselessly paints a picture of truth if one intends to follow it."

"*Not* sure what that means, but it sounded cool when you said it." Shujin steadily nodded. "And 'Nataliya,' is it?"

"Sure is. Don't wear it out," she replied, a hand rubbing her chin. "What's the story with mystery man here? Care to answer some questions, Shujin? Clearly you've got the talent to address such a *simple* matter."

"Er, I...w-well," he stuttered, feeling intimidated.

Tsumisu made cutthroat signs that immediately warped into timid neck rubbing.

"Wow! So it really is a reunion!" exclaimed Arlette. "Too bad we don't have party favors, huh?"

"Balloons, safety scissors, walnuts—all those great items." Tsumisu sighed but eagerly clasped his hands together. "Let's go to the mall once we're done here, Arlette, because *apparently* we've got work to do!"

"Yay!" she cheered. "I'm gonna find all the sales!"

"Dude, stop encouraging her." Shujin wore a stale expression.

"*What?*" Tsumisu exclaimed defensively. "My wish list is overflowing, and goodness knows I've put it off for—"

"*Enough!*" Taras yelled, aiming his weapon at Tsumisu. "Grraaah! How were you able to escape my prison? Those parameters were in place to confine *all* forms of energy!"

He exhaled slowly in annoyance, looking at Shujin. "He's been like this the *whole* time, right?"

"I'm so sick of Taras right now, all I want to do is something *different* today," he replied in equally frank irritation. "It's the voice, you know?"

"Oh my gosh, I miss this so much," Tetyana muttered to Suzuka and grinned. "I swear I'm gonna record them one day."

"I highly agree," Suzuka replied. "However, you'd simply use the material for marketing purposes, would you not?"

"Pfft, *no*! Eh, well, not *really*, I wouldn't." She shrugged nonchalantly. "And what's wrong with a little exploitation?"

"Yeah, it's that *stupid* voice," Tsumisu continued, shaking his head in disgust. "That misogynistic assholery too, you know…"

"Ugh, *plenty* of that. By the way, thanks for looking after them, man."

"Anytime, my friend, though I will say we were looking after one another." Tsumisu threw out a thumbs-up. "We're a happy family here, right, ladies?"

Arlette instantly gave him a big hug. "We sure are!"

Nataliya eyed him mischievously. "Probably about to get *bigger* by the looks of it!"

"Whuuuhh, I have *no* clue…w-what you're talking about," he muttered, returning the embrace. "Say, I'll take you to *two* malls if you let me go."

"Hee-hee, it's illegal to bribe military personnel," Arlette replied. "But I'm willing to bargain with ya!"

Tsumisu slumped over in a wheeze upon her release. "*Thank you.* And *you* have to stop staring sometime today, Little Lady," he continued, noticing Nataliya at it once again.

"Oh?" she said, hands sassily on her hips. "Then make a deal with *me* and answer Taras's question there!"

"Weeellll," he began, wincing in thought, "since I've got absolutely *no* respect for him and he's never answered *any* of my questions today, why don't *you* ask me, Little Lady?"

Nataliya gasped with glee. "You see how we get along? It's gotta be the prettiness factor! So *fuck you*, Taras!" she suddenly yelled harshly, flipping him off.

"I'll make you suffer for that smart mouth!" Taras was seething inside, though realizing with Shujin and Tsumisu present, his agenda was slowly coming to an end.

"Come say that to my face, *asshole*! Well, handsome?" Nataliya turned to Tsumisu in a calm, sweet demeanor. "How'd you do that *nasty* dimension in? Go on! We don't have all day now."

"*Whoa*," Tsumisu remarked in astonishment, beginning to stretch his legs. "Dear diary, how to annihilate a dimension, by Tsumisu…um…"

"Turkeyhands," Shujin suggested in a whisper.

"Tsumisu Turkeyhands. Thank you, sir."

"What? You *destroyed* it?" Taras couldn't believe what he was hearing. "You lie, boy! There ain't no way—"

"December eleventh," Tsumisu began, speaking as if he were literally writing something down. "Today, Taras was smart enough to manipulate Little Lady's power and build a *very* isolated dimension into the *Leviathan*, nearly preventing me from finding the source I needed to destroy that stupid place." He scoffed. "But he wasn't smart enough to stop me altogether, because I found a generous lady in the mood to help a guy out."

Taras frowned. "You found…Evelyn? She was your source?" He slammed his fist on the floor. "You're a damn liar, boy! Ain't nobody in the galaxy capable of doing that, and even then, it would be impossible to connect—"

"Then Taras *assumed* I wouldn't be able to connect with Evelyn for some stupid reason," Tsumisu continued, doing push-ups, "allowing me to have the best opportunity to set the energy parameters *just* right and blow the dimension to smithereens." He rose to his feet after finishing his calisthenics. "Ha, *the end.*"

"Shujin…the Mark was the key." Taras pounded both fists against the floor, this time furious. "I underestimated that little shit!"

"Makes you mad, doesn't it? Because of Shujin's ability to be, um, badass?"

"Yo, I appreciate that." Shujin nodded with a smug grin.

"Dude, we're getting fish nachos later." Tsumisu bumped fists with him and continued, "I was able to use *his* spirit to connect to Evelyn's while everything else in the physical dimension was cut off." Tsumisu smirked as white ethereal energy swirled around a valiantly clenched fist. "If only you *listened* to me on earth when I offered you 'spot in gulag'!"

"That is absolutely incredible," whispered Suzuka to the group of women. "*Only* those of the Devonian Royal Family can connect to Goddess Evelyn; however, it is certainly not on the scale we've just witnessed!"

"So either the big guy is Devonian," Tetyana began, eyes narrowed in thought, "or he's some messed-up half breed."

"Hmm, makes me wonder about *full* breeds, Tetyana," said Arlette. "Can *you* do all that stuff Tsumisu did, Suzuka?"

"She is the Mother of Souls—by what means *could* I do such a thing?" Suzuka exhaled, trying to piece things together. "And besides, interactions on such a scale are strictly forbidden!" She leaned over to the eagerly attentive scientist. "I implore you, *how* was it possible for Tsumisu to do that?"

"I was about to ask *you* the same question!" Nataliya whispered back intensely. "Could it be he's some sort of warrior-wizard with sorcerer-like powers? But that's just *crazy* talk, like unicorns..."

Arlette gasped and frowned. "Unicorns are *real,* Nataliya!" she scolded. "Don't say things like that!"

She wore a straight face. "If only in your head, dearie," she nonchalantly responded.

Shujin turned to them in address. "You ladies stay here, all right? Me and Tsumisu will deal with Taras...once and for all." His tone was earnest yet soft as he nodded to the princess.

"Indeed you shall, Prince Shujin." Suzuka smiled, eyes filled with admiration. "We shall remain until you are finished."

"Don't take *too* long now." Tetyana sent a wink his way.

Shujin nodded amiably to each of them and walked over to Tsumisu's side.

Arlette clasped both hands before her. "Wow!" She sighed. "How *dreamy...*"

The Mark of Evelyn and the Sonzai commander bore their weapons and stood guard before the group of women, staring down their foe.

"Glad to know you were here all this time, Tsumisu," Shujin began. "Makes me feel a whole lot better."

Tsumisu wore an expression of deep gratitude. "I'm glad to see you back, brother. I almost lost hope a little while ago." He chuckled. "That suit really *does* look good, by the way."

"Ha, thanks man. Er, nice T-shirt? Wait." Shujin raised an eyebrow. "Is that a *goat?*"

"Ehhh, it makes sense when you hear the album."

"Ah, OK. So what's the plan?"

"Give me..." Tsumisu paused, running mental calculations. "Five minutes alone with him."

Shujin shrugged. "That's it?"

"I estimate that's sufficient time to exact a little retribution. *I* will make him suffer in this world before his demise, Shujin." White energy slowly began emanating around the Sonzai commander's body. "Then…it will be *you* to rightfully take Taras's life in exchange for yours."

"Hmm, I like that plan." Shujin nodded in satisfaction, dematerializing his blade. "A blow from me would be a quick, honorable death. And we all know *this* guy—"

"Lacks honor," they replied in unison and bumped fists.

"I'll keep watch of the girls." Shujin grinned, patting his comrade's back once. "Make him pay, brother."

"Ooohhh, I *will*." Tsumisu sheathed his weapon and left it levitating behind him. "Ha ha ha ha…"

Taras growled, overhearing their conversation. "You think you can *mock* me to my face? I ain't done with you yet, *boy*!"

"A ship to destroy *planets*, they said." Tsumisu cracked his knuckles, not bothering to summon his exoskeleton armor. "He has…terrorized *countless* across the galaxy, they said." An intimidating chuckle swelled from underneath his words. "He plans to obtain *power*, they said…" Tsumisu raised an energy-laden fist. "I have one question for you: Are you prepared to suffer?"

Taras stood firm with weapon drawn. "I don't know who the hell you are, but I'mma kill you just the same!"

"K-*kill* me? Ha…ha ha!" The Sonzai commander grew wholeheartedly amused. "Little Lady!" he called, eyes dead-locked on his enemy. "Five minutes on an atomic clock *please*?"

Nataliya's expression lit up in pleasant surprise. "*Me* give you a simple numerical device? Coming right up!" With a wave of her hand, the Ordovician scientist summoned a holographic clock with red numbers. "There ya go!"

"Thank you, Little Lady!" Tsumisu called back. "Foreign thoughts *consume* me…I have a hatred for those who commit evil callously throughout the world—people like *you*, Taras. You utterly sicken me."

"Oh, shut the fuck up and fight! Graah!" Taras charged forward and attacked but stopped upon realizing his strike simply *missed.* "H-how is that possible? Raagh!"

Taras tried once again and furiously slashed away, but reality was a cold awakening indeed for the fear-stricken cyborg.

The Sonzai commander's body was flowing with white ethereal energy becoming manifest as a flame enveloping dry vegetation. He had *never* moved from his position during Taras's assault.

"Taras can't…touch him." Tetyana looked on in amazement, unfolding her arms as she recalled memories of Tsumisu's talents. "No fuckin' way. Did he flinch?"

"No, I don't think so." Shujin smirked confidently. "Let me know when it gets too much for any of you ladies, OK? It *might* get ugly in a minute or two."

"Or five!" Nataliya happily replied. "Hee-hee, like that, don't ya, Shujin?"

"Oh, uh…I don't, um…" he stuttered, not particularly knowing how to respond.

"And yet he *isn't* using the power of Devonia," remarked Suzuka, looking on as well. "I say, I'm at a loss for what's going on."

Taras swiped his weapon in the air, unwilling to give up. "Stop your toying, boy, unless you wanna encounter my wrath!"

"Wrath?" Tsumisu inquired, clenching his right fist to dispel energy. "With my bare hands, I will show you no mercy! Such that *hell* shall fear my wrath! Time!"

Taras howled in pain as a violent blow struck his face, sending him into the floor with a mighty compression wave to follow. Casually walking up to the cyborg, Tsumisu patiently drove a mighty fist into his face, time and time again, making a deep crater in the seemingly impervious floor with each impact. Yet in the next moment, Taras managed to escape and darted across the room, attempting to gain an advantage.

"You think you're stronger, *boy*?" Taras roared with bloody face and crazed eyes. "Prepare to *die*!"

Standing erect, Tsumisu closed his eyes and took one step forward—single-handedly catching Taras by the throat, taking him *out* of energetic pseudoform and choking him.

"Nuts, bolts, flesh, *and* you still have a wretched soul," the Sonzai commander seethed, strings of energy encompassing his vision. "I will torment your useless existence! This is for those who have cried!"

Without hesitation, Tsumisu focused his energy to target Taras's soul *and* physical form by sending torrents of near-fatal waves, lighting up the entire hall.

"Nooo! Aaaarrggh! *Heeeayaaaaghh*!" were the continuous, excruciating yells of Taras, suspended in midair.

"For those who have been oppressed!"

He shoved five fingers into his chest, dramatically increasing the degree of torturous energy. Taras's blood ran down his hand as the hall became severely illuminated by Tsumisu's unrelenting ferocity. But darkness was sinking in for Taras, as Tsumisu began pulling against his rib cage while clinging to his throat.

"Aaagghhh! Just kill meeee!" he yelled in unyielding desperation, unable to control his body.

"Ha! Ha ha ha!" The Sonzai commander released his grip from Taras's throat, slammed him into the floor repeatedly with his buried hand, and maintained his electrocution. "Death is too *good* for you…" he seethed, ripping Taras's flesh to release him.

Taras writhed in unbelievable pain, powerless to stop screaming. "Go to hell! I…aaaggh! I…I'll never submit to the likes of you! Geeeyyrraagh!"

"That's good. Keep that will going, Taras!" Tsumisu paced around quickly, cracking his bloody knuckles once more, eyes mercilessly flaring. "The imprisoned victims that *you* tortured ran out of hope, and you left them to *die*! Didn't you?" he roared and stomped on Taras's right arm, snapping it with a sickening break. "So you kept their dead bodies as a prize?" His next attack was a violent stomp on his left leg at the femur, crushing it. "Answer me you *sick*! Fucking! Bastard! *Answer* meeeee!"

Not able to witness any more, Arlette hid behind Shujin, covering her ears. "J-just tell me when he's done! This is too scary!" she cried in a whimper. "Is-is that really Tsumisu?"

"Oh *shit*." Tetyana's eyes were still, a frown covering her face as she couldn't help but watch. "Tsumisu is, uh…kinda pissed off, yeah, Shujin?"

The Mark of Evelyn continued to stand with folded arms. "That's one thing I know about him," he began. "Tsumisu won't show mercy to those who hurt his loved ones."

Suzuka tried to watch but grasped on to Shujin during certain moments. "Let us be grateful a power like his is on our side, for certain," she said.

"Woohoo! Yeah! Go, Tsumisu!" Nataliya was rallying with pom-poms and throwing confetti everywhere. "Hit 'em again for me! You're gettin' what's comin' to ya, Taras! Oh, three minutes left, Tsumisu!"

The sinister cyborg, meanwhile, tried to catch a moment's reprieve, and Tsumisu, remarkably, let him have one.

"Arrgh…what…what are you boy?" he wheezed, blood pouring from his mouth. "I…ain't ever seen a power like yours…"

"And you *never* will again." Tsumisu stood over him, placing a foot on his profusely bleeding chest wound. "The name 'Nyugo' sound familiar to you, asshole?"

"Grah…*fuck* you—"

In the next second, Taras flew into the air, and Tsumisu came from behind and rammed his elbow straight into the middle of his back and punched his stomach in repetitive sessions, making it as if Taras were a Ping-Pong ball in midair. With each hit, Tsumisu was yelling out.

"How-dare-you-kill-my-friend-and-lock-that-pretty-lady-up-for-eight-hundred- years!" Fury encompassed his tone as blood flew in all directions. "You-will-*pay*-for- making-Suzuka-Arlette-and-Tetyana-cry!"

Finally, after twenty or so brutal sessions, Taras simply fell back to the surface in a collapsed heap, barely able to move.

"Amazing!" Tsumisu approached again, kicking him in his back. "You're still *alive*, asshole! *See* how this works? Countless years of suffering drive your victims to pray for death, doesn't it? Seems like a *fantastic* option right now..."

Taras coughed up a pool of blood, spitting it onto Tsumisu's boots and pants. "Look at you..." he snarled, pain searing throughout his body. "You...you're no better than *me*..."

"Hmm, you're right." Tsumisu casually took Taras's shirt to wipe the blood away. "I could turn it up a notch to *surpass* you!" he yelled, grabbing him by both legs. "Count with me now!"

Taras realized that Tsumisu was rendering all power sources available to him within the *Leviathan* inoperable. This time, *he* was the one cut off.

"You fuckin' earthling!" Taras screamed. "You'll rot in *hell*!"

Tsumisu picked him up as if to swing him away, but instead and to everyone's surprise, he lifted Taras over his head and slammed him to the ground.

"That's *one*! *Two-hoo*! That's for hurting Tetyana!" he yelled. "You fucked with the wrong earthling!"

Taras howled in excruciating pain as each impact made a deeper and wider crater within the floor, yet the intense violence was clearly *not* bothering Tsumisu.

"*Three*! I can't *hear you*! *Four*! That's for Arlette! *Five*! That's for hurting Suzuka!" the Sonzai commander furiously declared, eyes burning with insatiable rage. "See? Shouldn't have done that, motherfucker! *Six*! *Graaah*!"

Being struck with *fear* now, Shujin finally unfolded his arms as he continued to watch the brutal spectacle. "Oh my God..." he muttered, noticing how badly Taras's skull was split open. "Is-is anyone else seeing this?"

"Trying!" Tetyana replied, clinching her eyes with each impact.

Nataliya seemed overecstatic. "Such raw power...astonishing..." she whispered, having to clench her eyes every once in a while too. "Suzuka, keep your eyes open, my dear! You're witnessing a rarity indeed!"

"I'm just fine, Ms. Nataliya!" she cried, joining Arlette in hiding behind Shujin.

Arlette continued covering her face. "I've never seen this from Mr. Tsumisu!" she said. "Is he OK, Shujin?"

"I'm really not sure," he replied calmly, "but this is *exactly* what he had in mind. I just don't know how Taras could *survive* after this—"

Shujin stopped in midspeech when he witnessed Tsumisu take Taras by his *broken* leg and began swinging him around—viciously slamming him headfirst through *everything* with a sickening "smack," akin the sound of a bullwhip. Tsumisu's deadly rage left behind a horrifying trail of blood- and tissue-soaked circuits.

"*Seven*! That's for intimidating, brutalizing, and killing *innocent* people!" he continued. "What gives you the *right*? *Huh*? *Eight*! For *Evelyn*! *Nine*? *Ten*!"

Tsumisu finally tossed Taras through the air, as one would casually throw a rock, allowing the false gravity of the *Leviathan* to do the work for him.

At once, the hall became silent, and upon his final approach, the nerve-struck Sonzai commander knelt down to the utterly ruined, half-dead cyborg.

"You…tell all of your associates as you burn in hell that there exists a power stronger than you, *Leviathan*, and Evelyn *combined*," Tsumisu seethed, standing upright. "Thank you for giving me something to *break*, Taras…ha ha ha, breaking your fucking soul." He smirked and walked away.

Taras groaned loudly as he tried to speak with a dislocated jaw. "N-no! Aaghh!"

His face was wholly disfigured. Nearly every bone in his body was shattered. No circuits functioned; his chest and skull were opened and badly bleeding, and his soul *burned* in agony.

"Tell me! Who are you? Who are yooouu?"

Taras's scream echoed through the still air, and no response was given.

Clenching his eyes and exhaling deeply, Tsumisu muttered a prayer underneath his breath as he approached the others. "Shujin?" he addressed him solemnly. "It's on you, brother."

Shujin acknowledged with a nod and walked over to the fallen Taras, materializing his weapon.

Removing his shirt, Tsumisu began wiping off his hands. "Isn't he just a *badass* with that form?" he stated brightly, watching Shujin stand over their enemy. "Bastard neeever saw this one coming, though. Um…" The Sonzai commander noticed the stares from the women. "Right…Little Lady, did I go *over*time? I-I tried to be punctual."

Nataliya scoffed but grinned in cognizance. "Two seconds to spare! You wanna go back and finish it?" She casually nodded in Taras's direction. "And you might need *this*." She snapped her fingers, bringing up a sink.

Tsumisu nodded, grinning at her with appreciation. "Wow! Thanks! That's…eerily convenient. And uh no, this is all for Shujin now." He began washing his hands. "Thanks for keeping time, by the way—"

"I've, um," Tetyana began, interrupting with folded arms and a telling expression. "I've never seen anyone do *that* before. Goddamnit, you've got *a lot* of explaining to do, big guy, 'cause I *knew* you were hiding something!" She pointed at him.

"Let alone exploding dimensions?" Tsumisu smiled at her in confession. "It's crazy though. I hear you…*I* went crazy…but Taras shouldn't have *done* those things to any of you." His tone was sincere as he gazed into each of their eyes.

"Indeed, such crimes are unforgivable, though his punishment was nevertheless frightening as well, Tsumisu," Suzuka frankly replied, a little shaken, though not wanting to show ingratitude. "That display of power, as you say, should definitely send a message to those who wish to cause harm."

Nataliya was eyeing him very, *very* intently. "Sooo…you're sure you're human?" Her inflection was raised. "Or perhaps a branch of it that evolved into a stronger breed? Care to take a DNA test right now?"

Tsumisu scooted away from the eager-beaver scientist, drying his hands as he realized his shirt was mysteriously clean now. "Uh, yeah, Suzuka, I didn't mean to scare you girls, honestly…though the outcome would be obvious, I suppose," he replied, looking at Nataliya cautiously. "So I hope you forgive me?"

"It's OK." Arlette stood beside him with a smile. "Taras got what he deserved!"

"Sure did, and he's *about* to get more." He pointed to direct their attention.

Shujin placed his sword on Taras's neck. "I have no sympathy for you," he sternly remarked.

Taras coughed and could barely speak anymore. "Just…kill me." He spat up blood, another circuit popping. "I'll admit you are one of a kind, boy, and he…please tell me, what *is* he?"

"He is my friend." He lifted his weapon. "That's all that matters. Be gone, Taras!"

Shujin let his weapon fall and decapitate Taras, the resulting blow disintegrating his body in flames, eviscerating the evil cyborg until nothing was left. The Mark of Evelyn took a much-needed sigh of relief with Taras finally defeated, and he regressed to his normal form as Suzuka, Tetyana, Arlette, and Nataliya met up with him.

"Shujin!" Tetyana cried, giving him a big hug. "Gosh, I'm so happy you're OK!"

"You were wonderful, Prince Shujin!" exclaimed Suzuka with hands clasped in front of her. "I'm so proud of you!"

"I'll say!" Nataliya exclaimed suggestively. "You really gave it to Taras!" she started punching the air. "I know I can sleep better tonight! Wait! Am I *still* chewing this?" she rolled her gum up and tossed it, noticing it hit Tsumisu in the forehead. "Sorry! Call it fertilizer!"

"Thanks!" he yelled from behind them, sitting cross-legged and waving. "It smells weird! I-I don't know how to feel about this!"

Shujin laughed in amusement. "You didn't have a foil wrapper? Ha, I'm kidding. Thanks, girls! I'm just really, *really* glad this is over. Know what I mean? I'll never complain about a final exam again," he joked.

"Yay! And we can go home!" Arlette cheered brightly; however, her celebration paused as she was struck with recollection. "No, wait…I'll have to file a report about this…aww."

"Oh yes!" Suzuka remarked in realization. "I'll be interested in reading that, Arlette. Think you can provide a copy?"

"That's if I provide the original first," she lamented, arms drooping.

Tetyana couldn't stop staring at Shujin. "What to do for celebration, I wonder?" she sighed in his ear.

"Ha! Whoa! What was that, Tetyana?" Shujin replied nervously, taking astute note of her unrelenting gaze. "I mean, I'm happy to see you too—er, Tsumisu! What're you doin' over there, dude?" he started pointing to Tetyana, then making circular motions with his fingers.

"What?" Tsumisu cupped a hand over his ear. "*What*?"

Nataliya giggled conspicuously. "Oh? Shujin doesn't *know,* does he? Wooww, talk about keepin' a secret—oops!"

Tetyana kicked Nataliya over and sat on top of her, laughing. "Oh no! Why, Nataliya, whatever do you mean?"

Suzuka was observing the situation, closely. "Doesn't know what? Prince Shujin, what is this about?"

"I, uh…have no idea, I promise, Ms. Suzuka!" He shook his head. "Seriously!"

"Tetyana is mmmfff!" Nataliya was trying to tell him, but Tetyana covered the scientist's mouth.

"*Ha!* Ha ha! Just checkin' her temperature! Shut the hell *up*!" Tetyana's face turned vampire-like as she pulled Nataliya's face to hers. "You're gonna ruin it!"

At that moment, Dahlia appeared, standing directly beside Tsumisu with a bright smile. "Thanks, Mr. Tsumisu!" she said, getting a hug from him. "Shujin! Big Sister! Guys!"

"Dahlia!" cried Suzuka as they ran to hug each other. "I'm so glad to see you're safe!"

"I'm all right, Big Sister! I'm glad to see you too!" She giggled and then granted Shujin a hug as well. "Wow! You really did it!"

Shujin smiled brightly. "Hey, yeah! Isn't it great? But, uh, where'd you come from?"

Dahlia pressed a finger against her lips. "Shhh! You can't tell anybody!"

Tsumisu finally joined the group, nodding his head as if he knew something top secret.

"Trust me, I'm just shamelessly gaining needless attention." He smiled, being humored by the responses. "See? I got'cha there, Little Lady."

"All right. But maybe one day, I'll get *you*!" Nataliya peered at him. "Heh heh…heh heh…"

Tsumisu tried to wipe that creepy but well-meaning smile from his memory. "Whoa…so yeah, what's that you were saying about earlier?" he asked Shujin.

He raised an eyebrow and pulled him to the side. "Tetyana's hiding something, and she got *all weird* just now…"

Tsumisu covered his mouth. "Oh snap! Information?"

He shrugged in earnest absence of knowing. "*That's* why I need your help!"

"All right," he muttered, looking around suspiciously. "The *origin* of my power is uh…the sierra of mist…We'll talk this over back home, yeah?"

"Stop doin' that!" Nataliya stomped her foot. "Urrrghh…"

"Oh my, what's got you so huffy, Nataliya?" Arlette innocently asked. "It's the *air* in the ship, isn't it? It's on your face!"

Dahlia giggled. "I really missed you guys! You're funny!"

"Aww, we missed you too, Dahlia." Shujin grinned, rubbing the top of her head. "So how do we get home? Did we bring the *Diablo* today oorrr…"

Tetyana slid over to her beloved, wearing an inconspicuous grin. "Why, Shujin! I thought you'd never ask!" She put an arm around him. "Would you like to be my copilot?"

Suzuka leaped like a soccer goalie, swiping her arm away. "Do not touch him, Tetyana!"

"Oh my *gosh*, did I ask you, Princess?" Tetyana dropped her arms in exasperation. "Why can't he learn how ta fly the freakin' ship?"

"I see your advances on Prince Shujin!" Suzuka was seriously shaking a finger at her. "I have figured you out!"

Nataliya approached the two warriors, hands on her hips and wearing a very *suspicious* smile. "A heh…heh heh!" She narrowed her eyes at Shujin and then Tsumisu. "So which—"

"Ah! I didn't do it!" Tsumisu fell backward suddenly, only to rise up in an awkward sitting position. "Sorry, what was the question?"

She lifted an eyebrow and folded her arms. "Is *that* where you'd like to be during the examination, Mr. Tsumisu?"

"Ha! Only if you want me there—no wait, that ain't right." Tsumisu held up a hand, eyes clenched in regret. "Tetyana? Let's, uh…get the *Diablo*?"

Tetyana was busy pushing Suzuka in the face, while *she* was doing the same. "F-fine! Cut it out, Princess!" she said.

"You…grah…must cease first!" Suzuka said in retaliation.

Shujin smiled but grew several dozen sweat droplets over his head. "At least it's back to normal," he muttered, watching the scuffle escalate.

"It'd be a good idea to get into a *real* big hurry," commented Nataliya. "Provided Taras was interconnected to this junk-barge, this whole place should render itself destroyed in saaayy…three minutes?"

Everyone looked at Nataliya, shocked.

"Exactly! Follow me!"

Nataliya guided them through alternate routes to the makeshift port where the *Diablo* sat, and they immediately boarded and took off back home. And sure enough, the *Leviathan* self-destructed and incinerated into nothing—receiving the same fate as its malevolent owner.

During Tetyana and Suzuka's inevitable attention-grabbing showdown, Shujin remarkably found some time to reflect, watching the *Diablo* reenter earth's atmosphere. What the *hell* happened that day? Did he…die? Unfamiliar scents from the ship and the somehow intoxicating aftermath of nearby warrior ladies seemed to prove that Shujin was *indeed* alive and well. The only thing he could remember was Taras staring him down and then nothing.

Well, Evelyn appeared—said she was the "Mother of Souls," charged with assisting Shujin, her "Mark." He recalled a blinding white light, and she emerged—reassembling his spirit and body. Man, what *was* Evelyn? And more important than that, what was *he*? At any rate, Shujin guessed there was a much greater purpose behind all his powers. But for now, with what he did understand, it was enough to save the day—and Shujin was fine with that outcome.

CHAPTER NINE

Shujin greeted his father and grandmother with news of Taras's defeat and introduced Nataliya as the newcomer to the household—where she was happily accepted. Arlette didn't have much time to stay, as she had to report back to her post, so she said her goodbyes and sent for her ship to depart.

Tsumisu was silent for most of the time, allowing Shujin and the others to explain what had happened; he went outside to stand at the lake behind the house, a place that reminded him of the Sonzai encampment's stream. Bodies of water always brought him peace while things were on his mind, so he sat before it with a setting sun peering through a breaking overcast sky, smiling.

"Everything happens for a reason," Tsumisu thought aloud. "Shujin fell to rise again. Perhaps this means equally for me..."

"Hey, bro!" Shujin suddenly called while approaching. "We were wondering where you went, man—Grandma and Dahlia tagged-teamed to get dinner ready!"

"I knew I smelled something freakin' *spectacular.*" Tsumisu looked at him over his shoulder. "But I don't think I'm staying, bro; gotta head back and attend to some business."

"Aww, c'mon now! You couldn't wait until you've celebrated with us? It would make this entire occasion complete. Right?" Shujin smiled warmly with an outstretched hand.

"Yeah, what's the point in being a missing piece to the party." Tsumisu grinned, taking hold. "Let's get some of that dinner, dude!"

Upon going inside, Suzuka was busy assisting Dahlia in setting the table as they all took their seats; the aroma of the food was more than enough to keep Tsumisu around.

"I was about to miss out on this too," he said to Shujin, nudging him. "Can you believe that?"

He chuckled, looking at him tellingly. "I was wondering if I was talking to the same Tsumisu, but I see nothing's changed, thank goodness."

"Never will, man." He patted his shoulder. "We're still the same guys who couldn't flirt if our lives depended on it. Well, at least *you* couldn't..."

"Don't start with that, dude," Shujin warned. "We've been through that."

"You can sit over here, Shujin!" said Tetyana, a cushion saved right beside her.

Suzuka quickly dragged it by her. "Or you could sit over here, Shujin!"

"Uhm, that makes *two* places actually," he pointed out casually. "So where's Tsumisu gonna sit?"

He nudged him again. "Then you try and drag me into it—I see how you live."

"What? I told you earlier I needed some *help*," he whispered.

Exhaling, Tsumisu wiped a hand over his face. "OK. You and I will trade places after ten minutes or so. Keep it off kilter, know what I mean?"

Shujin shrugged nonchalantly. "No idea, but I'll take your word for it, sir."

"Awesome. Now go sit with Tetyana first; I'll sit beside Suzuka."

"Yeah, c'mon, son!" cheered Mr. Iwato.

Tsumisu walked over and casually sat by Suzuka, while Nataliya sat directly across from him.

"We're going to trade places in a little while; don't worry," Tsumisu addressed the princess, noticing Nataliya kept *staring.* "Aaand…you've got *lovely* pink eyes, Little Lady."

"How nice of you to say that, Mr. Tsumisu," Nataliya replied, instigating. "How nice *indeed.*"

"Uh…" Shujin was handing a dish over to his grandmother. "Did something happen between you two that I don't know about?"

Tsumisu started to chuckle at that moment. "I have no idea, man. I just said that 'cause she reminds me of morganite in a daylily garden…Plus, she was staring at me *first,* sooo…"

"Daylily garden, huh? I *like* the sound of that," Nataliya remarked, putting food on her plate. "Perhaps I should look forward to more of it, hmm?"

Tsumisu shrugged, arranging his plate as well. "I don't know really, because when I see Suzuka, it's like a calla lily hosting an *aggressive* pool party. Tetyana is a honeybee pollenating a hydrangea flower. Arlette is a sunflower wearing a sapphire jewel…not present, but oh well. Meanwhile, Dahlia here is an ambitious tulip." He took a bite of an eggroll. "But like I said, *I don't know* really."

"Wow! Are you serious?" asked Tetyana, giving him a curious glance. "You *are* serious, aren't ya?"

"Unknowingly serious." He winced.

"Aggressive pool party?" Suzuka remarked, sounding appreciative. "I've never heard the like, Mr. Tsumisu."

"Well, *you're* the one hosting it, so I'm waiting for an explanation," he jested. "*Just* saying."

Shujin smiled. "That's awfully nice of you, Tsumisu," he said. "I mean, there's unorthodox parallels that come to mind—"

"Hey," Tsumisu said, his mouth full, "don't talk as if *you* didn't tell me first! After all, I get it from you, dude."

"Wha-what?" His voice broke. "N-no, you don't! No, you do *not*!"

Suzuka clasped her hands together. "Prince Shujin said that about us?"

"I knew you were good in your literature classes, but I didn't know you were *this* good," remarked Mr. Iwato. "Nice goin'!"

"Dad, I don't know what he's talking about!" he tried to defend himself. "Seriously!"

"Come now," Tsumisu said as convincingly as he could. "You told me when you came to get me from outside, remember? Got all Shakespeare with the sunset—"

Shujin shot him an annoyed glance. "Would you cut it *out* already?"

"Play along!" he mouthed the words, making a circular motion with his hands. "I'm gathering info."

"You know honeybees don't sting, Shujin," said Tetyana, grasping his arm with an infatuated demeanor. "Well at least not *much*."

Shujin's eyes widened. "Hey, n-now, wait a second!"

"Tetyana! Release him this instant!" cried Suzuka, reaching over Tsumisu to halt the situation.

Tsumisu put a hand over his mouth to restrain his laughter. "He's got a way with words too. Tell 'em more, Shujin!"

"Tsumisu! Dude, cut it out!" His exasperated tone intensified.

"OK, man," he admitted, "you *might* have said that stuff. And I honestly observe you ladies in that manner because there aren't a lot of women around who so accurately fit the description." He turned to Mr. Iwato. "Now that was being *honest*, wouldn't you say so?"

"Saying a lot more than I would've said," he replied with suggestion. "Hey! Aren't you the one who tossed Taras around like a salad?"

"Noooo, they didn't tell you that story already, did they?" Tsumisu turned his sight to Nataliya. "Bet it was the little lady, wasn't it?"

"Mm-hmm," she snickered in confession. "Wouldn't ya know it?"

"I was looking forward to hearing it from you, actually," said Mrs. Himaki. "As I've heard both you and Shujin were on opposite sides and experienced separate events."

"Yeah, tell him what you said too!" said an amused Tetyana. "It was like insult to injury!"

Tsumisu rubbed his forehead with the back of his hand. "Well, sure, I had some…misplaced aggression after my ordeal with that *Leviathan* ship—*it* having an alternate dimension, which I stumbled on, cutting me off from assisting Tetyana and Suzuka; *it* having *no* energy whatsoever, which means I couldn't get back to *this* dimension, meaning I had no choice but to destroy the alternate dimension. But!" Tsumisu grinned as he shook his head. "Taras was such a…despicable man, you know? I uh, just wanted him to know what it was like to feel some pain." He nodded, looking at his plate.

"So you beat him up before Shujin took him out?" asked Mr. Iwato.

"He didn't just 'beat him up,'" Nataliya began with enthusiasm, her tone in storytelling mode. "Remember when Shujin *totally* dusted his shoulders of that explosion? He dueled with Taras for a little while, and Tsumisu came up and told him he wanted to make Taras suffer before Shujin killed him."

Tetyana scoffed, shoving food into her mouth. "Man was that *ever* an understatement," she said. "Shujin was handlin' the bastard left and right, then here comes Mister *Mysterious* over here, wiping the floor with his face! Literally!" she threw her hand out in expression, shaking her head as she recalled the vicious scene.

"Indeed," concurred Suzuka. "In all my battles, it was a display the likes of which I've never seen before."

"When he got to him?" Nataliya used a napkin for show. "Taras literally looked like this thing—Tsumisu took him by both legs at first and wham! Hit 'em against the ground and kept counting like, 'One! Two! Three! I can't hear you!' I'm serious!"

Tsumisu looked at Shujin while pointing to Nataliya. "See how amiable she is?"

Shujin winced. "I-I dunno what you're talking about?"

"The fight escalated when Tsumisu took Taras by one leg." Nataliya held up one finger. "Then he started slinging him around through pillars and on walls; just like I'm doing this napkin now!" She snapped it in the air. "Wham! *Wham*! Oh my goodness, I can't begin to express the amount of strength to exert such *force* and execute something like that; it's astounding!"

"Yeah," began Shujin, "and it was something to think about because he did it...*effortlessly*. So I just wondered what he could've done if he hadn't been holding back, you know?"

"One reason that made it more frightening, to *me* at least," Suzuka remarked, politely eating an eggroll, "showing" Tetyana how to do it. "See? Prince Shujin admires eloquence."

"Pssh," she retorted in dismissal, "that ain't necessary for what *I* want him to eat..."

Suzuka's expression rose in comical realization.

"My point exactly, Shujin!" Nataliya enthusiastically continued. "Shujin's transformation made him much stronger than Taras, yet it seemed that Tsumisu might have been stronger all the while and was just unable to kill him any sooner...at least that's what *I* assumed."

"Say that *is* something to think about." Tetyana seemed to recollect something. "You remember me sayin' you were hidin' stuff from me, big guy? Out with it already!"

Tsumisu held up his hands. "And do you remember my answer? I'm not hiding anything!" he innocently replied. "What you saw is what I can do—well, Shujin just mentioned I was holding back so I see the issue."

"Oh gracious, that does sound very dramatic indeed," said Mrs. Himaki. "Did you not have your weapon with you, Tsumisu?"

"Yes ma'am, I did; 'Akari' is its name. Had it since I was a boy—dude, did I lay it around here?"

Shujin pointed in its direction. "It's on the wall rack over there, remember?"

"Oh yeah, thanks." He quickly got up to retrieve it and returned. "That food makes you forget things, huh? Ha! Let's see... it's just about as pretty as all the girls in this house," he said humorously and unsheathed it.

"Whoa! Careful where you swing that thing." Tetyana ducked her head. "Hey, I remember seeing that up close; it's got those weird designs in it."

"Appears to be lightning," said Suzuka as she inspected it. "Where might've you gotten this weapon, Tsumisu?"

"The grandmaster of my clan." Tsumisu held it perfectly still before the curiously observing others. "The Sonzai clan to be specific."

"A clan?" Mrs. Himaki sounded surprised. "As in a group of warriors perhaps?"

Tsumisu nodded. "That's correct. We've been around for hundreds of years completely tied to secrecy, so I can't divulge *why* we're hush-hush...Little Lady."

"What would you mean by that?" asked Nataliya, her mental wheels turning. "Might there be enemies out there as strong as you?"

"Oh, *far* stronger," he replied firmly. "So, my training continues, and I've got a long, long way to go evidently."

Tetyana stared at him in thought, chopsticks in her mouth. "So what's your peak? Any idea?"

"Well, since you ask and getting back to the sword, the grandmaster says there's another one just like it; kinda like a polar-opposite so to speak. Although it will complete the things necessary for me to finish my training, the man says I'm not ready for it yet."

"Man..." Shujin looked at him, bearing subtle disbelief. "If you're not ready now, I don't know what you'll become when you *are*."

"It's funny I told myself the same thing, dude. But it's just like this sword." Tsumisu displayed it. "The grandmaster allowed use of Akari due to my mastery of its capabilities—like second nature to breathing, fortunately. Even so, what point is there to knowing this sword when I don't even know what I can do first? The inner strength that I yield, right? Shujin here is a great example."

He raised a curious eyebrow, noodles hanging from his chopsticks. "I am?"

"*Yeah*, dude, don't act as if it's *not* you." Tsumisu nudged him. "You're the Mark of Evelyn, for crying out loud."

"All right! Geez...can't a guy be modest?"

"Uh, how about no?"

"I see," Mrs. Himaki replied in a wise tone. "After all, a sword is no more than an extension of the wielder, not the potential of the wielder."

Tsumisu nodded with a smile. "Absolutely. You were right about this sword not being ordinary, Grandma—I can call you that?"

"Of course, dearie." She grinned pleasantly.

"Great. Now the, uh...the sword is 'alive' so to speak. So, as I get stronger, it gets more active, and we sort of feed off of each other."

"Interesting," remarked Nataliya, her scientific discipline showing. "Normally, weapons are, as you just explained, used as a tool; however, this one seems to have a life of its own...and you share a symbiotic relationship. Hmm, what of the other one again? Why aren't ya ready for it?"

"It's far too powerful, to put it bluntly," Tsumisu succinctly replied. "I've got a greater risk of dying from *it* rather than busting up another dimension."

"Is that due to the direct opposite of the sword you wield now?" Suzuka had her warrior wheels turning.

"In a nutshell, Princess Suzuka," Tsumisu acknowledged. "Think of Kuroi as Akari's evil twin…and I do mean *evil.*" He emphasized the word. "I mean, how would you feel having to handle a sword wanting to control your soul and you're not done training yet?"

"Even when you're done," Shujin began with apprehension, "isn't the risk still present? If you get stronger, it might want your soul more than ever!"

"See, what I mean by 'training' is strengthening my spirit," Tsumisu explained, looking at everyone. "Because the whole purpose in the end is to take the powers of both swords into myself. To do this, I *must* attain the balance of power between Akari and Kuroi, who in the event of conflict will battle for dominance of my soul." Tsumisu grinned with internal humor. "It sounds really far-fetched, but I can't explain it any other way!"

"That would happen if you wielded them both, correct?" Suzuka was clearly catching on.

"Exactly, borderline fight between good and evil. Yet," he instructed, "you must understand that life cannot live without either, so with that knowledge you have to respect one and the other power in order to attain that balance."

"Very true, Tsumisu," Mrs. Himaki said. "This is the structure of life itself."

"I guess that explains where most of your power comes from, hmm? A mutual display of power between yourself and the swords," Nataliya expressed, appearing to type things down. "Would that battle have been significantly different if you had used Akari?"

Tsumisu shook his head slowly with widened eyes. "*No one* wanted to see that," he said and sheathed the weapon. "As much I as wanted to kill Taras, I didn't feel it was my place in the name of honor. Shujin was rightfully supposed to kill him, seeing as Taras took his life first."

"Think I should learn some of those warrior codes?" Shujin asked, grinning. "I mean, I really appreciated what you did, regardless of the…gruesome nature, know what I mean, dude?"

"I mean…" Tsumisu shrugged. "Suzuka and Tetyana kinda made an interesting spectacle earlier—"

"Yeaaaah, but we weren't preventing him from doing that healing thing," replied Tetyana. "Amplifies the violence a bit on *your* behalf, don't it?"

"*Not* publicly admitting to that?" he said in rebuttal. "Aannd *yes*, Shujin, I'll teach you until you pass out, brother," he continued, patting his shoulder. "I think Grandma here may know more than I do, however."

She smiled humbly. "Well my memory sometimes fails me, Tsumisu," she said. "Those days of Kendo are long over for me, so I think it best if you taught Shujin yourself."

Tsumisu nodded. "Then I'll turn him into an encyclopedia in no time."

Shujin held up his hands with a timid expression. "Now I think that's going a bit too far," he began. "I-I mean, I only wanted to know a few things."

"The knowledge will make you stronger, man; trust me," Tsumisu reassured him. "I'll write it down or something and make it easy. Oh! A metal song…like uh…"

Nataliya appeared to be thoroughly enjoying her documentation. "Mm-hmm, so with the assistance of your sword you were able to determine the center cluster of the dimension, thereby connecting through it and using your own ability to draw the energy necessary to destroy it?" she asked. "Catch all that?"

"Y-yeah bits and pieces—what're you doing again?" Tsumisu tried to look over the table. "What's in your lap? Is that pimento cheese?"

"And jarred olives!" she continued, putting on a big grin. "Now I need specifics pleaasseee!"

"You're gonna explode with all this info. Why don't you give it until tomorrow after sleeping on it all?"

"That's what I'm talking about," Tetyana concurred wholeheartedly and drank a swig of sake. "Besides, I'm getting dizzy already."

Shujin observed her closely. "No, it might just be the *sake*," he said. "Exactly how much did you drink, Tetyana?"

"Only a few cups' worth, Shujin!" she innocently proclaimed. "What? You wanted some? I saved some for you…"

Nataliya cleared her throat. "If you don't mind, I'm in the middle of gathering some very important information?" she said. "It's practically equivalent to impeding a gold miner from mining gold *right* in front of him."

"Well, excuuuusse me, *Nataliya*, I was in the middle of offering Shujin some sake," Tetyana replied while pouring a cup, with Mr. Iwato leaning over to gather what she was spilling. "That's like what? Tripping somebody up as they're running to the bathroom or somethin'?"

"Um, no thanks, Tetyana." Shujin smiled courteously. "I-I'm fine right now."

"Precisely," said Suzuka, taking the bottle from Tetyana. "You've had enough as it is."

"Hey! No fair! Give that back, Suzuka!" She tried reaching for it.

Suzuka drew it away. "I most certainly will not!"

Tsumisu gently took the bottle from Suzuka and handed it to Tetyana. "Here you go."

"Hey, thanks." Tetyana raised the bottle to him as if to make a toast. "You want some?"

"Nah, you got it, girl." He reached over to nudge her shoulder.

Suzuka looked at him in surprise. "Why did you do that, Tsumisu?"

"All in the context of evading conflict, my dear. Something you two are *familiar* with." He coughed. "Pardon me."

"But—" Suzuka sounded desperate.

"I *know* you wanted to keep her from trying to get Shujin to drink some when he didn't want to, and that's because you're sensitive about him—which a lot of women are sensitive, so that's to be expected and you are not to be blamed for it." Tsumisu tiredly laid his face within his hands. "Oh, curse my convoluted presuppositions..."

Shujin bore a sweat drop. "Um, am I taking notes now?"

Tsumisu sat upright again. "You probably should, dude. And not to get off topic 'cause Dahlia is just left out." He chuckled and smiled at the little princess. "You OK over there?"

"Oh, I'm fine, Mr. Tsumisu!" She smiled brightly, granting a little wave. "I don't mind you guys talking 'cause I'm not sure what most of it is about anyway."

He gave her a thumbs-up. "Well, you're too young for it, and you've got like hundreds of years—is that right Suzuka?"

"Excuse me?" she politely replied, trying to follow Tsumisu's piecewise rambling.

"Yeah, hundreds of years ahead of you to write your own cook-book! So, for you to lie awake at night, goodness forbid, regretting not understanding *anything* of this conversation is not worth it." He winced. "Hope that makes sense, Dahlia."

"That part does, Mr. Tsumisu!" She giggled in reply.

"I wouldn't say not worth it entirely," said Shujin, correcting him. "You know the stuff you said about how you and the swords relate to life? That could help her."

"Yeah, such is true, my friend," Tsumisu humbly agreed. "I guess she'll have the little lady over there to help explain...seeing as they are both *short* and initially think on the *same level*!" He broke out in laughter and immediately stopped with a sigh.

Dahlia continued to laugh. "Whatever you say, Mr. Tsumisu!"

Mr. Iwato chuckled. "You hear that? 'Cause, they're both short...That's funny!"

"He normally does that?" Nataliya cheerily directed the question to Shujin.

He nodded with a grin. "That's just him," he replied. "I hope he doesn't rub off on me 'cause I've been catching myself *a lot* lately."

"Resistance is ultimately futile." Tsumisu slapped his shoulder. "You hold it in? It becomes too much. Tetyana knows what I'm talking about..."

"Actually, I was lost," she said with crimson cheeks.

Mr. Iwato thought for a moment. "I've got a general idea, but it's related to the bathroom." He laughed heartily. "I figured it was pretty simple!"

Tsumisu laughed with him. "It sounded like it, right? Had to think about it for a moment myself! Because if you hold it in?"

"It becomes too much!" they said in unison.

"Oh, guys," Shujin groaned. "We're eating, for cryin' out loud!"

"Oops, sorry about that, son. Guess we got carried away!" He broke out in laughter again.

Tsumisu fell backward and held his stomach. "I suppose he had to *let it go*!"

It took a few minutes for them to compose themselves, and Tsumisu sat back up, trying desperately not to think about it anymore.

"All right, I'm done. What about you, Mr. Iwato? Can you hold it in?"

He cleared his throat. "I don't think I'll be releasing it anytime soon."

"Tetyana, I know you're about to hit me, but this is the last time," Tsumisu explained to her. "I solemnly swear on this lovely table of food that I will speak of it no longer."

"I was gonna hit you anyway, big guy!" she said, keeping her word.

"Ow!"

Shujin laughed, being humored by their interaction. "You guys are wild. I never knew you had *that* in you, bro."

"It happens every day!" Tsumisu leaned to his friend and in a screaming whisper, said, "Just like figuring out the little lady was *diabolically* planning on ruling the world!" He snapped his fingers. "Every ten minutes, you learn something entirely new."

Suzuka placed a hand over her mouth as she began to laugh now.

"See? It's contagious! All right…" He gave Nataliya an honest gaze as he addressed her. "I know you were going to ask me something else, and I'm sorry, OK? You being super smart just kills me in a good way. But go ahead…seriously."

"I'm not complaining!" Nataliya replied, eyeing him pleasantly. "It's a relief to know somebody like you isn't an all-serious-headed guy with no personality; keep 'em coming!"

"You're saying like regardless of who we are or what we're capable of, we're all just normal people on the inside?" Shujin asked. "I-I'm just trying to get some clarity…"

"That's right!" Mr. Iwato declared. "Take myself, for instance—"

"Er, thanks for that example, Dad!" Shujin wisely interrupted the jovial man. "Whew, that was close."

Tsumisu nodded in agreement as he put more food, particularly the roasted chicken, on his plate. "Shujin just made a really good point; who knew he'd pull that Mark of Evelyn stuff off? I know he didn't. I know *I* didn't," he explicated, mouth half-full. "Who knew I could destroy dimensions? I know he didn't. I know I *really* didn't. Who cares? We're still the same vir—I-I mean, same guys! Same *guys*."

"Yeah it's what we can do but not exactly who we are altogether…or is it what we can do doesn't determine who we are?" Shujin was trying to phrase it right. "It's somewhere in that area."

"I understand, Prince Shujin." Suzuka gave him a smile. "Such is the reason why I admire you so."

"Whoooa, hey!" cried Tetyana. "I caught that!"

"I can hit on Shujin if I damn well please!"

"*On* the subject of destroying the dimension as well as Shujin's Mark of Evelyn form," Nataliya began most inquisitively, readjusting her seat as a sophisticated laptop computer came into view. "I'm curious as to *how* you destroyed the dimension in its entirety *without* interfering with this dimension and perhaps preventing Shujin from reaching his Mark of Evelyn form…care to explain, Tsumisu?"

"Well, we certainly don't want this good food to get cold, do we?" Tsumisu replied in jest. "Dahlia might transform into Optimus Dahlia and…toss me through the window or something."

"Aww, I wouldn't do that, Mr. Tsumisu!" She laughed. "Besides, we placed the food on warmers!"

He pointed to his head. "Never hurts to think ahead either, right?"

Nataliya propped a hand under her chin as she leaned on the table, peering. "So why don't you continue? I'm *fascinated*."

"Hey, well, I know you are," Tsumisu replied nervously, "being a genius and everything, a subject like *this* would automatically grasp you like sticky paper to adhesive." He demonstrated by clasping his fingers together.

"I smell trouble," Mr. Iwato commented.

Shujin got his attention. "Hey, dude, if you're tired, you don't have to explain if you don't want to," he suggested.

"I appreciate it man, but tired is having to destroy a dimension in a certain amount of time *before* the energy kills you." Tsumisu grinned and exhaled in relief. "Heaven *knows* I'm fine with it—"

Suzuka laid her chopsticks down, taking another thought at what Tsumisu mentioned. "Are you saying you could've died before the attempt was complete?" she asked, her tone indicating subtle alarm.

"He certainly *could* have," Nataliya instructively responded. "I'm not sure if anyone here realizes what it *really* takes to destroy a dimension and the factors that need paying attention to; first, you must have a sufficient amount of energy to connect to the dimension; then you need to lock onto its source and penetrate its cluster center...all of this *after* you've determined which parameters of the dimension are the core energy strands of the cluster center!"

Tetyana burped loudly. "The hell is a cluster center?" she said. "Sorry, I don't remember you sayin' anything about it back then."

"The direct source of energy that contains the parameters to sustain a dimension," Nataliya patiently explained. "It exists *only* on the subquantum level. If you find the cluster center, you are able to either use it to travel through it, or destroy it...which, theoretically, is impossible."

Tsumisu was eating and nodded in realization. "Wow, I should be writing this down," he muttered. "Is this some kind of *chai* spice, Grandma?"

Mrs. Himaki smiled. "You've certainly got a talent for taste, Tsumisu," she replied.

"Look, close that Hot Springs Inn business—*you* and Dahlia could rule all Eurasia with this chicken. *Alone*."

Shujin scratched his head. "Then what would it take to destroy a dimension after finding the cluster center, Nataliya?" he asked. "Wouldn't it take a lot of energy to get that far in the first place?"

"Indeed it would, an *infinite* amount too. Yet! Where it grabs me most is the energy stabilization necessary in order to *remain* at the cluster center as you proceed to destroy it." Nataliya peered at Tsumisu, who looked back with some noodles hanging out of his mouth. "Which brings me to this conclusion: it would take an *ungodly* power to accomplish the entire process, then be able to keep the parameters of time and space from ripping each other apart, subsequently causing a chain reaction of disturbances in other dimensions, while making it back *alive*...only being short of breath." She smirked. "Oooo, did I make somethin' obvious for ya, Mr. 'Tsumisu'?"

He stifled his laughter. "I swear, *everything* you said sounded unbelievably cool, but I'm not hiding anything!" he said. "I'm being honest here!"

"Why're you laughing, Mr. Tsumisu?" Dahlia asked, inspecting his disposition as Nataliya was doing the same. "Seems like you're aware of a couple things, right?"

"Naw, it's 'cause she *knows* so much, I can't help it!" he exclaimed, looking at the young princess. "It makes me giggle inside for some...unknown reason. OK, stop, Tsumisu."

Shujin grinned, though he was desperately trying to figure out the background dynamic between Nataliya and Tsumisu. "Well, it helps to understand what happened better, even though I probably didn't get half of that," he remarked. "If only I had my smartphone, I could've recorded this conversation very *easily*, man."

"OK..." Tsumisu dropped his chopsticks and sighed. "Why are you bringing up old issues again?"

"Bringing up—it's been *weeks* since you said you'd pay me back!"

Nataliya's expression rose with piqued interest. "And a cheapskate too," she muttered, typing. "That can't be good."

"No, delete that," Tsumisu said timidly.

"Do what now?" she asked, turning to him. "Oops! I think it's saved!"

"OK, *don't* delete that." He winced in acceptance. "I'm not cheap..."

"Don't you have one of those 'smart' things?" Tetyana smirked, wiping her mouth with the back of her hand. "You can't lie! Don't you do it!"

"I borrowed it from cap—my *mom*." Tsumisu caught himself. "It wasn't mine anyway, so I gave it back. Look, this isn't the point!"

"Dishonesty ill suits you," Suzuka added her two cents in jest. "Now, what were you explaining before, Ms. Nataliya?" she continued. "That Tsumisu might be in relative terms to, as an example, Evelyn or greater in association with power?"

"*Exponentially* greater," Nataliya began with whispered enthusiasm. "Tsumisu, what happened when you made contact with Evelyn?"

"First," the Sonzai commander said, holding up a hand, "did you ask Shujin what transpired when Evelyn took hold of *him*?"

"I *did*. That's why I'm asking *you* now." She smiled knowingly with narrowed eyes.

Gathering goose bumps, Tsumisu took a cautious scoot back. "Right…Why-why didn't you tell me?" he whispered, leaning to his friend.

"I dunno. I thought it wasn't important!" Shujin replied in an equal whisper. "What's wrong? I-is there something wrong?"

"Don't worry about it! *Well*!" Tsumisu began, rubbing his hands together. "To answer your question, Little Lady, when I first sensed Evelyn's power, I could immediately detect she was an excellent source to connect to the core of that 'prison' dimension." Tsumisu held a hand over his mouth as he burped. "Pardon. The issue was *she* wasn't sure I existed because Taras made the dimension a one-way street. In energetic terms, it's the same as a mirage. So when I tried full communication, I guess I made her suspicious of me."

Suzuka was pondering, fascinated by his encounter with the sacred entity. "Why would Evelyn be afraid of you?" she asked. "Well, aside from the obvious display on Taras…"

"Ha, point taken. Seriously though, it's probably because not many beings reside in the same realm as Evelyn. So, somebody she doesn't know contacting her so easily would be pretty scary, I suppose. Probably thought I was gonna hurt her when she felt my presence, but I told her not to be frightened because I needed her help."

"What you speak of realm accessibility is true indeed," Suzuka continued. "Did Evelyn ask who you were by any chance?"

"Oh yes." Tsumisu nodded in the affirmative. "I told her I was a friend of Shujin, and that I was trapped inside a dimension. In response, Evelyn wanted to see me, and right then I was thinking, 'How the hell am I gonna do that?' considering the energy constraints, right?"

Nataliya wasn't missing a beat. "Definitely. Exchange *should* be impossible to accomplish. So what did you do?"

"I told Evelyn the only way she could see me was if she tried to reach me, that being a little suspicious." He winced. "Fortunately, Evelyn left her 'mailing address' pipeline open so I could send her proof via 'postcard' greeting. It's that simple."

"You're using those analogies on purpose to distort my database, aren't ya?"

"Ha ha, and you catch on quickly too, Little Lady!"

Dahlia giggled. "That's pretty mean, Mr. Tsumisu!" she said. "Try throwing somethin' at him, Ms. Nataliya!"

The diligent pumpkin-haired scientist gasped with glee. "Like a *dart*?" she asked. "Dip it in a smidge of neurotoxins?"

"Dahlia?" Suzuka smirked. "No conspiracies at the dinner table, my sister."

"Yes, Big Sister," she replied, giving an encouraging wink to Nataliya. "*Sleeping* neurotoxin too…" she whispered.

"Thank you." Tsumisu graciously patted the warrior princess's back. "I owe you like sixteen muffins or something."

"Rest assured, I meant not to intervene on behalf of your fate, Mr. Tsumisu," Suzuka retorted, jesting again. "Only such that I spare my sister any premeditated behaviors—"

"It's *fine*, Suzuka," Tsumisu groaned and ran a hand over his face. "Sh-should we talk about this? No, Shujin, you talk to her."

"Whuh-*hey*! Why me?" he exclaimed. "I'm not a part of this, man!"

"Lies, you live here! And because of that glaring fact, *how* are you gonna allow me to get shot with a, I quote, 'dart dipped in a smidge of neurotoxin'?"

"Um, that's easy." Shujin pressed his lips together. "I'll just get out of the way. That's how."

"I trusted you, dude."

"*You* should answer the phone!"

Tsumisu paused. "*So* I personally wrote up a card, nicely prearranged with 'connect-the-dot' images," he continued, dismissing Shujin's statement. "When Evelyn *received* it, she was able to determine—OK! Oh my gosh, I'll do it right!" he exclaimed, indeed dodging an object from Nataliya. "Geez, you're a lady of your word."

"Oh? So you noticed, huh?" Nataliya replied, balling up some typing paper Tetyana had previously given to her. "Also, I don't ask *twice*, Mr. Tsumisu."

He twisted his mouth. "Tetyana, is this some vengeance thing fooorr—"

"You were outside for like thirty minutes, big guy!" Tetyana unabashedly confirmed. "There's no telling what we've discussed regarding everything you're *still* not saying. Know what I mean?"

"Yeah, I learned about that secret conversation," Shujin added. "Ha, your 'mom'? She let you wear that T-shirt too, right?"

"*She* said it was cute," Tsumisu admitted in a feeble voice. "All right, Evelyn established an energetic conduit…"

"O*K*…" Nataliya was closely following along. "Keep going."

"By which I submitted a portion of my energy to her along said conduit…"

"Oh my goodness! We make such a great team, handsome! Now what happened when she received your energy?"

"She called and said I should take a nap—I'm kidding!" Tsumisu cowered away. "Ha ha! I couldn't help it, Little Lady!"

"Especially when you're paralyzed from the neck down!" Nataliya replied cheerily. "You want me to jump across this table?"

"I would *love* to see that…Upon Evelyn's reception of my energy, she knew I didn't have any evil or wrong intentions toward her!" Tsumisu blurted and then wiped his brow. "Sounds like a first date, huh, Mr. Iwato?"

"Ha! You won't be getting to second base either with that much trouble!" The jolly man ripped out a laugh.

He laughed with him. "Might as well just go home! Not happening tonight, dude!"

Mrs. Himaki had to laugh at that particular joke.

"Nope! Oohhh gosh, OK." Mr. Iwato noticed a glare from Shujin. "What? It was funny, son!"

"Dude? Don't encourage him," Shujin lamented.

"Man, you'd better be taking notes," Tsumisu pointed out. "Where was I? Yeah, at that point, we began to connect with each other; I saw Evelyn emerge from a realm of pure white—silver hair, violet eyes, and she wore a *really* stunning dress. Sound familiar to anybody?"

Shujin snapped his fingers. "That's her!" he announced. "It felt like you were about to go blind, didn't it?"

"Yes! Twice! I mean, even though it was terribly nice of her to meet me, I was kinda thinking, 'OK, turn down the brightness, ma'am.'"

"*Or* provide some sunglasses."

"Sunscreen"—Tsumisu was counting on his fingers—"umbrellas, beach towels, *something*."

Suzuka was simply amazed. "So the both of you witnessed Mother Evelyn?" she asked. "This…this is by no means any random event! Only legends of Devonia tell of Evelyn's appearance to generations past; your witness *and* interaction with her weighs tremendous importance indeed!"

"My point exactly, Princess!" Nataliya concurred. "This is why I'm trying to gather as much tangible information from you-know-who and derive parallels between him and Shujin!"

"Yaaaay! I'm not the only one being scraped for information!" Tsumisu cheered. "Woohoo!"

"Put your arms down, man." Shujin shook his head.

"I was finished anyway."

"Say, I've got a question. When did all of this happen again? 'Cause if Evelyn was still around, I must've just arrived on the ship. Right?"

"Yeah, I think it was around that time," Tsumisu acknowledged. "Virtually, I was pulling her toward me as I was a power source in the prison dimension. Remember, this is a one-way street. So the *other* half of the battle is exchange with Evelyn to break that dimension wide open."

Suzuka nodded. "Yes, I see, but how in the world could you not only reach her from the prison dimension but still keep contact with her throughout all of that time?"

"I asked myself the same question!" Tsumisu shrugged. "Gaining Evelyn's trust *had* to be solidified; after all, she'd have to work to maintain contact. Now what about me, you say? Well, that's where I needed a link to reach Evelyn's power in the other dimension."

Nataliya snapped her fingers. "Bingo! Shujin comes into the picture," she said. "You mentioned utilizing him as a source to get to Evelyn—how so?"

"Shujin, showing off his swagger…"

"Thanks, I appreciate that." He nodded smugly. "I'll get you an autograph."

"You're too kind, sir. Shujin was creating an *independent* source of power that was more than sufficient to overshadow the *Leviathan*'s constraints," Tsumisu proudly explained. "I found his energy to function as Evelyn's 'publicist,' so to speak, which granted me the key to the *door* to get to Evelyn. Whew! Does any of that make sense?"

"Yes, yes, I see it makes perfect sense!" Nataliya exclaimed valiantly. "Or in other words, Shujin was the switch to complete the energy circuit!"

"Yeah! Y-yeah." Tsumisu raised an eyebrow. "OK, calm down…"

"My word, though you detected Prince Shujin's powers, how did you know the manner by which to utilize them?" asked a continually fascinated Suzuka. "Certainly they do not directly mimic Evelyn's!"

"You'll have to call his 'mom,'" joked Tetyana. "Which is your *clan* right?"

"*Yes*, Tetyana!" Tsumisu scoffed in exasperation. "Are you happy now?"

"Nope! You're not even *close* to coming clean with me!" Her aggression had piqued because of the sake. "And from now on, the minute I see some fish nachos in your hand, they're automatically mine! End of story!"

"Pfft, you and what army? Agh! Don't hit me!" Tsumisu rolled backward to evade Tetyana's fist. "I'm kidding! Geez…agh! What're you doing?"

Tetyana rose up to give chase. "That ninja stuff won't work on me! Get back here!"

"Try to bait him this way, Tetyana!" cried Nataliya, wadding up a ball of paper. "I've got something for him!"

"Get him, Tetyana!" cheered Dahlia, granting applause. "Go for the legs!"

"Suzuka! That's a sign!" Tsumisu declared, failing to dodge his pursuer. "Intervene for your sister's sake! Waaah!"

"Now take a look at *that*, son," said Mr. Iwato, trying to give Shujin advice. "It never pays to cover yourself in too many lies."

"Um…" Shujin winced at the sight of Tetyana pinning Tsumisu down. "Don't you mean it never pays to lie, Dad?"

"Nonsense! If you do it too often, ain't no way to sell it!" He chuckled. "It's part of the business!"

"Shujin, your honeybee is stinging!" Tsumisu cried, parrying her fists away. "Your honeybee is *stinging*!"

"Talk!" Tetyana demanded, a fist cocked and ready. "Who was that before? You didn't walk away all macho-like for nothin'!"

"All right already! It was one of my clansmen, OK?" Tsumisu held his hands up in defense. "Can I get more eggrolls, please?"

"No! Are you gonna keep dodging questions? Well, are ya?"

"Y-you mean *yours* or Little Lady's? Because I can easily do both—ow! I can't help it!"

Suzuka was studying the scenario. "Are you holding back, Tetyana?" she asked.

"Pfft, what? As if!" she answered, letting her barrage of attacks continue. "Help *this*!"

"OK, I'll be serious! *Ow!*" Tsumisu laughed. "This is serious Tsumisu from now on, I double-promise!"

Tetyana finally let him up. "Fan-freaking-tastic!" she brightly exclaimed. "Next time, I'll have Nataliya tag in, got it?"

He dusted himself off. "What are you, her ambassador—kidding!" he instantly bucked his eyes in fear. "Sitting down. Glad we talked."

Shujin winced as the two retook their seats. "I wanted to lend a hand, but…" he said.

"Dude, how much toxic revenge are you accumulating tonight?" Tsumisu muttered, slightly annoyed. "Rough estimate."

"About three months' worth. *And* everybody's pulling for me, if you haven't noticed."

"Gross." Tsumisu sighed and turned to Mrs. Himaki. "Are your springs open late, Grandma?"

She gave a humble smile. "At the rate of your scuffles, I'm willing to make an exception," she said.

"Room for anybody else?" asked Nataliya, clearly instigating. "*Somebody's* gotta provide adult supervision after all."

"I think you'd be the *perfect* accommodation for Tsumisu, Ms. Nataliya!" Mrs. Himaki excitedly concurred. She gasped. "In fact, why don't you stop by later?"

"Aww, you think so?" Nataliya's eyes glittered. "I think I'll do *just* that!"

"Err, Grandma, you don't have a mixed-bathing section." Shujin grinned nervously. "I mean…"

"Oh, it's fine, dear," she reassured him. "There's a first time for everything—"

"*OK*, serious Tsumisu says he doesn't need water wings," Tsumisu remarked, giving Nataliya a blank expression.

"Aannnd serious Nataliya disagrees," she immediately retorted. "*C'mon*."

"More important, Evelyn's in-your-face megawatt flashlight granted me 'sight' of the prison dimension's cluster center," Tsumisu continued with trepidation. "Thus, I gathered the exact energetic parameters just as Little Lady explained. Because if you screw up? It's all over. Hooray!"

"Exactly! There was absolutely no room for error," Nataliya added, a chopstick in her mouth as she resumed her data entry. "But as the saying goes, 'practice makes perfect'; I wonder if you've done this before? And for what reason?"

"Ha! Oh boy, that was uh…a *first* attempt. And Dahlia? This food is freakin' awesome. I shall stuff my pockets thoroughly tonight."

She giggled. "Nooo! I can just give you a container, Mr. Tsumisu!"

"What?" Suzuka looked at Tsumisu in shock. "That was your first time? What would've happened if you had made a mistake?"

Tsumisu patted her shoulder. "Now, calm down. I never said I didn't know what I was doing," he explained. "Once you know the rules well enough, it's very possible to make it on the first attempt. Most of the time, it's best *not* to try it, but in this case, I had no choice."

"Wow, I see what you mean," said Shujin, exhaling at the thought of what could've been. "Man, aren't you even tired?"

"Are *you* tired, Mr. Mark of Evelyn, sir?" He smiled, nudging him unnecessarily hard. "You and I both know we're too good for that, plus this food replenishes all that ails you…besides other things that sit among us…" He quickly looked over to Tetyana.

"Wha-wait! Hey don't start anything! What's gotten into you?"

Mr. Iwato raised a cup of sake. "Well, he's right, son, and it's about time for you to—"

"Will you be here tomorrow, Mr. *Tsumisu*?" Nataliya gave a really forced but really beaming expression.

He scooted back some more. "Uh, that *is* my real name, and *no*, I'm afraid I'll…be busy, Little Lady," he replied. "Perhaps the day after?"

"Aren't ya gonna ask why I asked?"

"Oh nooo!" He chuckled knowingly. "Because some things… dude, take note…are best left unquestioned. Like your intentions, for instance—which I believe are good; don't get me wrong!"

"Mm-hmm." She nodded in understanding. "Yet you're implying I might be doing something *bad*, is that it?"

"*No*!" Tsumisu wildly shook his hands in gesture. "No, no, no, the whole point is—and Shujin will tell you too, when he can't get in contact with me? I'm somewhere else and that's all there is to it."

"S-stop throwing me in this, man!" Shujin was clearly in panic mode. "I swear, is it the sake fumes or somethin'?"

"Sorry, baby," Tetyana replied, holding a half-empty bottle. "I worked it all off earlier so I gotta get started all over again!"

"Mr. Tsumisu likes you, Nataliya!" Dahlia happily concluded. "Am I right?"

"Do you think so?" she responded with a cheeky grin. "I hope it's enough to where he can break away from his oh-so-busy schedule tomorrow, just to see this 'Little Lady'!"

Tsumisu turned to Shujin. "You know Dahlia automatically assumed that, don't you?"

"Uh, I really wouldn't know at this point." He shrugged. "But I've got an idea: I can just call tomorrow and see what you're up to, and…that'll settle things, I guess?"

Tetyana finished the bottle. "I mean, if you're busy and everything, it's no problem," she began. "Can't force the guy to be here if he can't make it, right?"

"No," sighed a disappointed-looking Nataliya. "I suppose you can't. C'mon, Dahlia. Let's put some dishes up."

"OK," the little princess responded, noticing the scientist's suddenly changed demeanor. "What's wrong?"

"Oh nothing! Just…" She glanced at Tsumisu, saddened. "I had my hopes dashed; that's all."

As Nataliya and Dahlia went to the kitchen, everybody was left wondering what troubled her so suddenly.

"What's gotten into her?" asked Mr. Iwato.

"For some reason, she wants Tsumisu to return tomorrow," Suzuka stated in her educated tone. "I'm not sure why."

"Hey, you don't see me moping!" Tetyana opened another bottle. "If he's busy, let 'em be. Besides, I'm sure you're just tired, right, big guy?"

Tsumisu pushed his hair back. "I certainly didn't mean to kill her mood," he replied, being in fear of overthinking his actions. "She uh, she *might* be sensitive so let me make a notation of that. Like, Arlette is sensitive to the existence of mythical beasts. Wait… Is this the same category?"

Shujin leaned in to his friend and whispered, "Want me to go talk to her?"

"Nah, she's probably listening right now, watch—if it makes you feel any better, I'll be back tomorrow, all right?" Tsumisu brightly called to the kitchen.

Nataliya came rushing to the table. "Really? Do you mean it?"

He grinned, clearly amused. "Now, I didn't think it was that big a deal, but if it means that much to you, I'll come back, Little Lady."

"What a nice thing to do!" Mr. Iwato said in adoration. "Anybody else feeling warm and fuzzy? Tingly maybe?"

Tetyana put an arm around Shujin's neck. "I know I am. How about *you*, Shujin babe?"

Suzuka's ninja senses sky-rocketed. "Take your arm off of him!"

"Yeah, that's right." Tsumisu remembered something and rose to his feet. "We were supposed to switch places! So there you go! Have at it, Warrior Princess Suzuka!"

"Why, *thank you*, Tsumisu," she politely acknowledged and then started to tussle with Tetyana. "Did you not hear me? Cease this behavior at once!"

"Hey now, c'mon, girls!" Shujin was trying to get them to stop. "W-why'd you do that, man? Waahh, noo!"

"Countertoxic, dude." He shrugged, picking up some dishes. "And *you* have to live with them. I'll be right back though..."

"Ha ha! C'mere, Shujin!" Tetyana pushed Suzuka away and aggressively took hold of the poor fellow. "There's no escape!"

Shujin was flinging his arms around like a desperate swimmer. "Tetyana! Aghh! Noo! Tsumisu, wait! Help me!"

Mrs. Himaki bore a smile. "It's good to see Shujin finally interacting with some girls, don't you think?" she asked her son.

"Like a dream come true." Mr. Iwato was about to shed a tear. "Make sure you take some pictures so I can show the guys at work, OK, Mom?"

"Oh, I wouldn't have the time," she replied with clasped hands. "Perhaps you could ask Tsumisu?"

He snapped his fingers. "Good idea! I hope he didn't get too far..."

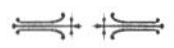

Meanwhile, Tsumisu was on his way to the kitchen; however, he ran into some resistance.

"I'm, uh...still here," he said with Nataliya standing in front of him, arms outstretched. "Say, I remember you doing this before. Why are you doing that again? It's making me paranoid."

"The idea!" she said mischievously. "*Buuuut* I'm willing to make a compromise with you if you're willing to cooperaaaate!" she sang.

"Please hold for the next customer service representative." Tsumisu held up a finger. "Mr. Iwato, were you gonna ask me something?"

"Uh, I will before you leave, OK?" he replied. "Make sure I don't forget!"

Tsumisu nodded. "OK, I won't! Now what were you talking about, Little Lady? What compromise? I haven't agreed or bargained with you about *anything*," he continued.

Nataliya finally ended her barricade and folded her arms as she spoke. "Well, the thing was you said you were coming back tomorrow, right?" she asked.

"Yeeeeah, that's right." He scoffed. "What? Did you change your mind about seeing me tomorrow by divine intervention?"

"Oh, of *course* not!" she confidently answered. "By all means, come back, but I was just curious as to whether or not there were certain terms or conditions on *my* end I had to uphold for you to return…maybe?"

He smiled. "Now why would I do a thing like that after nearly breaking your poor heart? You looked so *pitiful* when you went to the kitchen. I felt like a dumbass like, 'just *visit* the lady tomorrow,' know what I mean?"

Nataliya grew a sly grin. "Just for lil' ol' me? You're nothing but a big softy inside, aren't you, handsome?"

"I suppose, or just um…too blind to see reason." Tsumisu winced with a shrug. "Either way, it *is* one reason why I took it easy on Tetyana the first time we met; she was 'attacking' Shujin and tore up our school in the process, so I ended up helping him out. But she was so darn *pretty* I didn't wanna hurt her…"

She was pleasantly surprised. "You fought against Tetyana? Ha! To think she never stood a chance."

"She seems OK with it now." He ducked something that Tetyana threw as the tussling continued. "But anyway, that's been and done. You really created her?"

"Absolutely," Nataliya affirmed. "In a sense, she's like a daughter of mine...hence the copious degree of cooperation between us, yes?"

Tsumisu envisioned the process. "So sugar, spice, and everything, blue food-coloring; bring water to a boil; and pow: instant Tetyana?" He paused, observing her (and appreciating how the dress contoured her body...Was she braless?) "You really *are* a scientific masterpiece; I can see it in your demeanor."

"Oh?" Nataliya gave him an intuitive sideways glance, striking a little pose. "My demeanor? Am I that obvious to you, Mr. Tsumisu?"

"Ha!" He forced himself to stop appreciating.

"Like what ya see, huh?"

Oh God...

"Go ahead." Her eyes narrowed. "Looks like you need a minute."

All right, though the situation is certainly on track to derail, what stands before you (literally) is the *first* opportunity in your life where you can set things straight! Disregard any other moment where thinking wasn't prioritized *prior* to speech and handle this, Commander! This is *your time.*

"You *are* admittedly sexy—I mean!" He clenched his eyes in severe regret. "Let's just say I can guess pretty well about people... H-how about that?"

"Wow!" Nataliya chuckled, blushing a bit. "Well, I should expect nothing else from somebody like you. Such talents for energy manipulation must grant a knack for in-depth dispositional observation *somehow.* Hmm, there's no *telling* what else you're capable of...until I *get* to ya that is."

"See?" Tsumisu balanced dishes on one arm as he shook a finger at her. "There was this feeling circling around the reason why you wanted me back tomorrow. I mean, I didn't want to say it..."

"Nothing wrong in being honest is there? You've *just* proved that, handsome."

He blushed, looking away. "I-I dunno what you're talking about."

"Riiiightt! And I'll tell you one thing, Mr. Tsumisu." Nataliya pointed assertively. "It's better for you to come *here* than for me to come to *you*, got it? I mean, I'll hunt you down, stalk your closets—*whatever* it takes!" She exhaled patiently in conclusion. "Yep! Are ya scared now?"

Tsumisu rubbed the back of his neck, sensing some stalwart decision making that mirrored Arlette's—similarly frightening him.

"Whoooaaa…I guess so, Little Lady. But hey, I might be looking forward to that—" Strike *three,* Tsumisu! You die! "Oh God, please scratch what I just said!"

"Ha! *Nope*! And you've got until, oh, say…noon to make it here. Remember that now 'cause I'll be timing youuu!" she sang.

"You're timing me now?" Tsumisu scoffed. "C'mon! Just because you're short doesn't mean your patience has to be."

Nataliya eyed him. "Are you implying something again?"

"Naaah, I know better now." He cleared his throat, realizing those ominous words of Lieutenant Kadochi just *might* have been manifesting into reality. "Oh yeah, whatever that device was you put in my food was fairly tasty, but my stomach didn't call for technology. Girl, you really got me now…" he began to sing and walked toward the kitchen.

"Damn it!" Nataliya snapped her fingers and thought to herself. *That was made to trace him if he were late—the time-activated system would pinpoint his location by using his body's own electrical field. But he couldn't have known that*! Nataliya smirked, a finger on her bottom lip. *Little does he know, I'll have the last laugh*! "Ya hear *that,* Mr. Tsumisu?" she yelled to the kitchen now, catching everyone's attention suddenly.

"Uh…w-what?" he called back, banging some pots and dishes as he ran dishwater. "Say that again?"

"I said I'll have the last laugh!" Nataliya cupped her hands over her mouth. "You're not as clever as ya think, ya know!"

"Fantastic!" Tsumisu incongruously responded. "I'll tell Shujin about your class—Wait…What?"

Later on, Tsumisu prepared to leave for his apartment quarters, or return to the Sonzai encampment, which he didn't specify for scientific reasons. The entire group met him outside and stood at the front door to wish him goodbye.

"See you, man," Shujin said and shook his hand. "Thanks for everything. We're all more than grateful you were here to help us out."

Tsumisu grinned. "It's no problem, dude. What kind of friend would I be if I didn't help my buddies, huh?"

"Nah, you're like part of the family," he replied. "I mean, just like always, you're welcome anytime you feel like stopping by."

"Thanks, man. I'll be in need of Dahlia and Grandma's dinners; they kick all kinds of galactic ass," he joked. "Oh wait…Your dad wanted to talk to me about something before I left."

"Really? OK, Dad! Were you gonna talk to him?"

Mr. Iwato smiled innocently. "I sure was! Say, um, can we go around the house for a second so we can talk?"

Tsumisu shrugged in honesty. "Not sure why when I'm gonna end up telling him anyway."

"I mean, this isn't a *secret* thing. It's just…" Mr. Iwato was looking over his shoulder at the women. "It has to be between *you and me*; that's all."

"If you say so, Mr. Iwato." He put a friendly arm around his shoulder. "Might be something very important, you know? Like development-wise?"

Shujin raised an eyebrow. "I hope that conversation won't go where I fear it will…"

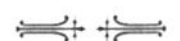

When Tsumisu and Mr. Iwato reached the other side of the house, Mr. Iwato cleared his throat attentively.

"Well you see, Tsumisu, as a father—"

"Yes, as a father..." He nodded in understanding.

"I'm awfully proud to see Shujin, my son, progressing in his interaction with women. Females, yes? So, as a *proud* father asking a friend, would you take pictures to document it?"

"Ha! *Really* depends on what I'm documenting." Tsumisu folded his arms with a twisted mouth. "Not that it's a bad thing 'cause I can see why you're proud. I'm just not sure if this is directly related to a child's first steps toward walking...Then again, it is. I see."

"Great!" He gave a thumbs-up. "So will ya do it?"

"As much as I'd like to, I-I *can't*, Mr. Iwato," he began to explain. "It's best you do it yourself or just have cameras set up around the house. Then that would be like spying..."

"Hmm, I guess you're right." Mr. Iwato began devising alternate methods. "Video cameras then?"

Tsumisu laughed aloud. "High-definition, Dolby surround sound too! Mr. Iwato, that's the *same* thing. Besides, Shujin might not be OK with it, so I'd suggest just keeping these kinds of memories in your head or your heart. Who're you gonna show the pictures to anyway?"

"Err." He grew a huge sweat drop. "Nobody really. Just like for a picture book, I suppose. I get what you mean, Tsumisu; these types of things are especially for memories kept inside."

"Great! Besides, half of those images would have nosebleeds and...no. Now let's get back to the others."

⇹

Around the corner were Tetyana and Suzuka, attempting to eavesdrop.

"Did you catch anything?" Suzuka whispered, taking things too seriously.

Tetyana's ears twitched. "Not much, just some stuff about pictures and cameras. I really didn't get it!"

"What're you two doing?" asked Shujin as he approached from behind, startling them. They fell on top of each other.

"Nothin', Shujin!" replied Tetyana with an innocent smile. "We were just, um, checking to see if any poisonous critters were around!"

Shujin narrowed his eyes in suspicion. "Yeah, I'm sure." He helped them both up as his father and Tsumisu approached.

Tsumisu grinned as Suzuka and Tetyana dusted themselves off. "The hell happened? I didn't feel any earthquake," he remarked.

"W-well, we were inspecting the ground—" Suzuka began.

"It's all right. No explanation necessary." He walked past with a pat on her shoulder. "Lavender is an excellent color for you, Princess."

"Oh!" Suzuka said in pleasant surprise. "Well, thank you."

Tetyana tapped Tsumisu on the back as she followed. "What was that flower you said I was again?"

"Hydrangea," he responded informatively. "It's a certain breed that has your color, but I'm gonna talk to Shujin about growing a garden with all those flowers I mentioned tomorrow."

"Wow, that's really nice of you, man," Shujin said, overhearing. "Think we could start tomorrow if we manage to find the seeds and bulbs?"

"Hell yeah, we could!" Tsumisu responded with a celebratory smile. "Plenty of space out there around the lake. I'm a nice bastard, ain't I?"

"Well you can't help it apparently!" Nataliya remarked suddenly, hands on her hips. "I can see it in your 'demeanor,' ya know!" She winked.

"*Ha*! Ha ha…" Tsumisu stopped in his tracks, putting a hand over his heart. "Yeah, you scared me, Little Lady. I just didn't expect you to be in front of me so *soon*."

"Aww, am I scary to you, Tsumisuuu? Does that make you nervous sometimes? Will my face *haunt* you in the night?" Nataliya stood on her tiptoes and wiggled her fingers at him. "*Wooo-oooo*!"

"Whuuhh!" he cried, comically cowering.

"Mwahahahaaa! I'm already winning!" she proclaimed. "But ya see now? That's why you're coming back tomorrow, right?"

The Sonzai commander took a step back, checking his pulse and noticed he was sincerely feeling intimidated. "You know what? You're waaay too pretty to scare anything!" he stated to build some integrity back. "Sure, I might be in subtle, subconscious fear…but, um, Shujin here has rubbed off on me a lot since we've known each other!"

Shujin smiled as he placed a hand behind his head. "Well, I wouldn't say *that* much, but it shows, I guess…in terms of niceness. Agh, you give me too much credit, dude."

"Mm-hmm, he wasn't nice when he tossed Taras around!" Nataliya chirped with a grin. "*Were* you, handsome?"

Tsumisu pointed to Nataliya as he looked at Shujin. "See it's only been a few hours, and I like her already; she's got a lot of whatever she has, and I can't get tired of it. Ever."

"Sounds like you want to take her with you." Shujin poked at him with slanted eyes. "But I mean, be my guest—"

"*God no*! No, no, no, you've got it under control here, man." Tsumisu wiped his forehead. "And you're catching on quick, dude! I need to *watch* myself…"

Nataliya ran up to the Mark of Evelyn with puppy-dog eyes. "Could I go with him, Shujin? Pleeaasseee?" she begged. "It'll be like the friendliest, most *educational* sleepover ever! A heh heh heh…"

Shujin was at a loss for a decent response. "Uhm, I-I was just kidding around with him, Nataliya! Er, I mean, did you *want* to? Or—"

Tsumisu *immediately* escorted Shujin a few meters away, stumbling in the process. "Don't instigate anything, dude! She's friggin' serious, and if I say no, she'll be all sad, and I'll end up feeling bad about it. Then I'll end up saying yes, and who *knows* what'll happen in the morning! I only have one bedroom, remember?"

he whispered desperately. "*One*! I've *just* resolved my inner guilt in this *same situation* with Arlette!"

"OK, OK, I'm sorry! Geez!" Shujin exhaled, trying to figure things out. "So what should I do now?"

Tsumisu glanced over, noticing she was approaching casually. "Tell her maybe some other time, OK? Or do you want me to do it? No, she asked you; that's right. OK, go."

They both returned with friendly smiles.

"No, not tonight, Nataliya. I'm sure he's got some stuff to do tomorrow before he comes back," Shujin explained.

"Okeydokey, if you say so! But that means I *can*, right?" she pointed out, looking to the both of them. "In the future?"

"Ah, uh…" Shujin looked toward Tsumisu, who was slowly shaking his head with widened eyes. "I-I'm not s-supposed to say," he replied in absolute doubt.

"Hmm, that's strange," Nataliya replied with skeptical eyes. "Oh well, when you figure it out, let me know, OK?"

"Dodged," said Tsumisu with a sigh. "OK guys, I'm outta here! Anybody want some hugs or somethin'?"

"I do! I do!" said Dahlia, raising her hand with a smile. "I love hugs!"

"OK, here goes!" Tsumisu said while picking her up to swing her around. "Weee! Ha ha!"

"Yaaayy!" the little princess cheered.

"Aww, how adorable." Suzuka smiled.

Tsumisu held up Dahlia by his right arm and stretched the other out. "You might as well join the party, Suzuka!" He smiled. "C'mon! Let's get Big Sister in here!"

"Yeah, c'mon, Big Sister!" Dahlia laughed. "This is fun!"

Shujin folded his arms and grinned. "Are you gonna swing her around too?"

"Ha ha, watch me!" Tsumisu winked.

Suzuka stepped back. "Now, wait! I'm not sure if it's safe—waahh!"

Tsumisu grabbed Suzuka and swung her and Dahlia around a few times. Then he set them both down and laughed. "You should've seen the look on your face!" He laughed.

"Wasn't that great?" said Dahlia.

"I was not ready for it." She timidly wore a smile. "Thank you anyway, Mr. Tsumisu."

"Ah, you'll get used to it, and you're welcome." The Sonzai commander turned around. "Now, Tetyana, I won't do *that* to you because, uhh…you don't look so well."

She scoffed with a smirk, achieving her optimal level of tipsy. "I'm just fine, big guy. Gimme a hug." They embraced, and Tetyana patted him on the back. "Thanks a lot, for everything, you hear? Be careful out there."

He grinned, nudging her shoulder. "Hey, you're beyond welcome, Tetyana. Thanks for being the most awesome, bloodthirsty fighting partner a guy could ask for. Let's go stab like *eighty* deer right freakin' now."

"Now *that's* what I'm talkin' about!" Tetyana grinned in appreciation. "And you're welcome, big guy."

"Hey, if you need *anything* you can get it from Shujin. But if you need anything from *me* you can ask him for my phone number."

"Hmmm, really now? Could you get me some more sake when you come back?" She bent over to eye him, hands on her hips.

Tsumisu smiled in humor. "Yeah, I'll see what I can do."

"All right…at least bring *one* with you." Tetyana punched his chest.

"Would you do the same for me?" asked Nataliya, standing behind him.

"Sure, I would!" Tsumisu turned around and picked her up. "I mean, it wouldn't seem fair that something so intelligent and *freakin' pretty* did not deserve an unreturned favor or two from me, you know?"

"Yeah!" Nataliya smiled brightly, her arms on his shoulders. "So why not do me a favor right now?"

"Well, uh, you see," he began, covering his nerves, "I'm currently working with another client right now..." He nudged his head in Tetyana's direction. "So as soon as I'm done with *her,* I can get to *you.*"

Nataliya gave him those darn puppy-dog eyes. "But all I wanted was for you to swing me around. Could you, pleeease?"

Tsumisu looked over to his amused friend. "You hear that, don't you, dude? I'm gonna spoil every last one of them before you get a damn chance."

Shujin smiled with arms folded. "By all means, go ahead! I'll have my chance sooner than I know!"

"Ha! Funny thing is you're *not* prepared! OK, Little Lady, here goes!"

Tsumisu held her by the waist and twirled her around several times as she laughed with enjoyment and then set her down.

"Why that bastard locked you away is *beyond* me!" He sighed, kneeling before her. "That's another reason why I wanted to hurt him like I did...between you and me." He grinned with a whisper.

Nataliya's eyes turned empathetic. "Aww, ya big old softy."

"You got that right," said Tetyana, strolling up with a grin as he arose. "I was surprised we got along so well after we fought each other, but I guess he never didn't like me? Is that how you say it, Shujin?"

"Er..." Shujin shrugged, unsure. "We'll accept that until further notice?"

Mr. Iwato put on a grin. "Say uh, Tsumisu, you don't need a ride back home? It's kinda dark and cold out here, ya know! Say, where *is* home for you?"

"Nah! Nope! I've got it, Mr. Iwato, thanks." Tsumisu grinned, briefly glancing at Nataliya. "Long as I got my legs I can save on some gas. See you guys!"

"Goodbye!" they said in unison and waved.

"I'll call tomorrow and see what's up, OK?" Shujin shook his friend's hand and pulled him in for an embrace, and they snapped their fingers.

"Absolutely, brother, you know how to reach me." Tsumisu made a comical face. "Oh! And I'd be *very* careful if I were you," he whispered.

Shujin whispered in response, "Huh? Why?"

"Well, if you don't know, I'm gonna let you figure it out on your own—it'll make you stronger." Tsumisu nodded with confidence. "Remember? Running and hiding *just* like the majestic lemurs?"

He scoffed. "W-why bring this to my attention when you *leave*? Now I'm gonna be paranoid!"

"You'll be just fine!" He patted his shoulder and took off running down the main driveway. "Nothin' to worry about, dude!"

"You're *lying* to me, dude!" Shujin called back, shaking his head but chuckling. "I swear…"

Tsumisu laid Akari over his shoulder, darting into the night, whistling the little tune he sang before as it echoed into the forest. Yeah, he thought while observing the stars, you really got me now indeed…

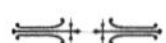

The hour was late, and all was quiet in the Iwato household. Shujin stood in his room, meticulously scanning the surroundings; was anything shuffled out of place? No? Check. Anything in his closet? No? Check. All right, time to inspect his bed. Shujin patted it…nothing. He stood upright, arms folded and unconvinced.

"Tetyana? Are you in here?" he said. "C'mon now, say something if you are."

Nothing. Still not convinced (and still trying to defeat paranoia), Shujin strolled around the place, sniffing—Tetyana wore a perfume of some kind, clearly extraterrestrial. Or was it just how she smelled on average? Gosh, combine that with her latex body suit—*Stop*! Keep checking your room, Mr. Mark of Evelyn.

Four minutes elapsed, and his sniffer was satisfied: no trace of Tetyana. Shujin approached his bed once more and patted *everywhere*; he even created a funky conga beat as he did so. Good thing nobody was watching him.

Finally, with the lights off and standing at the foot of his bed, Shujin prepared for his favorite nightly ritual—falling facedown to accept the sweet embrace of sleep. Arms outstretched, he took the dive…only to find his face buried between invisible, sweet-smelling breasts.

"I was wondering when you'd give up, baby," said a devious-sounding Tetyana, becoming visible, arms wrapped around him. "Ready for bed?"

Shujin exhaled deeply, too tired to resist. On the bright side, she was warm and comfortable and the strength of her embrace could've melted away every horrible memory. Heck, after a day like his, maybe this was what he needed.

"Not putting up a fight?" she sounded surprised. "What's wrong, babe?"

He shrugged. "I've done enough of that," he said, voice obviously muffled. "Know what I mean?"

"Hmm, true," she agreed. "I'm…so happy you're back, Shujin. Honest."

"Well, I'd hate for you to be hurt because of me." He managed to prop his head up, catching her gaze. "So…knowing you're happy means I'm happy too."

"*Aww*!" she whimpered, mussing his hair. "Don't make me cry."

"Ha, not trying to do that either." Shujin humbly grinned. "Say, um…w-were you planning on sleeping *here* or…"

"Well, I'm not sleepy just *yet,*" Tetyana continued, pulling down the straps of her gown to reveal herself. "But I think you can help me get there, Shujin..."

On second thought, this was *not* what he needed! Mission *abort*!

"Tetyana! Ooomff!" he cried, his face smothered and nose bleeding. "Let's talk about this!"

"Shhh." She rolled on top of him, instantly fondling his crotch. "Mmm, big, strong *hero* lookin' after me, huh? Well this is what you get, sweetie—"

Suddenly, the door slid open violently. "Halt!" announced Suzuka, donning an attractive nightgown with weapon in hand. "I suspected your schemes! You shall not soil my prince, mercenary!"

"What? I'll soil my baby three times *over,* Princess!" she retorted, pinning him down. "Now get the hell outta here! You missed your chance!"

"Never! Prepare yourself!"

All that quiet, all that preparation, all the strength Shujin *wished* existed had led up to a small-scale battle in his room. Was *this* what Tsumisu warned him about? He should reach for the phone. Wow, Suzuka cut it in half. And so, the Mark of Evelyn just assumed the position and became a humanoid Frisbee. Who knew? Maybe that was the way things had to be from then on.

CHAPTER TEN

"All done!" said Nataliya, her tone bright. "The results are *just* as I expected."

"Hmm, really?" asked Shujin, sitting on a counter in a doctor's-office-style environment. "That was awfully fast, Ms. Nataliya. What were you able to find out?"

"Yeah, I was wondering the same," said Tetyana, standing by with arms folded. "I thought you were gonna have laser beams and fog machines going on."

"Ha! Science is a *bit* more subtle I'm afraid." Nataliya wrapped a stethoscope around her neck, standing before him in a pink sundress and lab coat. "Turns out, Shujin dear, that you've got Devonian *and* Ordovician genes."

Suzuka gasped. "Lineage from both civilizations?" she asked, wearing a white blouse and long skirt. "But...how can that be? When did this happen?"

"Yeah, the ban of intermixing between civilizations has been a standing order since time began," Nataliya explicated.

"Unfortunately, I can't determine *yet* when 'it' took place…but 'it' certainly happened!"

Shujin rubbed the back of his neck, blushing. "Pretty sure you got your point across," he muttered.

Arlette adjusted the straps of her blue camisole. "Wow, so that means there's a *whole* lot more to his powers, right?" she asked, hands curiously clasped behind her back now. "If Shujin has mixed blood, then maybe the same goes for Tsumisu? And that's why they could contact Evelyn?"

"Oh the hypotheses could blossom for *years*," Nataliya replied, her tone eager. "Needless to say, the implications are extraordinary, but I've got a hunch as to why Shujin can do what he does."

"Really?" he asked. "Even with the basic tests you ran?"

A wise grin spread across her face. "Trust me; I *know*!" She nodded.

Shujin felt intimidated. "Hey, I can sleep better knowing that," he nervously replied.

"So what now, Ms. Nataliya?" asked Suzuka. "Will your search intensify in the near future? Any results you produce may very well restructure the balance of the empire."

"Yeah, maybe I'm supposed to *unify* the two civilizations instead of just serving one?" said Shujin, scratching his head. "I dunno; it's a lot to take in at one time. I'll be honest."

"Well, not to worry. We've got plenty of time to figure it out," Nataliya said warmly. "OK folks, I'll need a few more minutes with him. After that, let's eat, OK?"

"Yaaay!" cheered Arlette. "C'mon, guys, the sooner we leave, the sooner we can chow down!"

"See you in a bit, babe!" Tetyana winked, bending over slightly to show cleavage courtesy of her tank top. "I'll save a spot for ya—"

"Prince Shujin shall accompany *me* this morning," Suzuka retaliated as the group left Nataliya's lab.

"Pfft, in your *dreams*! Shujin was staring at *me* this whole time!"

As the door closed, the silence became awkward. Nataliya and Shujin met eyes.

"Ahrrm," he began, "so…what else do you need to do?"

"Just give you some simple questions, Shujin," she said, but her face suddenly turned dark and sinister. "*Where's your friend?*"

"Whuuuaaah!" he cried, jumping back into a cowering position. "I-I dunno!"

"You gotta do better than that!" she growled. "Where is he? *Now*!"

"Waah! I swear I dunno anything!"

"Oh! *What*? Ack! Ack-ack!" Nataliya coughed as she calmly reformed herself. "Ack! Woo, excuse me! I was only asking where Mr. Tsumisu was located. Have any idea, dear?"

Shielding himself, he wasn't sure how to respond. "Uhh…he…I mean, typically he's asleep about now," he said cautiously. "In…his apartment?"

"Yeah? Think you can call him and…leave a reminder about our scheduled appointment today? I would do so myself," Nataliya said innocently, flinging some hair behind her. "Yet I wished not to impose."

"Oh…well, of course." Shujin dropped his guard. "Sure, I'll give him a call, but I don't expect he'll answer."

"Why's that?"

"Well…" He finally sat upright. "Tsumisu *really* makes use of the answering service. That's just how he is."

Nataliya's eyes narrowed as a finger pressed against her bottom lip. Contemplation saturated her ambitions like a *bad* habit. "Just how he is, huh?" she snickered. "Thanks, Shujin, you're free to go…"

He wasn't comfortable with her tone of voice, yet he retrieved his wits and made haste to the door.

"See you at breakfast?"

"Breakfast…will be *served*…mwahaha…" She chuckled. "Mwahahahaaa! Hmm? Oh! Yeah, yeah! See you in a second, Shujin!" She beamed, waving.

With widened eyes, Shujin slowly closed the door and stared.

"What?" she cried. "*What?*"

"N-nothing!"

⁂

Tsumisu flung the covers off his bed as the alarm clock rang. Eleven thirty in the morning; Birds were singing outside with children playing at the apartment complex's playground; people were commuting here and there as their weekend began.

Rubbing his face and shaking the sleep off, he headed to the bathroom to freshen up only to find his radio mysteriously turned on within the living room. Of course, he didn't sense anything or anybody nearby (or in the apartment for that matter), so he shut it off without paying it another moment's notice. Maybe wear and tear was getting to it.

Tsumisu's casual dismissal of technological mishaps changed when he turned the bathroom light on…and it flicked off *by itself*. Now he took some greater consideration into these mysterious occurrences; knowing this wasn't just any sort of practical joke, Tsumisu wondered if anything related to the power grid running through the complex had something to do with these events. Yet a power surge can't cut a light switch off, duh. So, Tsumisu turned the light on again and waited…but nothing happened. The conclusion? No conclusion. Whatever, it wasn't as if he were trapped in that prison dimension again, so why sweat it?

Done with his morning hygiene ritual, Tsumisu went into the kitchen and saw the light on his phone blinking, indicating received messages. With the fridge door open, he grabbed the phone and pressed a few buttons to reach his voice mail. Among them were messages from Shujin, Asaka, and a click.

"I hate those," he mumbled and deleted it.

The next message was Shujin's.

"Hey man, you're not up yet? When'd you go to sleep? Anyway, if you still plan on coming over, give me a call. I've got some stuff to tell you that you, uh...might wanna know first. All right, see ya."

"Stuff I might wanna know, huh? I think it's related to that warning I gave him last night." He grinned with insight, turning on the stove. "I told you, man, but I won't say that to your face."

The next message was from Asaka; normally, he had information on the latest rave or club event. Tsumisu told him before he wasn't interested, but if it kept Asaka busy, then Tsumisu didn't mind the questionable-activity updates. So, Asaka insisted on letting him know in the most colorful manner.

"Yo, man! They got it tonight!" the message began. "So bring that money for tha hunnies, a'right? Lemme know if you can make it, man! Peace!"

"Money for the honey..." He laughed aloud as he deleted the message. "That's not right, man, on any level. Bet Tetyana would enjoy that, however...*No,* weird thoughts of Tetyana twerking it." Tsumisu sighed regretfully and shook his head. "OK, I'll call Shujin later. First thing I have to do is *eat.*"

As he stuffed a tart in his mouth while placing a pan on the stove, the phone rang. Caller ID showed "Iwato, Komaru." Shrugging away his willingness to delay an urgent conversation, Tsumisu picked up the receiver.

"Hey, if it's mentally detrimental man, let me get something to eat first. All right?" he answered nonchalantly.

"And good morning to you *too*!" said a very bright, extraordinarily ecstatic voice. "Did ya sleep well, handsome?"

Oh great merciful heavens help him. It was Little Lady, Nataliya. Why? The first thing in the morning, God? Why?

"Ah, the majestic power of redial!" he cordially replied, looking over his shoulder now. "Yeah, good morning. Sorry for the introduction—I did sleep pretty good, Little Lady. How about you?"

"Suuuurre, just like a log! Best sleep in eight hundred years, thanks to a very certain somebody, yeah?" Nataliya maintained her cheeriness. "Say, um, you notice anything when you got up?"

Tsumisu scoffed in nervous denial, sweating under his arms. "*No.* Why?"

"Hmm, I see," she replied, instantly aware he was a terrible liar. "Reason I asked was because you can't be too careful with *radios* and *light switches* nowadays; there's no telling *what* could happen, ya know? Crazy flickering and stuff like a rave party!"

"Yeeeeah!" He yawned loudly, figuring she scanned his messages too. "Yikes! Sorry again, still waking up."

"*Oh?*" Nataliya's tone piqued suddenly with unusually deepening interest. "Need some bedside stimulation soon to get your blood goin'? You needn't look far, Mr. Tsumisu."

"Ha! Whoooooaa, that's *not* caffeine, I'd imagine, Little Lady!" Tsumisu wiped his forehead, not believing the sudden nature of the conversation. "Hey, I-I know that was you screwing with the stuff in here."

She gasped in delight. "Why, Mr. Tsumisu, I thought you *didn't* notice my outstanding efforts! What a surprise! Do ya realize how much better I feel?"

"Ha ha, on *that* I wouldn't dare provide a supposition." He cleared his throat. "But do *you* know how your 'efforts' make me feel?"

"Paranoid? Sound about accurate?"

Tsumisu wiped a hand over his face, still attempting to wake up, hoping to accelerate the process. Problem was his semidelirious state, he deduced, granted easier psychological access for the little lady. And for all he knew about her remarkable genius, she was *precisely* aware of such a fact; therefore, she *really* didn't need avenues of mental tactics made simpler.

"So, um, is this entire…*thing* some statement in the neighborhood of 'I know where you live'?"

"Hee-hee! Pretty much! Alsoooo!" Nataliya said in a singsong tone. "If you don't make it here in about sixteen minutes, you can expect an *awfully* pretty visitor soon!"

Tsumisu grew fearful all of a sudden; paranoia was a derivative of fear anyway, right? Naturally, then, he *should* feel that way.

"Well, I-I just got up. You can't grant me more time?" he requested. "Besides, I gotta eat something—"

"You could just wait until you get over here; lunch is coming up soon, right?" Nataliya politely suggested.

"Little Lady…"

"Hmm?"

Tsumisu sighed. "When I get over there, you can talk to me as long as you want. Right now, I need to speak to Shujin, OK? Stop delaying, please, my dear?"

Nataliya exhaled heavily, disappointed. "*OK*. Shujin! Phone for you!"

"Oh, he's outside, Nataliya!" replied Dahlia in the background. "Want me to get him?"

"No! *Nope*! That's *OK*! Thank you, Dahlia! Eh heh heh heh…"

Tsumisu smiled and shook his head. "But I'm returning his call, don't you think you should let him know?"

"He'll know; trust me," she said almost reassuringly. "And he won't get upset either. Shujin and I sort of…bonded over the past couple of hours."

"Bonded?"

"Yeah! Ya know, like a mutual understanding of each other and our positions?"

"Well, uh…I'm not sure I follow, so I won't say I understand." Tsumisu sounded unconvinced. "What do you mean by 'positions,' Little Lady?"

Nataliya giggled mischievously. "Do you *really* wanna know? I can always show ya the best positions if you're so eager to learn, Mr. Tsumisu."

"*Wow,* that sounded *really* sordid," he muttered in the affirmative. "If your instruction involves any riddles, bribes, or schemes, I'd best figure it out by myself, Little Lady."

"*Damn,* you're a tough cookie! And here I was thinking I had a plan too. I bet if you said that to my face, you couldn't resist knowing, could ya?"

"I'd probably run away just to avoid the temptation!" he joked. "I'm glad you noticed my weakness though. Now, I'll have to delay my visit another three to forty-five days—"

"No! Don't do that!" Nataliya instantly pleaded. "My analysis can't wait that long!"

"Ah *ha*! That's what I figured—'positions' as in scientist and test subject, right?"

She paused in long silence. "You know that wasn't fair! You did that on purpose, didn't you, Tsumisu? Ooooo, you're a *mean* one!"

"I sure did!" he said proudly. "So exactly what happened between you as the scientist and Shujin as the test subject? You played 'house' with the poor fellow?" Tsumisu could envision it and stifled his laughter.

"What do you mean 'what happened'?" Nataliya said in a stalwart defense. "Nothing happened other than both he and I agreed that I'd give him a simple series of tests, and then that was the end of it! I promise!"

"Oh boy," Tsumisu groaned. "I'd hate to take your word for it… but you sound so *cute* when you say it, it's hard for me *not* to believe you."

"Mm-hmm!" She snickered deviously. "Maybe we should talk in different 'scenarios,' huh? Seems to me it'll work both ways..."

He let out a huge fake sneeze. "Pardon me, Little Lady, just uh...had a case of innuendo; that's all."

"Hey! It happens, Mr. Tsumisu! It's even better at *night*, you know that?"

Another sneeze. "Weeeeell, I'm gonna go now! Lots of preparations today, that big unknown out there just waiting to be seized—"

"*Ha*!" Nataliya scoffed in severe amusement. "You're damn *right* I'm gonna seize it! Ha-haaa! You walked straight into that one!"

"*Wow*!" Tsumisu was floored. "OK, Little Lady, I-I'm hanging up now."

"Well, *you* just get your tail over here right now, OK? And I mean, as soon as you hang up the phone, go straight out the door."

Tsumisu found himself looking over his shoulder *constantly*. "Not to give you any brilliant ideas, but it's not as if you're watching me..."

Nataliya's tone was confident. "Yeah, but how would you know I'm not? Hmm, *Mr. Tsumisu*?"

"D-don't try and psyche me out, Little Lady." He attempted to stand up for himself. "Just because you rigged my radio doesn't mean you put a surveillance system in here...Er, that shouldn't be too far removed from your technical capabilities, I suppose."

She laughed with a sense of knowing something. "All right, whatever you say! But you do look *pretty nice* in a body shirt, wouldn't you say so yourself? Oooo, what's that about seizing that 'big' opportunity? I think I see somethin' big...right...*now*."

Tsumisu looked down and shuddered at her accurate observation. All that dirty talk got him *activated*. "Look, I won't ask how you installed your equipment in here so *silently*—"

"*Scared* now, aren't ya?"

"*No*!" he proudly declared but soon slowly exhaled, only to speak in a whisper. "...yes."

"Well, all right then!" Nataliya replied in unbelievable cheeriness. "See you *soon*, Tsumisu! Eh heh heh heh..."

"A-all right!" he cautiously replied.

"*OK*!"

"Yeeaaah..."

Tsumisu hung up the phone. He tried not to become paranoid but decided to take his clothes elsewhere to change; he never knew where a camera might be now.

After dressing in a dark closet and returning to the kitchen, Tsumisu proceeded to stuff another tart into his mouth, only to get the incredibly unnerving sensation of being *watched*. See, there's a difference between camera lenses and actual eyeballs—sweet mercy, to the Sonzai commander's utter horror, *every* poster and *every* framed symbol representing the Sonzai's creed was holographically overlaid with an intently observing *Nataliya*. Nothing but her face showed, and she grinned with simmering intent to subdue. Tsumisu was surrounded...

"Um," he began, accidentally knocking his keys over because of the jitters. "Damn it! Whuh, is-isn't this illegal?"

"A heh," the greater than twenty projected Nataliya's simultaneously snickered. "A heh heh...you only have *seven minutes...*"

Tsumisu quickly retrieved his keys and bolted out of the apartment, shutting the door behind him amid Nataliya's vocally layered sinister cackling.

"Ya better *hurry up*!" she called. "Time's a-wastin'! Mwahahaaa! I'm coming for *you*, Tsu-*mi*-suuu!"

"I *really* wish I could set this place on fire and start over again," he mildly jested, thinking of ways to avoid prosecution for arson. Sighing afterward, Tsumisu gained enough courage to press forward. "That's right, dude," he thought aloud, "just pretend she's not in your head..."

A few people passed Tsumisu by as he went to his motorcycle. Did...one of them look very similar to the Little Lady? No, that was just *crazy* talk. Still, rather than use foot-engaged boosters, Tsumisu figured not using his energy to travel would limit the chances of Nataliya tracking him…*if* she really was tracking him.

Tsumisu took off and headed for Shujin's—not exactly feeling the worst was to come, but something wasn't right altogether. Why he felt he needed to stay sharp wasn't a question of his judgment but instinct. Nataliya wasn't just any scientist; she was probably the best between two civilizations. There was *something else* about her that made for cautious skepticism.

If she likes me, it's only because I'm a big experimental project in her head, he thought, *but I'm no lab rat for anybody. Still, I can't be mean to her and then feel bad in the morning…I curse my sensitivity sometimes.*

He pulled up to a flower stand with a merchant busily watering his display. Tsumisu asked for certain flower seeds and bulbs, and sure enough, the man had the exact ones—blue hydrangea, sunflower, calla lilies, tulips, and daylilies. Decision made, he handed the merchant fifteen hundred yen and thanked him, continuing toward Shujin's house.

Twenty minutes later (yes, he was keeping time), Tsumisu arrived at the turn to get to the driveway but decided to cut the engine and roll the motorcycle just a little bit up the driveway and out of sight; it was worth evading Nataliya because he needed to speak with Shujin first. Taking a path through the woods and reaching the garden, he spotted Shujin yet again at work and approached.

"You'd think stuff wouldn't sprout in the snow," he said while looking at the clouds.

"Oh, h-hey, Tsumisu! When'd you get here?" Shujin was surprised to see him. "Did you get my message?"

"Yeeeaaah, I got it." He sighed, recalling the grotesque beginning to his day. "Thing was, Little Lady pushed redial and started an…*interesting* conversation. I asked to speak with you, but she took the opportunity to let you know 'later.'"

Shujin shrugged. "Whenever that was, 'cause she hasn't told me anything about that. Wonder why?"

"Obviously hiding something…rather, planning something. Say, what was that you wanted to tell me before I got over here?"

Shujin calmly shoved his aerator into the ground. "OK, well…" He sighed, looking troubled. "First off, I *hate* to say you told me so, but you did."

"Tetyana attacked you, didn't she?" Tsumisu asked. "All that Mark of Evelyn strength struck *notes*, dude! You didn't check your environment?"

"Man, I-I checked over and over!" Shujin exclaimed. "Apparently, she was just waiting for me to finish. Next thing I know, her boobs are on my face…again."

"Naked?"

"Do I have to be specific?"

Tsumisu sympathetically patted his shoulder. "Continue, my friend," he encouraged.

Shujin stood in a slump. "I think I slept like four good hours after she and Suzuka duked it out…*again*. In my room."

"Consider me impressed." Tsumisu nodded in appreciation. "Those ladies are ripped *and* hormonal nuclear power plants. *Did* she get anything? Did the battle involve sacrificing your helpless body?"

"Uugggh, c'mon, Tsumisu! That's *not* what I'm talking about!" Shujin shook his head in disbelief. "I swear, where does your brain go sometimes?"

"Public works sewer! So that's a no?"

"*No.* Nothing happened, thank God…"

Tsumisu chuckled. "Suzuka didn't try anything? She hides her intentions, man. I'm just saying…"

"OK, you're not wrong. Sure, she 'saved' me, but I got the feeling Suzuka wanted to initiate the 'unification.'" Shujin quoted, using his fingers. "And Tetyana beat her to the opportunity. Is it fair to say I'm not ready for this yet?"

"There's no popular fitness program on the market that could train you, so…" Tsumisu shrugged. "Either you install several locks and chains on your door, or *move*."

"That advice doesn't help me, dude," Shujin said with irritation.

"I can help you install the locks." He grinned. "Take it or leave it, sir!"

"You know, I should just let you go inside and figure things out on your own." Shujin's tone was of deep conviction. "See how *you* like it for once!"

"*Fine,* man, I'm sorry, OK? That ordeal must've been tough because I'm pretty sure the atmosphere is slightly awkward between the three of you." Tsumisu rubbed the back of his neck. "All right, *really* awkward."

"Can you or *can't* you provide assistance with this obvious situation today? At *least* for today, man?"

"Sure, I'll do it."

Shujin twisted his mouth in doubt. "I need some collateral on those words—"

"Dude, what *else* happened?" Tsumisu dropped his arms in a charade of exasperation. "Is there good news, or have you resorted to the freezing-cold garden to contemplate your life?"

"Don't judge me; it's my workout for the day," Shujin muttered defensively. "But yeah, Nataliya's made herself at home—took up the last guest room downstairs."

"Oh well, that's nice. You *really* needed another hot female boarding up—*kidding*." He cleared his throat. "Keep going; I won't say anything else. Except that she didn't have any luggage, soooo…"

"Dude, I'm not sure *what* Nataliya is made of, but apparently, she's a master at dimension manipulation." Shujin's expression shifted to confusion. "When you slide the room door open, you *immediately* step inside this crazy facility located on another planet!"

"Whaaaaat?" Tsumisu replied, his voice in a high pitch. "Like a bad Star Trek episode? Are there rocks and smokestacks of different colors?"

"H-ha, right? That was my first thought! But no, dude, she gave everybody a 'tour,' saying there are multiple laboratories she constructed over several centuries—totally hidden from the imperial government too!" Shujin rubbed his chin as he recollected. "From massive greenhouses to ocean habitats, power plants. You name it; she's got it."

"Essentially, Little Lady's got the earth's equivalent in space all to herself is what you're saying?" His expression rose in astonishment as he whistled. "That's a bad woman. No wonder Taras wanted to keep her around..."

"Yeah, that much is obvious," Shujin agreed. "Anyway, I got a doctor's checkup from her—totally what you'd expect with the basics. And with that, Nataliya found out I'm half-Devonian, half-Ordovician!"

"Dude!" Tsumisu was giggling inside. "I *knew* you were a freakin' alien! I knew it! Totally makes sense!"

"Aw, c'mon, man! What's *that* supposed to mean?" Shujin laughed.

"Coming back from the dead isn't an obvious clue? Let alone being the world's most socially awkward man? I'm surprised you don't have *beady* black eyes and slimy green skin!"

"You watched Star Trek last night, didn't you?"

Tsumisu sighed in humored relief. "There's truth in fiction, my friend," he said, as Shujin swiped his consoling hand away. "Nevertheless, I'm absolutely certain your origins carry a significant amount of weight."

"Yeah, that's what Suzuka mentioned." Shujin nodded, still turning over the ramifications. "Don't get me wrong; it's still great news to know 'that' part of me, and of course, my dad and grandma are still the people I know...but I guess it's the uncertainty behind what lies ahead. Know what I mean?"

"Yep, that's natural, man. Just know that Evelyn's got a higher purpose for you...and she's smoking hot *too,* if I might add—"

"Stop that."

"Stopping."

"I've got some bad-ish news though," Shujin began, his tone foreboding. "And yeah, it's regarding why I called you earlier."

"Uh-oh." Tsumisu was rubbing his hands. "Let's hear it."

"Nataliya...she's planning something against you. I dunno what it is. But she went all *vampire* mode on me when she asked about where you were." Shujin shuddered in recollection. "I-I still don't know how to feel about that moment."

Tsumisu raised an eyebrow. "What?" he asked, a bigger picture painted in his head now. "Was she just messing with you?"

"No!" Shujin made himself clear. "*No.* Nataliya was all like, 'Breakfast is served,' and some other creepy stuff! I mean, she was *stupid* nice to me, but I get the feeling you're not gonna be so lucky!"

"Breakfast? Oh hell naw!" Tsumisu shook his finger. "Dude, I am *not* going in your house. Not going!"

"I know, but I'm just worried that you'll get sympathetic again and change your mind after saying that to her face." He shrugged with a wince. "You *always* do that. Admit it."

"Shut up with your truthfulness." Tsumisu pointed at him. "That's why I'm going to have you tell her I'm not going inside *for* me."

"What?" Shujin was stunned. "You can't do it by yourself? C'mon! Don't do me like that, Tsumisu! I've been through enough already!"

"Yeah, I know, man." He plopped down in the snow. "It's close to lunchtime too, and over the phone, I said I was gonna eat something before I came over. The little lady said that by the time I got here, lunch would be ready." He exhaled, facing internal indecision again. "I hate to break my word…"

"Oh no," Shujin said, fearing the worst. "You made a promise?"

"Are you crazy? Hell *no,* I didn't make a promise," Tsumisu scoffed, almost sounding offended. "I might as well sign my *balls* over to her. So what should I do? Just go inside and refuse?"

"That's up to you. I mean, she's obviously waiting right now, and I'm not sure if she knows you're here…?"

"She doesn't." He quickly shook his head, clearly unsure. "Uhhh, at least I *hope* she doesn't. I came on my bike, but it's parked at the far end of the drive. Oh yeah, I got the flowers too."

"Hey, great!" Shujin grinned as Tsumisu handed them to him. "I got a lot of pots around the shed we could use, and after that, we can set them inside on the windowsill."

"Yeah, can't wait for that." Tsumisu rose up with a little sigh. "Well…here goes. You might as well come with me since lunch is ready, I'd imagine."

"All right." Shujin built up his courage once again. "I'm about done anyway. If you need any backup, just ask."

"I'll be fine, probably." He patted his friend's shoulder. "If there's anything to negotiate, I've got it covered."

CHAPTER ELEVEN

They continued to converse as they entered the house. Tsumisu kicked his boots off and threw his jacket over his shoulder, while Shujin put his shoes away and headed toward the bathroom.

"W-wait! You're gonna leave me alone?" Tsumisu sounded afraid.

Shujin looked around. "What's the worst that can happen in five minutes?"

"Ha, need I *remind* you what I accomplished in five minutes, sir?"

"I mean, well..." He shrugged. "Sorry, dude! When nature calls, it can't leave a voice message."

"Yeah, don't hold it in; that'll cause damage." He mashed his lips together in thought, a slight frown coming across his face. Tsumisu tried plotting some solutions for his worst-case-scenarios. "You think I'll make it if I stand still?"

Shujin grinned. "Good luck with that."

Defeating his reluctance to remain inside, Tsumisu strode into the living room and encountered Arlette and Suzuka watching television.

"Hey, Tsumisu! Yay-haaay!" Arlette greeted him happily and jumped from her seat to hug him tightly. "Oh my gosh! I didn't know you were coming today!" She was blushing, her eyes dancing with excitement. "Yaaay, Tsumissuu!"

"H-hey, Arlette! Watch out now!" He grinned and hugged her back, surprised as he had to brace himself. "I thought you went back to base, but Shujin told me what happened."

"Yeah, I didn't have enough energy in my ship to make it there, so I just came back! Hee-hee!"

Perpetually adorable as she was, Tsumisu had a burning suspicion that *something* about Arlette's quick attachment behavior stemmed from some past event or series of trials in dealing with said event. Well, after the recent emotional bludgeoning *each* lady endured surrounding the Taras ordeal, the Sonzai commander decided it was best to submerge the notion to ask the lieutenant about some potentially disturbing history, even if the opportunity for such an inquiry presented itself weeks from now.

Besides, if a lady wanted to reveal *anything* about her past, she'd make an unambiguous effort in doing so. Whoa, where did *this* train of thought stem from? Right, the inadvertent, sentimental teachings of Shujin-ism. *Oh, you should probably respond to Arlette, given the magnitude of her confused stare, sir.*

"Sometimes the best course of action when in doubt is to make the first decision on impulse," he said. "But uh, you're OK, right?"

"Yes! *Yeah*! Even *better* now!" Arlette beamed sincerely. "Ha, wow, Tsumisu, you're so *warm*…"

Tsumisu nodded in the affirmative, trying to resist any physical reaction to her apparently subconscious rubbing against him. "Ahrm, yeah, gotta…stay warm-blooded. Say uh, you wanna let me go now?"

"*Oh*!" She blushed again. "Sorry! I didn't notice!"

"Nah, it's cool with those big blue eyes of yours." He gently rubbed her shoulder, grateful to detect her spiritual condition lift. "And how are *you* doing, Princess Suzuka?" Tsumisu inquired kindly, turning to her. "Get some rest, my fellow warrior?"

Suzuka smiled humbly, taking enjoyment in his light nature. "I am fine, Mr. Tsumisu. Thank you for asking. How do you fare today?"

Granted, she was so *freakin'* polite with clearly conditioned royal mannerisms, Tsumisu found it beyond amazing that Suzuka, crown princess of the Devonian Empire, had such fierceness. Maybe it assisted her greatly during many missions of conquest. Well, it was as he had openly professed to everyone the night before: every attribute a woman might or might not possess was to be recognized and appreciated, not held as blameworthiness toward her *or* used against her. Uh, wait, did Tsumisu say *all* of that, or was that just how he felt about the matter? Regardless, didn't everyone have a hidden talent?

Gosh, what was with this train of *thinking* all of a sudden? Tsumisu swore on all that was good in the world to confront Shujin with a stern handshake of gratitude—after the man washed his hands.

"Oh, I couldn't complain too much even if I wanted to. For example," he replied, pausing momentarily, "I did *not* wake up sore! Imagine that!"

The princess was genuinely surprised. "After such an event, that is truly remarkable!" she said. "Aren't you the least bit fatigued?"

"Nah. Say you feel 'OK' after working hard or something, but it's *misleading* because when you wake up the next morning, you're all like, 'Uughh, *God*, what did I do?' Right?"

She smiled with pleasant insight. "Yes, that is precisely it. I suppose Ms. Nataliya's assessment stands?"

He nearly flinched at the mention of her name. "Seems it does! Thanks for asking too, Suzuka. Well uh, I guess Tetyana is upstairs messing with Shujin since I don't see her around…"

Suzuka frowned in sudden realization. "Oh, she had better *not* be!"

"Now, calm down. I was only making an assumption. Oh *right*, I wanted to ask you, where's uh..." He bent down and whispered, "the Little Lady located at the moment?"

"Perhaps she's still in her laboratory," she replied, wondering why he was being discreet. "Is something the matter?"

"Nope! That's all I needed to know. Thanks, Suzuka, you're a perpetual life-saver. Dahlia is about done with lunch?" Tsumisu smiled inconspicuously.

She snapped her fingers. "Thank you for reminding me, for I need to help set the table. I'm so silly being drawn into this show I somehow forgot."

Tsumisu looked at the television screen in reproach. "What is this, a soap opera?"

"Yep!" Arlette happily answered. "This guy named Itaki is dating a girl he just met over the Internet, but he's cheating on poor Mayume—"

"I was just wondering if it was a soap opera, dear." He chuckled.

"Ugh, why don't you ever sit down?" Arlette asked in quite the serious tone, cheeks slightly puffed. "Every time I see you, you're *always* standing!"

Tsumisu, needless to say, was a little surprised to hear her concern. "It...bothers you that much?"

"Um..." She thought for a moment, demeanor immediately allaying. "Yes! Yes, it does! Here, sit by me and watch!"

He grinned in acceptance, throwing his hands up. "Why the hell not? All right, Arlette. Maybe it'll take my mind off some stuff."

"Yaaay!" the lieutenant was beyond elated. "You'll enjoy it! I promise, Tsumisu!"

They sat for a minute or two as Tsumisu observed, while Arlette was very into the program.

"Did you *see* that?" she exclaimed in her storytelling tone. "How could Amidako do that to her?"

"Is, uh…Amidako the bad guy?" Tsumisu inquired, detecting her depth of engrossment.

"No, see, he's an accountant at a wealthy bank."

"Same thing, they're all criminals in there," he joked. "But go on, I'm listening, Arlette."

She smiled in return. "Well, in *one* episode, he was on trial for money laundering but wasn't convicted because his lawyer was a friend of one of the jurors. I really didn't like that episode, because he should've gone to *jail* for that."

Tsumisu folded his arms as he sat back in the couch. "Since he did that crap, you would think Ama-something would have a tough time finding a steady lady, right?"

Arlette snapped her fingers. "I thought the same thing! But see, his girlfriend's name is Neio, and she was his high school sweetheart—"

"Well, *well*! When did *you* make it over here, 'Mr. Tsumisu'?" Nataliya made her entrance into the living room suddenly with hands on her hips. "A heh heh…heh…"

Fight-or-flight response kicking in, Tsumisu quickly rose to his feet and stood at the other end of the couch.

"Hold that thought, Arlette! A-and the very moment I realized my mind wasn't under a state of emergency anymore, Little Lady!" he replied. "That's the, uh…*precise* moment, I believe!"

Nataliya's expression was stunned, her mouth open in expressiveness. "Why *ever* would that happen?" she replied, slowly walking in his direction. "You're a pretty level-headed guy; can't get shaken up by little things, right? You proved that *yesterday*!"

Tsumisu strolled around the couch, keeping his distance. "Sometimes even the *little* things, *Little* Lady, can turn into bigger ones! So uh, best to stay on guard all the time."

"Yeeah, I guess!" Nataliya shrugged and pretended not to follow, though she maintained her pace with him. "But hey! Can't you, at the same time, take things *too* seriously and blow it out of proportion? Reaching a *misunderstanding* on occasion, ya know?"

Arlette was ducking and dodging around them to continue watching the program.

"Say that's, uh, very possible!" Tsumisu replied with an instructive finger, wondering how long she was going to keep this up. "Yet you have to be aware enough to distinguish what's worth paying attention to and what's being overanalyzed to the point of disregard…such that you balance those proportions."

Nataliya shuddered as she grew an unbelievably sly grin. "Oooooo! Mr. Tsumisu, I take *enjoyment* in the way you think. You like talking to me like that? Full of *reason* and *logic*? C'mere! Say it closer to me, why don't ya?"

"Ha ha! *No.* No, Little Lady, not if I wanna die…I mean, get trapped…I mean, *damn it*!"

Tsumisu clenched his eyes, painfully aware that his nerves were slowly getting the better of him…and realizing he had returned to his seat. Was that *his* doing?

"Aww, you don't wanna 'talk' to me anymore?" Nataliya stood beside him, leaning against the armrest. "Maybe I could learn a thing or two from you, hmm?"

"I could send you a lesson by FedEx." He nodded affirmatively, sweat beading on his brow. "Probably would be *safer* that way too."

Her eyebrows flinched. "Oh? But you *realize* that depends on what you mean by 'safe,' Mr. Tsumisu," she said, whispering in his ear. "And I'm *harmless…*"

"*Oh*-kay, I'm hot for teacher!" Tsumisu exclaimed in a brief moment of delirium. "Uuhhh, is lunch ready yet?"

Fortunately for Tsumisu, Dahlia came out of the kitchen with her sister.

"Certainly, Mr. Tsumisu," Suzuka responded, setting out the food. "Has Prince Shujin returned?"

"He hasn't, and I'm going to check on him *right* this minute! Everybody just wait here," Tsumisu replied and hurried to the stairs. "Gives me an excuse to leave, 'cause I wasn't ready for that shit…"

"I only asked if Shujin returned," Suzuka remarked, watching the Sonzai commander scurry away. "That's odd of him to leave so quickly."

"Well, don't look at me!" Nataliya innocently smiled. "He and Shujin have been acting weird lately; perhaps it's a side effect of their powers?"

"Side effect?" asked Arlette, hands on her cheeks as she looked at the genius curiously. "Like that sleep medicine I've been hearing about that gives you nightmares? Or makes you suicidal!"

"Yeah, something like that," Nataliya replied, tapping her foot and carefully observing Tsumisu's track. "Only this time, this side effect clouds your judgment!"

Meanwhile upstairs, Tsumisu stumbled on the bathroom he believed Shujin was still using. Unfortunately, the door was carelessly left open, the light remained on, and the faucet was running.

"He must've escaped like I told him to." He grinned. "Shujin! You up here, dude?"

"Shh!" he said from around a corner. "Tetyana came in while I was trying to wash my hands, and I just freaked out! Gosh, she's trying to find me, but I just feel so nervous I can't *think*."

"Ha, you look funny hiding behind there, but I won't give you away. Although you can't stay there forever 'cause lunch is ready. Um…" Tsumisu mashed his lips together, realizing he should provide moral support. "You'll get over it?"

Shujin sighed and approached. "Hopefully. But maybe I'm hungry…hungry enough to come out into the open…"

"Like that *one* gazelle leaping into that ridiculously long grass?"

"Dude, those shows." Shujin shook his head in recollection. "Let me tell you, there's so much knowledge you can gain from watching like…black widow spiders."

"True b-but don't think about it too much." Tsumisu patted his shoulder. "Your brain burning on nothing will make a situation worse than it already is…like mine!"

Shujin patted his face as if he were a washed-up boxer. "All right, let's go get some lunch. I feel bad running away now, you know? I feel guilty."

"Tetyana is a big girl; she'll be fine…but she *will* ask why you ran. But don't tell her *why*, just cover your ass with a bunch of excuses—which I know you're not good at."

Shujin looked at him in surprise. "I can't just lie to her, man; I'd feel even guiltier."

"Yeah, yeah, I know. I was kidding anyway." Tsumisu stuffed his hands into his pockets, letting a moment pass. "Little Lady is downstairs, by the way…"

"She's downstairs…and *you're not* in her lab? Hmm…"

Tsumisu remembered her words floating in his ear. "Not *yet*, I'll be…"

So the two (clueless) gentlemen traversed downstairs and into the living room, where everyone was at the table, sitting on comfortable cushions—Dahlia at the facing end, Suzuka to her left, and an empty seat. Tetyana was next with Arlette on her left and Nataliya on the other side with another empty seat to her right, which would put said seat between her and Arlette.

"All right, you sit with Nataliya," said Shujin, "for obvious reasons."

"I don't feel any more comfortable than you, dude," Tsumisu replied calmly. "But I wasn't tortured last night, so yeah, I gotta work on my sentimentalism…which I learn from you. How odd."

"Shujin! Where were you?" asked Tetyana, her expression was covered in worry. "You ran out of the bathroom, and afterward I didn't see you. What happened?"

"Uhm I-uh-well—" he stuttered while taking his seat between her and Suzuka. "You just kinda freaked me out. Sorry about that."

"OK, just making sure nothing was wrong, you know? Aww, poor baby."

Tsumisu casually took his seat. "Man, this food looks good. I won't even ask what it is because Dahlia is just that friggin' *awesome*." He grinned eagerly.

"Hey, thanks, Mr. Tsumisu!" She giggled happily. "I was hoping you'd come by today!"

"That makes *two* of us, Dahlia!" Nataliya cheerily responded and instantly eyeballed the Sonzai commander. "Sooooo, Tsumisu!"

"Oh noooo, Little Lady!" he joked in reply.

"Plan on doing anything in particular today?"

"I mean, I was gonna take out the recycling…in Mongolia?" Tsumisu forced a smile, but it was truly a grimace. "So I gotta head back in a little bit to take care of that business. Woo, save the planet!"

"Woo!" Shujin followed up in meager support. "The power is ours!"

"It is *definitely*…ours." Tsumisu nodded in all seriousness.

"Hmm, I see." Nataliya took a bite of her food, casually wiping her mouth afterward, confirming his *habitually* poor lying. "Could you squeeze in a little time to pay me a visit in the lab?"

He chuckled. "What? You just wanted me to *look* at it? 'Cause I can do that…looking."

"Actually…" She wasn't one to stand for being denied. "I wanted to look at *you*!"

Shujin choked on his food but managed to swallow anyway.

"L-look at me?" Tsumisu smiled warmly. "Well hey, you're… uh…looking at me right *now*, Little Lady! And if you want, I could just take a picture—"

"Mmmmm, nope! I don't think so."

"Yeeeah…"

Nataliya gasped in sudden realization. “You seem *tense*, Mr. Tsumisu. I wonder why?”

Shujin coughed twice.

“Are you all right, Prince Shujin?” asked Suzuka, lightly patting his back.

He nodded quickly and continued eating.

Nataliya looked at him and then turned to Tsumisu again. “Did he tell you something?”

“Aannnnd it just doesn’t look like she’d *do* anything.” Tsumisu grinned at her. “Probably wouldn’t hurt a fly and is just as harmless as, oh, saaay…Tetyana on a good day. What’re your good days like?”

The mercenary smirked. “Blood and vengeance, big guy. Thought I told you that yesterday,” she replied.

“Could’ve asked *me*, Mr. Tsumisu,” Nataliya remarked. “I created Tetyana, after all.”

He was about to spill into laughter. “Maybe Little Lady is the one who came up with sliced bread too!” His voice broke, yet he kept eating. “I’m good.”

Arlette laughed. “You’re funny, Tsumisu! Why don’t you make a joke about me?”

Tetyana shook her head. “I think he picks his targets, and Nataliya is the one for the week. Ain’t I right?”

“You catch on quick, girl, and I like that about you!” Tsumisu pointed at her enthusiastically. “However, and if I may, it’s just innocent fun.”

“You crack jokes about yourself sometimes,” Shujin remarked kindly. “It’s a wonder you don’t write comics.”

“*Innocent* fun, you say…” Nataliya muttered with a sly grin.

“Uh, excuse me, ladies and gentlemen in the crowd.” Tsumisu looked directly at Nataliya, as she was clearly plotting in the back of her mind. “Please ignore the black bars at the top and bottom of your screen.”

"But I *can't*, Mr. Tsumisu. After all, it's just *innocent* fun, right? Ooooo!" Nataliya shuddered as she narrowed her eyes. "This is fun for me *too*, ya know."

He exhaled heavily, wiping a hand over his face. "OK. W-what are you getting at, Little Lady?"

"*Ha*!" she exclaimed, getting in his face. "What's your last name?"

"D-d-don't try and confuse me 'cause you do that a whole lot!" Tsumisu replied with unusual desperation, and he grabbed a chicken spring roll. "Besides, what's *your* last name?"

"Oh?" Nataliya flicked her eyebrows again. "Well, I'll tell you *mine* if you tell me *yours*."

"Hmm, come to think of it, even I don't remember," Tetyana commented, witnessing the very interesting scene between the two. "But what *is* your last name, big guy? Hell, I'm curious too!"

Shujin grew a wide, none-too-suspecting smile. "Could've sworn I told you before, Tetyana!" he said. "It's Maruwaka!"

Tsumisu slapped his forehead. "Thanks, man! Now Little Lady's gonna try and pull me up in her infinite database," he groaned. "Fudge-nuts on a stick."

"Oh…" Shujin winced. "My bad?"

"Hee-hee!" Nataliya snickered. "Thank you, Shujin. Now we'll see if you've got something to hide or *not*, Mr. Maruwaka!"

"Yeeeaaah, that's not my real last name." Tsumisu smiled knowingly. "We were only kidding! But we exposed what you were gonna do, see?"

She gasped deeply. "You big meanie! Ooohh! You big fat meanie!" she cried, nudging him in the side.

"Ow! Ohh! Ow!" Tsumisu reacted, rolling backward and stumbling around to collapse on the floor. "Ow…ouch…wow! You wouldn't think something so *short* could do that!"

"Dude, really?" said Shujin, shaking his head. "Isn't that the routine that got you kicked out—"

"Shh! Shut up! Ow!" Tsumisu turned onto his side, squirming around in a circle. "Oh *Lord*! What unholy, sadistic madness is this?"

Dahlia giggled, fully entertained. "Are you gonna be OK, Mr. Tsumisu?" she asked.

"Nah!" he wheezed. "That was a liver shot…li-*ver*. I needed that!"

Suzuka politely laughed. "What's gotten into him today?" she began. "Elevated blood sugar, Ms. Nataliya?"

"Pfft, *and* a bad case of 'rub some dirt on it,'" Nataliya replied dismissively, smirking. "Hey! That was a latent-effect attack, so you're gonna feel an electric shock in a second!"

"Well, you heard the lady," Tsumisu muttered, lying on his stomach now. "The Ordovician Fist of Shortness…agh! It's in my… *pancreas…*"

"Oh no! Tsumisu!" Arlette began to grow concerned. "It'll be over soon!"

Tetyana laughed with hilarity while Tsumisu struggled to reach the table, stretching a hand out in "desperation."

"Not…going to…*make it…*" he said, falling still.

Tetyana fell backward in laughter. "Man, that looked so real! Oh my gosh! Did everybody see that?"

"Yeah, unfortunately," Shujin jokingly commented. "You're gonna vomit if you keep that up, man. And you'll be cleaning it up too!"

"All right, all right!" Tsumisu sat up and went back to the table to mild applause. Then his expression became instantly struck with insight. "Wait! Wasn't that my first hit-on by a lady?" he asked, turning to Shujin in laughter. "Man, we absolutely *suck*!"

He laughed as well. "Whoa! You're right! At least it *finally* happened, huh?" He threw up his arms in exclamation. "Hey, when push comes to shove, you gotta take what you can get!"

"Yeah, I know!" Tsumisu patted his left side. "Oh snap, life sometimes…"

Suzuka smiled, humored. "I wouldn't have believed it if you two hadn't said it yourselves!" she remarked.

"What?" cried Tetyana. "Are you kidding me, babe?" She shook her head and muttered. "Pshh, don't let *me* catch you in a dark alley somewhere…"

"Uhm, well, uh," Shujin stuttered, realizing there may have been some drawbacks to their outburst of reality. "I mean, the absence of receiving hit-ons isn't for a lack of trying. Wait, no."

"Such *handsome* boys too," Nataliya immediately remarked. "I guess girls around here are blind as bats!"

Arlette giggled. "Aren't they cute?" she said. "We must be lucky to meet two at one time!"

Tsumisu looked at Shujin, concerned. "Lucky, yeah, but the *weather* is nice *too,* right? Cold but tolerable at the same time!" He made his voice like a cheesy weatherman's. "So *get* on out there an' enjoy it!"

"Y-yeah!" Shujin joined in on his friend's diversion. "You could wear shorts, I guess?"

Tetyana grabbed hold of Shujin. "Aww, don't be shy, Shujin! I could be your first kiss, you know—"

"Release him!" Suzuka immediately protested and took hold of Shujin. "He will not bear the first kiss from you, Tetyana!"

Shujin was once again physically helpless. "Hey now, girls, cut that out! Just think about the weather!"

Arlette had chopsticks in her mouth as she watched, captivated. "Wow, this looks like when Takame found Numo with Ishi!"

Also witnessing the scene, Tsumisu nodded in agreement. "Something tells me you're not the *only* one influenced by such programming, Arlette."

"Um, Big Sister, I think you're hurting him," said Dahlia, trying to get her attention.

"Well, what if he *does* want it from me first?" said Tetyana, tugging him one way. "You don't know that, do ya?"

"Waah!" Shujin hollered, not really knowing how to remove himself from this all-too-familiar situation. "Girls, wait a second!"

"Fate has already decided, Tetyana! You cannot change that!" Suzuka retaliated and pulled him the other way.

"Waaahhh! Let's talk this *over*!"

"Ha! I'm glad you can't do *that* to me," Tsumisu remarked to Nataliya.

Her expression lit up in unadulterated delight. "Are you now?" she asked.

"Yup!" he brightly confirmed. "See, you being inextricably *vertically challenged* takes away that advantage...Now, uhhh, don't let me stimulate any ideas."

"*My*, Mr. Tsumisu, shall you risk underestimating the femme fatale of science? I have my *ways*," Nataliya replied with a clever smile. "Heh, wanna see?"

"Not sure if I do!" *That's right, dude; reject any and all bizarre offers. You're awake now.* "As a matter of fact, I'm certain I don't. Because *if* I do...or did, what will happen?"

"C'mon! Let's see those science-y skills, Nataliya!" Arlette cheered her on. "Yay! I'm sure you can nab him in no time!"

Tsumisu's cardiovascular system seized up.

"Arlette, that is really not helping, yet I *adore* your encouragement slash positive reinforcement!" he complimented her rapidly.

"Aww, you're such a *sweetie*!" Arlette said with twinkling eyes. "So does that mean I can help Nataliya nab you too?" She readily cracked her knuckles. "You might as well stand *still*, Tsumisu!"

The Sonzai commander shuddered in fright, still having that blood-circulation problem, and quickly glanced at the supremely eager scientist and then back to the lieutenant.

"Uuhhh, I-I regret to inform you, Arlette, that *this* is beyond capable of—"

"How serendipitous!" Nataliya exclaimed excitedly, wearing an innocent smile. "A heh, *'this'* can take *all* the help 'it' can get! I heard about your wrestling reputation, Lieutenant!"

"Yep! First place, each and every time!" Arlette stated proudly. "And I've *always* wanted to use my winning technique on him, but he *always* gets away—right under my nose!"

She smirked, eyebrow raised. "Case in point?"

"Hm? *Hey*! Tsumisu!" Arlette pounded her fists on her yoga pants. "Where are you going? Get back here, mister!"

"Errr," he began with uncertainty. "Provide me a moment while you ladies work that conversation out?"

Indeed, removing himself from his precarious situation, Tsumisu excused himself to the other side of the table, dragging Shujin out of *his* predicament.

"Oh my gosh!" Arlette said, flustered. "You see how Tsumisu is a sneaky one?"

"Yup!" Nataliya nodded in agreement, briefly typing some information into her now summoned computer. "Data is *duly* registered! Eh heh heh heh…but he ain't sneaky *enough*."

"All of that motion could mess with his *equilibrium*, ladies," Tsumisu calmly instructed, easily assisting his friend. "You have to be careful about that."

"And I need what I have left," Shujin murmured, disoriented. "*Thanks*, sir."

"Hey! Why'd you do that, big guy?" Tetyana cried in frustration. "I almost had him! Nataliya was right—you *are* mean!"

"Noooo, mean is doing *this*!" He bent down, picked Tetyana up, and put her over his shoulder—appreciating her flare-cut slacks. "Right?"

She instantly began flailing her arms and legs around. "Lemme go! Put me down!" she cried, the jingle of her bracelets furious. "Shujin, tell him to stop!"

Shujin, regaining said equilibrium, had an amused grin on his face. "Dude, what're you doing?"

"Saving your ass—sorry I said that, Dahlia! I'll bake you cookies!" Tsumisu *instantly* turned to her in apology, comically avoiding Tetyana's knees, yet he was inadvertently smacked in the face. "S-stop!"

"No! *You* stop!" Tetyana demanded, purposely smacking him.

"Ow!"

Enjoying the elevated degree of entertaining activity, Dahlia only smiled. "It's OK, Mr. Tsumisu! I'm learning to ignore 'those' words!" she replied honestly.

"Whew!" Tsumisu felt wholly relieved. "Aaaand, Suzuka? Give Shujin some air please, dear?"

"Oh, very well then." The princess pouted, folding her arms. "I suppose it is the 'right' thing to do."

"Hey, big guy, put me down, please?" Tetyana asked nicely. "I won't do anything to Shujin, I promise! Just a tiny misunderstanding!" She put on an incredibly innocent face.

Tsumisu patted her back like a drum. "Oh, I know you *will* later on, Tetyana. I'm just proving a point." He then set her down. "I forgot to bring you that sake too, and *now* I owe you—damn it."

"Ha! Accept it, dude!" Tetyana pointed victoriously, punching him in the chest for vengeance. "That's *three* bottles now!"

He exhaled in defeat. "*Accepted…*"

Arlette smiled in ecstatic anticipation. "That looked like fun! Can you or Shujin pick *me* up next?"

Shujin was still on the floor. "No, sorry, Arlette. My back still hurts," he grunted, taking in a sharp breath. "I'm not sure how Tsumisu keeps this up!"

"I told you already, man." Tsumisu instantly collected himself, sat down, and took a bite of food. "Fortified muffins *every* morning. Now, uh, where was I, if I was?"

"Mmmm, where *were* you if you *were*?" Nataliya playfully remarked, a hand placed underneath her chin as she watched him. "So many curiosities abound in the universe…"

Tsumisu smiled, barely able to swallow his food, and shook a finger at her. "You know? I get the feeling you're trying to start *something*, but somehow, *someway*, I'm not allowing you to."

"Me?" Nataliya sat erect in her seat, hand on her hip. "Well, look who's talking here! I'm not the one picking on somebody because of her height in 'innocent fun,' as ya put it. And ya keep doing it at that!"

He gasped as he leaned away, faking his surprise. "Me? Do that to lil' ol' you?"

"Yeah, you did!" She stuck her bottom lip out. "I think you like me because you keep picking on me!"

"You *do* like Nataliya, Mr. Tsumisu!" Dahlia matter-of-factly pointed out. "I can at least see that much!"

"But, uh, what *kind* of like?" Tetyana further implied, testing Dahlia's knowledge. "There's differences, you know, little Dahlia!" Her smile was telling.

"Um, I'm not sure what you're saying, Tetyana," Dahlia replied, confused. "Like the people on the TV shows?"

Suzuka cleared her throat politely. "That's quite enough of those programs for you, Dahlia. I shall have no more *influence*"—she shot a sharp glance at Tetyana—"on my sister until she has reached the appropriate age."

Arlette blinked pretty much a thousand times. "You mean… boyfriend/girlfriend like?"

"Oh hoooo, further than *that* too! Ha ha ha!" Tetyana continued to get Suzuka's goat. "She's gotta learn, Princess! What do ya want? It's a parta life!"

Suddenly Shujin was wiping his forehead with a towel. "For once, I have to agree, Tetyana—a part of life. Dude! Wait…why are we answering?"

Tsumisu rolled ninja-style backward from his cushion, scurrying over to his comrade. "What? You mean a danger-zone-type situation?" He knelt beside him as if they were behind enemy lines.

"Over *here*!" Shujin intensely whispered as they conversed in the living room. "You got any painkillers? Like headache meds?"

"Uh…" Tsumisu reached into his pocket and drew out a few coins, two white tablets, and a strange metal device that had spring-roll pieces stuck to it. "You want the metal or the meds?"

Shujin gave him an incredulous blank stare.

"You got *choices* in life too, dude."

"Stop messing around, please, sir?" Shujin took them from his hand. "What the heck is *that* anyway?"

"Shh! It's all…mysteriously showing up in random food items… on *my* plate!" Tsumisu pointed to the floor frantically.

Shujin's face lit up in fear. "What?" He checked his stomach. "Oh God, what…what if…"

"It's so *quiet*, just like a *small* golf tournament!" Nataliya called from the table, the other women giggling thereafter. "Aannd a swing-and-a-miss from Shujin! Oh! Sooo close! Comin' up to the seventh hole, Mr. Tsumisu!"

"Yay!" Arlette clapped. "Ooo, wait! *Golf* tournament…yaayy…" she then whispered.

"D-don't look over there." Tsumisu awkwardly grabbed his friend's face and guided it to the window. "Now, *this* is a tracking device—see it blinking? It *blinks*!"

Still looking at the pretty snow on the ground and not the device, Shujin sighed. "So…that's Nataliya's?"

"Ha! No, it's your grandma's. Just-a-hint-of-a-metal-spice-a!" Tsumisu faked a horrible Italian accent. "Sir, I'm not gonna make it. My brain is cracking *wide* open, and then the local news will be at *your* door."

"Seriously, can I turn around?"

"Yeah, go ahead. Be my guest."

"Shujin?" called Tetyana, stifling her laughter. "Is everything OK in there, Shujin? Come back and eat! What are you two conspiring about in there? G—ha ha! Golf? Ha ha haaa!"

Tsumisu was trying hard not to glance toward the table, but with all those eyes over there...

"J-just a second!" he cheerily responded. "OK, how do you feel?"

"Nauseous," Shujin scoffed rhetorically. "It's just a Saturday for cryin' out loud, right?"

"Hey!" He patted his buddy's shoulder. "At least the sun hasn't set. Now, limited answers as you said, indirect diversions, and we survive, got it?"

Shujin blew an exasperated raspberry. "Yeah, yeah, I got it! Let's do this."

"Get it *done*, big man," Tsumisu encouraged, and he followed him to the table.

Upon taking their cushions again, the women inconspicuously eyed the two of them. Of course, Tsumisu wasn't the *best* at keeping information discreet.

"Just had to, uh," Shujin began, nodding his head to gain self-confidence, "refresh my mental oxygen levels. Makes sense, right?"

Suzuka smiled with understanding. "Absolutely, Prince Shujin," she said. Her fiercely sharp blue eyes seemed softer. "Such is necessary for a developing Mark of Evelyn. Care for a spring roll?"

His eyes flew wide as tiny sweat droplets appeared on his brow. He looked at the princess as humbly as humanly possible. "Er, give me a sec to settle down?"

Tetyana had a huge lump of food in her cheek. "Shujin? You can have some of mine if you don't want hers!" she offered. "After digging all those *holes*, ya gotta eat, babe!"

"She's so *right*!" Nataliya gasped suddenly, handing a plate of food to Tsumisu. "A heh...would you like some, Mr. Tsumisu? I made sure they're *warm*."

He blushed. Their proximity granted him a bird's-eye view of Nataliya's cleavage courtesy of her sundress; cute freckles peppered her chest. *Oh God, did she catch you looking?* Averting his gaze and placing a vertically aligned right hand to his face, the Sonzai commander began praying.

"And so, diligence ensures victory for all," he said. "*Yeah,* uh, Little Lady, I am so…so very happy for all of you to be so…"

"Thoughtful?" she remarked with a raised eyebrow, knowing he was looking. "So thoughtful to *observe* your train of thought, handsome?"

"You got it! Thoughtful! Er, a-and so dang thoughtful for bringing up the *word* thoughtful…for it takes much *thought* to do that…I think." Tsumisu nervously smiled as the scientist eyed him, slowly shaking her head with a *subtle* grin. "Whew! All that *thought* process is stored in that hair, I'd imagine! Shujin, did you notice that, sir?" He single-handedly made circular motions in the air.

Holding onto the spring roll of doom, Shujin noticed his friend's signal. "Oh, uh, y-yeah! The resilient power…um…within all the women before us *must* be associated with uh…the hair. See?" He tugged on his short cut. "Not much going on here! Couldn't hold a Mark of Evelyn form if I tried!"

"How astute, good sir! Even Suzuka's got long hair. Dahlia's got it. Tetyana over here does 'cause she got it from *her.*" Tsumisu forced a grin at Nataliya, who simply slid the plate of food closer to him. "Then Arlette just has it…kinda pinned up, yet it's *a lot* of hair." He scratched an eyebrow. "Geez, this is kinda ubiquitous."

"I wonder what *else* you noticed about me." Arlette remarked with strong, infatuated inquisition. "I'm *aaall* ears."

"Whuuhh—I was just…"

Sensing danger, Shujin knew he had to react quickly. "H-how do you think they keep it looking like they do?" he asked.

"See, if there's *one* thing we learned in school, it's that you never question how a lady keeps up her hair." Tsumisu gave a grateful thumbs-up. "Now, I've never seen Tetyana engage in hair management. You don't tend it often, do you?"

"Not really; it just grows natural," she said, messing with it but clearly enjoying the awkward spectacle. "What about *yours*, big guy? Huh? Got some special shampoo for all that dimension-bustin' power?"

"Shh! It's on sale today, and I don't want everybody knowing about it." He looked around suspiciously. "But, uh…when you look at Little Lady over here, and heaven forbid—"

"Oh, *heaven forbid*, Mr. Tsumisu!" she exclaimed enthusiastically.

"*Heaven* forbid, I continue to utilize her talents, for you see, this 'do' is *unreal*! Um…" Tsumisu paused to calmly gather his idea formulations. "This is gonna sound weird…but could you turn around?"

She gasped in utter shock. "Oh *my*! If you wanted a special *favor*, don't say it in front of *everyone*, Mr. Tsumisu!" she exclaimed. "That's inappropriate!"

"But I thought a favor was like borrowing something?" Dahlia inquired innocently.

"Ha! There are *lots* of favors in the universe, Little Princess, lemme tell ya!" Tetyana pointed at her with a telling wink. "Ain't that *right*, Shujin babe?"

"Tetyana! I dunno what you're talkin' about—waahh!" Shujin desperately tried to explain but was cut short.

Suzuka instantly grasped on to him, interrupting by putting his neck in an awkward position. "Leave him be! The only favors he shall receive are mine alone!" she declared.

Once again aligning his hand before his face, Tsumisu exhaled. "Due diligence. That is *not* what I was talkin' about—"

Arlette smiled brightly as she suddenly got an idea. "Ohh, I think you're too shy to say it! Did you wanna see somethin' special, Tsumisu? Like my *butt*?" she said, blushing. "Maybe it's only fair 'cause I *was* staring at yours."

Shujin was fervently making cutthroat signals to his buddy. His hand motions actually created a subtle wind on Suzuka. "Oh sorry, Ms. Suzuka. Just…getting more oxygen!" He nervously laughed, remaining in her inadvertent choke hold. "Dude! Ix-nay!"

"Trying!" Tsumisu said through gritted teeth and an odd smile. "Ha ha! Arlette, my dear, your butt is just *fine* today—oh gosh, poor choice of words. I-I mean, that's not necessarily saying your butt *isn't* fine, because it really is. I think?" He continued, addressing her with explanatory hand motions. "However, I am *not* publicly acknowledging the fact that it *is* fine…today."

Shujin could only stare at his buddy in profound disbelief.

"Aww! Thanks, Tsumisu!" she replied with a bashful giggle. "Does that mean we can stare at your butt anytime?"

"Yes!" Shujin declared, but he realized he had answered too quickly to diffuse the conversation. "Wait! Ms. Suzuka, don't look at me like that—I don't really stare at any—"

"Prince *Shujin*!" the princess exclaimed, a blush coming to her now as an elegant hand lay over her chest. "I had no *idea* I drew your eyes in such a manner!"

"N-no, wait! I-I mean, not say that I don't find anything about you that isn't—"

"So *that's* why you're so dang quiet every time we're watchin' TV!" Tetyana concluded with suggestive intent. "And you're always behind me! Mmm, get a little *entertained*, yeah, Shujin?"

He was sweating millions of bullets, knowing Tetyana lay on the floor, butt *indeed* wiggling from time to time as she watched. "Whuuhh, th-that's not the reason why I sit there!"

Dahlia giggled brightly, eyeing him. "Aww, you're a *bad* boy, aren't ya, Shujin?" she remarked. "I think Mr. Tsumisu learns it from you! Hee-hee!"

"Ah ha ha!" Tsumisu exclaimed aloud, like a cheesy game-show host. "That's not exactly *true*, Dahlia—"

"See? Dahlia made you admit it! So you're hankerin' to see my butt, huh?" Nataliya inquired in a provocative way, hands sassily on her hips. "Or would you rather *devour* the rest of these spring rolls, Mr. Tsumisu?"

"Yeaaah, can I see what's behind door number three instead?" Tsumisu casually replied with a wince-grin. "Didn't you hear Shujin just now? We're not *trying* to look…wait…that's actually admitting we are—"

"You're staring at my butt *too,* big guy?" Tetyana wore a wide, amused smile. She was floored. "Well, that's *one* mystery we figured out about ya! Ha haaa!"

"*Ooooo*!" Nataliya shuddered once more; this time, it seemed involuntary. "My, you're one to move *quickly*. I *like* it!" She chomped at him. "*Rargh*!"

"Whuh!" Tsumisu held up his hands in horrified defense, staring into her threatening eyes. "Sh-Shujin, let's go get dessert! Now!"

"D-dessert?" he replied in terror, voice breaking.

"Yes! Exactly. *Dessert!* Now, Shujin and I are going to the kitchen to get dessert, aren't we, my good man?"

"Uh-ah, yeah, we are!" Shujin caught on to the escape plan. "OK, we'll be right back. You girls just sit here! Please?"

"Yay, how nice!" Arlette remarked in excitement. "Now we get to watch their butts *and* get dessert! Go on now, Tsumisu! And bend over again, cutie!"

"Arlette!" Suzuka scolded the lieutenant. "That is quite enough! You'll ruin Dahlia's imagination! *You* as well, Ms. Nataliya!"

"Huh? Are you kiddin'? Just look at that gluteus maximus!" The eccentric woman pointed to Tsumisu, trying to slap his butt. She barely missed as she fell over. "*Oop*, get back here! Mwahahaaa!"

"Quickly, sir!" Tsumisu incoherently muttered in panic. "We must *flee*!"

Reacting like a bear trap, Tetyana grabbed Shujin's hand as he walked by. "Think I found my dessert right here! C'mere, Shujin!"

"Waaah! Oh no!" he cried.

Tsumisu swiftly plucked the ensnared man away. "Very good, Tetyana! Very good…" He sighed in appreciation as the two fearfully strode off.

"Hey!" She looked at her hands curiously. "How'd he *do* that? Urgh…"

"Woo!" exclaimed Nataliya, getting her hair together after sitting upright. "I haven't had this much fun in *years*, ladies. Certainly works up an 'appetite'!"

"Oh my gosh, I know, right?" concurred Arlette. "You think the boys are having fun too?"

"They seem quite nervous," commented Suzuka, leaning over to try to peer into the kitchen. "*Very* nervous."

"I wish they weren't so damn polite all the time!" Tetyana chuckled. "It's like they think we're gonna *do* something to 'em. Know what I mean?" She shook her arms. "How can we get 'em to loosen the hell up?"

"Perhaps you are *too* loose, Tetyana." Suzuka smirked with narrowed eyes. "Prince Shujin is not interested in the floozy type."

"A *what* type?" she retorted with a clenched fist. "No! Say it again, Princess. I'm listening!"

"Oh, cut it out, girls." Nataliya grinned, appreciating the quarrel. "Neither Shujin *or* Tsumisu has a clue about what they like in a lady." She scoffed. "My God, hasn't anybody…and I mean *anybody*…noticed they're virgins? *Blatant* virgins. It's not even funny!"

Arlette *instantly* raised her hand. "Oo! Me! I noticed!" she chirped. "It's like coaxing a turtle to come out of its shell—they're soooo cute!"

"That's a *fantastic* analogy." Nataliya pointed to the lieutenant. "Ooo, the big question: what's it gonna take to give it up, right?"

"Exactly!" exclaimed Tetyana. "Initiative? Motivation? Bribery?"

"What's a virgin, Nataliya?" Dahlia cheerily asked. "Isn't that a kind of olive oil?"

Suzuka gasped and zipped over to her little sister, covering her ears. "*Yes,* Ms. Nataliya, that point is glaringly obvious." She grimaced. "Nevertheless, such a possession of Prince Shujin's will be *mutually* granted for release…Tetyana."

"Don't even start with me," she said, shaking a finger. "Remind me: *Who* was at Shujin's door last night with a weapon out again? Who even carries a weapon to bed?"

"Can you let me go, Big Sister?" Dahlia timidly requested.

Suzuka's cheeks were puffed. "Defending Shujin's virginity from the likes of *you* does not compare to your obvious intentions!" she protested.

Arlette gasped, mouth covered. "You tried to *take* it, Tetyana?"

"Yeah, I did! So what?" Tetyana replied, comfortably propping both hands behind her to lean back. "Shujin is *so* lucky. You freakin' ruined it, Suzuka! What the hell?"

"Still sore, Tetyana?" Nataliya had to ask. "Why don't you drink some electrolyte fluids, dear?"

"*No.* That crap gives me nightmares."

"Precisely, you'll have something else to think about."

"Hmmm." Arlette continued to contemplate, staring at the ceiling. "Well, Shujin seemed to be OK with it," she muttered. "Maybe I could try it with Tsumisu?"

CHAPTER TWELVE

Seeking much-needed salvation within the kitchen, Tsumisu and Shujin leaned against the counters, exhaling simultaneously.

"How much sleep did you get again?" Tsumisu looked at him with a telling expression.

"I can't remember now," Shujin responded, recollecting Tetyana taking hold of him…and his nosebleed. "Yikes…will I get sleep *tonight* is a better question."

"Correction, that is a *brilliant* question, 'cause Little Lady knows where I live now so…"

Shujin scoffed in shock. "No way! How's that possible?"

"She's the 'femme fatale of science,' that's how." Tsumisu threw air quotations as he replied, "All right, so this dessert thing…"

"Yeah, thanks for that. How do we go about this plan?"

He looked around. "You know those tarts I keep buying?"

"Yeah?"

Tsumisu reached for them. "Get some saucers, and what we'll do is set a scoop or two of that vanilla bean ice cream—you still got blueberries, right?"

"I got plenty of them left." Shujin was getting his culinary brain into gear. "So we put that on top?"

"Precisely." Tsumisu pointed to his temple. "This is all in the name of evasion, man; just trying to save our asses. Agh..."

"They want our *asses* now, you hear that?" Shujin pointed to the living room. "I mean, I've seen them bend over before, but uh...I never, uh...paid much attention to um..."

"You don't have to answer that. If your sight copped a feel on *any* of those booties up there, I don't think we'd be in this kitchen right now. Understand what I mean?"

"Ha, you sound like Asaka." Shujin chuckled, trying to scoop the ice cream. "Stay clear of that guy, you hear me?"

"I am! I took your word for it a long, long time ago." Tsumisu nodded in affirmation. "You know, it's only been like twenty-four hours, and...Little Lady is already causing psychological problems for me?"

Shujin shook his head slowly. "No...dude, c'mon. What's happening? More devices? Are you not telling me something?"

"All right." He wore a solemn expression. "I've grown to realize that there are many degrees of cute. Yesterday, Arlette asked if I had a girlfriend, right?"

"Ha! No way! On the *Leviathan*?"

"Shh!" Tsumisu ran up to him and covered his mouth. "They listen even now...I've *not* had the time to contemplate the implications of Arlette's inquiry, yet I can only tell you that Little Lady's cuteness is on par with Arlette's, though they are both advancing in different ways...ways that I *can't* control."

Shujin removed his buddy's hand from his face. "So...Nataliya's 'advance' is getting into your head?" He chuckled. "You really like her that much?"

"Dude, don't single me out—we both like all the girls." Tsumisu wore a straight face. "C'mon. Remember that short girl in history class with the *big eyes*, whom you met *once* and basically ran away from? Leaving the girl—"

"See, that has nothing to do with this." Shujin twisted his mouth. "OK, yeah, I remember. What about her?"

"I apologize for my ridiculing of your disposition that day, for I, Tsumisu, suffer the same thing but worse...worse as in the amount of *fire* in Little Lady." He shivered. "See that? Goose bumps."

"Yikes." Shujin's expression was of surprise. "That's pretty intense, dude. Well, I'll admit that I do feel awkward if I stare at Tetyana too long...not saying I have, but even if she's like normal right now, I can see what you're saying. Suzuka's eyes make me nervous—what am I talking about here?" He dropped his arms.

"Ha ha!" Tsumisu nodded as if he had accomplished something. "Dahlia is wrong: I'm rubbing off on *you*."

"Unfortunately." He sighed. "Somebody here has gotta mitigate the chaos that happened just now, right?"

"Certainly, man, but the whole time I figured no harm, no foul." Tsumisu scratched his head in thought. "*Then* I forgot about understanding the intuition of a female..."

"Which, again, nearly got us in trouble," Shujin added while putting blueberries on Dahlia's saucer.

"Hey, I put my neck on the line and saved both of us; took a lot of guts doing that," Tsumisu said, pointing a fork at him. "Well, looks like all of them are done. Which ones are you taking?"

Shujin shrugged. "I mean, whatever; they all look the same."

"Sure, but which one of us will be handing *which* saucer to *which* girl? See, that's the conflict."

He shook his head with a smirk. "There's always a 'conflict' or something with you, man. There's not *any* conflict right now."

"Yeah, there is!" Tsumisu threw his hand out in gesture. "Say you take three saucers—to Suzuka, Tetyana, and Dahlia—and end up handing the first one to Tetyana. Guess what Suzuka is gonna do?"

"Ooohh, well, I see what you're saying. Sooo...why not hand over two at the same time?"

"Precisely." He gave a confident nod. "I've got the rest, so handle it well, bro."

Shujin scoffed. "I'll try…if I don't get pulled over again."

"I think you should prepare yourself for that anyway. Due diligence!"

"Due diligence!" Shujin repeated, following him out of the kitchen.

At the table, the women appeared to have been sitting there for the entire time they were gone and smiled when they saw the two of them with desserts in hand.

"Oh wow!" said Dahlia in delight. "You guys did that?"

"Pretty neat, ain't it? Oh, the hidden culinary talents…" replied Tsumisu, and he handed one to her. "Enjoy, Dahlia!"

Her expression was truly pleased. "Wow, thanks a lot!"

"Man, that stuff looks good!" Tetyana exclaimed, rubbing her hands and licking her lips. "What is it made of, Shujin?"

"It's probably best to let you figure it out, Tetyana." He smiled, setting the saucers in front of her and Suzuka simultaneously.

Nataliya smiled ever so innocently as Tsumisu set saucers before her and Arlette. "Ya know something, Mr. Tsumisu?" she began with suggestion.

"Perchance, what shall I know on your observation, Little Lady?" he replied in humored eloquence.

"I thought that entire dessert thing was a hoax! Imagine that, huh?"

"Oh really?" he replied, albeit nervously. "What a crazy, mixed-up world we live in!"

"Awfully crazy it seems!" Nataliya concurred, still eyeballing him as he took a seat. "I see you're a man of your word regardless of *how* suspicious you are!"

Tsumisu gave her an odd expression. "Yeah, I…sure *am*, Little Lady! Nervous? Yes. Suspicious? Nooo. Now you just enjoy that stuff, and Shujin and I will take these *other* dishes out of you ladies' way!"

"Aren't we lucky to have them around?" said Arlette brightly, brooding over her plate. "I've never had something like this before!"

"You haven't had dessert before?" asked Shujin, trying to collect the used dishes.

"Um…I think I have, but I really meant the treatment!" She beamed.

"And you *deserve* it, Arlette!" Tsumisu gave a friendly thumbs-up, with a smile to match. "That's why we made it from scratch!"

The lieutenant blushed, sighing dreamily. "*Yeeeaah…*"

"Uhhh…wuuhh—"

"This is so *delicious*," commented Suzuka, and she placed a modest portion on her fork. "Here, Prince Shujin, you should try some."

Tetyana immediately got a healthier sample on hers. "No, you can try some of mine, Shujin!"

"I asked him first!" she protested.

Tsumisu shook his head at Shujin as if to say "reject the offer."

At a loss, Shujin went ahead and took his advice. "Um, I'm fine, thanks! You girls just enjoy it!" he said, mildly sweating.

"Aww, c'mon! You sure you don't want any?" Tetyana tried to press it to his mouth. "It's really good, babe! You know I'll make it better!"

"I will give him some, Tetyana. Back away!" Suzuka brought her sample to the other side of his mouth.

"Well, uh, um, I'm not hungry anymore? Right now?" he timidly pleaded.

"Man…I didn't see that one," Tsumisu mumbled, pulling his chin. "*Man…*"

Nataliya couldn't help herself as strange noises came out of her because of the dish. "Mmm, it is simply delightful! But, oh my, weren't you having some as well?" She turned to Tsumisu in inquiry. "Unless you 'forgot' to get yours from the kitchen?"

"Well, we, uh...kinda just *ran out* of ingredients, so we just figured the girls deserved some!" Tsumisu replied, feeling like a magician with the amount of tricks he had pulled out in the past ten minutes. "See how considerate we are?"

"*Oh*? How sweet of you! But you boys *deserve* some just as much as we do. After all, have you forgotten what happened yesterday?" Nataliya gave a cheeky smile, offering a *huge* portion to him. "Now come on and open up that handsome face for meee!"

"She's right!" expressed Arlette in agreement, doing the same. "If you want, you can have some of mine, Tsumisu!"

"Whuh, that's awfully nice of you, and I *really* appreciate it, Arlette! Er, but if you ladies let me explain, and I think Shujin... *Shujin*! Dude! Sit still so I can tell you this," he desperately whispered.

"I'm kinda busy," he said with a mouthful, having eaten both samples.

Tsumisu pointed to his head. "Wise decision, Admiral. All right. I was going to say that we've already gotten what we deserved: that's *you* girls!" He gestured to them all. "So I don't know...what more we need."

Tsumisu's statement made them all smile, and Tetyana gave him a peculiar glance.

"Saaaay, are you gettin' mushy on me, big guy?" she asked.

"Damn *straight* I am! Take it!" he proudly proclaimed.

"Man, that was really kind of you," Shujin remarked, finishing the overwhelming bite. "I'll have to admit, I look at it the same way!"

"Really, Prince Shujin?" said Suzuka dreamily.

"Of course he does! Hero of the weak, defender of justice—anyway, Little Lady here was asking why you and I haven't had dessert, Shujin."

"Oh yeah? Well, uh..." Shujin nodded, unsure of what the response would be. "How shall we answer, good sir?"

Tsumisu snapped his fingers. "How to answer that, you say? Our dessert is already *here*; we just haven't eaten it yet! Oh wait..." He clenched his eyes in regret once more. "All right...wait."

Nataliya let out a very amused laugh. "Oh *yeah*! Shall I personally serve your plate, Mr. Tsumisu? Or will you *take* it from me? Ha haa!"

"No! That was a very rhetorical comment; trust me! Ugh, I'm just going to stare into the sun now."

Dahlia had a confused expression on her face. "What does that mean, Shujin?"

"*Tsumisu*! Dang it, dude! Um, I wouldn't worry about it right now, Dahlia!" He grinned nervously. "Besides, I honestly don't know what he's talking about!"

"Are you kiddin' me?" said Tetyana, wearing an intrigued expression. "There's no telling *what* you guys talk about when we're not around! And we're just lucky *he's* got a big mouth!"

"N-no! I swear, Tetyana! I have no—"

She blew a kiss at him. "Would you like my *cream* filling, Shujin? I'm makin' it as we speak..."

When it finally hit Suzuka, she grew red all over. "Oh my goodness," she whispered and placed both hands on her face. "Prince Shujin! Is this *true*?"

"Now, j-just hold on a sec. I never said stuff like that before in my life!" Shujin tried his best to defend himself. "I'm sure he got that from, uh...Asaka or *somebody* at school!"

"You got it!" called Tsumisu while lying down on the couch. "It's all Asaka's fault!"

Arlette counted on her fingers. "Uuumm, so are *we* ice cream then?"

"Denial is the first step to honesty, Shujin!" said Nataliya cheerily. "You shouldn't hide your feelings, for it leads to terrible physiological functionality and depressive mood swings!"

"But I'm not even *hiding anything*! God, now I'm sounding like him." He sighed in self-confession. "W-why don't you come and straighten this out, man?"

"I mean, I *said* it was rhetorical, didn't I?" Tsumisu sat up, throwing his arms out in exclamation. "What do you want me to say? Ice cream *doesn't* have different flavors? And we all know *that's* a lie! At present, there's black cherry flavor, orange flavor—surprise! Banana split! We got sea salt…"

"Shut *up*, dude! I swear to—shut *up*, dude!" Shujin was gaining in embarrassment points, his thoughts in a loop. "You're *not* helping here!"

"I'm *hibiscus* flavor, Shujiiin!" Tetyana remarked in a singsong tone.

"Well, this is actually flattering for you to reveal such information, Prince Shujin!" Suzuka gazed on him with great infatuation, though she was shy. "Perhaps this is how you're comfortable expressing your feelings?"

"*No*! I-I mean, yes, but this is *not* how I express my feelings at all!" he declared, rising from his seat to stomp over to a contemplative Tsumisu. "What the *hell* just happened, dude? Are you insane? Have you *gone* insane?" he intensely whispered.

Tsumisu began childishly flinging his hands at Shujin. "I dunno! That's why I'm over *here*! You're drawing the wolf pack!"

Shujin fought back. "See what I mean about your chaotic mouth? C-cut it out!"

"I shall defend myself!" he proclaimed in a high-pitched, voice-breaking English accent. "Man, you got better at this! Are you pulling energy from Evelyn?"

Shujin laughed aloud. "What?" He instantly stopped, dropping his arms to his sides, and exhaled. "Look…you gotta…find a way to *stop*, OK? I'm on the edge enough as it is!"

Tetyana suddenly appeared before the two, swinging around Shujin. "On edge? Aww, why, babe? I can ease *a lot* of that tension, you know." She swept a hand across his cheek.

"Whuuah! Well, Tetyana, I-I'm just taking vitamin supplements for that!" Shujin was freaked out by her inherent magic trick, trying to maintain his balance as she continued to spin. "Gotta stay healthy, r-right?"

"Did ya know consistent copulation helps maintain your circulatory system too, Shujin?" Nataliya casually strolled up to the two, hands on her hips with a cheeky grin. "This is why a *total* physiological examination is necessary, Mr. Tsumisu! Oooo, didn't think I heard ya when you came up the driveway earlier? *Ha*!" She raised an instructive finger with victory in her disposition. "Nothing escapes me!"

"Uh-um-ah, it couldn't hurt to *try*! Hee-yah!" Tsumisu performed a hapless forward roll from the couch to perhaps evade whatever impending danger lay ahead from Nataliya, only to land at Arlette's feet as she, Suzuka, and Dahlia joined the others. "Um," Tsumisu began, looking up at the curious lieutenant, "will you be around the rest of the day? You know, random morale boosting and whatnot…"

"Yes, I *will*, Tsumisu!" she excitedly responded. "Why? Is it the ice cream? Are we getting more?"

"I still don't understand what that means," Dahlia responded, looking to her sister for an answer. "C'mon, Suzuka! Tell me!"

Busy tackling the problem of Tetyana swarming Shujin yet again, Suzuka successfully snatched the man from Tetyana; his body went limp, however.

"Dahlia! This is not the time, my dear sister!" she replied. "Tetyana, you shall not lay another finger on Shujin! I am to be his dessert, not you!"

"Ha! Think you can back that up?" She pointed to the princess in defiance. "At least I've got amenities!" Tetyana further declared, grabbing her breasts and shaking them. "See *these*? Cherries on top!"

"Uurrgghh!" Suzuka dropped Shujin on the floor and clenched her fists in frustration, steam blowing from her ears and eyes. "You take that back, you *spiteful* woman!"

"Can't deny the truth, sister!" Tetyana took a victorious stance and laughed heartily. "What's that old sayin'? The way to a man's heart is through his stomach?"

Dahlia was assimilating many of the nuances. "Oh wow!" she exclaimed. "Is she talking about—"

"Sure *is*, Dahlia!" Nataliya turned to the little princess. "So when you get older, remember to maintain your *entire* menu; otherwise, it'll be difficult to entrap individuals like Mr. Tsumisu here!" She demonstrated by sitting atop his chest and crossing her legs. "See that? Ha haaa!" She folded her arms, feeling very proud.

"But why would Mr. Tsumisu try to run away?" Dahlia continued to ask, knowing this was the best learning moment she had.

Nataliya's faced blossomed with gratitude. "Why, Dahlia! I thought you'd *never* ask, my dear! You see—"

"A little help would be *great*." Tsumisu was still outstretched on the floor, looking toward Arlette as she just stared at the developing situation. "Know what I mean?"

"I never knew entrapment worked in this manner." She knelt down to meet him with a smile. "Typically, people go to jail for that!"

"Or worse!" Nataliya leaned toward the conversing Arlette. "*As* I was trying to explain, Mr. Tsumisu is trying to break his promise to me!" She suddenly threw on the best sad face ever known.

Dahlia and Arlette instantly grew worried.

"Mr. Tsumisu!" Still crouched over the helpless man, Arlette shook her finger at him in scolding. "For *shame*! Breaking promises!"

"You could hurt someone's feelings by doing that, Mr. Tsumisu!" Dahlia also walked up to him with a slightly distressed expression. "You know that, right?"

"Whoooaa, w-wait a second!" Tsumisu's arms were at least free to maneuver around. "I don't quite recall promising Little Lady anything...recently! I promise—well, there goes a promise I used in a figure of speech soooo..."

"You see?" Nataliya had crocodile tears running down her cheeks. "And all I wanted to do was give 'em a little, tiny, itsy-bitsy checkup! And he won't let meeee! Waaa-haa!" She began rubbing her eyes. "He *promised* I could! It's not fa-ha-haaaiirr!"

Falling back on the "uphold the right thing to do" side of her military training, Arlette gave an altogether cute scowl at Tsumisu. "I am disappointed in you, mister!" she remarked, proceeding to sit on his chest as well. "Now, you say you're sorry to Nataliya! Or I'm *not* getting up! Hmph!"

Not quite believing how quickly the situation turned in Nataliya's favor, Tsumisu found out the genius had simply adapted her methodology to ensnare him into her laboratory. Why do it alone when you can twist the truth and gain support for your cause? Ha, Little Lady would make an *outstanding* politician.

"Uh, wait, Arlette, Dahlia! You gotta listen to me!" the Sonzai commander pleaded. "Little Lady, d-don't cry like that, OK? Seriously, it's not—"

"Waa-haa! He still won't apologize!" For an instant, Nataliya's waterworks shut off as she glanced at him with a *most* cunning smile and then instantly resumed her charade.

"Oh sh—did you guys see that?" He tried pointing it out. "Seriously! Did you *see* that?"

"No excuses, Tsumisu!" Arlette cried, slamming her bottom on his chest. "Say you're sorry, and make it up to her!"

"Ow!"

"You *have* to, Mr. Tsumisu! Please?" Dahlia implored. "See how sad she is?"

"All right, OK! Little Lady?" Tsumisu addressed her kindly, severe apprehension within his expression.

"Yeeesss, Mr. Tsumisu?" Still atop him, Nataliya immediately lay on her stomach, lifting her legs up and down as she propped her chin with both hands. "You have somethin' ya wish to tell me?"

His entire vision was pretty much taken up by Arlette's, Nataliya's, and Dahlia's faces. So those moments, Tsumisu recalled, where he could look away and think about starting a horse farm in Mongolia to escape, just weren't available now. How sad.

"Uh...I'm s-so..." he stuttered, trepidation building.

Nataliya's eyes got wider and wider. "Yes? *Yes*?"

"I'm sorr—man, can't we just reach a compromise?"

"No!" Arlette and Nataliya exclaimed in unison.

Well, at least Suzuka got the better grip in her battle for supremacy against Tetyana, Tsumisu noticed, simply because they were *right* beside him. Hmm, where was Shujin this whole time? And *what* was that gurgling noise? No matter.

"OK!" Tsumisu gave a cautious stare to the both of them, who seemed to team up all of a sudden—his female intuition awareness was severely lacking. "So, I'm, uh...sor-sorry for n-not keeping my pr-promise..."

It was as if Nataliya were listening to the best music in the world. Her face grew with such immaculate delight she could've exploded. "Promise? *What* promise?" she asked.

"*Don't* make me say it! I don't wanna say it," Tsumisu whined, shaking his head in desperation. "Arlette, do I have to say it too? Can't we just be on the level and call it square?"

"Hmmm..." Arlette's expression lightened up; it was never really the opposite anyway. "Well, Nataliya, what do you think?"

She shook her head, unconvinced. "Nope! If he's gonna come clean, he's gotta come *clean*. Right, Arlette?"

"Right!" Her tone of justice returned.

"So spill it! What promise?" Nataliya crept up to him, her face mere centimeters away. "*Hey* there, handsome..."

"Wow." Tsumisu could inhale the carbon dioxide composition of her exhalations, and it made him feel *weird* and tingly. "So since I'm not *fully* aware of certain…information surrounding the circumstances of the promise…"

"Mm-hmm?" Nataliya didn't blink as she eyed him down, letting him know the inevitable was near. "Yeah, I'm coming for ya…"

"Oh God…I-I elect to maintain my ignorance…in the face of such uncertainty and declare I've kept my promise to keep promises!" Tsumisu exhaled deeply, blowing hair from his face. "*Wow,* that was hard."

"Stop dodging the truth, Mr. Tsumisu!" Arlette further scolded. "I'm listening to you!"

"Ooooo, don't back out of it *now*; otherwise, you're gonna find yourself in a *deeper,* oh so much *deeper* predicament, Mr. Tsumisu." Nataliya brought her face ever closer to his. "Right?"

His eyes dilated in submerged fear. "I promise to let Little Lady give me a checkup," Tsumisu quickly mumbled incoherently.

"Wha-huh? What's that?"

"I…oh *God*!" Tsumisu was fighting the bad thoughts: the stereotypical extraterrestrial probing devices, the hands over his body doing things that would haunt his senses at night. "I promise to allow Little Lady…to give me a checkuuuuupp!" he said aloud, banging the back of his head against the floor repeatedly.

"Hooray! Yaaayy!" Nataliya cheered, flailing her arms and legs in celebration. "See how much *better* you feel?"

"Yaayy! I was about to say the same thing!" Arlette grew a bright and proud smile. "It's like a big ol' weight has been lifted off your chest!"

Dahlia applauded the Sonzai commander. "Yay, Mr. Tsumisu! I *knew* you could do it!" she said. "Sometimes Big Sister has troubles too, but eventually you come around!"

"A heh…" Nataliya began to snicker, a devious grin reaching her lips. "A heh heh! They *all* gotta come around sometime, Dahlia…"

Oh wait! That sound is Shujin! Tsumisu finally came to the realization that he might be lying facedown on the floor, unable to cope with his previous ordeal…on top of *this* ordeal. Anyway, Tsumisu was either officially screwed or otherwise. All those diversions, all those times he *probably* should've kept track of his thoughts—did it matter? Did Nataliya have an alternate plan this entire time? Why did she start laughing like that?

"Wow, I've never seen her so happy!" Arlette was very appreciative of the ongoing expression of emotion. "Well, guess you two better get going! After all, checkups are important. Especially for a man like you—using *all* that energy to save us! Who knows how you were affected, right, Dahlia?"

"I agree, Arlette!" Dahlia said warmly. "And since Nataliya is so smart, you're in the *best* hands, Mr. Tsumisu!"

Tsumisu, encapsulated in the moment of severe, unrelenting irony, could only laugh aloud with Nataliya. "Yep! The best hands, Dahlia! Couldn't have said it better…"

Having swallowed her saliva down the wrong pipe, Nataliya started coughing. "You…ack! I *told* you…ack! I was gonna…have the last…ack-ack…laugh!"

Gently patting her head and back, Tsumisu only nodded calmly. "Yes, this revelation was astutely brought to my attention previously. Thank you for reminding me, Little Lady. May I have another prediction?"

CHAPTER THIRTEEN

Time was a majestically enigmatic creature; some days, it stood in your favor. Other days, time laughed in your face with spit flying in your eye…and mouth. Seven elapsed minutes brought a downpour to the Sonzai commander's mouth as he and a clearly overambitious, self-proclaimed scientific *slash* fatally dangerous Nataliya stood beside each other, facing her bedroom door dual-occupation laboratory entrance. They hadn't spoken a single word, though the background calamity of Tetyana and Suzuka continued to fill their locally electrified air of anticipation. Tsumisu wore profoundly anxious reluctance on his expression, while Nataliya's captured profound satisfaction. She looked up to the Sonzai commander, hands on her hips.

"Are you ready, handsome?" Her tone was awfully cheery.

"Huah! Sorry, you startled me." He then muttered, "Man, I have *got* to keep it together somehow…" Tsumisu turned to her. "OK, let's just get this over with, Little Lady. I know what you did back there, and I commend you wholeheartedly for exercising such brilliant manipulation."

Nataliya winked. "Hey! It's my business to make sure I get what I want. Tough job but somebody's gotta do it."

"Yeah, you're welcome too." He gave her a forced smile. "So, uh…how many times have you, uh…done something like this?"

"Hmm, *never* on somebody…or some*thing* like you, since we're being specific here." Nataliya folded her arms and explained succinctly, "Are you interested in knowing what I intend to find today, my ready and willing victim?" She subtly licked her lips. "Mmm, I can *taste* victory already."

"Whuuhhh!" Tsumisu blushed, finding her gesture grotesquely inviting. "OK, uh, I can only imagine with the amount of detail and coercion you put into your work, so why not?" he replied, still trying to cover his nerves. "Lay it on me, Little Lady."

"Ha! The way you talk sometimes makes me appreciate what I do, Mr. Tsumisu." Nataliya gave him an insightful smile. "Well, all that stuff you told me on the *Leviathan* wasn't fluff—and I *know* that. Thing is, I need—and I mean, I *need*—some solid, tangible, undeniable, verifiable evidence to ascertain what ya did, how ya did it, why ya did it, et cetera."

Tsumisu nodded in realization, knowing this scientific exploration shouldn't involve messing with his "nobunaga." "Hmm, I can definitely see how the way *you* talk makes me appreciate what I do, Little Lady."

"Ooooo." She shuddered, arms displayed. "See that, handsome? *Goose bumps.* Now please entertain my notions…" Nataliya narrowed her eyes. "Unless you don't believe me when I say I'm *watching* you."

Oh dear God, she's been listening to everything that's poured out of your face, dude! She knows what you said about her advancing! And all about her being cute!

That reality nearly gave Tsumisu a diabetic seizure. He hoped he could help the pumpkin-haired lady find a secondary hobby outside of…wait…did she *have* one? She might appreciate badminton.

"Um…"

"Cat got'cha tongue?" Nataliya stepped toward him.

"N-no! Of *course* not!" Tsumisu simultaneously stepped back, having to adjust his disposition. "I was only saying that in my line of work, the 'stuff' or 'evidence' before me really has no names—it just exists. So, it's nice, albeit a little bit on the-*the*…" He let out a fake sneeze. "*Frightening*! Whew! Excuse me."

"Little bit on the *what*?" She stared blankly. "C'mon; you said something. Spit it out."

"I *shan't*…" Tsumisu responded but wasn't sure about his depth of confidence. "Um, it's nice to meet someone who can relate things in a tangible, solid manner. Provides a sense of…" He exhaled, recalling the moments he stared at every last energy strand from the *Leviathan*'s prison. "A sense of familiarity with what I do, despite the naming conventions," he concluded with an honest smile.

Nataliya gained a thoughtful expression. What Tsumisu found mysterious about her was equally what she didn't understand about *him*—such a similitude made them, in a sense, one and the same.

"So." Nataliya grinned, shuffling her foot against the floor. "Guess that's why I grab your interest as much as you do mine?"

"It explains why I relentlessly pick on your inexplicable degree of shortness," Tsumisu affirmed. "And damn it, you *are* short."

She laughed in amusement. "I swear, I'm gonna hit you if you keep doin' that! I'm not that dang short!" she protested. "You just think you're so *tall*, don't ya?"

"This, my tallness, is a fact," he said, arms proudly folded. "And consider this, Little Lady…"

"Oh?" Her tone was inquisitive. "Do tell? Another advantage of yours that I shall eventually defeat?"

"*Perhaps* I plot and plan as much as *you* do…but I, uh, won't look at you…while you sleep." He stepped back for a moment in caution.

"Hmmmm, maybe I'll look forward to that, Mr. Tsumisu." She smirked slyly. "What? You don't wanna see me in a different 'condition' every once in a while?"

"Sweet heavens, I just *saw* you in the past twenty-four hours." Tsumisu used his hands in exclamation. "Let me get accustomed to what…and how…you know?"

"Ha! You won't have a choice if I decide otherwise—just consider *that* for a moment. Now, after you then!" She directed him toward her open room door.

"Nooo, ladies first."

"Oh, but I *insist*, Mr. Tsumisu!"

"And I don't have eyes in the back of my head, Little Lady!" He laughed. "Ladies first."

Nataliya exhaled heavily. "There you go not trusting me again. What's it gonna take to get you to realize I'm not gonna do anything…bad?"

Tsumisu exhaled as well, building confidence. "Look, you touch 'true north' downstairs, you have to use him, OK? Wait… nooo, wait! That is *not* what I—"

"*Nope*! You said it now! Can't take it back! Ooooo, I *love* it!" Nataliya celebrated. "Let's go, shall we?"

Aversely, Tsumisu walked inside her laboratory. Shujin wasn't lying; the place was simply *huge*. Exotic technology was scattered in just about every place he looked. Massive computers, or what looked to be computers at least, connected to wires that crisscrossed everywhere; generator-type machines hummed as they exerted no doubt enormous quantities of power; and there were huge screens as wide as football fields. Essentially, whatever Nataliya had going on in terms of processing power and data crunching, this place was it. Fortunately, it was well lit and brought some small sliver of comfort to the Sonzai commander. At least he could see his path to *doom* rather than guess where he'd end up later, right?

As the two entered, he continuously looked over his shoulder, watching Nataliya as she followed.

"What?" she asked, slightly exasperated, and she threw her hands up. "You act like I'm gonna *kill* you or something!"

"Trust me; it's nothing like that. I just...all right, look." He faced her, hands before him. "Shujin told me what happened this morning. Vampire mode ring a bell?"

"Yeah, and...?" she replied, making the door disappear suddenly behind her with a snap of her fingers. "You're *looking* at that vampire now, handsome."

"D-did you just seal the dimension portal off?" Tsumisu really didn't want to ask the obvious, yet that fight-or-flight problem was controlling his mouth now.

Nataliya giggled mischievously. "I suuuure did! And it's only temporary! So don't *worry*, Mr. Tsumisu! As long as you cooperate, there should be no problems." She winked. "Nooo problems at all..."

"Crap."

"A heh...heh heh..."

"Stop that." Tsumisu pointed at her with conviction. "Y-you're *not* getting to me without a challenge, Little Lady!"

Nataliya gasped in overdramatic surprise. "Oh? Is that *so*? Please, tell me more about your grand plan to negotiate your terms." She shuddered in brief exhalation, eyeing him intently. "I should be asking *you* to stop that..."

Still having that fight-or-flight problem, Tsumisu winced in thought as he brought a vertically aligned right hand to his face. "Don't ask her 'what'...fine. Stop *what*?"

"Stop making me *wet*, Mr. Tsumisu! Ha!"

"I *object*, Your Honor!" he protested immediately, not really knowing how to respond. "I-I am not doing anything to change your moisture concentration, Little Lady! What do I look like, a humidifier?"

"*Oh*? You dare doubt what the femme fatale of science says? *C'mere*! I wanna show ya!" Nataliya began running toward him at full speed. "Mwahahahaaaa!"

Wow, shit just got real. At the tone, please start running, Tsumisu.

"W-wait a minute! What about the negotiations?" he yelled.

"Then you better start talkin', handsome!" Nataliya yelled back in a demanding tone, showing her athletic prowess in maneuverability as they rounded a corner. "Bwahahaha! Come back here!"

"Whoa!" Tsumisu was thoroughly impressed but had to turn up the heat to gain some serious distance. "Listen to me!" he called, darting atop the giant machines. "It doesn't have to be this way!"

"Yeah?" she yelled back, stopping in her tracks suddenly. "I guess you've got a point! I'll give you a head start, Mr. Tsumisu!" She brought up a holographic stopwatch beside her and smirked. "Now..." she lowed. "I'll close my eyes and count to thirty..."

Get ready for the most intense game of hide-and-seek you've *never* played. Eyes wide, Tsumisu gave the apparently crazed Ordovician former chief scientist a last look and darted away as she began counting down.

"Thirty, twenty-nine, twenty-*eight*..."

"Ah, man, where to hide?" he muttered, sweat beading on his forehead as he frantically searched. "I've got plenty of crevices around, but that's the *first* place she'd look..."

"*Twenty*, nineteen..." she continued, her voice echoing against the metallic environment.

"I wouldn't mind a dumpster right now; if I make a racket and trick her into thinking I hid inside, I could use a crevice and then... maybe?" He looked and found nothing in the immediate vicinity. "What? Where does she throw her trash out in this place?"

"I can *smell* you!" Nataliya announced. "Hm-hmmm...eleven, *ten*!"

Tsumisu rubbed his hands fervently. "Uuugghh, I don't have a choice..." he muttered, scurrying toward his hiding place. "I hope this works!"

"Three...two...*one*!" Nataliya sent her stopwatch away. "Ready or not, here I come, handsome! Get it?"

Tsumisu dragged a hand over his face. "*Yes*," he whispered. "Leave it to *her* to violate something innocent."

In the ambience of machines beeping, hard disks writing, and the humming of electricity, he could hear footsteps and nothing else. This was the first time Nataliya had been so quiet. To the Sonzai commander, it indicated she was *indeed* taking this occasion very seriously. But *how* seriously? Was she just...messing with his head this whole time? Uh-oh, her footsteps came closer...

"Strange," she said, checking a scanning device. "Mr. Tsumisu should've been close by."

A piece of equipment sporting rubber flaps around its edges provided the equivalent of "hiding under the bed" for Tsumisu... yet Nataliya was standing right next to him. His training kicking in, Tsumisu controlled his breathing and stilled his body, fearing to blink as sweat dripped from his brow.

"Oh, has Mr. Tsumisu beaten me this day?" Nataliya began dramatically. "What *ever* shall I do if he's escaped? Hunt him down?" She leaned against the equipment, smirking. "And if I *catch* Mr. Tsumisu...whatever shall I do with him?"

Tsumisu began sweating more.

"The possibilities are endless, I guess," she continued, detecting his nervous system's electric field at her feet. "Force an 'examination' within the hot springs? I wonder if he remembers that offer he so *casually* left on the table last night..."

Tsumisu clenched his eyes tight in regret; that was never resolved. Maybe a quick talk with Mrs. Himaki could prevent Nataliya's plans from reaching fruition. *Maybe*.

"It'd only be fair. Mr. Tsumisu seems to take an interest in my anatomy anyway…" She giggled. "It'd be a learning experience for both of us, no doubt."

Damn it. Nataliya knew he was checking her out like a supermarket clerk getting overtime. And what was she trying to do? Did she know he was there?

"I can make this easier for the *both* of us, handsome," Nataliya said in a *deep* and seductive tone. "Either you come out now, or I'm coming in there after you. Wouldn't you like that? Intimate proximity with me? I'll be gentle with you…and *vice versa*, I'm sure."

Ouch. Nataliya had a *wicked* aroma too. *Cool it down, Commander. Cool it down. Don't listen to her. Shujin said she went "vampire mode," remember? Sure, those creatures aren't real* (it was worth consulting Arlette about that). But in the unlikely event Nataliya proved otherwise, Tsumisu focused his mind from derailing into the gutter.

"One more thing, if you try and run away from me"—she giggled again—"you seal your fate. Understood? You belong to me either way."

He remained quiet. Either choice didn't end in his favor apparently.

"Again, if you run…" She blushed. "Pray I don't catch you, Tsumisu. OK?"

She was foreboding yet sounded so sweet! Madness! Tsumisu noticed his pants were all but reduced in real estate downstairs. Was *this* the reason she was the self-proclaimed "femme fatale of science"? Nevertheless, he had to steel his resolve! Was he a man or a mouse?

Well, mice hide under things, soooo…

"Wah!" she cried, startled by his sudden scurrying away. "Bad move, handsome!"

"For the record, I wasn't *trying* to check you out, OK?" he replied, blushing hard. "And what…what *are* you? A siren or something?"

"You're about to find out..." Nataliya snapped her fingers to assemble a lightweight exoskeleton flight suit. "I've already predicted this happening, Mr. Tsumisu!" she said while gaining elevation, eyeing him down. "And now your time has come!"

"Say, that's kinda neat!" he exclaimed, knowing her combined agility with that technology would prove challenging in her *own* arena. "You could dry your clothes that way since you're so wet—*oh my God*! I didn't mean it like that! I was talking about the springs!"

"You dare tease me?" Nataliya charged after him. "Come to *Momma*!"

Just the sense of determination—or *whatever* it was—confirmed to Tsumisu that his only option was to run now. Good thing he had slapped on some extra deodorant that day. Scaling tall rows of what appeared to be computer cabinets, he noticed Nataliya was doing well to close their distance—but that *look* on her face just made him shudder.

"So wait!" he called back. "*If* you catch me, I succumb to your every whim?"

"You mean *when* I catch you, right?" Nataliya was darting in and around the massive wires and structures almost as easily as Tsumisu, trying to pull up beside him. "And I like the choice you made! You must be pretty confident to sacrifice yourself so easily!"

Tsumisu stopped in his tracks, standing erect to evaluate his bearings. "A bit stupid too! Don't forget that!" He folded his arms, watching her pass by. "Bye, Little Lady! I, uh, I guess I win!"

"Ooooohh," Nataliya muttered to herself, shifting her extremely accurate thrusters to change directions. "Keep it up, Mr. Tsumisu!" she yelled, their distance about seventy meters as she levitated midair. "I could lubricate your whole *body* from my excitement! Yes! Keep running!" Her eyes narrowed (and darkened), and her grin became *really* devious.

Paying attention to her rapidly deteriorating condition, Tsumisu suddenly realized he had made the greatest blunder in the history of blunders: running was a *plus* for Nataliya, a rather *arousing* plus. This, in systems theory, was positive feedback! Well, Tsumisu recalled that from some article he read during a long wait at the dentist's office one day—*Time* magazine, was it? Ah well. Nataliya was barreling toward him like a woman possessed. What to do? Stop running? No, that would be surrendering at this point.

Dashing to his right, Tsumisu managed to evade the maniacally flying Nataliya but continued in his thought process. "So what happens when you lose?" he yelled.

"Mwahaha! Who said I planned on *losing*, handsome?" Her side thrusters illuminated her well-meaning-but-sinister face.

At that moment, she summoned forth a legion of extendable, three-prong metal claws to her exoskeleton. Probably numbering in the tens of dozens, they did not affect her flight stabilization in the least.

"Mr. Tsumisu! Today is your submission to me!" she declared. "I will dominate your body and *reap* the information I seek!"

He flinched at her epic statement. Wincing, he said, "I mean, maybe you should calm down—"

"In all the galaxy…in all the *universe*…I've never seen something like *you* before!" Nataliya's voice was raspy yet excited as she stared him down. "You think you can just *waltz* in here, and I won't take you apart, piece by piece? After destroying dimensions, subjugating energy at will, and contacting powerful entities like it's second to breathing? You're *mine*, Mr. Tsumisu! You understand me? All *miiine*!"

Tsumisu's eyes widened; he was officially afraid, for he finally realized Nataliya had reached the edge of an endless canyon and jumped over *just* to enjoy the fall. "Oh, what a difference twenty-four hours can make…" he muttered, taking a step back. "*So,* just to be clear, when you lose, I'll just find my way out, OK?" he yelled, pointing to the last known location of the lab door. "I mean, you'll obviously need some time to…you know, recover—"

"Now, start *running* for me, handsome…*ruuuunn*!" she screamed. "*Nooow*!"

Tsumisu scratched his neck nervously and summoned his exoskeleton armor. "Well, you heard the lady." As he darted away, she pummeled toward him once again.

"Ha ha haaa!" Nataliya maniacally cried. "Yeah! That's more *like* it!"

At once, Nataliya ordered her mechanical arms to reach for Tsumisu, yet he simply evaded their attempts to capture his arms and legs while never losing sight of Nataliya as they danced around midair. Undeterred, Nataliya snapped her fingers to summon *hundreds* more from random portals scattered across the laboratory. The vicious clanking of thousands of claws shook the air, and Tsumisu had to think quickly to determine a pattern to their movements—if a pattern existed. Observing his moves the previous day, Nataliya had evidently calculated some techniques to circumvent Tsumisu's speed. This observational data came in handy, for Tsumisu managed to make one misstep and fell into a transparent void. Instantly, the hundreds of claws surrounded him, clanking vibrantly to subdue their target.

Nataliya knew if the preprogrammed machines had accomplished their task, they *shouldn't* be continuously reaching for Tsumisu. As she exhaled deeply, a wide grin came to her lips, and she sharply turned around.

"Very *good*, Mr. Tsumisu!" she said. "Such proficiency in understanding delicate energetic patterns in my algorithm—which are absolutely *random,* by the way! Oooooo…" Nataliya shuddered. "Keep it up! Yes!"

Though proudly standing with his arms folded, Tsumisu *finally* figured out what was happening each time she did that…thing. "Look, Little Lady," he began, "if this is getting too—I dunno how to say this—*physiologically intense* for you, let's just hold up here and start over again—"

"Mwahahaha!" She defiantly ignored his pleas. "*Never*...oh, you *wish* I would stop, don't you? This is just the beginning!"

She sent forth a wave of cages that materialized from literally everywhere, all extending toward him at tremendous velocity. Tsumisu took off into the air and launched from wall to wall, yet everywhere he landed, there was a waiting cage barely missing him. Knowing this strategy wasn't working, Tsumisu suddenly turned invisible as he performed an array of blind maneuvers—essentially using his speed to mask his physical presence.

When Tsumisu initiated his new strategy, the materializing cages began to chase at random rather than follow his movements, losing their trace of him completely. Nataliya lost sight of him herself yet was very quick to transform the entire area of the laboratory into a heat-sensitive receiver, meticulously observing where he would land before making her next movement. Tsumisu wasn't able to tell what she did, as his surroundings didn't change, yet he caught on to the reactions of the cages. One nearly got ahold of his leg as he attempted to push off a nearby wall and managed to throw him off for a split second to decrease his speed. For that instant, Nataliya got a clear view of where Tsumisu was located and then commanded another wave of mechanical arms embodied with energy caps to subdue him as *she* barreled after him as well.

Tsumisu noticed a horde of arms drawing nearer from all sides while he was heading for a catcher's-mitt-shaped cage.

"This is gonna be interesting!" he exclaimed as the ensnaring arms bore down on their target.

From Nataliya's point of view as she checked the status on her holographic heads-up display, she calculated Tsumisu had a 1 in 500,000 chance of escaping her brilliantly devised plan.

"Yes! Momma's comin' to get'cha, handsome!" she screamed as the screen flashed *subject captured*. "Ha ha! Oohh, now I shall consume my hard-earned *prey*...mwahahahaa!" Taking her time to close in on her catch, she levitated toward the entangled pile of metal. "Do you see, Mr. Tsumisu?" Her breathing was heavy as she was savoring the moment. "I *told* you I'd have the last laugh..."

Yet the moment she attempted to retrieve Tsumisu, the holographic screen read "subject not detained." Sounds of slashing came from inside the seemingly inescapable trap as bits of metal and material fell from around Tsumisu—his weapon, Akari, rested on his shoulder as he exhaled deeply, eyes opening to stare at his hunter.

Nataliya pleasingly stared right back. "Very, *very* good, Mr. Tsumisu." She contemplatively shook her head, biting her bottom lip. "Oooooo..."

"Oh God," Tsumisu lamented, face dropping into his hands. "This is going to go on all *day*, Little Lady! I'm *asking* if we could change both our strategies, please? Please? I'm begging you for the love of everything sacred in this world!"

"Ha! And relinquish my opportunity for your capture? Especially when you've shown me how much ya like to play *rough* with me..." Nataliya teased. "Mmm, I *love* it rough, handsome."

"I swear, I am *not* trying to 'play rough' with you! I'm trying to..." Tsumisu helplessly threw up his arms in exasperation. "Look, I-I dunno *what* I'm trying to do, OK?"

"You are *mine*, and there is *no* escape for you...ha ha ha..." With sudden dramatics, lightning bolts flashed around her in ferocity as she cackled quite sinisterly, illuminating an epic silhouette that Stephen King would've been proud of. "Mwaha-ha-haaaa!"

That's when reality hit Tsumisu.

"Kadochi...you jinxing bastard," he muttered in disbelief.

Then Nataliya transported them both into a massive arena that looked like it had been abandoned for centuries. Not having a moment's notice to prepare, Tsumisu witnessed many strange and unusual obstacles of sorts—each looking untrustworthy. In the next moment, the entire area went pitch-black, and Tsumisu could see nothing. What was worse, he felt the ground beneath him completely give way and began tumbling through a void of darkness. He was unaware of which direction went where.

Not panicking yet, Tsumisu devised a light source to guide him. He drew on his energy to envelop himself within a glow of white aura, and the radiance revealed that he remained within the arena, which was turned on its side. Gaining a light source did a lot of justice, for Tsumisu was barreling toward a massive blockade, shaped like a runner's hurdle. With no time for evasion, Tsumisu took his weapon to slice through it, sending metallic debris in all directions.

"Wow, glad I wore some armor," he muttered under his breath. "If it's *this* easy from now on, I've got nothing to worry about."

Seconds later, countless large, energetic spheres came shooting through the "ground" of the arena. They fired off like bullets in a turret gun and were larger than three-story houses, yet these spheres were comprised of energy with a capacity to immobilize. This realization occurred in very little time, as Tsumisu was still under the threat of oncoming obstacles that varied in size and mass—as if the stakes weren't high enough, the resummoned horde of mechanical arms appeared from the pitch-black void, just out of reach of his sight.

Tsumisu couldn't *believe* the magnitude of Nataliya's ambition; however, it didn't take a genius, so to speak, to realize this was providing tremendous satisfaction for her. So, the longer it went on, the *better* the experience. Take note, Tsumisu. Take note. Was this the second base Mr. Iwato had spoken about the previous night? Nah, th-that was just crazy talk. The reality behind Nataliya's behavior was just a by-product of a lady really taking enjoyment in her work…or something. OK, maybe the benefit of doubt didn't *quite* apply here. After all, those are some *huge* spheres of energy coming for your neck. Nevertheless, Tsumisu surmised that Nataliya's impressive show of scientific—actually, *supernatural*—ability to transform matter and dimensions was immensely commendable, and it was worth exploring what *else* she was capable of...despite the overwhelming dangers.

Meanwhile, with such adversity surrounding him, Tsumisu had to devise another strategy. He took off past dozens of large spheres, which continued to fire off relentlessly, so he headed toward a randomly appearing stone monument of Nataliya. Breaking through it created large debris, disjointing the ravenous mech-arms. Although the plan was successful, the number of mech-arms that continued to arrive made it seem like a wasted effort.

Then, without *any* sort of warning, the broken debris he generated materialized into giant nets that flew with one objective: capture and subdue. Was that *clever* or what? Dozens upon dozens of nets bore down on Tsumisu, swarming in accordance to their preprogrammed formations. To his surprise, a crazily maneuvering net managed to catch on to his left arm, disrupting his inertia to send him into an uncontrolled spiraling motion. Quickly, he cut the net but ended up falling backward through a wall, placing Tsumisu face-to-face with an energy sphere *with* a barrage of mech-arms speeding toward him.

In the back of his mind, or maybe it was really all around him, Tsumisu could hear Nataliya laughing triumphantly, as his capture was inevitable; yet as the spheres, arms, and nets drew closer, Tsumisu turned up his energy gauge to streamline his body.

"It's *over*, Little Lady!" he yelled, glowing a brilliant white.

Aiming Akari before him, Tsumisu's internal power boost accelerated him to become a potent beam of energy that pierced through anything in proximity. At the same time, by disrupting the flow of energy in the scientific genius's arena, he could easily pick out the flow of surrounding energy. Now, seizing his opportunity, the Sonzai commander and Akari tore a gap between the void he fell through, subsequently reversing the formula used to summon the spheres and mech-arms. Seconds later, Tsumisu hit the far side of the arena, sending a blinding wave of energy that made the once dubious environment nonexistent.

When the light dissipated, Tsumisu and Nataliya were transported back to the laboratory, where they had stood before each other at the inception of the chase. Tsumisu was catching his breath as sweat dripped from his chin, while Nataliya caught hers as well and stared.

"Well," Tsumisu began, a certain smile on his face, dematerializing armor and sword sheathed, "I guess I win…Little Lady."

"Nooo! *Noooo*! This can't beee-heee!" Nataliya fell on her hands and knees and punched the floor, exoskeleton suit detached. "Nooo, I almost *had* you! I was so close! How could I let you slip through my fingers? *Hoooowww*?"

"Hey! Hey, don't worry; I've got good news for you, Little Lady!" He held his hands up, not wanting her to cry.

"Yeah, yeah, I know. I don't get my information, and you walk away a free man," she replied in utter defeat. "God, I can't believe I said 'free.' Uuugghh…"

"No, I'm actually going to *tell* you what you need to know."

Nataliya looked up in surprise. "You're gonna what?"

"Guess you forgot about my sensitivity, huh?" Tsumisu knelt down before her, an arm propped on his knee. "You need information, and I'm willing to provide it…under *my* terms, at least." He grinned.

"Do you mean that?"

"Sure do, Little Lady." He picked her up, giving her a one-armed seat. "Sorry to get you all—*whoa*! What the fu—gracious! Um, er…I-I'm uh! Uhhh…"

Nataliya narrowed her eyes and grinned slyly. "I *told* ya so, Mr. Tsumisu…" she said, arms around his neck.

Now being awkwardly close to the half-siren, half-vampire, *fully* crazy scientist, Tsumisu could definitely *feel* the magnitude of his actions. Was she wearing panties under that dress?

"Y-yeah, um, I-I, uh, really don't know w-what to say..." Tsumisu stuttered, suffering a mild anxiety attack.

"Oh? You don't have to say *anything*." Nataliya widened her eyes and began continuously shifting her seat. "See? Splish-*splash*, Mr. Tsumisuuu!"

"Oh my God! Cut it out! I get the point!" He exhaled, knowing he'd have a phantom warm, moist sensation on his arm forever now. "I should put you down—"

"No! A heh heh! No, I, uh, *like* it up here!" She gave him an innocent smile. "Soooo...you're gonna tell me some stuff, huh?"

"Yeah!" he exhaled in a shudder, still not knowing about her underwear situation. "A-all that drama from me earlier was purely to *test* you, Little Lady."

"Ha! No way! This whole time?"

"Nothing wrong with testing *the* femme fatale of science, is there?"

Nataliya grinned and sighed. "Hmmm, well, I guess not," she said with an acquiescent tone. "I'll admit, you're pretty good to escape all of that—I honestly thought I had you cornered a few times!"

"And I underestimated *you*!" Tsumisu responded humbly. "If I let my guard down at *any* moment, you would've had me in a paper bag. Easy."

"Aww, really? You're not just saying that?"

"Nope!" Tsumisu gave her a big smile. "To be honest, you were a hell of a lot more challenging than Taras. What can I say? You're a *badass* scientist."

Nataliya giggled and gave him a hug. "Well, at least I'm getting what I want..."

Tsumisu blushed, feeling her breasts press against him. "Ha... yep. Say, why not open that dimension again?"

She rose up, placing her hands against his cheeks. "Because," she began in a whisper, their eyes meeting, "you're not going *anywhere*, handsome."

"*Help*," he feebly muttered, pupils dilated.

At that moment, Nataliya released an electromagnetic field that ensnared him, causing Tsumisu to collapse on the floor and rendering him unconscious.

CHAPTER FOURTEEN

Sometime later, the Sonzai commander awoke to find himself strapped to a table by restraints composed of an energy complex hooked to twin *giant* generators that sat a few meters from him. Large cables were connected to the bottom of the table and provided the energy necessary to keep him still, whereas the restraints themselves were at his ankles, knees, wrists, elbows, neck, and forehead. Wow, spare no unnecessary risk, he supposed. Extravagant arrays of wires, labeled with patches at the ends, were attached to his body in nearly *every* location.

Tsumisu also noticed that most of his clothes were gone—his boots, socks, pants, and shirt specifically—but he was *lucky* to have his boxer-briefs on. *Wait…what's this?* It was an uncomfortable sensation, seeing a certain wire—the *only* wire, that is—running directly from Nataliya's terminal and into his underwear from the front opening…

"Hey, ya finally came to!" Nataliya greeted him from behind an array of screens visualizing information. "I was beginning to think I overdid it! Whew! What a relief, huh? Since you have such an…

exquisite power output, it was difficult, to say the least, to determine a safe voltage gradient."

Tsumisu could only sigh audibly as his eyes drifted to her position. "How long was I out, Little Lady?" he asked patiently.

"Only for about thirty-five minutes, I guess. *That* in itself is amazing," she casually replied, typing away and analyzing data. "Hope you're not mad at me."

"Mm," Tsumisu muttered, looking at the ceiling.

"Are you mad at me, handsome?"

"Nah, not really."

Nataliya finally glanced over. "Well, I can't see how, unless that shock did something to your judgment. After all, I *did* kinda trick you." She winced. "Aaaand take advantage of your kindness…"

"I know," Tsumisu replied understandingly. "I probably wanted you to anyway."

"Probably?" Her tone was of clear surprise. "Are you trying to make me feel guilty?"

Tsumisu chuckled. "Never! You've got enough stuff to worry about."

At that moment, Tsumisu watched Nataliya walk down from the platform where she stood and approach the table, and he chuckled in disbelief.

"What the hell is going on?"

Nataliya was sporting a black-lace corset, complete with matching stockings and garter belts, *dangerous* heels, a long white lab coat, and glasses. This…was *worse* than Shujin had described earlier.

"You, uh, honestly wear glasses, right?" he asked.

"Call it coincidence," she retorted, hands on her hips. "What do they call this? The 'dirty librarian' look?"

He pressed his lips together. "Probably just a dirty look—uh, *yeah*, that's what they call it."

She leaned on the table Tsumisu was lying on with a little smile. "Your genetics *do* give me an indication of similarities between humans, Ordovicians, *and* Devonians," Nataliya began, her tone calm and calculated. "And although it's only been a few minutes into my analysis, I've come to believe your origins are none of them…am I right?"

"Are *yours?*" Tsumisu asked in return. "After all, who has an enormous amount of natural orange hair and can transform portals intradimensionally every few milliseconds?"

She laughed and started playing with his hair as it hung over the edge. "Well, that's for *me* to know and *you* to find out, isn't it, handsome?" she replied.

"Careful. I'll hold you to that, Little Lady."

"Mmm, I hope *so.* Before ya do, first answer my question," she said, bending over to meet him face-to-face. "Why give me an answer? Because I've never seen *anything* like you before. Neither have I seen anything produce that kind of *power* before without severe biochemical damage or having its body traumatized by unimaginable forces. Ha, I don't even have a trace of your genetic code anywhere in my database." Nataliya's stare was intense, filled with the promise of discovery. "I *must* know what you are if it takes me all day and night or the next few centuries, Mr. Tsumisu." Her voice was low and soothing. "You understand? I won't take my eyes off ya even for a *second…*"

So he was a "thing" now? Tsumisu gave her an odd glance. "I see reasons behind your obsession, but now I feel like you're gonna be watching me all the time…like another level of *all* the time."

"Oh? You mean longitudinal observation? Yes, I will be!" she happily declared. "Remember what I said about stalking your closets?"

"It is my undying wish *not* to remember," Tsumisu frankly replied, clenching his eyes, "but it appears I don't have a choice."

"That's *right,* you *don't* have a choice!" Nataliya nodded steadily. "Glad we're on the same page, Mr. Tsumisu. And now that we've reached this echelon of understanding, you can expect that I'll know when you sleep, when you wake, when you eat, when you pee—"

"I've got one!" he cheerily interrupted. "When I dream?"

Nataliya leaned in closer. "And when I give ya *nightmares…*" she said with widened eyes.

Tsumisu honestly shivered. "Er, how nice of you?" he feebly replied.

To his extended detriment but not surprisingly, Tsumisu's physiological responses, like respiratory and cardiovascular functions, were being monitored. Nataliya caught his increased pulse rate and blood pressure from the corner of her eye—gaining instant gratification as a result.

"Feeling afraid, handsome?" Nataliya began. "Awwww, well, don't worry; Momma's gonna take care of you."

Everything she does is just epic, Tsumisu thought, hoping his thoughts were safe from her prying instrumentation. *Like epic-mistress. But it's like…where did this* come *from*?

"Now, my sweet victim, please answer my question." Nataliya leaned on the table once again, continuing to play with his hair. "What race of being are you? Why do your genes, aligned as they are, produce a body such as yours?"

"First, you gotta promise something," Tsumisu jokingly remarked. "You on board with that?"

Nataliya's expression showed piqued interest. "Oh?"

"Yeah! You gotta promise *not* to eat me once you're done," he said, chuckling in disbelief. "Gastronomy can't possibly equal anatomy!"

Without moving, she tightened the restraints on him. "I'll consider it, Mr. Tsumisu," Nataliya replied, smirking.

"Oh sh—soooo…you noticed I've got a pretty sturdy body, huh?" he replied, wondering if he should quit provoking her. "I'm sure you paid attention to the muscle and bone composition."

Nataliya observed him closely, looking into his eyes. "I certainly did: your bone density is greater than what I found in Shujin's, and your muscles create twenty-six percent more protein than average. You realize what that can do?"

"Given the right genetic sequencing, it could make them 'tougher,' I suppose?"

"Oooo, don't you *dare* talk science back to me." She stroked his chin.

Tsumisu mashed his lips together. "Yes, ma'am."

"But you are exactly correct—a *lot* tougher," she continued to explain. "What baffles me is, your body is structured like any typical humanoid species, yet your genes say otherwise. Ha, I must be repeating myself…"

"*Now* you've got something to think about, gorgeous." Tsumisu smiled. "Aside from 'dominating' my body…ahrrm, besides! The matter is *so* simple, I needn't explain anything to you."

Nataliya scoffed in amusement. "I thought your sensitivity weakness implied instinctive niceness to me."

"See, I would be *nicer,* but I have to make it difficult for you in some way, right?" Tsumisu grinned, trying to state the obvious. "I-I mean, look at me in all these restraints. W-what's all this for? I'm *completely* defenseless here, Little Lady."

"That's the idea, Mr. Tsumisu." Nataliya smiled with narrowed eyes and playfully hopped onto his chest, knocking wires away. "In order to make sure you couldn't escape from me, I had to make sure you couldn't run in the *first place.* Please don't take it harshly…"

Even though Tsumisu absolutely enjoyed the nature of Nataliya's voice, crisp without the slightest hint of uncertainty, there went that warm, moist sensation again—no panties. He exhaled deeply, trying to absorb the reality that her "state of affairs" was on him.

"Maybe I'm the one to be asking who's trusting who?" His tone grew suspicious.

"Oh, I trust you, but this is all part of the deal. If I capture you, you succumb to my every whim, right?" Nataliya pointed to her temple. "Or did you *forget*, Mr. Tsumisu?"

He groaned in recollection of the agreement that he *did* accept. "All right," Tsumisu began in admittance, "I decided *without* knowing—"

"How far I was gonna go?" Nataliya replied deviously.

"Exactly! Because frankly, I-I don't see how attaching a wire directly to my *crotch* could possibly give you any important information." Tsumisu maintained a straight face. "Know what I mean? Sure you could think of it like a hydraulic system…the shaft goes up, goes down—"

At that moment, Nataliya's monitor alerted her to movement detected from the specialized sensor.

"Oh?" She intuitively chuckled under her breath. "Up and down, huh? In and out? Back and forth?"

"*Wow.* L-look," Tsumisu stuttered, struggling with idea formulation and getting chills. "Such data is *subjective,* not *objective.*"

"Not quite what you expected on your first occasion being alone with a lady, is it?" Nataliya continued to pick his brain, her tone sultry. "Aww, don't be shy; you can share your naughty secrets with *me,* Mr. Tsumisu. I won't tell…"

"Oh sweet merciful heavens," he muttered, having a virgin nerve struck. "I-I-I-I…" Tsumisu gulped aloud, wondering if his face provided more pathways for Nataliya to meticulously gauge how to assault his conscience.

In the next moment, she bent over on her hands to meet him face-to-face. "I need every bit of information to crack your code, Mr. Tsumisu," she said. "Your secrets, your functions, your *life*—*nothing* is rendered useless in the name of science. And guess what I'm pretty good at."

"Er, *science*?"

Trepidation seeped into his disposition like water into an ambitious sponge, for Tsumisu noticed a moist, pooling sensation arriving on his chest from her. And could somebody shut off that *damn* monitor already?

Resorting to laughter to stifle his nerves, Tsumisu looked at the perpetually staring genius. "If I may," he began, politely clearing his throat, "it seems like *you're* the device collecting my data—not your computers, Little Lady."

"Hmph, I wouldn't say that's a *total* lie." Nataliya rose up again with a mischievous grin. "After eight hundred years frozen in a box, how would *you* feel?"

"A literal 'Alice in Chains' as it were…" His tone was conclusive. "So I'm the best of both worlds for you then?"

"I'll *never* tell you that," she firmly replied. "But I'm not ignoring your plight either, Mr. Tsumisu. Such is the reason why I'm giving you a little something now, see?" Nataliya flung open her lab coat, blushing. "You like my outfit? I'm certain you've *felt* my personal gesture of 'no harm intended' by now."

"Uuuhh, I can't say I'm not appreciating your efforts." His face beet red, Tsumisu's reply reflected cautious admiration as he wondered how she got her boobs into that corset. "Yup…" He averted his eyes to focus on the ceiling lights, visually confirming her sans-panties situation. "All kinds of appreciation."

"I know you like what you see, for you'd be a liar if you said anything to the contrary," Nataliya suggestively remarked with a raised eyebrow. "Wouldn't you agree?"

"Nevertheless, I-I refuse to *publicly* agree with you." Tsumisu wasn't sure if that statement made sense. "Only because we're not *exactly* even, Little Lady."

"Weeeelll…" She looked at his crotch and grinned slyly. "Your rather *large* specimen might've prompted me to…"

Tsumisu's fearful eyes widened like saucers. "OK, w-wait! How long was I out again?" he cried. "You wouldn't! Aww, no, y-you *wouldn't dare*!"

"Bwahahahaaa! Are ya *scared*, Mr. Tsumisu?" she gloated under the alarm of his pulse skyrocketing. "Oooo, that burning question: Did I or *didn't* I take advantage of your offer to gather *objective* data?"

"C'mon, Little Lady! Say it ain't so!" Tsumisu exclaimed, clearly distressed. Since she'd obviously been pantyless, the fact that he'd been unconscious, and it only took a minute. "Oh God!"

Nataliya cackled in pure elation, sitting on his chest victoriously. "You poor *thiiiing*! Mean ol' Nataliya hooking you up with wires and restraints, huh?" she rhetorically sympathized. "Well, to tell you the truth, it's quite arousing to see you this way."

"Oh come now," he muttered in exasperation, hoping her response equated to the negative. "What *haven't* I done today that aroused you? A-and what if I was in pain 'cause of these things holding me down?"

"Then you would call me a *masochist*," she replied, quickly meeting him face-to-face again. "Comfy?"

"Couldn't be freakin' cozier!" Tsumisu laughed aloud in self-confessional incredulity. "Whoa, what've I gotten myself into, Grandmaster Sonzai. Um, you've got awfully pretty eyes, Little Lady," he continued as she kept staring.

"Why, thank you. Flattery makes me aroused, handsome." She winked.

Praying as hard as he could internally, Tsumisu hoped that one day he'd understand that shutting up was the best, if not *only*, option in the context of extraterrestrial kidnappings by potentially masochistic, clearly maniacal, yet altogether cute superscientists. Still, he needed to escape…soon.

"OK, well, I'd break these restraints, but I'd feel guilty doing it, you know?" Tsumisu explained, sensing Nataliya's growing objection to his words. "So…that's the only reason why I'm still here. I-I'm just saying—"

"Mmm, no that *isn't* the reason why you're here," Nataliya remarked instructively. "Those restraints are powered by three hundred billion volts of electricity, which have joined individual electrons together to create a single beam of energy that harmlessly holds you down. Yet if you attempt to break that chain of electronegative consistency, I'm afraid you *will* get harmed."

"I mean, that's *very* impressive and all…"

"I'm serious now, Tsumisu. Don't try it." Nataliya pointed a strict finger at him. "I don't wanna see you get hurt, OK? Well, not much." She shrugged. "Even if you *are* my victim. So if you just stay *there* until I'm done, everything'll be fine."

Tsumisu pressed his lips together, thinking. "How long is this gonna take, really?"

"Two hours? Two weeks? Two thousand years? What difference does it make?" Nataliya replied in dismissal of his concern. "The fact of the matter is that you belong to *me*, and there's no getting away." She grasped his chin with authority. "*Never.* Ya got it?"

"B-belong to you?" he asked, voice cracking, as his mind couldn't cope with this region of the unknown. "W-what are you talking about?"

Nataliya nodded steadily with overambitious eyes. "*Yeah*," she replied with a psychopathically crazed grin. "You hear me?" She began aggressively bouncing on his chest. "Mine! Mine! *Mine*! Mwahahahaaaa!"

"Aaahh! Aaahhh, nooo!" Tsumisu hollered in panic. "Cut it out!"

"You're never gettin' away! Never! Never! *Never*!"

So…if the heavens were listening and looking in on Tsumisu's situation right then, he deduced the heavens were being absolute *jerks* for allowing Nataliya's mentally and physically strenuous attacks to perpetuate. After all, just *what* did he do to deserve *this* kind of treatment? With his physiological responses blaring incessantly from Nataliya's equipment, Tsumisu felt very much at her mercy. Wait! Was she creeping backward?

"Tell me! Tell me! Tell me!" Nataliya continued in joyful laughter, centimeters away from his waist.

"What? *What? Whaaat?*" Tsumisu screamed in horror. "Tell you *what?*"

"Say it! Say it! *Saayy iiiit!*" she playfully sang, *barely* in the proximity of his groin.

"All right, *OK!*" Tsumisu blurted hastily, feeling her body heat on his awkwardly extended hydraulic shaft. What was worse, he wasn't able to wipe Nataliya's psycho expression from his memory or the torturous splashing sensations. "OK, you *win*…Little Lady," he said, breathing heavily.

Nataliya granted him some reprieve. "There's a good boy," she replied, her tone one of satisfaction. "I *always* win. Mmm!" Reprieve over. "So *warm*. What else?"

"Whuhh!" Tsumisu flinched at the sensation. This was *bad*. "Wuuhh! Uh-um! Little Lady! You can't do that!"

"*Ha!* I do what I please, Mr. Tsumisu!" She tightened her grip. "Now what else?"

"Aghh! Y-you can…have the last laugh?"

"Damn *straight* I can." Nataliya flared her eyes. "You never stood a chance against me, Mr. Tsumisu. The moment you set foot in here, you sealed your fate." She finally released him. "And let's get something else straight: don't think for a second you could *ever* outsmart me. Understand?"

Maaaan, why is she so intimidating? he sincerely wondered. *Should I tell her I'm* totally *freaked out, but this is disturbingly sexy? Naaah, I've already taken too many risks today—*

"Understand?"

"Whuh! Y-yes, ma'am! I understand!" Tsumisu frantically replied. "Um…permission to ask a question?"

"Be careful what'cha ask for…"

"*Oh.*" Tsumisu didn't expect that response, and it slightly derailed his sense of self. "What happens next now that I've submitted to your whims?"

"Hee-hee. *I'm* going back to work!" she gladly proclaimed. "Aren't you excited, handsome?"

"Woo, sure am!" Tsumisu pseudocheerily said, shuddering afterward. "Happy working, Little Lady. Thanks for the, er...gift."

"It was my pleasure, ha!" She raised an eyebrow and smirked. "Do ya get it?"

Tsumisu clenched his eyes in regret. "*Yes,*" he whispered. "I get it."

So as Nataliya hopped off of Tsumisu and strolled toward her array of computer terminals, she began to hear sparks flying and the sound of heavy strain from her generators. Turning around quickly, she *knew* what was happening and rushed to the table again.

"Hey what did I say?" she yelled amid the noise. "Cut that out, or you're gonna get hurt! Aagh!"

Nataliya had to retreat as sparks flew with greater intensity and flashed across the room. But despite the deadly electricity, Tsumisu bore no expression of pain as he raised his head up, pulling both arms as well as his legs free. When the danger passed, the generators lost all of their capacity and went dead while the wires attached to Tsumisu's body were fried. Tsumisu casually plucked off the sensor patches, taking care when he reached the one on his crotch, and then stood up from the table to stretch—without a *single* scratch on him.

Nataliya approached him again, this time in a highly flustered manner. "What the *hell* is *wrong* with you? Didn't you hear anything I said?" she said in well-founded frustration. "You could've gotten hurt or worse, Tsumisu! I swear, that is the *last* time you—oop!"

Nataliya's words were cut short as Tsumisu rushed in to give her a *kiss.* Her eyes flew wide in unadulterated shock. What just happened? Yet strangely, perhaps wrapped up in the essence of chaotic reasoning, she didn't pull away. In fact, Nataliya felt she *couldn't.* She lifted her hands to Tsumisu's hardened cheeks, holding the kiss, and closed her eyes. Tsumisu took the scientific genius in his arms and pulled her close; Nataliya wrapped her arms around his neck, releasing a few gentle whimpers of pleasure—a result of enjoying the Sonzai commander's taste as their tongues interlocked.

After a few more moments, Tsumisu gently pulled away. "*Now* we're even, Little Lady," he said in a softened tone.

Remaining in his arms, she blushed an intense crimson, as she was, at least for the moment, speechless, her rose-pink eyes gazing in wanting.

Giving Nataliya a tiny kiss to her seal acceptance, Tsumisu smirked with intuition. "Hmm, could you tell me where my clothes are?"

"Uh...y-yeah, right over there." She pointed in their direction. They were lying on an adjacent table nearby.

Tsumisu played with the hair that extended over her shoulders. "Thanks a lot. It gets cold in here. And I'd get the door, but that's more *your* specialty..."

Without looking away, Nataliya snapped her fingers and reestablished dimensional connectivity to the Iwato household.

"See?" he scoffed in amazement. "How'd you do that?"

"Shut up," Nataliya whispered in response, kissing him once again, speaking between passionate intervals. "Shut the hell up. I *hate* you...*so* much."

"That's a strong word," Tsumisu said, returning the favor. "I don't believe you, gorgeous."

"Ugh, you think you're so damn *strong*..." she continued.

"Ha, you think you're so damn *smart*," he replied. "You're mad because I led you on?"

Nataliya sighed with lips barely touching his. "Now you wanna be honest with me?" she said, biting his bottom lip. "You knew this *whole time*...jerk."

"Maybe," Tsumisu confessed, moving to kiss around her neck now, squeezing her bosom as well, "but I learned you're more badass than I thought."

"*Mmmm*! Compliments won't spare you from my vengeance, Mr. Tsumisu," she moaned with closed eyes, hands on his back. "I hope you know that you're still in trouble with me..."

"Then don't spare me. I *want* you as my perpetrator, Little Lady," he said, bringing a kiss on her once more. "Is that fair?"

"Mm-hmm," Nataliya concurred, rubbing his nose. "But I *still* hate you, handsome."

He chuckled softly. "As long as you're happy…"

Gently releasing Nataliya from his embrace, Tsumisu strode to his clothes and calmly dressed himself; Nataliya stood by, silent as she observed him retrieve Akari, strap the weapon to his back, and make his way for the laboratory exit.

"Who I am now is nothing compared to what I will become," he kindly remarked, turning to her. "*What* I am is not the purpose; however, my purpose is what I am—and in order to figure that out, Little Lady, a laboratory won't get you the answers."

"What do you mean by that?" Nataliya asked, her tone a little desperate. "Please, what are you trying to tell me?"

"This is why I like you: I *know* you'll find out." Tsumisu smiled and opened the door. "See you later, Little Lady."

The door closed, and Nataliya stood alone, remaining in a state of trance. A timidly outstretched hand clung into a modest fist, slowly drawn away and to her side; the femme fatale of science sighed contemplatively…and then banged her clenched fist against her forehead, *repeatedly*.

"Oooohh, what's *wrong* with me? It's just a stupid, insignificant kiss; that's all! Nothing special…yeah…" Nataliya started touching her lips and areas of her neck, recalling the warmth of their encounter. In the next moment, she cried out. "Aaarggh! This is *crazy*! What am I doing? The experiment comes *first*, and I'm letting him get away!"

CHAPTER FIFTEEN

With a snap of her fingers, Nataliya changed back into her normal clothes and rushed out of the lab. Frantically searching, she didn't see Tsumisu down the hallway on either end, so she bolted into the living room, where she found Tetyana, Suzuka, and Arlette watching television.

"Whoa-hoooaa there, what's the *hurry*, buddy?" Tetyana looked over her shoulder with a smirk. "Did ya lose somethin'?"

Arlette blinked a few times. "Oh my, you look upset, Nataliya! Did anything happen?" she asked sincerely.

"Never mind about that! Did *any* of you see Tsumisu come this way?" Nataliya demanded quickly.

"I think he went outside with Prince Shujin." Suzuka directed her to the back door. "They might be tending to some vegetation—"

Nataliya took off without a second thought.

"Hey, wait! What the hell were you two doing all this time?" Tetyana called as Nataliya shut the door. "For cryin' out loud," she scoffed and plopped back on the couch.

Outside, Shujin and Tsumisu were inspecting the pots they planned to use to plant their recently obtained flower bulbs.

"Well, I didn't mention that some of them were a bit overused," Shujin said while holding one and flipping it over. "But it won't hurt if it's just for a little while, right?"

"Nah, it'll be fine!" Tsumisu said cheerily as he collected the rest. "Let's just make sure we've got plenty of *towels* nearby when we need to dry up that water."

Shujin twisted his mouth in annoyance. "Har har, OK, we won't use *this* one."

"Exactly, no point in taking risks when you know you're thinking, *Hey, this'll do some damage*! *Ah well, let me do it anyway*. Makes no sense, bro. That's another thing to avoid when making decisions on the battlefield—" Tsumisu was about to explain, until Nataliya came running toward them, looking determined. "Uh-*oh*…"

"Wonder where she's going in such a hurry?" Shujin asked with a curious tone, setting his gathered pots down. "Say, didn't you just come out of her lab? Are you OK?" His eyes lit up in realization. "Did she *get* to you?"

"Nah, I'd call us square really." Tsumisu exhaled quickly, a grin coming to him. "But, uuhh, I kinda had to make out with her in order to escape, sooo…"

Shujin was epically stunned. His jaw dropped. "You did *what*?"

"Sshhh! It was bureaucratic! I'll explain everything later!" he said quietly as she approached, immediately composing himself. "Say, you need something on your head, Little Lady; don't wanna catch a cold! But with *all* that hair, I wouldn't think it'd matter much!"

Flabbergasted by his friend's report of what had happened, Shujin tried his best to observe the situation carefully. "Is uh…s-something wrong, Ms. Nataliya?"

"No," she responded, peering at Tsumisu, rather short of breath. "I'm fine, Shujin. I just…need to ask Tsumisu something."

Shujin quickly looked back and forth between the vertically disproportionate two. "OK, well, I hope it's nothing dramatic enough to having you running"

Tsumisu shook his head. "C'mon! She's big on information. I'd be running too—"

"Could I talk to you for a moment?" Nataliya asked him in a prompt interruption. "*Alone*? Please? Like right now?"

He noticed her demeanor was serious—not just serious, filled with sincerity, like it had been briefly when Nataliya had warned him about the dimension on the *Leviathan*.

"All right then." He smiled in acceptance. "Dude? I'll be right back. And if not, I'm sorry. If you want, just finish up with most of what you can, and I'll complete it later. Cool?"

"If you say so, dude," Shujin responded, obviously wanting to know more of what was going on. "I'll bring the plants in the house then?"

Tsumisu patted his shoulder. "Good idea. OK, Little Lady, let's go."

"Hey!" Shujin got his attention with a stern expression. "*No* antics, dude."

He scoffed as if his character were under attack. "And I look like that type of person, I suppose?"

"*Yes*!" Nataliya responded definitely and grabbed him by the hand to lead him away. "You *are* that kind of person! The worst kind!"

Tsumisu waved to his friend and then quickly pointed to Nataliya and shrugged with an expression of comical obliviousness. Shujin could only wonder what had been unleashed on the world.

With the stride of a woman on a mission, Nataliya took them back inside and past the living room, where Arlette observed closely.

"Hey, is everything OK, you guys? Why are you dragging Tsumisu around?" she asked worriedly, but her expression shifted to confusion. "Uuuumm, what're you doing, Tsumisu?"

He was making cutthroat signals, but Nataliya quickly looked up; Tsumisu stopped before she saw him.

"I've just gotta ask him a few questions; that's all," Nataliya replied calmly and quickly eyed Tsumisu as he once *again* made cutthroat signals. "I *see* you already!" she cried.

"What? Shujin told me *no* antics!" he said with a straight face.

"Nah, not by the looks of it." Tetyana had a hand propped against her cheek. "You guys were stuck in that lab for like an *hour* doing who knows what! So why are ya lookin' at him like that again?"

"As if it's much of your business anyway, Tetyana," Suzuka patiently responded. "Perhaps they were drawn into conversation."

"Oh, c'mon!" she exclaimed, looking at the princess. "Try explaining the lab being gone for all that time!"

Nataliya turned to her creation. "If I told you, nothing would make much sense anyway, seeing as I'm trying to figure it out myself. Now if you'll excuse us?"

"OK! Long as you two aren't mad!" Arlette said cheerily. "See you guys later!"

"Bye, Arlette! Thanks for your support, dear!" Tsumisu interjected casually before Nataliya led him away again and into her lab.

Temporarily sealing the dimension again, she confronted him with folded arms as he sat cross-legged on the floor with a grin, laying Akari aside. A few moments passed as they looked at each other, and Tsumisu started to laugh.

"*OK*, ask away," he said in confession.

Wearing a little scowl, Nataliya pointed in stern accusation. "First of all, that kiss you *stole* won't happen again—"

"Which you *enjoyed*, of course…"

"Ooohhh!" She instantly blushed but attempted to fight it off. "That's not the point, and you *know* it, Tsumisu! That was a…a cheap trick you pulled on me!" she exclaimed. "Grrr, you're such a bastard!"

"Hey, settle down!" Tsumisu held both hands before him. "Name-calling isn't necessary! And besides, you were kinda *asking* for it, right?"

"I didn't ask for *that*!" Nataliya stomped her foot and pouted. "Just tell me what you meant, and no more riddles this time!"

"But haven't you given my words some thought yet? Well, I guess not after…OK, you deserve a break, I suppose." He patted a spot beside him. "All right, gorgeous, best to take a seat."

Nataliya kept an eye on him as she sat down, waiting for a response. "Well? Start talking! I demand an explanation!" she fussed.

Tsumisu could tell she was a proud woman, though he sensed great apprehension, the cause of which was a secret she alone knew. "OK! Wow…let's get you in a different mode first," he suggested.

"I don't want your stinkin' help! I want answers!"

"C'mon now! *Deep* breath…" He adjusted his posture to sit upright, inhaling and then exhaling. "It feels annoying initially, but the second time usually starts chipping away the stress for me."

Clearly irritated, Nataliya closed her eyes and forcefully inhaled…then exhaled.

"One more time, Little Lady."

On her second meditative breath, Nataliya's bothered expression slowly dissipated, and she felt more comfortable in her seat, gaining a better posture.

"Say, you're right," she said.

"Oh yeah?"

"Yup," she quickly responded. "Typically the sound of rain works for me," she explained, "but my hands have to be *stupid* busy in order for my mind to get the idea I'm trying to relax."

"Got conditioned to the process," Tsumisu deduced, observing her.

"You're tellin' me." Nataliya's tone was confessional. "It helps a lot when work calls. Don't get me wrong, but a girl's gotta *unwind*."

Tsumisu was utterly fascinated. Imagine that: an individual, from an extraterrestrial race known as the Ordovicians, possessing power that literally bent reality at her beckon—what *was* she? As he contemplated earlier, Nataliya seemed exceedingly supernatural with her abilities.

After all, she couldn't have lifted all this heavy equipment alone or captured whatever planetary body they were located on with a dart gun…right? Did she enslave millions of people from some *other* alien civilization? Seriously, how the *hell* did Nataliya pull it off? Considering all she'd accomplished, it was beyond evident why Tsumisu was more than the next head trophy on her wall.

Therefore, in spite of the need to report back at the Sonzai encampment, Tsumisu felt it was necessary to obtain a greater contextual background on the Little Lady. For all intents and purposes, such information on an individual like *her* would be extremely invaluable indeed.

Meanwhile, Nataliya noticed how quiet it had become; she didn't hear Tsumisu engaging in breathing meditation like before, so she opened one eye and caught him gawking.

"What're you lookin' at?" she said.

"Duh, n-nothing!" Tsumisu cleared his throat to look straight ahead. "Nothing. I was, uhhh, just counting the number of stress veins disappearing from your face," he muttered. "Good news! They're all *gone*."

Nataliya mildly chuckled, amused at his horrible denial tactics. "And that's the best lie you could come up with?" she inquired, some sassiness in her tone.

"I mean, there are *literally* no veins—*yes,* it is," he said, turning to her in honesty. "But you feel better now?"

"Hmm, *yeah.* I'm not in the mood for crossing methods of capturing you off my mental list…if that's what you're saying." Nataliya narrowed her eyes tellingly. "Why? Got something you wanna say to me?"

"Yeah. How about we start over?"

"Two things, Mr. Tsumisu: You're still aware that I'm coming for ya, right?"

Tsumisu pretended to check things off. "Got it, Little Lady."

"And you're *still* my victim?" Nataliya asked firmly. "Like, there's *never* going to be a point in your life when I'm not stalking you?"

"That's not on the menu—I'm kidding!" He grinned. "Absolutely, I'm your scientific victim."

She gave a little grin too. "Okeydokey, Mr. Tsumisu, let's start over."

"Awesome!" He nodded, feeling relieved. "I'm surprised you haven't asked me for an apology for, um…you know."

Nataliya raised an eyebrow. "Oh? I said didn't ask for it, not that I didn't *enjoy* it," she said confidently. "I'm not a walking contradiction like *you,* Mr. Tsumisu."

Goose bumps. "Right," he said, suspiciously adjusting his seat as she stared. "Maybe I should work on that—"

"Are you afraid of me?"

Tsumisu chuckled with hilarity. "Not really?" he replied. "But you certainly scare my poor brain into oblivion! Like *pow,* I don't know who or *what* the hell I am anymore!"

Nataliya laughed aloud, politely covering her mouth.

Hey, she likes your dumb jokes, dude! Aww, she's got a cute laugh—stop. Reroute your thinking, Commander.

"Quit making me laugh!" Nataliya remarked. "I still wanna be mad at you in some way, ya jerk!"

Tsumisu shrugged with a comical expression. "Hey, *you're* the one sucking out my brain, soooo what would you call that?"

"I'd call that quit messin' around and start giving me answers," she said, nudging him. "Too bad for your brain! In fact—"

She snapped her fingers and changed their seating to a queen-size bed, complete with satin sheets, pillows, and a headboard. Her wardrobe changed again—Tsumisu curiously noticed his white button-down school uniform shirt on Nataliya; enough unattended buttons provided all degrees of imagination for Tsumisu as her cleavage stayed in with a prayer. Wait...How'd she get his shirt again? In addition, Nataliya's glasses made a return, but there was a glimmer of hope in her attire...

"Thank God," he whispered, shuddering. "I've never been so relieved to see panties before in my life."

"See?" she began, arms folded behind her head, her smooth legs crossed. "Isn't this more comfortable than sitting on that crusty old floor, handsome?"

"Definitely helps our back health." Tsumisu nodded, blushing once again. "Prevents early onset of sciatica and all..."

Geez, I'm leaving it out for him, but he's not making a move! Nataliya thought, biting her bottom lip. *Tetyana was right: these boys are too straight-laced. But how would you explain earlier? Grr, he's such a bastard! Can't he tell I'm* obviously *horny? That's why I was bothered!* She slightly shook her head, looking him over. *You can't just make out with a lady and leave her hangin' like this! Aaaghhh!*

"Er, you OK over there?" he asked cautiously.

"Huh?" she blurted. "Oh! Y-yeah! I'm...I'm great...ish."

"Hey, um...how'd you get my shirt?"

She chuckled. "Really?"

"Yes. That's called breaking and entering, Little Lady." He winced, still sitting upright. "Sprinkle on a little *theft* too, if you hadn't noticed."

Nataliya laughed aloud this time. "Oh my gosh, don't you like what I have on at least, Mr. Tsumisu? Stop being so damn polite with me!"

"Whuuh! I'm sorry!" Tsumisu looked away, though he questioned his actions as doing the *opposite* of what she requested. "What do you want me to say?"

"How about 'Nataliya, you're freakin' sexy. Could you stop jerking me around please, ma'am?' Sounds accurate?"

He was silent.

She turned over, head propped on her hand. "C'mon now…"

Tsumisu exhaled, grinning with internal hilarity. "Little Lady, you're *really* sexy. I couldn't stand another hard-on today. I'd appreciate your kind generosity to abstain from jerking me off—*around*," he instantly corrected himself. "Please, ma'am? Thanks."

And theory solidified! If you're that *tense, handsome, take it out on* me *for heaven's sake! I'm* right here*! Aaaaghhh!* Nataliya ranted in her head once again. "Hmmm, OK, handsome. Since you asked so nicely, I'll cut you some slack," she said.

Nataliya was capable of mercy! Tsumisu felt victorious, though he noticed her wardrobe was unchanged. Better not make mention of it.

"So…you're not gonna change? Gaahh, wow." He face palmed.

Nataliya confidently shook her head, pulling the shirt open. "Nope," she said, lying on her back. *That's right. If you won't make love to me, you're gonna have to deal with* all *of this.*

Waah! Why would she do that? Are there *no* Ordovician taboos? *Stop.* Forget you saw anything. You saw *nothing.* Eyes forward. "Uhhh, OK…you're familiar with spiritual concepts, aren't you?" he began, face fully red.

"Hmm, can't say I am," she said, smirking. "If it's not really scientific concepts, I don't pay much attention. Why?"

Tsumisu nodded bashfully. "I-I see. Well, reason I asked is because it would help you understand the whole 'what I am is not the purpose, and my purpose is what I am' thing…th-that I said earlier."

"Sounds more like a riddle than spiritual philosophy to me." She shrugged. "Which is practically the same once you look at it."

"Overall, I agree with that assessment," Tsumisu agreed, having to stare at his boots. "Nevertheless, what is life but a myriad of clues that one must accumulate to construct and solve his or her own puzzle?"

Nataliya grinned in appreciation. "You can say stuff like that, handsome?"

"Oh yeah." Tsumisu pointed to his head. "Can't leave that thing weak. Now, to the point of 'what I am is not the purpose'; this means I could be any form or being, hold some certain characteristic that may define me as different in comparison to *another* form or being in some particular aspect," he explained. "But regardless of my physical relation and possession of all this power, figuring out what my power *does* isn't the point of what I *am*."

She crept closer to him. "Mm-hmm. So you're saying my analysis of your physical aspect is irrelevant?" she asked.

He scratched his head, feeling her body heat. "Whuhh, no? It depends on what you're trying to accomplish," he replied, accidentally getting a full view of her bosom again. "Don't *faint*…OK. For *example,* if you're investigating how I tick, I mean, that's *fine.* However, such investigation won't provide you any indication as to *why* I'm here and *what* I could be doing here in the first place… seeing as you can't find anything like me in your database, am I right?"

"Yeah, you're virtually uncharted territory as far as genetics are concerned," Nataliya agreed, enjoying his reactions. "Well, in terms of power too. Yet you've gotta say if my physical analysis wasn't observed, no one would've known that you were uncharted territory in both respects."

"No, no, no, I'm not debating *that*, Little Lady," Tsumisu clarified. "Only thing I'm saying is, if *that* was all you were aiming for in your research, that's all you'll get."

She scoffed, granting him a gaze of skepticism. "Don't ya realize who you're talking to here? I'm a *scientist*, Mr. Tsumisu."

Damn that was hot. He caught that stare of hers, and all she did was grin. Would she stop that?

"Brings a whole new dimension to 'pillow talk,' huh?" she poked with a giggle. "I'm enjoying this as much as *you* are, handsome."

"Coming from an individual that *loves* dimensions," he muttered. "OK, I-I wasn't trying to patronize you, Little Lady. Sometimes my explanations can be convoluted such that the meaning comes out wrong..." He paused in his thoughts, tapping his forehead. "All right let's clear the water." Tsumisu laid his right hand out to her, extending his pinky. "And this time, I'll *remember* this promise."

Surprised at his gesture, Nataliya looked on the mysterious man, grinning at her with strong sincerity...despite his enormously sheepish demeanor. Of course, she was all too aware of the meaning behind *pinky promises*—but it wasn't so much that she didn't trust Tsumisu to keep it; she wasn't sure if *she'd* be able to. What a hell of a time to question oneself.

Well, considering she masterfully manipulated a few individuals to twist Tsumisu's arm into coming to the lab initially and then took full advantage of his kindness to place him in those powerful restraints, there were grounds for doing so. Nataliya *knew* this about herself anyway, and with all due respect, *he* was certainly aware of her deceptive characteristics. And yet, there he lay—offering her a *pinky promise* of all things, no hesitation or apprehension.

What did it mean? Was *this* a core structure behind what granted him his abilities? Or maybe...Tsumisu was just showing her how simple it was to continue having *faith* in others, despite what they might have done or continued to do. The Ordovician scientist exhaled, her expression changing from scrutiny to solace as she raised her right hand, extending her pinky and locking it with his.

"Now," Tsumisu calmly began, "let's promise that neither of us here wishes to change who we are, only that above *all* things in this great universe, we would love nothing more than to learn so much from each other." He gave a kind but soft laugh. "Hopefully, it bodes positive for each party concerned..."

Wearing a smile of her own, Nataliya pulled his pinky toward her. "I promise, Mr. Tsumisu," she said.

"And I promise as well, Little Lady. Oh..." He paused with stifled laughter building. "I *also* promise you're ridiculously short—ow! Hey, I'm *sorry*! Hahaha! I'm sorry! Cut it out!"

She *instantly* began punching him repeatedly. "I'll show ya who's short!" she declared through a flurry of fists.

"OK! *Ow*! I take it back!" Tsumisu said, brought on his back while gently parrying her fists away. "You wanna continue talking or what?"

"Yeah, but call me short again and see what happens!" she laughed, pushing him one last time. "Jerk!"

Tsumisu leaned away from a psyche-out threat of hers. "I'll try to be good, all right?" He cleared his throat. "Also...can you just look *that* way for a second?"

"Ha! Why?"

"It's for the best, I swear."

Nataliya peered at him, suspicious. So she crept even *closer* just to make sure Tsumisu wasn't planning anything. "Remember what I said about thinking you can outsmart me," she began. "Is that what're you're doing, handsome?"

"*No*! No, furthest thing from it." He nodded, wiping some blood from his nose. "Furthest thing..."

So Nataliya (stylishly) turned her head to the right, and the *instant* she did, Tsumisu's lightning hands buttoned up her shirt.

"Hey!" she exclaimed, though impressed. "What's the big idea?"

"My salvation!" Tsumisu chuckled with defensive hands raised before him. "What's that look for?"

Nataliya wrinkled her nose at him. "Salvation, my foot," she replied. "I'll be nice this time."

Tsumisu released a sigh of relief.

"But if you fail to convince me by the end of this conversation..." She grinned deviously. "Well, you can figure out the rest, Mr. Tsumisu."

It was like the heavens had programmed Nataliya to *always* find an advantage, no matter the scenario. Was it advantageous to lie shoulder to shoulder with her? Seriously, Nataliya displayed these *pockets* of nice that were mixed in with incredible underhandedness. Tsumisu just couldn't figure it out; he didn't know what to anticipate, how to brace for the next *thing*. Nothing of his Sonzai training availed him against her...and maybe she knew it? Or maybe Nataliya was simply reading his face.

"What'cha thinking about, handsome?" she asked, her tone soothing. "Yeah, I know when you do that *too*."

"J-just my response!" he said, trying to reestablish his thoughts. "Um, the goal is applying a spiritual component to the overall equation," he continued. "So if you sat down and thought, 'Well, gee, this guy is mighty strange...What could he be doing here?'...It doesn't necessarily have to be all 'wise-man' type of thinking; however if you begin to apply a *tiny* attribute of that additional spiritual component, you could perhaps form the relation of 'why' instead of 'how' in a manner that attempts to solve a puzzle like mine."

Nataliya's mental wheels were turning as she was biting her bottom lip. "Wouldn't that be the same as asking what your purpose is?" she inquired.

"Precisely, gorgeous," he said and snapped his fingers, reaching into his pocket to whip out more chewing gum. He handed her a piece. "It's 'wintermint' this time."

She had figured Tsumisu was keeping quiet about his ability to read her. "Ha, what is it that doesn't get past your observation, hmm?" Nataliya shoved the gum into her mouth. "That's a *direct* question, Mr. Tsumisu."

He also began chewing a piece. "Oh! Well, uh, the energy spheres, dimension conduits, this planet-size laboratory..." He counted on his fingers, having a comical, matter-of-fact expression. "Metal claws, Tetyana, et cetera...basically *all* that science you do." Tsumisu showed Nataliya his tally. "I'm being brutally honest here."

"Don't worry; I know you are," Nataliya responded confidently, grinning. "How do I know?" she propped herself up, bringing her face to his. "You smile when you're honest, but ya *sweat* when you lie. Anybody ever tell ya that?"

Yes, Tsumisu, it was *that* obvious.

"Aaahhrrm!" Tsumisu adjusted his position politely, still feeling intimidated. "In *any* event, I figure that 'spiritual' attribute is part of my 'job,' so to speak...which leads me to this point: my purpose is what I *am*," he explained. "It may not seem like a rational idea at first; however, when the conventional method of thinking does not suffice for the answer, then you must question what is not apparent."

"Care to clarify a little bit, handsome?" Nataliya popped a tiny bubble, lying on top of him now. "Oh! *Ooh my*! Haven't settled down yet, have we?" she said, having to make room. "Where are ya gonna put that, huh? I've got an idea..."

It'd be great if she'd stop pointing out the obvious. "*To* clarifyyyy," he began, blushing intensely, "*why* does my body resemble a human yet my blood doesn't? Why do I have so much power? *Why* am I so damn nice to you and everybody else?" Tsumisu shrugged. "Try and tie those inquiries together for me, Little Lady. In fact, try to remember some of the things I said on the *Leviathan* and last night, then tie the rest of that together; it may seem like a lot, but it'll be easy for a brilliant lady like you." He gently nudged her.

"Okeydokey!" Nataliya laid a hand on her chin, her head comically bobbing up and down as she worked over her gum. "To question your purpose and why, then from what I observed as a part of the equation to solve it..."

Some moments passed as Tsumisu patiently waited for Nataliya's response.

"Hey," she began, "you mentioned there were enemies stronger than you, and in order for you to defeat them, you would have to complete your training, right?"

He nodded once. "That's right."

"Then you mentioned there was a second sword—'Kuroi' or something. It's basically an 'evil twin' of the sword you currently wield, yes?"

Tsumisu grinned with intuition. "Yeeah, you're getting warm, as if you weren't hot enough," he replied. "Do you get it?"

Nataliya smiled and continued thinking. "With that in mind, you said you weren't ready to wield Kuroi under the condition of its power, yet it's *necessary* to complete your training. If I'm not mistaken, didn't you mention the sword you're carrying is sort of like the 'good' twin of the two?"

"Exactly." He nodded. "Keep going."

"All right!" Nataliya was getting excited. "OK, let's see here, you also mentioned that another part of your training was finding the balance within yourself in order to attain both powers within yourself? Is that right?"

"The concept sounds a little screwy but definitely accurate. I'm, uh...loving your comprehension, and don't mind my flattery; it's your hair."

"You could make my day and *kiss* me again." Nataliya glanced at him momentarily. "Waah!"

Tsumisu swiftly turned over and lay atop *her* this time. "And play into your hands?" he said, fingers interlocked with Nataliya's to pin her down. "You underestimate my ability to adapt, Little Lady…"

Folks, that was *the* greatest "favor" Tsumisu had given Nataliya this whole occasion. As she lay beneath him, her cheeks were red, mouth slightly open, eyes wide…thoughts blank.

"You were saying though?" Tsumisu knew he took an *enormous* risk pulling that move. "Sorry for interrupting—"

"*Just* give me a second." She shuddered, eyes clenched briefly before looking at him once more. "I hate you so…damn…much, Mr. Tsumisu."

He scratched his temple. "News flash: I can live with your hate, Little Lady." He winced.

It's OK, Nataliya, she meditatively contemplated. *Repress the rape. Eliminate the rape…He deserves—no! No* rape*! I'm gonna rape him!* She cleared her throat aloud. "Well! You said the power of the swords is an extension of what you are, and you are the same way with them; in the relationship of them being virtually good and evil, could it be a mechanism of your conquering good and evil within yourself in order to complete your training?"

"Whoa! And *if* I kissed you right now, what would you do?" Tsumisu excitedly exclaimed. "Because you're making my day!"

"Then do it already!" she screamed at the top of her lungs. "*Dooo iiit*! What? Ack! *Ack-ack*!"

Needless to say, Tsumisu was startled, yet he rolled over to roll *her* over and pat her back. "We've gotta get you some Ricola or something," he muttered.

"It's! Ack! Your damn fault! Ack!" she cried, waving off his assistance as she lay on her back to sigh. "Gosh…" Her eyes drifted to him. "You haven't won this battle, just saying."

"I had *no* idea we were at war!" Tsumisu nervously chuckled. "Seriously!"

Nataliya grinned intuitively. "*Liar.* But I'll get back to the subject 'cause I'm nice." She lay on her side. "So I'm tying this stuff together: your purpose and your enemies, who so happen to be stronger."

Tsumisu did the same. "If you would like for me to clarify, I will. Maybe I can make it simpler," he suggested.

"No, wait!" Nataliya held a finger up to him. "I'm assuming that naturally your enemies would be evil, and that makes them stronger, so your purpose is to simply defeat them…right?"

"You've got about seventy-eight percent of it this time, but it's like this in spiritual terms." Tsumisu used his hands to illustrate his explanation. "Evil has a strong influence on the conscience whether we realize it or not, and so often is it strong that evil drives a person to make the wrong decision or do the wrong thing—while *we* seldom take the harder road of *not* accepting said evil influence." He grew a slightly furrowed brow. "Ever wonder why it's so hard for anybody to just…damn it, do the *right thing*?"

"Yeah, many times," Nataliya responded, her tone sounded as if she'd experienced that on another level.

Tsumisu nodded. "Well, just as I've explained, it takes a lot more emotional capacity to continuously do the right thing or make the right intention. If that individual isn't careful, they could end up lost…Case in point? Taras."

Nataliya rubbed her chin in thought, similarly wearing a slight frown. "Takes some serious insight to deduce a bastard like *that*; nevertheless, it makes sense what you say, Mr. Tsumisu."

"And, hey"—he took hold of her hand—"I apologize for what you endured."

"Well…" Nataliya looked away, trying to smile, though her expression was clearly a somber one. "I certainly appreciate it…"

Tsumisu didn't want Nataliya to begin resurfacing any painful memories, lest he violated his incongruent train of thought from earlier in the day. Nataliya was a powerful woman in both scientific prowess and character; just *what* took place prior to her capture truly must've been traumatic for her.

The Sonzai commander, and no doubt Shujin as well, wished to remove the painful memories from *each* of the women for that matter. Perhaps they were already doing that, provided the frequency of laughter shared among them. Still studying a silent, contemplative Nataliya lying beside him, Tsumisu had to assume his intent to alleviate the spiritual burden she possessed was manifested through his actions—he stayed with her this *entire time.* And, by the looks of it, Nataliya was grateful.

"Here's another example, Little Lady," he began, hoping to bring the original topic back. "You ever heard of the phrase 'quick to happy'?"

The scientific genius turned her eyes back to him, an eyebrow raised. "Don't you mean 'quick to anger'?"

"Nope. See how *difficult* it is to justify why the former phrase would be of common acceptance?"

"Wow, that makes sense too." She pointed, sighing with inner release. "I'll admit I never thought of it that way."

"Takes a lot to be happy, so why not choose the easier road, right? It's not a general rule, yet it is widely understood among those who observe this concept that 'evil' comes *so easily* to the soul; it's the stronger force of the relation between good and evil."

"That's the reason why your enemies are stronger than you are now?"

"Precisely," Tsumisu confirmed. "And seeing as I'm trying to accomplish the power of good…or rather the balance of good and evil, which creates a *greater* force, it would take me longer because it's of the 'lesser influenced parameter' of the soul—although being a much more powerful force than evil itself at the same time."

Nataliya sat up and immediately brought out her laptop to jot down information. "It all ties together, yet scientifically speaking, you wouldn't be able to realize it because it's not focusing on the physical aspect of the relationship," she said. "Correct?"

"And not ashamed to say it." Tsumisu smiled warmly. "Now if you really want to make it interesting, you would ask, 'Why is this sort of evil here?'"

"Hold on a sec," she said and continued typing, chewing her gum on overtime. "All right, you bring up a very interesting question indeed: Why would something that evil exist? And for how long has it been around? How long has *your* power existed if the case be the evil counterpart was present as well?"

"Longer than anybody could imagine really," Tsumisu replied definitely. "I'll say probably before anybody was even born, but that's another subject and I'm not really sure about it."

"Did you just hear that question though? Where exactly did your power originate? Certainly, it didn't just sprout right out of your body; there must've been a consequential event on a level so immense that it must be in serious ancient times." Nataliya suddenly gasped as she turned to him with an exciting discovery. "That's it! You have a power so ancient that neither humans, Ordovicians, nor Devonians were even conceived to inherit it! That explains why your genetic makeup is different from theirs, yet your power has somehow adapted to your body, which received a human gene but kept the stronger gene as its dominant DNA!"

"Aren't you glad I got you thinking in a different perspective?" Tsumisu replied with a humble smile, preparing to roll out of bed. "Now I can't disprove or verify that hypothesis, but you're a dynamo of thought now! So that means I can help Shujin with these flowers—"

Nataliya grabbed his shirt sleeve. "Ooohhhh *no* ya don't! You're staying *here* until I'm finished!" she ordered, placing him back down. "I've still got more questions to ask, and you've got more things to tell me!"

"B-but—"

"*No* excuses!" Nataliya gave him a bit of a pout. "You're *staying,* and Shujin will get somebody to help him!" She instantly switched to a cheery disposition. "Besides, don't you enjoy *my* company…*Mr. Tsumisu?*"

Tsumisu rubbed his forehead, remembering how…*aroused* she became earlier. "Yeah, and you're obviously enjoying mine, but only thing about it is I'll feel guilty not getting back, yet that's who I am. So I suppose it wouldn't hurt to stay."

"That's right! Now since I've figured out you more than *likely* possess an ancient power and it provides a basis for your genetic makeup versus your physical structure, it doesn't completely tell me what that other 'part' of you is." She eyed him.

"Oh no." Tsumisu sounded worried, and his expression said the same. "Don't tell me I've just stirred that 'particular' interest even more?"

"Hee-hee, what did you expect, handsome?" Nataliya asked confidently. "Changing my mind or something?"

"Well, not *really,*" he replied, hands behind his head. "Just figured all this knowledge sharing could assist your scientific abilities, perhaps assist you as a person…um, only *adding* to the wonderful attributes that you already *have,* of course."

"Oh yeah? I'm glad you were thinkin' about me." Nataliya leaned over him with a grin. "Makes the whole occasion worthwhile, doesn't it?"

Tsumisu looked at her, smiling as well—trying to remember how harmless she *wasn't,* given the right environmental conditions. But Nataliya was really beautiful and downright sexy. Wasn't she extraterrestrial though?

Dude, you're staring at an alien—just stop staring, Tsumisu. It's rude.

"Yeah!" he said finally. "N-never a dull moment, trust me."

"I'm impressed by your resolve, by the way," she remarked, a hand stroking his cheek. "Just know the offer always stands. OK, Tsumisu?"

Man, her touch was *stupid* soft. In that moment, Tsumisu found himself comforted by Nataliya…even though he couldn't figure out what *that* meant!

"Er…" He paused, uncertain. "Th-the hot springs?"

"So adorable!" she exclaimed in awe. "*And* know that only a thread separates the abduction of your innocence from *me*."

"Are…you thinking about pulling that thread, Little Lady?"

She giggled. "It's not the *only* thing I wanna pull on," she remarked with narrowed eyes. "Soooo, what's the story about the 'other' part of you, hmm?" Nataliya essentially sat on his shoulder with laptop still in hand. "Are you related to a secret entity that passed down this power from generation to generation? Is it fundamentally the same as Shujin's power? Or what?"

"I'm, uh…not really sure myself, come to think of it," Tsumisu responded with a sudden realization, though still baffled (more like shell-shocked into a state of denial) by her earlier statements. "As far as I know and from what I've been told, I have the gift and ability to attain the power I seek. But being related to the source of the power? I have no clue."

She snapped her fingers, apparently deleting something on her database. "Hmm, that's too bad. Think there's a way you could find out for me? If you don't *mind,* of course…"

Tsumisu scoffed with a grin. "Hey, I didn't mind lying on that table while you took advantage of me, did I?" he joked. "Oooo, got'cha thinking…"

Nataliya threw her hand at him in severe dismissal. "Whatever! I *caught* you and that's that!" She muttered afterward with folded arms. "Got'cha thinkin'…the *nerve*."

"Listen, I'll try to find something out. Stop pouting, Little Lady," he responded and rubbed her back.

"You'd better!" She glanced at him with a subtle scowl. "Tryin' to take my victory away. Hrrmm, that's not fair…"

Yikes! Nataliya was sore about that? Tsumisu figured playing nice would serve him better since she obviously didn't want to talk about it. "Throw another question at me," he stated in a friendly tone, trying to catch her gaze again. "I might have an answer this time!"

Nataliya exhaled, arms outstretched to adjust her mood. "Yeah, I wanna ask about your swords," she said. "Where did they originate from again? All those pretty designs on that blade weren't put there by an eccentric swordsmith; I know *that* much."

Wishing he could've eaten his last words, Tsumisu stifled his wince. "Now, uh…that's a *fantastic* point; in addition, you're *really* getting into something I'm not—"

"Uurrgghhh!" she lamented, falling backward in a heap. "Crap, Mr. Tsumisu! Is *everything* a big secret? You'd think with all that power, you'd have some…instruction manuals! Aaaarrrhhgg…" She laid her hands on her face. "Waa-haa-haa! I'll never get my information now! Waaaa!"

Oh God, not again. Did Nataliya's captivity release occur simultaneously with *that time* of the month? And if so, why did the heavens pick *him* to be around? Hey! He didn't say it aloud this time! Won't Shujin be proud? No matter. Tsumisu took in a deep breath and forced himself to emotionally proportion the allure of her false moment of extreme despair. So he gently patted her head as she started kicking.

"Now, now, Little Lady. With all that power, it's best to keep it a secret," he sympathized. "Besides! Imagine some incompetent fellow strolling by with those swords lying around—not a good thing to leave a manual lying about, yeah?"

Nataliya instantly dropped the charade, a hand on her chin. "Hmm, *yeah,* I see your point. OK, now." She rose up, eyeing him down with authority. "You are strictly *forbidden* to tell me you don't know from now on, got it?" She pointed a stern finger. "*Got it?*"

"Yes! Wow, I've got it!" Tsumisu replied desperately, exhaling deeply, as it was getting harder to relax. It had to be premenstrual syndrome on a *bad,* extraterrestrial level.

"Great!" She beamed brightly. "What about the, um...Akari is its name, right?"

"Uh, yes, it definitely is. Don't wear it out."

"Ha! Explain to me the reaction it has to certain types of power—like *you*, for instance."

Tsumisu thought about her question for a moment; it seemed odd. "I'm not sure what you mean, Little Lady...n-not saying I don't know the *answer*, of course! Ah ha ha!" He laughed nervously. "Sorry..."

Nataliya narrowed her eyes, waiting for him to slip up again. "See...when I subdued you, your sword became 'active,' so to speak, and when I attempted to get it for examination, it created a barrier around itself and prevented me from touching it."

"Ooohhh! Akari is overprotective as well; I forgot to mention that—"

"That's not the end of it, however," she continued, interrupting him. "All of *that* happened so quickly, I presumed you were trying to trick me, right? So as I approached, something in the back of my mind said 'purify those lost.' And I know I wasn't just *thinking* it, because I experienced it as if someone *literally* spoke to me. It was so strange. I didn't know what to make of it!"

Tsumisu quickly sat up, concern in his expression. "Wait! It *spoke* to you?"

"'It'? The sword, you mean?"

"Was that all it said to you?"

Nataliya was beginning to grow *really* worried by the tone of his voice. "Y-yeah, that's all it said! 'Purify those lost.' Is there anything wrong, Tsumisu?"

"Huuhh, that's not a good sign," he began, mumbling to himself. "Or maybe it is? Gosh, perhaps my constant use of power has caused it to awaken—or maybe when I destroyed the dimension? Agh, there are too many variables..."

"Any that I should be aware of?" she asked, trying to listen in.

Tsumisu shook his head. "No, no, it's fine," he replied, not looking at her as his thought process continued.

Nataliya was certainly unconvinced. "Doesn't sound like it. Something happened, and you're *not* telling me…"

"It's nothing you should be worried about; trust me," he replied calmly, rising to his feet. "Could you reestablish the door, please?"

"I mean, sure, but c'mon! What are you hiding from me, Tsumisu? What are you about to do?"

"I've, uh…just gotta do *something*." Tsumisu finally turned to her, his expression calmer now. "We'll finish up this conversation later, yeah? I really, really love talking to you, Little Lady."

"Hey, wait!" Nataliya got up and bolted to the door, standing in his way. "If this has anything to do with me, let me know, all right? I don't want that sword to place a curse on me!"

He sighed. "Worse things could happen, and it's a bit difficult to explain right now. I ask that you please forgive me."

"But…" she said as he gently moved her aside. She watched him leave. "Tsumisu? Tsumisu! Come back!"

Tetyana was walking down the hall, sipping on a bottle of soda, when she heard Nataliya call to him. "Wonder what that's all about? Hey, where ya goin', big guy? Everything OK?" she asked as she approached.

Tsumisu was strapping the sword to his back. "I'll return soon, Tetyana. Tell everyone bye for me. And make sure nobody follows, cool?" he asked, looking straight into her eyes.

"All right, if you say so, but I'm sure *nobody* could." She chuckled but saw Tsumisu wasn't amused. "Hrrmm, you look kinda bothered. Anything happen to ya?"

"Yeah," he muttered and walked away with calculated footsteps. "It's *awakened*."

Tetyana stood with a straw in her mouth, puzzled in her attempt to figure out what he meant. Upon turning around, she noticed Nataliya behind her—dressed normally, leaning against the frame of her room door with arms folded.

A hand on her hip, Tetyana looked at the scientist. “You get any of that?” she asked.

Nataliya shook her head. “He said it’d be too difficult to explain. How? He just won’t tell me…” she replied.

“Big guy said ‘It’s awakened’—the hell does that mean?”

⟞⟝

Walking down the stairs, Shujin overheard Tetyana’s words; soon, he heard someone close the front door. Not giving it much attention, he continued into the hallway toward the kitchen before meeting Tetyana and Nataliya—where he expected to see a Tsumisu-Nataliya combination.

“What’s up, guys?” he greeted the Ordovician duo, albeit cautiously on account of not seeing his friend.

“Hiya, Shujin! Did you talk to Tsumisu outside?” Tetyana asked, granting him a smile.

“Yeah, I did, but I’m not telling you what was spoken in fear you…uh”—he cleared his throat—“might take it the wrong way.”

“Nah, it’s nothing like that, Shujin. He just acted kinda weird before he left,” Tetyana continued to explain. “All *serious* and stuff.”

Shujin shrugged, trying to think of possibilities. “Maybe he just had something on his mind? And I thought he was with you, Nataliya?”

“Well, he *was*,” she replied, clearly in deep thought. “It was going great, but when I mentioned his sword, Tsumisu just switched moods on me.” She sighed. “Gosh…I knew something was eating at him this whole time.”

"Switched? I don't think he's really moody. Are you sure it wasn't something you did?"

Nataliya gave him a straight stare. "Really?"

"Duuuhh, I only meant in terms of diplomacy!" Shujin immediately explained.

"That's the thing!" Tetyana exclaimed, trying to figure out the situation. "It wasn't really a *bad* moody, but it's *off* to see Tsumisu, and he ain't crackin' a joke. Know what I mean?"

"Wow, that *is* pretty serious." Shujin got the idea, having successfully evaded a counter from Nataliya. "W-what about his sword again? Did he get…*upset* about it, if that's the case?"

"I mean, he wasn't *raving* mad," explained Nataliya informatively, giving Shujin her sincere attention. "He just seemed like some event occurred with his sword to make him concerned enough *not* to smile—and he *always* smiles. As a matter of fact…" She paused, rubbing her chin. "Doesn't that sound like bipolar disorder to you, Shujin?"

"Uhh," he nervously began, a sweat drop looming on his brow. "N-not that I'm aware of, Nataliya?"

She scoffed. "Then what gives?"

"Hey, let's all give him a little space," Shujin said with reassurance. "I'll give Tsumisu a call later on and see what's troubling him. In the meantime, try not to worry, OK? Knowing him, I'm sure everything is fine!"

Nataliya's expression lifted a little, struck by the similarity of benevolence between him and Tsumisu. "If you say so. Thanks, Shujin."

"Once you find out, lemme know, OK, babe?" Tetyana took another sip of her drink. "He *still* owes me that sake."

He nervously chuckled. "Er…maybe it's best to take a break from it?"

CHAPTER SIXTEEN

Tsumisu made his way toward the Sonzai encampment with one thing on his mind: Akari. The ancient weapon was awakened by an event he couldn't determine. Maybe it was because of him trying to reach Evelyn, the Mother of Souls, or his destruction of the dimension, or Nataliya attempting to capture him—whatever the reason, the soul of Akari connected spiritually with Nataliya and *spoke* to her.

Akari, the Sword of Light, typically reacted in defensive behavior in the event its wielder, being Tsumisu, was brought under some degree of harm—let alone incapacitation. Further, the weapon would *only* awaken given a spiritual event or encounter of great magnitude. Now, Nataliya was not harmed, nor did Akari realize Tsumisu was in some particular danger, so the question was obvious: What could this all mean? This and more, Tsumisu wished to divulge to Grandmaster Sonzai, for if this indeed happened again, Akari could defend or endanger lives of others completely outside of Tsumisu's volition.

In about an hour, the Sonzai commander reached the mountains and heavily forested hills of Okayama, where the encampment was located, traversing down the cold and barely trickling stream that led directly behind the irrigation fields. After a few kilometers, he came to the clearing in the forest where the main, modern-in-design encampment sat beneath a hill. Other clansmen, some with their families, could sense Tsumisu drawing closer and turned their attention to the stream along which he traveled.

"He's back already?" asked Lieutenant Wanako. "I don't remember Grandmaster saying this was the last period of investigation, do you?"

Captain Goshinfuda shook his head. "No, it's likely something else—must've been due to those great surges of power we detected the other night," he replied.

"Yeeeaah, what a spectacle *that* was!" Wanako nodded matter-of-factly. "I'm still woozy from the epileptic seizure I suffered…at least I *think* that's what it was."

"You're asking the wrong guy," the captain scoffed, "but I guess we'll find our answers soon enough."

Tsumisu walked across the field and waved. "Greetings, brothers!" he said. "What's got you out here in the cold? Lieutenant, you…*hate* the cold, right?"

"Funny you mention that, Commander!" He laughed rhetorically. "See, this is the *captain's* fault here, so, uh…"

"Welcome back!" Goshinfuda proudly patted Tsumisu's shoulder. "Yes, I've dragged the lieutenant and everyone else out for team organization."

Tsumisu raised an eyebrow. "More team organization? I wasn't aware we'd be moving out again. Well, my communicator fried out, so that'd probably explain things."

"I know, but you'll be brought up to speed soon, Commander."

"Better than trying to catch a cold," remarked Lieutenant Kadochi, joining the group. "Commander, you've returned awfully early. What's happening out there? The array detected some outrageous degrees of energy disrupting multiple spiritual complexes on the planet."

Tsumisu exhaled with a grin. "This would sound on par with a poorly scripted science-fiction series, so bear with me." He held a hand up. "Ready?"

"Nope!" Wanako humorously responded. "Go ahead though, Commander." He dramatically sniffed the air, interrupting himself. "Um, I'm not tryin' to get into your *business*, but…have you been around something exceedingly *floral* recently?"

"That was my *next* question," Kadochi remarked, bearing an insightful grin while adjusting his glasses. "A garden of epic proportions indeed."

The captain's expression rose in profound inquisitiveness. "*More* female troubles, I presume?" He smirked with folded arms. "I'd like to know the woman capable of *that* level of potency, Commander."

"Eeerrr, gentlemen…" Tsumisu realized Nataliya's southern-hemispheric essence had been substantially enhanced by his on-foot journey. "B-between us, I'd like to shove that event to the back burner right now."

"Ha *haaaa*, she *hit* you, didn't she?" Wanako began snickering. "Didn't she?"

"Cut it out, dude!" Tsumisu pushed his shoulder. "*No*! Well, I-I mean *maybe* she did? All right, *technically*, she did. But I stood my ground, and that's the bottom line."

Kadochi nodded in immediate understanding. "Congratulations on your escape, Commander." He applauded. "She must be a hell of a woman as the captain asserts; I can tell she differs greatly from the military woman. Overall, that makes *two* incidents—"

"Kadochi, I am *not* confessing anything to you *today*." Tsumisu knew they all could easily read his demeanor. "But thanks, I guess. All right, this goes on the back burner. Are we clear, gentlemen?"

"If only temporarily, Commander." The captain chuckled with an amused sigh.

"Fantastic. Now, I was explaining all those surges were a result of an extraterrestrial cyborg tyrant," Tsumisu tallied, "a kidnapped super scientist, mystic entities overseeing an alien empire, *and* a hidden power within our abnormal lead, Shujin Iwato."

"I *knew* it was him." Goshinfuda nodded in cognizance. "So, after three long years of investigative work, your instinct proves your case, Commander. Seems Shujin is significantly more influential to the spiritual realm than previously assessed."

"I just couldn't figure out how." Tsumisu smiled, feeling proud of the Mark of Evelyn warrior. "Nevertheless, it proves he's a good man, and the Sonzai have nothing to concern themselves in terms of his abilities."

"Hey..." Wanako patted the commander's shoulder. "Any friend of yours is a friend of ours, homie."

"Indeed," the captain concurred. "About this, uh, 'cyborg tyrant,' as you put it, he is no more?"

"Dead as a doorknob, courtesy of Shujin," Tsumisu acknowledged. "Such a despicable wretch...Taras Ganymede was his name. He was stupid enough to run into me and paid for it."

"Amen! That's what I'm talkin' about!" Wanako exclaimed, bumping fists with him. "He must've been one *eeevil* bastard."

"A predator and killer of women as well." Tsumisu clenched his eyes in disgust at such an atrocity. "I assure you, my brothers, Taras received a blue-plate special of punishment before leaving this physical realm."

"Of *that*, I am most certain." Captain Goshinfuda nodded, having a family of his own. "May he find no reprieve..."

Lieutenant Kadochi handed the commander a standard piece of paper. "This is a summary of the signature levels with respect to the event just outside the earth's atmosphere," he explained. "One of them, a subdimension, arrived and disappeared violently with *this* degree of energy."

Wanako and Goshinfuda encircled their comrade in observing the analysis they had no doubt seen before.

"Aha, see that?" Wanako pointed out. "That signal went 'poof'! Gone. Now, I *know* what that means..."

"Yeah." Tsumisu shook his head, getting a better idea of the events after seeing it visualized. "I didn't use that energy on Taras. *This* particular signal was in an effort to...well," he whispered, "destroy a *dimension*."

"Which is ill-advised, Commander Tsumisu," responded Grandmaster Sonzai, entering the crowd of clansmen.

The aged warrior stood one meter six and possessed long, completely silvered hair that was tied into a ponytail, matched by a silvered goatee and connecting mustache. His pale-blue eyes were wrapped in wrinkles, no doubt a physical representation of the countless events he had witnessed that brought great wisdom. He wore a judo-style outfit, white in color, with the clan's golden crescent-moon insignia on his chest.

"Though, by the account of your testimony, I trust you did it for good reason," he continued.

"I apologize for disobeying you anyway, Grandmaster." Tsumisu, as well as the other clansmen, placed a hand atop fist and bowed to the aged Sonzai warrior. "I was regretting the entire occasion."

Sonzai's grin grew wise. He knew Tsumisu better than the young warrior knew himself. "I understand. It is good to see you back, Tsumisu," he said, propping himself against his sword-cane.

"I'm glad to be back...I'm sure you're aware on short notice."

"Indeed. Much has transpired since your departure."

"If I may, Grandmaster," Goshinfuda began. "We've begun reorganizing our teams, for we've pulled the global profiling operations, Commander. So, congratulations: no more school suspension notices."

"Well, that's a relief on my conscience." Tsumisu wore a grin but in apprehension. "Yet that means we've encountered a very strong potential, yes?"

Grandmaster Sonzai nodded in the affirmative. "Australia. A disturbing entity has arisen among the populace, unbeknown to all."

Tsumisu knew full well what this occurrence meant. "Do we have an idea of this being's strength? The degree of his possession perhaps?"

"It's powerful for a certainty," the captain responded. "Yet the matter is obvious. Nyugo is finding a way to reach into the physical realm."

"I shall divulge more details soon, Tsumisu," Sonzai remarked. "Come, we have much to discuss. Captain? Continue in preparing our teams as planned. I will send the commander forth with additional information upon the conclusion of our discussion."

"As you wish, Grandmaster." Goshinfuda nodded.

"See you gentlemen in a few." Tsumisu bowed.

After some time and tea, Grandmaster Sonzai pertinently briefed the commander. Unfortunately, as the captain had mentioned earlier, the Sonzais' global operation for tracking spiritually at-risk individuals, particularly those who were in their youth, was halted altogether because of disturbing events occurring in the southern region of the planet.

Indeed, the inevitable they strove to prevent had occurred: a malicious being, emanating a clear spiritual signature of possession, arose without warning. The lack of warning made the situation far more complicated and worrisome. For even with all of their resources, the Sonzai clan could not indicate the initiation of possession for this case. Typically, with them being specialists in spiritual energy manipulators, detection of such a malevolent event was not a grand matter by any stretch of the imagination. Yet this was not just *any* subjugation of a human being's soul; this was *Nyugo*—the foul, debased architect of wickedness they endeavored without fatigue to keep away from the physical realm.

Nyugo's hand in causing spiritual damnation only meant he was beginning a resurrection. The adversity in ascertaining his evil methodology would surely be immense, for if he mastered the ability to manipulate the darkness of man's soul while circumventing the spiritual energy encompassing the physical realm, by what means would the Sonzai go about *finding* him? Where would they trace him? Essentially, their one lead would have to be the newly tormented soul that had arrived—and asking it a simple question would not suffice. No. This demanded soul extraction through purification—if possible.

Tsumisu was tasked with the objective of utilizing Akari to control the possessed one's soul. By attempting to render the person under the entity within the weapon, Tsumisu could use the soul as a literal tracer back to the source of Nyugo. Likely, Nyugo had not the strength to sustain his existence for very long. This was evidenced by there being only *one* soul under his possession out of the several *billion* humans. Thus, it stood to reason that early detection would prove beneficial for the Sonzai.

As the grandmaster informed him of what was necessary to accomplish his goal, Tsumisu was reminded of Akari's recent interaction with Nataliya.

"Grandmaster," Tsumisu began, setting his cup of tea before him. "I have news with respect to Akari's condition..."

"Please, go on," the Sonzai grandmaster quickly acknowledged, his expression firm.

"The imprisoned one freed from Taras's grasp, Nataliya, informed me that the weapon spoke to her."

Sonzai nodded, stroking his beard. "So, it reached contact with her soul, *direct* contact..." he muttered. "This is rare indeed; however, I cannot deduce detriment or benefit unless you can relate to me specifically what it mentioned. Indeed, these entities do not speak without reason."

"As I assumed, Grandmaster," Tsumisu stated assuredly. "It said 'purify those lost.' I've gone over the phrase countless times. What could it mean?"

"Consider that Akari did not act against her," Sonzai began with instruction, "and instead gave her an order."

Tsumisu rubbed his chin. "An order…to purify? But that would mean she has—"

"*Much* spiritual significance behind her, Commander," the grandmaster completed. "*You* must find out what that is, for the sword speaks in transparency."

"As you command, Grandmaster." Tsumisu nodded to him humbly. "What are my orders?"

"You shall proceed to the continent of Australia. Our coordinates are troublesome, as the energetic parameters saturated the entire region—likely a masking tactic implemented by Nyugo. Therefore, it is on you to isolate the source."

"It shall be done. Any time restrictions?"

"One month; if longer than that, it is acceptable. Finally," Sonzai continued, rising from his seat, "you are to determine the trace of Nyugo using the possessed one's soul per my instructions of handling Akari…and stop Nyugo by any and all means necessary."

Tsumisu arose as well, taking in a deep breath and slowly releasing it. "Forgive me, Grandmaster, but I must ask this question."

"You have permission, Commander Tsumisu, as always."

"Will I get frequent-flier miles on this assignment?" he asked with a sudden flash of humor.

Sonzai gave a wise but raspy chuckle. "Not one moment removes your alacrity, Tsumisu," he remarked proudly. "May the Ancients protect you on your journey."

Tsumisu gave their clan's greeting, wearing a smile. "Farewell, Grandmaster…oh and uuuhh…I'll take a shower before I head out."

"That would be advisable."

"*Wasn't* my fault—just saying."

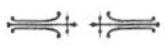

Somewhere in the galaxy, there existed a completely terraformed planet. Its caretaker, Nataliya, stood within a meadow before a flowing river—a setting sun painting a hue that matched her hair. She directed her gaze to the sky. Two gas planets showed above in mysterious opacity, and her dress moved with the warm, gentle breeze of the evening.

With partially outstretched hands, a smile making its way across her face, Nataliya began to glow with a prominent gold aura—rose-pink, tribal-appearing stripes formed on her cheeks, one on each, curving with her jawline. As if one observed a holographic display, a majestic blue dress overlay her attire, its woven material mimicking that of the river currents, and a beautiful golden tiara with inset rubies graced her forehead. With clasped hands resting on her bosom, Nataliya released a deep breath.

"Sister Evelyn," she said, tone calm and sincere, "I'm certain you can hear me, yet I long for the day to mutually hear your response."

A gust of wind captured the moment, and Nataliya briefly closed her eyes.

"Our time must be running short," she continued, "for I've seen your mark. He is *powerful,* Sister, and beyond capable of executing his destiny. Such a force warrants my concern, however…what threat stands before us? Sister Nikita?" Nataliya slowly opened her eyes. "Even so, the presence of your mark comforts me."

She strode closer to the river's edge. "I am struck with internal convolution, Sister; I don't know if perhaps I should be hopeful or…be fearful. The one named Tsumisu…I-I can't *see* him, Sister Evelyn. His essence is wholly *unlike* your mark. Why? How can this be?"

Nataliya observed the river. She noticed some currents moving in reverse despite the powerful flow in one direction, but they were forced to spiral out and join the main current.

"Yes," she said, "I see you face the same challenge. He possesses *immense* spiritual power, and that frightens me. He commands weapons of imprisoned beings, such that it spoke to me." Nataliya paused, briefly shaking her head. "What entity in this universe could perform such a thing without transgressing dimensional boundaries…unless it *transcends* such boundaries? Despite this, Tsumisu is wrapped with kindness, conviction, and purity of heart." Nataliya blushed. "I feel so *drawn* to him, Sister. Insatiably drawn. I…I wish to be near him. Is he…the Restorer of Equanimity?"

An even *stronger* gust blew across the meadow, persisting for a few moments, making Nataliya's heart race momentarily. She gave a wise smile after.

"My, it's great to know someone *else* feels the same," she replied, eyes narrowed. "But I don't want us to get our hopes up too soon, Sister. I realize the evidence is staggering, yet once I've conducted a thorough enough investigation, we'll know for certain. And I may reveal who I am to him." Nataliya sighed once again, her aura fading. "In the meantime, try not to worry…and I'll do the same. Goodbye, dear sister, Evelyn. Your sister—*Rosaria*."

CHAPTER SEVENTEEN

"So what was the most famous duel of the Edo period? Recall the date..."

It could've been another day setting up produce stands for his grandma, Shujin thought, staring out the window of his history classroom. Fingers lightly drummed against the mundanely ubiquitous desk that brought familiarity. Despite the instructor's droning, Shujin felt comforted knowing a laser beam wouldn't barrel through the walls and he needn't survive a head-on collision on board an extraterrestrial vessel...while trapped in a mysterious energy bubble. Or deal with space cyborgs. *Space cyborgs?* Wha-what the hell was his life turning into?

"Mr. Iwato!" addressed the teacher.

"Whuh! I-I'm sorry!" Shujin jolted from daydreaming. "What was the question?"

Gosh, how many times, dude? Ignore the giggles from that group of girls and the jeers from those guys who hate how you never lose a pant crease. Throw a curveball and spare yourself further humiliation.

"Miyamoto Musashi against his rival, Sasaki Kojiro," said a girl, bearing a royal diction. She turned to him with a wink. "Correct?"

"Uh..."

Dude...that's Suzuka in school uniform. Those thigh-high socks doe...

"R-right! That's exactly what I was gonna say—"

"Damn it!" seethed another girl beside him, furiously scrolling through a smartphone. "Now I gotta find another answer..."

Shujin's expression showed deepening confusion and fear.

"She won't beat me to the punch again, babe!" Tetyana puckered a kiss at him. "Why don't ya pull your seat closer?"

Shujin, take note: fear, if left unchecked, can lead to paranoia.

"Why do you think she's so blue?" whispered a male student to another.

"M-maybe a skin disorder?" he replied.

"Very good, Ms. Devonia!" said the teacher. "Despite it being your first day at Okayama High, I can tell you're acclimating quite well."

Suzuka nodded. "I certainly appreciate your courtesy," she replied. "And might I point out Ms. Ordovicia's violation of the school's dress code? Apparently, she left her handbook at home."

"Keep talkin', and I'll leave my hand in your face," Tetyana retorted. Indeed, she had her blouse (braless) tied at the front. "And might *I* point out Ms. Devonia's ability to get in other people's business?"

"If it were any other time, you'd be penalized, Ms. Ordovicia," the teacher said firmly. "But because it is your first day, I'm willing to let this pass—"

"Can I go to the bathroom?" Shujin chirped suddenly, pointing in an arbitrary direction. "Because I need to...you know..."

Without affirmation of his request, Shujin hastily (and awkwardly) escorted himself away.

Head doused with water, he stood at a mirror and tried to make sense of reality: Suzuka *and* Tetyana were at his school! *Why*? Why? Did they follow him? Did Grandma drop them off in an effort to escalate some matchmaker ambition? Another douse. This wasn't right. This couldn't be ethical. How did they register? Why wasn't he informed?

"Ugh, and I've got like a million classes left today," he muttered, sighing heavily. "Just keep it together. Play along, and maybe school won't be destroyed…again."

The minute Shujin regathered his wits, he turned around to find a now-uncloaked Tetyana. Two seconds seemed like eternity sometimes…

"Hey, sugar," she said, smirking.

"Oh my God! Why!—"

She pushed him against a wall, interrupting him, a hand covering his mouth. "Don't wanna attract unwanted attention, now do we?" she continued, her tone low. "To answer your question, baby, it so happens Suzuka and I had similar agendas."

Shujin's eyes widened. "Similar?" His words were obviously muffled.

"Yeah. I don't want any of these human girls staring at you to get any ideas. That being said"—Tetyana's eyes narrowed—"don't think you can flaunt all your hotness around and feel safe." She leaned in. "I'm the predator, and *you* are my prey…"

Doom lasts for eternity, right, Shujin?

"Now get back to class before I change my mind, baby."

He *bolted* out of that bathroom as if a biohazard had broken out.

That catchy little "dong-*ding*-dong-dooonnng" signaling the changing of class periods seemed so haunting now. At his locker, Shujin shuddered. A textbook fell to the floor and made him jump. This was *ridiculous.* He lived with Tetyana and Suzuka all the time…so why were his nerves absolutely compromised?

"I'm the predator, and you are my preeeeyyy..."

C'mon! Why'd she have to say that? He retrieved some headache meds and closed the locker—only to find a patiently waiting Suzuka.

"*Wuaah*!" he cried, immediately face palming. "Sorry..."

"Apologies aren't necessary, Mr. Iwato," Suzuka began. "I noticed you in class and decided to say hello. Given that I *am* a transfer student, it is the polite thing to do."

His eyes drifted to the Devonian warrior princess in stale wonderment. Why the charade?

"Oh! It seems you've dropped some materials here..."

"I-I mean, it's fine. You don't have to—"

Suzuka turned, bent over *slowly*, and retrieved the textbook. She handed it to him. "Here you are," she said, eyes narrowed. "You must pay more attention, Mr. Iwato."

With a bloody nose, he really didn't. However, white with pink lace was burned into his retina now, so...

"Are you two gonna be here all day?"

"*And* night, if necessary." She smirked, walking away. "See you in class, Mr. Iwato."

Maybe...you should just leave, Shujin. This can't end well. This probably won't end at all. Do they still make pay phones? Agh, it wouldn't matter. Tsumisu wouldn't answer anyway—*or* help.

"Shujin!" called a girl from the end of the hallway. "You're gonna be late, silly!"

"Uhhh..." Tetyana's threatening words of "similarities" might come to reality. "I-I'm on my way, Hitomi! You go on without me!" he replied.

"Great! Maybe afterward we can meet for lunch—aghh!"

"Oh *no*!" cried Suzuka (acting surprised), dealing a back fist that sent Hitomi into a janitor's closet. "Someone call the nurse! She's suffered a nasty spill indeed!"

Immediately, a crowd stood witness to debris scattered about as dust audibly settled.

"Wha-what happened?" asked a shocked male student.

"She probably didn't notice the Caution sign," replied Tetyana smugly, hands on her hips. "Well, don't just stand there! Go get the nurse!"

"Y-yes, ma'am. OK!"

Shujin's pale, petrified face caught Suzuka's and Tetyana's confident glares.

⸻

"After our second differentiation, given the original equation, we'll use substitution..."

OK. Nobody died. Suzuka had had enough restraint to cause only bruises. Still, Shujin figured violence wasn't necessary. Could he stop either of them? Or maybe he could warn all the students somehow. Shujin recalled that scene in *Batman Begins* where Bruce cleared everybody out by acting drunk and throwing insults...nah. A stunt like *that* would get him expelled, and then the warring duo would exact vengeance on everybody.

Speaking of war, their desks were *awfully* close to his. As a result, Suzuka kept stroking her leg against his. Tetyana retaliated with an attempt to stomp her foot and take over—sometimes succeeding, sometimes not. The sensation was incredibly distracting *and* disturbingly comforting all at the same time. Glancing at Suzuka, he saw she wore nothing but a sly grin. Couldn't she cut it out? What was she trying to say anyway? Calm down, sir. You're *not* on fire!

Nevertheless, Shujin was impressed on several levels: first, barely anybody noticed, and second, neither Suzuka nor Tetyana dropped their acts of paying attention. Seriously, folks, that takes *skill.*

"Mr. Iwato, can you tell us how we'll find our roots?" asked the instructor.

"Y-yeah," he replied, feeling something creep up his leg suddenly. "We'll use the quadratic *equation*!"

The instructor cleared his throat, a bit of sweat appearing on his brow. "Correct. Thank you for your enthusiasm."

"Anytime," a *super* blushing Shujin comically acknowledged and then glanced at Tetyana.

The mercenary shot him a seductive wink.

Suzuka wore a frown, having caught on to her shenanigans. Tetyana poked out her tongue in jest.

"Wait!" Shujin frantically whispered. "This isn't the right time, girls!"

Suzuka tried slapping Tetyana's hand away but kept missing. Tetyana wasn't letting up, having finally gotten hold of the *situation*.

"Desist…" Suzuka seethed.

"Nope," Tetyana retorted. "He *likes* it…"

The battle escalated and was like some ferocious variation of "slap hands." Shujin had a burning suspicion as to who would be the ultimate loser.

"Now, can anybody recall what type of equations we're solving? Ms. Watanabe…"

"Of course," she replied. "Our equation takes the form of homogeneous—"

"Heeeyyyyyyyeeaaahh!"

Eyes widened, a high-pitched, continuously monotonic whine accompanied Shujin's uncomfortably declining posture. His face landed between Tetyana's strategically placed breasts.

Crimson on her cheeks, Suzuka gasped and realized her death grip was *tragically* miscalculated. "P-Prince Shujin!" she exclaimed.

"See what you've done?" scolded Tetyana, mushing his face even more. "Good thing I was here to protect him! Isn't that *right,* sweetie?"

"Aahrrm!" began the instructor. "*Do* you have something to share with this class, Mr. Iwato?"

A weary hand lifted into the air. "C-can I go to the bathroom?" he muffled out. "I kinda just..."

Douse. Wait...That wasn't a good one. *Douse.* Why him? *No sense lamenting. You're in the thick of it now.* Gosh, he'd have a funny walk for at least two hours. *Suck it up, sir! You can do this...possibly.*

⇹

"Ugh!" Shujin banged his head against the mirror. "I just can't figure out these girls' motives. Are they trying to get my attention? Prove something?"

If it helps, here's a newsflash: a Devonian princess and Ordovician mercenary just fought over handling your stuff. Douse.

⇹

Ahh, sushi and vegetable fried rice. Mrs. Himaki certainly made sure his nourishment was taken care of. Dahlia threw in a brownie. Ha, maybe she *knew* this was gonna happen today. Surprisingly enough, Shujin hadn't vomited once, though his body hadn't been subjected to Caesar salad tossing *yet.* If he cut the brownie into a circle, it could substitute as a personal medal...

"Is this seat taken, Mr. Iwato?" asked Suzuka, lunch in hand.

"Er..." What could he say, folks? "It's not, Ms. Suzu—Devonia."

She smiled. "Why, thank you." She was close as she arranged her food. "I certainly hope you've forgiven me for...well...*earlier.*"

Shujin adjusted his seat in recollection. "Agh, it's fine. Could've happened to anybody!I think."

"Did you truly enjoy what she was doing?"

Damn, that was frank. "I-I'm not at liberty to answer that." He shrugged. "C'mon. Tell me what's going on with you two, please? This is crazy!"

"Make way! Comin' throoouuugh!" remarked Tetyana, sitting opposite Shujin. "Mmm, that looks good, babe! Mind sharing?"

"I've signed up for the ladies' volleyball team, Ms. Ordovicia," Suzuka began, politely eating. "Mr. Iwato seems to enjoy spectating."

He blushed. "O-OK, it's not what you think—"

"Yeah?" she remarked with a smirk. "Seems I've signed up *too.* Tryouts are scheduled after lunch…You're goin' *down*, Princess."

"Oh, I sincerely disagree, Mercenary." Suzuka's eyes narrowed. "And for your information, he *isn't* sharing."

"You're damn *straight,* he's not."

"Huh, well, what do ya know!" Shujin began jovially. "I conveniently portioned out *three* serving sizes! Ah *ha* ha! Ehhh…"

Just let things play themselves out, bro. You can't stop this train.

⸻

"OK, ladies, take your positions!"

It wasn't the fact Suzuka and Tetyana seemed a *bit* out of place among the other girls; it was as if everyone knew it and didn't have the heart to mention anything. That aside, Shujin really hated how the team uniforms displayed their *stacked* physiques. *No! You didn't volunteer your time and mental integrity for sightseeing!* OK, sure…they had the whole Xena-meets-Wonder-Woman appeal, but a glaring fact remained: as Suzuka and Tetyana stood on opposing ends, the air held their Wild West stare down. Needless to say, the coach was miffed; it was only the first leg of tryouts.

"Did you play at your former school?" a girl asked Suzuka.

"Yes," she replied, volleyball tucked under an arm. "You could say that I…*slaughtered* my competition."

"S-slaughtered?"

Tetyana was ready, arms folded in an aggressive stance. "Word of advice." She smirked. "Let me handle this. Got it?"

"N-not gonna argue with you," the girl replied, smiling nervously.

Shujin still felt guilty for *not* warning everyone that Devonia's and Ordovicia's most powerful warriors were about to throw down. Then again, he'd have to educate them on extraterrestrial civilizations, the reality of mind-bending strength and powers, and so on. And so, sitting among several others in the stands, the poor man rubbed his sweaty hands together, subtly rocking back and forth.

"Er, you all right, buddy?" someone asked. "You look like you've seen a ghost."

"Huh?" he blurted. "Oh! Uh…yeah! I-I'm fine. It's just a severe anxiety attack. It'll go away."

"First team to six points moves to the second leg!" the coach explained, and she blew her whistle. "Let's go!"

Suzuka wasted no time and sent a *powerful* serve across the net; Tetyana blocked and leaped to strike back. Suzuka anticipated the location and countered, sending the ball just on the court's edge—leaving a crack.

The gym was silent.

"F-first…first point to the blue team!" stammered the coach. "Am I seeing things?"

Shujin clapped furiously (and somewhat maniacally). "Woo! *Yeah!* Let's go, girls! Show 'em your stuff!" he cheered.

"Bruh, did you see that?" asked the person from before. "Don't draw their attention! That could be *us* next!"

"I'm *trying* to find my inner peace here!" Shujin desperately remarked, still clapping. "You wanna survive? Join me!"

All twelve-plus participants immediately gave enthusiastic applause.

Tetyana punched the court and gritted her teeth. She shouldn't have missed that ball. A cold glare passed between her and Suzuka.

"H-here, Ms. Ordovicia," stuttered a girl, handing her the ball. "Th-that was amazing."

Tetyana rose up. "Hmph," she replied. "You ain't seen nothin' yet."

In an instant, Tetyana served a blistering strike, and Suzuka couldn't get there in time. It was an *ace.* A valiant roar and clenched fist emerged from the mercenary as she stared Suzuka down…and *everyone* cleared the court.

The coach shuddered. "R-red-red team…first point…" she whispered. "How *remarkable*!"

"Get back!" cried a girl, escorting the coach away. "Your insurance doesn't cover this!"

"Blast!" the warrior princess grunted. A violet aura furiously emanated around her. "You shall pay!"

Tetyana charged her golden aura. "Bring it on, sister!" she declared.

A result of their power-up was a fierce wind that displaced anything *not* anchored down. All that wasted Gatorade…

"Oh…oh my God!" Shujin grabbed his head. The worst *was* coming true. "Girls! Girls, you can't do that here!"

"*Graaah!*" cried Suzuka, sending a serve.

"*Rrraaaghhh!*" Tetyana retaliated with a roundhouse kick. "C'mon!"

And soon it was no longer about scoring points (or playing the game, for that matter), as the two warriors traded blows via volleyball. Deafening booms echoed in the gymnasium, blowing out every window. Cracks appeared all over the place. The net was on *fire.* The net posts were mangled, and the few spectators questioned their reasoning as to *why* they remained sitting. Oh, the exits were blocked.

"Call the cops, somebody!" someone cried. "Or the government!"

"A heh heh!" Shujin waved goodbye to his wits. "Or maybe a camera crew, right? Could you imagine the ratings?"

A male student grabbed him by the shirt. "Ratings? We're gonna *die*, man!" he yelled.

"*Not* if you keep clapping!" he cheerily retorted. "For what is life but a thrill ride toward that sweet embrace?" Shujin stood up, arms proudly folded, as the chaos continued. "Yep! You can ask all the important questions, but it doesn't matter in the end! None of this matters!"

And then the volleyball of fate smacked him square in the face.

"Prince Shujin? Are you all right, my dear?"

Amazing. At one moment in time, he was proclaiming the truth about life. The next thing he knew: darkness. So…life equaled darkness? Stranger still, Shujin found himself back *home.* Actually, this was Ms. Nataliya's lab…place. How long had he been out?

"Ugh," he muttered in reply. "Y-yeah, I think so." At least everybody was "normal" now. "What happened?"

"You didn't make the tryouts," joked Nataliya. "And don't worry; I've already written a doctor's excuse for you."

He chuckled. "I appreciate it. Is there a gym left?"

Suzuka sheepishly shuffled her foot, hands behind her. "Well… it isn't necessary for a *complete* rebuild."

Guess he'd have to do push-ups at home.

"So, um…" Shujin's curious peer befell the warring duo. "Can *anybody*…anybody at all start from the top?"

"It was her idea!" Tetyana pointed.

"That's simply not true!" Suzuka retorted. "I merely followed you to investigate!"

"Wow," remarked Dahlia, inspecting. "I can still see the logo…"

A sweat drop loomed over Tetyana's face. "Weelll, we certainly don't wanna make things *worse*, right, Little Princess?"

She giggled. "Guess not! Did you eat your brownie, Shujin?"

"Trust me, it helped," he said, rubbing his face. "OK, if you girls wanna know what I do on a daily basis at school, we can totally go about this a different way. Agreed?"

"Really? You would not mind, Prince Shujin?" asked a hopeful Suzuka.

"If it prevents fires and destruction and violence, I'm *aaallll* for it." He chuckled again. "Why'd you have to do that to Hitomi?"

Suzuka shrugged innocently. "Whatever do you mean? She merely fell."

"Awesome! Sooo I need more registration documents from *you,* buddy," Tetyana requested of Nataliya. "Gotta keep the act goin'."

"Ah, that's correct. I'll need an updated copy as well," Suzuka added.

"Shh!" Nataliya replied and forced a smile. "Why, ladies! Wh-what's this about? First I've heard of it! Eh heh heh…"

It dawned on Shujin that he really *was* the only one out of the loop. Well, at least his crotch didn't hurt anymore…agh, no. *Now* Shujin faced the mountainous challenge of decoding all the *weirdness.* Despite being the Mark of Evelyn, he found that this ongoing social experiment with extraterrestrial women wasn't exactly easy to acclimate to—contrary to *some* people's opinions.

AUTHOR BIOGRAPHY

Stone Abdullah graduated from Jackson State University with a bachelor's degree in earth system science. As an avid writer for more than sixteen years, Abdullah has published both poems and scientific research papers.

Abdullah has worked in research laboratories for NASA, NOAA, and the National Center for Atmospheric Research. Abdullah has spent time as a rock and metal guitarist and blues pianist; enjoys watching anime; and is a video game enthusiast.

Made in the USA
Monee, IL
25 August 2019